CW00519664

Never Too Late

by

Suzie Peters

GWL
PUBLISHING

First Published in 2020
by GWL Publishing
an imprint of Great War Literature Publishing LLP

Produced in United Kingdom

ISBN 978-1-910603-77-2 Paperback Edition

GWL Publishing
2 Little Breach
Chichester
PO19 5TX

www.gwlpublishing.co.uk

Also by Suzie Peters:

Escaping the Past Series

Finding Matt

Finding Luke

Finding Will

Finding Todd

Wishes and Chances Series

Words and Wisdom

Lattes and Lies

Rebels and Rules

Recipes for Romance Series

Stay Here With Me

Play Games With Me

Come Home With Me

Believe in Fairy Tales Series

Believe in Us

Believe in Me

Believe in You

Standalone Novels

Never Say Sorry

Time for Hope

Never Too Late

Dedication

For S.

Part One

Adam

Chapter One

I'll never forget that feeling of stone cold fear when my parents told me they were getting a divorce.

I was six years old at the time, and I tried desperately hard not to cry, even though all I could think about was that life was never going to be the same again. The familiar, happy safety blanket of my home, my mum and dad, and our family unit was fracturing right in front of me, and although they were smiling and trying to put a brave face on things, from that moment on, I knew I'd lost my sense of place. I didn't belong anymore.

"You will be alright," my dad said, trying to sound reassuring, but I wasn't convinced, in spite of his steady smile. "Nothing's going to change, not as far as you're concerned."

"So we're all going to live here still?" I asked, feeling more hopeful. My friend Dean's parents had divorced earlier that year and his dad had moved away to Dorchester to be with the woman he'd met, which meant Dean only saw him during the school holidays. I looked from Dad to Mum, noticing how they glanced at each other, and wondered if their divorce was somehow going to be different; whether they'd worked out a way to keep us all together, even if they wanted to be apart.

I wasn't sure how that was possible. But it didn't matter anyway; my hopes were misguided.

"Well, no…"

"Then it *is* going to change," I reasoned and Dad blinked, pursing his lips.

"What your father means is, that we'll both still love you." Mum gave Dad a hard stare and I felt the tears welling in my eyes.

"But it won't be the same. We won't be a family anymore."

"We'll always be a family." They spoke together, in perfect unison, probably for the last time.

To be fair, they made a good job of splitting up – although I didn't appreciate that until I was a lot older. At the time, it felt horrendous, but there was no fighting, no raised voices, no acrimony. They compromised, tried hard to agree on everything, and always put me first. They sat with me, both together and separately, on several occasions, whenever they noticed I'd gone a bit quiet, or was feeling a bit low, and explained that none of it was my fault; that it was nobody's fault really, that these things happen, that after nearly ten years together, they'd just stopped loving each other, and because of that, living together had become impossible. Neither of them wanted their relationship to turn sour, and they knew the best thing to do was to end it before the rot set in. Looking back, I know they did the right thing, but it didn't feel like that when I was sitting on my own, in my bedroom, thinking about a broken future, my time divided between them.

Unbeknownst to me, by the time my parents told me what was going on, they'd already set the wheels in motion, so their divorce came through within a few weeks, and my dad moved out almost straight away, having found himself a small flat in Newquay, which was about a fifteen minute drive away from our house in Carven Bay. It wasn't too far. It certainly wasn't Dorchester. Even so, there was never any question of me living anywhere other than with my mum, but because he was so close, I saw my dad every weekend, without fail. He never let me down; never changed our plans at the last minute, and never made me feel second best.

He continued his visits, even after he married Michelle, which happened just over a year later. The only difference then was that she was included in whatever he and I were doing. I didn't mind though, because I really liked her. She was a year or two older than Mum, who was five years younger than Dad, and she had the darkest black hair I'd ever seen – much darker than mine, or my dad's – with a pretty, smiley, round face. Without a doubt, the best part about Michelle – other than the fact that she made the most delicious fish pie in the world – was that she never tried to be my mum, or my best friend. She was just Michelle.

And she slotted into our lives as my dad's wife, like she'd always been there.

When Dad and Michelle sat me down quietly on one of my weekend visits though, I started to worry. They'd only been married for about six months; surely they weren't getting divorced already?

"We've got something to tell you." Dad's voice was quiet, just like it had been when he and Mum had told me they were splitting up, and I stared up at him, wondering what was coming next.

"You're going to have a little brother or sister," Michelle blurted out and I let my eyes wander back to my dad, unable to hide my confusion. How could I have a brother or sister without my own mum being involved? I was coming up for eight years old by then, and my rather limited understanding of where babies came from had been gleaned from George Harris, a boy in my class, whose mum had given birth to twins during the summer holidays. George had reliably informed us that there had to be a mummy and a daddy, if you wanted to have a baby, and that they absolutely had to be in love. I'm guessing, with the hindsight of adulthood, that his parents had told him that, but at the time, when my dad and Michelle broke their news to me, I was thrown into turmoil. After all, my mummy and daddy weren't in love. They weren't even living together anymore. So how could *I* have a brother or sister? It didn't make sense.

"What Michelle means," Dad explained, coming and sitting beside me, "is that we're going to have a baby, and that means you're going to have a half-brother or half-sister."

That didn't make a lot more sense to me. I wasn't sure I wanted half a brother. And I certainly didn't want half a sister. But I did at least realise that my own mum had nothing to do with it... and I felt relieved that the baby was Michelle's and not my mum's and therefore wouldn't be living with me. Still, Dad seemed happy about it, so I smiled and pretended that I didn't feel as though I was being replaced.

Amy was born the following June, roughly three months after Dad and Michelle moved into a new house. I had to skip going round to Dad's the weekend after she was born, and the one after that. Mum explained that Michelle wasn't well, and that she needed lots of rest, and although Dad still came to see me on the Saturday afternoons, it wasn't quite the same. Then finally, about three weeks after Amy's birth, I was allowed to go and stay with them again. My new little half-sister seemed to cry quite a lot, but she also had the same pretty, rounded face as her mum, and she gazed at me with the deepest blue eyes I'd ever seen... and then she gripped my finger really tight, which was kind of nice. Michelle spent most of that visit either in bed, or on the sofa, and Dad was kept busy looking after her and taking care of Amy. And, as I watched them sitting close together, Dad feeding Amy from a bottle, while Michelle watched them closely, I felt like an intruder in their family.

Mum's life was changing too. The Christmas before Amy was born, literally just a few weeks after Dad and Michelle had told me about her impending arrival, Mum had started seeing Derek, and when I first met him a couple of months later, I found that I liked him nearly as much as I liked Michelle. He was the same age as Mum, a bit thinner than my dad, and he sold insurance – although at the time I had no idea what 'insurance' was. I just knew that he travelled around quite a lot and sometimes had to stay away. I also knew that he made my mum happy; he made her laugh, and I got on well with him. About two months after Amy's birth, they announced that they were getting married and while everyone celebrated and congratulated them, to me, it just felt like another change in my life.

I hadn't been involved in any of the planning for Dad's marriage to Michelle, but was astounded by how much needed to be done before Mum and Derek could finally tie the knot that November... between the invitations, flowers, dresses, suits, venues, cars, food, and cakes... the list was endless, and really, really boring.

On Bonfire night, a couple of weeks before the wedding, Derek came up to my bedroom, saying he wanted a 'quiet word'. The three of us had spent the evening on the beach, watching a big firework display, and had come home and had bowls of hot tomato soup and crusty bread. We'd had a really good time, but now, as Derek shut my bedroom door, a cloud descended and I felt uneasy. My 'quiet' talks with grown-ups up until that point had usually ended with momentous, often life-changing news, so I wondered what was going to come next, as he sat down on the bed beside me.

"I wanted to have a quick chat with you, away from your mother," he said quietly, a smile forming on his lips, which helped set my mind at rest a little. It couldn't be bad news, surely? Not if he was smiling. "I know a lot has happened around here lately, and you and I haven't really had time to have a talk, but I… well, I wanted you to know that I'm not looking to replace your father."

I frowned, wondering what on earth he was talking about.

"What I'm trying to say," he added, "is that I know you call Michelle by her first name, and I'm happy for you to do the same with me."

"You want me to call you Michelle?"

He laughed, throwing his head back. "No. I mean I'm happy for you to call me Derek."

I nodded my head, understanding at last. It wasn't something Michelle had ever discussed with me – maybe because I didn't live with them, which made it easier, I suppose. Still, it was nice of him to make it clear, and judging from the look on his face as he left the room, I don't think it had been an easy conversation for him to have.

Despite all the hurried planning, Mum's wedding was actually fairly small and quiet. My grandad had died a couple of years beforehand, so I felt really honoured when she asked me to give her away, telling me she'd be proud to have me do it for her. It seemed like a huge responsibility, but I knew Dad would be there too, along with Michelle and baby Amy, so I approached my role with a degree of confidence, and evidently carried it off perfectly. Even as I put my mum's hand into Derek's though, and she took his name, rather than mine and became 'Mrs Powell' and not 'Mrs Barclay', I wondered… I wondered what was going to happen to me. I'd just given my mum to another man. I was going to be the only person in our house with a different surname… so where did I fit in?

My uncertainty continued when Mum and Derek went on their honeymoon. They didn't go straight away, but waited until after my birthday at the beginning of December, and then flew to Thailand, returning ten days before Christmas. In their absence, I had to go and stay with Dad and Michelle, where I felt like Amy was the centre of their world, and I was a satellite – floating somewhere in the distance, vaguely visible in the periphery, but easily forgotten. I'm sure they didn't mean it to feel that way, but it did. It was what it was.

When Mum and Derek retuned, Christmas was upon us, and plans were made for a big family gathering, with all of us together.

"Derek and I have decided to invite your dad and Michelle over for Christmas lunch," Mum explained, the night after the school carol service. "That way you can spend the day with everyone."

I smiled at her, grateful that she'd thought it through, as I'd been dreading Christmas Day and having to choose between one or other of them. In previous years, I'd split my day in half, spending some of it with Mum and some with Dad, but now Amy was part of the picture, I wasn't sure if that would change and if Dad and Michelle would want to have Amy's first Christmas to themselves. Mum's idea seemed like the perfect solution.

Dad and Michelle agreed to the plan and, with great relief, I looked forward to the big day with a renewed sense of belonging, my misgivings from the wedding and its aftermath quickly forgotten.

Mum prepared an enormous turkey, with all the trimmings and, as we sat at the dining table, pulling crackers, telling bad jokes and helping ourselves to roast potatoes and Brussels sprouts, I glanced around, a smile settling on my lips, thinking that life really was pretty perfect.

It was only after lunch that Mum and Derek made their announcement… They were going to have a baby too.

My Dad raised his eyebrows and looked across the table at my mum. "Is that why the wedding was arranged in such haste?" he asked, and the room fell silent.

"No, Geoff, it isn't. If you must know, the baby's not due until late in the summer. It's very early days… we only found out the day before yesterday."

"Sorry," my dad said quickly, his face turning red.

Mum smiled. "Oh, don't worry. I have no doubt everyone is going to assume the same thing, but it looks like it's a honeymoon baby…"

I had no idea what that meant, and I didn't really care. For me, the point was that my sense of belonging had evaporated. Dad had his own family – him, Michelle and Amy – and Mum would soon have the same, with herself, Derek and their own child forming a similar unit. Even as they stopped talking, and everyone turned to me, awaiting my reaction to the news, I realised that I was the one on the outside. I was the one who didn't belong.

Nathan was born the following September. Nearly two weeks late, Mum was delighted that he'd finally put in an appearance, as was Derek, and Dad and Michelle were quick to come round and offer congratulations, the four of them admiring and pampering their babies, to the point where I drifted into the background, and eventually went upstairs to my room, unnoticed.

Mum became besotted with Nathan, doting on his every move, gesture and advancement, and Derek was almost as bad – when he was at home, that was – so I suppose it would have been about then that I started to surf a lot more.

I'd first taken up the sport as a hobby when I was seven, discovering a natural talent, a connection to the sea, and to the board, which seemed to become an extension of my body when I was on the water.

To me it seemed like the natural place to go, as my two families became entities in their own rights, and I floundered somewhere between them. I turned to surfing for solace, for the peace of actually belonging to something... anything. It didn't matter to me what it was, I just wanted to feel at home, somewhere.

What's more, it got me out of the house, away from a baby who, despite my mother's devotion, appeared to me to do nothing but cry, and then as the months turned into years, a toddler who was into everything, and threw a tantrum whenever he didn't get his own way. I suppose Amy – being just over a year ahead of Nathan – had lulled me into a false sense of security. Admittedly I didn't live with her all the time, but she seemed like a happy baby and an easy toddler, and she and I always got on well. She liked to play, she giggled a lot and she loved cuddles. Nathan was completely different, and no matter how often I told myself that it was me, that it was my fault, that I was being impatient, resentful of him taking my place, irritated by his control over my mother, I knew deep down, that wasn't the case. Nathan was just a pain.

I was almost relieved to start at secondary school, even though I didn't relish the prospect of extra homework, and I took the bus every day with my friends from the village, most of whom surfed, like I did, and formed my third family, with whom I hung out at the beach whenever I could.

I got on well at school, and one of the advantages to being quite sporty, I soon discovered, was the instant popularity. At first I found it a little bewildering to be surrounded by girls at almost every turn. After all, what was the point in them? All they seemed to do was giggle, and whisper to each other, flicking their hair and gazing at me through fluttering eyelashes. It probably wasn't that bad, but it felt like it… until the beginning of year nine, that is, when everything changed. I was thirteen then, just coming up for my fourteenth birthday, and it was like the confusion – the fog in my head – suddenly cleared, and I saw the light. I'm not for one second going to claim that I miraculously understood girls – that concept was way beyond me, and still is – but in that moment of clarity, I realised that there really was a point to them after all; that even if their whisperings, and gazing, and fluttering eyes still didn't make sense, there was something attractive about them… and they were definitely worth spending time with. Well, some of them were, anyway. Shelley Ellison certainly was.

She had long blonde hair, which she usually wore tied up in a pony tail, and pale blue eyes, and although her nose tipped up a bit at the end, which made her look a bit like a pixie, she was really pretty. And I liked her. She seemed to like me too, from the way she kept catching my eye. And because I liked her, I asked her to come surfing with me. She smiled and accepted, and we arranged to meet that weekend, on the beach near where I lived.

I was nervous and excited at the same time. I'd spent quite a bit of time over the previous few weeks studying Shelley, and I found her lips absolutely fascinating. They were pale pink, quite full, and whenever

8

she licked them, they got a kind of shine on them which made me want to kiss them. The problem was, I wasn't completely sure how. It started to worry me. Actually, it started to dominate my every waking moment, and as my date with Shelley approached, I ended up watching a couple of films with Mum and Derek, in which there were kissing scenes. It wasn't intentional, it just happened that way, and as I cringed, sinking into the sofa and wishing they'd vacate the room and leave me to myself, I studied the techniques out of one eye, noting the angle of the man's head compared to the woman's and how their lips met. I took note of how the man caressed the woman's face and I even spotted, in one of the films, that the couple's tongues touched, although I wasn't sure about that. Was that expected, I wondered. Either way, I hoped Shelley would give me a chance to work it out... and that I wouldn't make a fool of myself.

Saturday soon came around and the weather did me a favour by being sunny, with a good strong breeze. I got to the beach a little early, just to make sure I could keep an eye out for Shelley, and when she arrived, I waved. She waved back and made her way over to the spot I'd chosen.

The first thing I noticed was that she was wearing tight jeans and a pale pink jumper, and that she wasn't carrying anything other than a small shoulder bag, which struck me as odd. I mean, I could understand that she might not have a board with her... I'd actually brought a spare with me, just in case. But what I couldn't fathom was that she hadn't brought anything else... and I mean nothing.

"You... you haven't brought a wetsuit?" I asked, once she'd put her shoulder bag down beside the beach mats I'd laid out on the sand. It was late October, and too cold to go surfing in just a swimming costume... not that Shelley seemed to have brought one of those with her either, judging from the size of her bag.

"A wet suit?"

"Yes."

She smiled as realisation seemed to dawn. "Oh... I don't actually want to surf."

"You don't?" In that case, why was she there?

"No. I'll watch you though."

That seemed a little silly to me. Surely the whole point had been for us to do something together, hadn't it?

"Is it because you can't surf?" I asked, wondering if that was her reason. "Because if you want, I can teach you."

"Oh, no. Don't worry about that. I mean, I can't surf, but to be honest, I'm not that interested." She sat down, looking up at me. "You go ahead, and I'll wait here."

I felt a bit self conscious walking down the beach with my board under my arm, knowing she was watching me – or at least assuming she was – and I wasn't gone for too long, just in case she got bored waiting and decided to leave.

She didn't, and when I got back, I sat beside her for a while.

"How long have you been surfing?" she asked.

"Since I was seven."

She nodded. "You're very good."

"Thanks." I smiled at her.

"I mean, I don't know anything about surfing, but you seem to be very good to me."

I half chuckled at the way she'd turned her own compliment around, although she didn't seem to notice. She was too busy staring at me.

I decided the moment was too good not to take a chance and, leaning a little closer, I reached up with one hand, cupped her face, and kissed her. Her lips were soft against mine, and she seemed to like what I was doing, moaning gently until I pulled back, at which point I noticed her eyes were still closed, and her lips were still slightly open and pouting, as though she was waiting for more. And who was I to disappoint?

It was only over dinner that evening that my mum pointed out the error of my ways. She'd asked about my afternoon, and I'd decided to tell her that I'd met up with Shelley. I didn't give her and Derek any details – obviously. I didn't tell her that we'd kissed, or that touching tongues was a lot nicer than I'd anticipated. Instead I focused on the fact that Shelley had come surfing and hadn't actually wanted to surf, which I was still finding a little odd.

"Maybe she couldn't go in the water," Mum said, trying to get

Nathan to eat with a spoon, rather than his fingers, and to stop throwing his food onto the floor. He'd turned four the previous month and it seemed to me as though he should have mastered those small feats by now... but what did I know?

"What do you mean?" I looked up at her. "You think she might be scared of water? Well, in that case, why accept an invitation to go surfing?"

She smiled at me. "That's not what I meant, Adam. Think about it. You're nearly fourteen now... you're old enough to understand that there are times of the month when some girls prefer not to go swimming... or, in this case, surfing."

I felt my brow creasing as I tried to work out what on earth she was talking about, and then the light dawned and I wondered if I was blushing, because I realised how inconsiderate I'd been. Why hadn't I thought of that? It was so obvious. "Oh... I see..."

Her smile widened. "Maybe you should leave it a few days and ask her again?" she suggested.

"A few days?" I asked. "Is that long enough?" I had no idea about such things. Obviously I knew about periods. It had been a couple of years since Mum and Dad had sat me down and given me separate 'talks' about girls, and boys, and puberty... and at school we had lessons that focused on sex education, relationships, and personal development, but I didn't claim to know everything.

"For most girls, yes," she replied.

That night in bed, I wondered how I was going to raise the topic with Shelley, but decided in the end that I didn't need to. I didn't have to ask her such a personal question, I could just invite her to come surfing again, and see what happened.

"You want to go surfing?" she said, when I asked her on the Monday morning, catching up with her outside the English room. "Again?"

Her reaction was disappointing. "Well, yes. Don't you?"

"Not particularly."

"Oh."

"It's really boring."

"Not if you're actually surfing it's not," I reasoned.

"Maybe not, but I'm not that interested." She moved closer to me. "I'm happy to do something else though." Her voice was soft, her lips enticing.

"Like what?"

"We could go to the pictures...?"

"Okay. If that's what you want." She smiled and, although it wasn't really my idea of fun, I found myself looking forward to it.

My optimism was ill-conceived. I stupidly let Shelley choose the movie, and naturally she chose something romantic, although I have no idea what it was. I didn't really pay much attention after the first ten minutes, being as there didn't seem to be much of a plot worth following, and I'd already worked out that the male lead and female lead were going to end up together by the end of the movie, so watching them get there, through various invented tribulations seemed like a waste of time... of two hours, to be precise.

Still, they were two hours during which Shelley and I held hands, and after which I got to walk her home, before catching the bus back to Carven Bay. She let me kiss her goodnight too, and during those few minutes, I somehow didn't mind the wasted hours so much.

We carried on seeing each other for the next six weeks or so, with Shelley always dictating what we did, where we went and how we spent our time. It wasn't long though, before I started to resent that. I longed to get back to the beach, or to walk on the headland, rather than sitting in coffee shops, or cinemas, or waiting for her outside changing rooms in airless clothing stores. I wasn't being myself anymore. When I was with her, I felt like I was a different person; and he wasn't a person I particularly liked. So, I ended it. I tried to be kind about it; I blamed myself. I think she did too. Probably quite rightly.

I felt like a weight had been lifted from my shoulders and that I could at least go back to being me again. Getting back onto a board was like going home, and I spent the next few weeks just enjoying myself... until I met Roberta.

With her, I decided to keep my surfing separate; to learn from my mistakes and not to include her, but not to give it up for her either, like I had with Shelley. I thought if I could keep a decent balance in my life, then things would be okay. And they were, for a couple of months, at which point she complained that I was spending too much time on the beach, and not enough with her.

I felt like I couldn't win.

That didn't stop me trying though, because after Roberta came Alexis, then Susan, and then Suzanne – which was complicated, and an unfortunate mix up of names brought that brief romance to a rapid conclusion. Then came Vicky, and Tina, and Alison… The list wasn't endless, but I suppose it was significant and every time, they would want me to spend more time with them, and less time on the beach.

"You're there every night."

"Can't we have just one weekend without you surfing?"

"I'm fed up having to compete with your surfboard…"

I did my best to make time for them, and I went back to trying to include them, suggesting that they could always come with me to the beach, that I'd teach them to surf – and that we could have fun doing it, and spend more time together. But in every case, they'd cite a reason not to join me.

"It'll ruin my hair."

"I'm not a very good swimmer."

"I'm scared I'll get hurt."

By the time I'd finished school at sixteen, I was bound to admit that, as much as I liked girls – and I really did like girls – they were a hell of a lot of trouble.

I'd stupidly assumed that they were going out with me because they liked who I was; not because they were trying to change me into someone else. But after nearly three years of trying, I was seriously starting to wonder.

Obviously, I did know girls who surfed. I knew quite a few of them, but strangely enough, I didn't find myself attracted to them, even though I saw them quite regularly, and usually in little more than a skimpy bikini or a body hugging wetsuit. For some reason, I saw them differently to the girls I went out with, admiring their abilities on the water, rather than their figures or their faces.

There was a group of us; a core group of maybe eight or ten, with a few others who came and went. Some of us – like Dean and I – had known each other for more than a decade, and although we didn't meet up all the time, we knew each other fairly well, and hung out whenever we could. And for a while, I stuck with my friends, and gave girlfriends a miss; at least my friends accepted me for who I was.

I'd already decided that I wanted to go to college. It wasn't that I was particularly academic – I wasn't – and I had no intention of going on to university, but I wasn't ready to face the world of work yet either, and besides, all my friends were going, so it seemed like a good idea at the time.

What I hadn't anticipated was that I'd only just scrape through my GCSEs, which made everyone, including my parents, question my judgement about continuing in education.

"You can come and work for me," Dad reasoned and I had to admit I was tempted, even though I knew he'd be a hard task-master. He owned a building company and I knew he'd start me off at the bottom, with no favours, that the work would be hard and unforgiving, but it would also be outdoors – which was my favourite place to be. The problem was, I was determined – well, I was stubborn, anyway, and I'd set my heart on college.

I'd only been there for half a term when I realised how much harder it was than school. Okay, so the hours were easier, but the lessons themselves were tough, and when I was at home trying to study, there were constant interruptions from Nathan, who was seven by that stage, and effectively ran the house. It used to really grate on me that Mum would let Nathan talk down to her, and occasionally even swear at her, and she'd write it off as a 'phase'. That boy had so many 'phases', it was impossible to keep up, but with each one, his behaviour became more and more intolerable. In his latest one, he'd introduced hitting and punching, which he'd never tried on me, but I'd caught mum nursing her arm one day, and Nathan running in the opposite direction. Despite her denials that he'd done anything, it didn't take a genius to put two and two together. I tried talking to her, I tried talking to Derek, but neither of them would listen, and so I carried on living under their roof and treading on eggshells, until one day I cracked.

Being as I knew I had a job lined up with my dad, and I had no intention of going on to university, I'd chosen A-Level subjects that I'd enjoyed at school, which meant I was studying Geography and Biology, and I'd added Psychology into the mix just because it sounded interesting. Over that particular weekend, I had a lot of reading to do, and none of it was sinking in, because Nathan was running around the house, screaming his head off, while Mum and Derek were out in the garden ignoring him.

After over an hour of that, I'd had enough and yanked open my bedroom door, grabbing Nathan by his arm as he bolted past, and telling him to keep quiet.

He glared up at me. "Make me," he sneered.

"Don't tempt me," I growled back.

His eyes widened in fear, I think, before he pulled his arm free and ran down the stairs, and relishing the peace and quiet, I went back into my room and settled down to read again… that is, until Derek knocked on my door.

"Nathan's really upset. He says you hit him." He eyed me suspiciously.

"No, I didn't. I just told him to be quiet. I'm trying to study."

"And he's just being a seven year old," he reasoned.

"Well, can't he do that more quietly?"

Derek shook his head. "One day, when you have kids of your own, you'll understand that it's not that easy."

I stared at him, wanting to tell him that it was; that all they needed to do was exert some authority over Nathan, like my dad had done over me. And that, if they didn't, he'd soon be completely out of control. But I didn't, because looking at the expression on Derek's face, I realised there was no point. It was an argument I was never going to win.

So instead, I packed up my books and a change of clothes and left, asking Derek to tell my mother that I'd be back on Sunday night.

"Where are you going?" He sounded worried.

"To Dad's."

"But surely Amy's just as noisy," he said, smiling complacently.

"No, she's not."

She wasn't. Amy was quiet, placid, and a lot more considerate. In fact, she was such a lovely child, and Michelle clearly relished motherhood so much, that I'd often wondered why she and Dad hadn't enlarged their family. I was relieved that Mum and Derek hadn't – with the way Nathan behaved, it was bad enough already. The thought of another rowdy sibling living in that house was terrifying. Not that what any of them did was any of my business. Obviously.

Dad and Michelle hadn't been expecting me, and when I arrived, having caught the bus into Newquay and walked from the bus stop to their house, I think I threw their weekend into turmoil. But Dad knew me well enough to know that I wasn't given to tantrums myself and, if I'd decided to leave like that, then something had to be wrong. He whispered something to Michelle and she and Amy went out into the back garden, leaving us alone.

"What's happened?" he asked and we sat down at the kitchen table, facing each other.

"It's Nathan. He's…"

"He's what?"

"He's annoying."

"A lot of kids are annoying," Dad explained. "That's no reason to throw your own toys out of the pram."

"I'm not. But you've got no idea what it's like. He… he's noisy, he's disruptive. He's inconsiderate."

"You mean he's a child?"

"No, it's worse than that." I knew I wasn't explaining it very well. "If he doesn't get his own way, he gets in such a mood… it's like he has no control. He rants and screams, and he swears all the time."

My dad frowned. "Intentionally?" he murmured.

"Yes. And he hits Mum and calls her names, and she lets him."

"He hits her?" I could tell Dad was shocked.

"Yes."

"What does Derek say about this?"

"Nathan only does it when Derek's not there."

Dad stared at me. "So he does have some control then? He can pick and choose when he misbehaves?"

"Yes… I suppose." I hadn't thought of that – but I supposed I should have done. It was obvious when Dad said it.

"Have you tried saying anything to Nathan, when Derek's not there? Or tried to stop him yourself? You're certainly big enough…" He wasn't wrong. My dad was a powerfully built man; he always had been, and that was one thing I had in common with him… that and our hair colour, which was a darkish brown, although he used to frown at the length I'd taken to wearing mine since I'd left school and gained the freedoms of a college life.

"Of course I have. I've told him off, and sometimes I've held him back physically as well, when I've thought he might be about to hit Mum, but then she tells me off, and says it's not my place to chastise her son."

Dad's brow furrowed again. "So what happened today?" he asked.

"I was just trying to get some reading done, that's all. Derek and Mum were in the garden and Nathan was running round the house like a seven year old hooligan. Even with my music on, I couldn't concentrate, so I went out onto the landing and grabbed his arm as he was running past, and told him to stop. He ran off, and the next thing I knew, Derek came up and accused me of hitting Nathan." I looked my dad in the eye. "I didn't."

He nodded his head. "I know."

I sighed deeply, running my finger along the edge of the pine table. "I appreciate that you weren't expecting me to turn up unannounced, and if it's too much trouble, then I'll go and stay at Dean's, but I'm trying to get my head around psychodynamics at the moment, and I need to concentrate."

Dad smiled. "I don't even know what psychodynamics are, but you don't have to go to Dean's. You can stay here. You know you're always welcome." He got up from the table. "Help yourself to whatever you want, and go upstairs for a while. We'll keep Amy in the garden for now, just to give you some peace and quiet… and we'll talk later. Alright?"

I looked up at him and nodded my head, feeling grateful that I had a few hours' respite.

Over dinner that night, it became clear that, while I'd been studying all afternoon, Dad and Michelle had been talking about the situation, because Dad made the suggestion that I move in with them... permanently.

"You mean for good?" I asked, making sure I'd understood him properly.

"Yes," Michelle said, I presumed to demonstrate that she was in agreement with the idea. "You need to be able to study in peace and quiet." She looked over at me, her eyes filled with concern. "And you need somewhere a bit more stable..."

"But what about Mum?"

"Your mother isn't your problem," Dad said, putting down his knife and fork and leaning his elbows on the table. "I'll go and talk to her — and to Derek."

"What will you say?"

"I'll tell them what you told me."

I felt a shiver run down my spine. "But... but they'll be cross with me for telling you."

He shrugged. "No they won't." I wasn't convinced by that, but before I could say anything, he continued, "From what you've said, I'm not sure Derek appreciates how bad things are, and he needs to. And your mother needs to realise that she can't allow a seven year old to run the house. It won't do her any good, and it won't help Nathan; not in the long run."

"I agree with everything you're saying, Dad, but I doubt if they'll welcome your... um..."

"Interference?" he suggested the word for me and I nodded my head.

"They don't even like me butting in, and I live there..." Well, I had lived there, because the more I thought about it, the more I had to acknowledge that the idea of living with Dad and Michelle – and Amy – was becoming really very appealing.

"You let me worry about their reactions," he said firmly. "If you like the idea of living here – or you think you might like to try it for a while and see how it goes – then I'll go and see your mum in the morning."

I looked down at my plate of half-eaten chicken, and then turned to Amy, who was quietly eating her own dinner, seemingly oblivious to the momentous change that was about to take place in my life. The difference between this civilised, peaceful mealtime, and the usual raucous, ill-mannered ones I'd become used to at home, was too marked not to notice.

"I think I'd like to try it," I whispered, even though I felt guilty for abandoning my mum.

Dad reached across the table and put his hand on my arm. "Okay," he said. "Leave everything to me."

I looked up at him, feeling ashamed that I'd put myself first. "She will be alright, won't she?"

He nodded his head. "Yes, son. Don't you worry. I'll make sure she's alright."

I didn't know what Dad did or said, but he returned from visiting Mum and Derek the next day with a suitcase full of my clothes and a sad expression on his face. When I asked him what had happened, he shook his head, and told me not to worry; Mum was okay and everything would be alright. I tried to feel reassured by that, but I still needed to see her for myself to make absolutely certain.

So, the following day, after college, I caught the bus back to my mum's house and let myself in. She was pleased to see me and gave me a long hug. Then we sat down, while Nathan watched something on television and she said she understood the situation; that I needed some space to myself and that Nathan was a disruption to my studies. I didn't suggest that there was something she could have done about that, and therefore kept me under her roof at the same time, and she didn't apologise for Nathan's behaviour. All in all, it wasn't a very satisfying visit, but I left feeling a little better than I had before. At least she wasn't angry with me.

When Dad had picked up my clothes, he'd also brought my surfboards, which he stored in his garage, and it was only on the bus ride from Carven Bay back to Newquay that I realised I'd no longer be able to walk to the beach to surf and to see my friends. I wasn't sure why it hadn't occurred to me before, but the prospect of being cut off from that part of my life was devastating, and when I arrived at Dad's he guessed immediately that something was wrong.

Assuming it was to do with Mum, he sat me down, a smile appearing on his face when I explained the problem.

"You're going to be seventeen in two weeks," he reasoned.

"And?"

"And then you can learn to drive."

I smiled myself then, although my smile soon fell. "Which is lovely, but I won't have a car."

He nodded his head slowly. "Well, we'll see about that…" I stared at him and went to speak, but he held up his hand. "We'll see," he repeated and I stayed quiet.

It seemed like the best thing to do.

It only took me a couple of months to pass my test and Dad bought me a second hand Toyota Land Cruiser. It was a beast of a vehicle, but ideal for carrying my boards – not to mention the one or two of my friends who lived closer to Newquay and, like me, preferred the surf at Carven Bay, to the more popular beaches at Fistral and Watergate Bay. In the past, they'd always had to get lifts from parents or older siblings, but over the course of that spring, I became the most popular guy in town.

I soon settled in to life with Dad and Michelle, and found it easier to study at their house – to the point where I wished I'd made the move earlier, being as it would probably have resulted in better GCSE results. Still, it was too late to worry about that, and instead, I focused on doing as well as I could at college – which I did, getting three Bs, and shocking even myself.

Finally, we reached the end of the summer after we'd all left college, and it was time for the group to scatter. Everyone else, other than myself and Dean, was going to university in various cities across the country. Dean had got a job in a car showroom, and I'd already started working for my dad's building company. As I'd predicted, he'd shown me no favouritism, and I'd gone in at the bottom, and although it was hard work, I was really enjoying it. I was working outside, with friendly people, creating something with my hands. What wasn't to like?

That last Saturday, towards the end of September, as summer really turned to autumn and the surf began to pick up again, we'd all agreed to spend the day together and in the evening, we had a barbecue on the beach. Everyone brought something, from beers to sausages, and we sat together, watching the sunset while we reminisced, and looked forward to different times. Terry and Christina had been together since year ten at school and, to my knowledge were the only ones out of all of us who'd even kissed, let alone gone any further – and, believe me, they'd definitely gone a lot further than kissing. They were both headed for Durham University, having purposely arranged it that way, desperate to be as far away from home as possible, to escape and have some freedom from the confines of their parents' watchful gazes. Everyone else, however, was going to somewhere different, and the atmosphere that evening was a mixture of excitement and nerves. That is, except for Rick, who had a reputation for sleeping with every girl he'd ever met – other than those in our group, as far as I knew – and was avidly looking forward to finding a fresh set of victims.

Slowly but surely, everyone drifted away, a couple of them going earlier than the others, because they were actually leaving for pastures new the very next morning, until the only people left on the beach were myself and Fiona. She was tall and very slim, with auburn hair, and while I'd known her for about four years, I couldn't recall having a serious conversation with her before… not about anything other than surfing, anyway.

"Part of me can't wait to leave," she said, surprising me with her wistful tone of voice. "But I think I'm going to miss the beach, and nights like this." She was sitting beside me and we were both looking out to sea. The sun had gone down already, but it was still just about light enough to make out the horizon.

"I know I'd miss it, if I ever left," I replied, contemplating the wrench of leaving the one place that had always felt like home to me. It was bad enough living in Newquay, but the thought of moving further afield actually made me shudder.

She turned and looked at me, and I felt her lean in a little closer, her arm resting against mine. "You'll never leave, Adam. Not really. You belong here. This place is in your DNA."

"Is that a bad thing?"

"For most people, it probably would be. Carven Bay is small and can be stifling. But in your case, I'd say, no… it's not a bad thing." I wondered if that was a compliment, or an insult, and how she thought she knew me well enough to judge, but before I could comment, she continued, "I love it when the beach is completely deserted, don't you? It gives you a feeling of ownership."

She looked around as she spoke, and so did I, feeling unsure about the idea of ever owning the beach. If anything, to me, it was the other way around – it owned me. Even so, I couldn't deny that I loved the seclusion, and the solitude. We literally were completely alone that evening, the backdrop of the beach shrouded in shadows, the lapping waves and our own breathing providing the only soundtrack. But then, as I turned back to her, she leaned in and kissed me, most unexpectedly. To start with, I wasn't sure what to do. I'd never thought of her, or any of the other girls in the group, in that way before, but as her lips grazed over mine and her hand snaked down my stomach and across the front of my board shorts, my body responded easily to her touch. I heard her moan, swallowing down the sound as she twisted around and straddled me, sitting on my lap, her arms coming around my neck. She broke the kiss, breathing hard, and the next few seconds became a frenzy of fumbling fingers, as her purpose became obvious and she pulled down my shorts, releasing my erection, while I attempted, and eventually managed, to undo the ties at the sides of her bikini, before I felt her lowering herself onto me.

My mind was a whirl of so many sensations, it was impossible for me to order them, but I suppose first and foremost there was pleasure, because there was no denying that everything Fiona was doing felt incredible. Despite that, there was also surprise, and an element of shock. After all, we'd only been sitting talking a few seconds earlier, and suddenly we were having sex… and while the setting wasn't exactly what I'd had in mind for my first time, I wasn't about to stop her, just for the sake of geography.

We drowned out the sounds of the sea, her sighs filling my ears, and it didn't take long before her breathing altered and I felt her thighs clench, right before she clamped around me and let out a low cry, throwing her head back, seemingly in the grip of ecstasy. She stilled for a matter of seconds, sucking in lungfuls of air, and then started to move again, climaxing for a second time within minutes. That was too much for me and, clutching her hips, I raised my own, groaning through my much-needed release, deep inside her.

I have no idea how much time elapsed between that moment and the second when I opened my eyes, but I know that in the instant that I did, the magnitude of what we'd done hit me… like a wrecking ball.

"Oh my God," I whispered. "We… we shouldn't have done that."

"Well, thanks." She climbed off of me, sitting back down again, and twisted around, trying to re-fasten her bikini bottoms.

"Sorry. I didn't mean it like that. I—I just meant, I should have used a condom, that's all."

She stopped what she was doing, no longer offended, it seemed, and smiled up at me. "Oh, don't worry about that. I'm on the pill."

"Great… but that's only part of the deal, isn't it? I mean, that may have been my first time, but unless I'm very much mistaken, it wasn't yours."

Even in the moonlight, I could see the way her brow furrowed, and the frown settling on her face. "Thanks… again."

"Sorry… again. But it wasn't your first time, was it?"

"No." She finished tying up her bikini and sat up straight while I waited for her to say something, but she didn't, and eventually, I felt I had to fill the silence.

"So?"

"So what?"

I sighed. "So, was it safe?"

"Of course it was. I don't exactly sleep around, you know."

I felt a little ashamed. In my momentary fear, I'd been far too quick to judge her. "Sorry," I repeated, for the third time. "I'm not very good at this."

"I'd noticed."

I felt myself bridle, and knelt, pulling up my shorts, only then realising that I was still exposed. "Thanks," I said, echoing her comment from earlier.

She turned and looked at me. "I was referring to your panic, not your performance," she said and I felt slightly mollified. "Your performance was pretty damn perfect," she added, and I felt a lot better than mollified. Even so…

"You're sure it's safe?" I needed to be certain, because whatever she'd said about my performance, my panic was still fairly overwhelming.

"Yes," she hissed. "Look, I've been with one other guy… Rick, if you must know."

"Rick?" I was stunned.

"Yes. I lost my virginity to him," she said with disarming honesty, staring out to sea once more. "I… well, I was intrigued by what it would be like, and I decided I may as well try it with someone experienced."

"And they don't come much more experienced than Rick," I murmured.

She chuckled. "No. Although you'd never know it. He's not as much of an expert as he'd have everyone believe. He was a bit selfish about the whole thing… and it was just a bit underwhelming really." I nodded my head, not daring to pass comment, in the sure and certain knowledge that my own inexperience would give me away. "But you can stop panicking," she added eventually. "I made him use a condom."

I heaved out a sigh of relief, which I'm fairly certain she heard, and then got to my feet.

She gazed up at me. "You're not going to be weird about this, are you?"

I felt as though I'd already been weird enough, but I didn't say that. Instead I asked her what she meant.

She didn't answer straight away, but stood up herself and dusted some stray sand from her legs, before straightening, our faces just a few inches apart.

"I think you're gorgeous, Adam, and you're sexy as hell... and quite how you've never had sex before, I don't know. But that's not the point... the point is that you've been a fantasy of mine for a while now."

"I have?" She'd hidden that well. I'd had no idea, and I didn't really know what to say.

"The thing is," she continued, before I had a chance to work out my response, "I've realised the dream now, and while what we just did was really, really satisfying, and everything I'd ever wanted it to be, I'm going to uni next week, in Leicester, and this is my chance to spread my wings. I don't want to be tied to one guy. Especially not here. I want to see what else is out there for me. I want to have fun."

As she was talking, I watched her lips – because I still had a 'thing' about lips, and about kissing them – but as her words filtered through my still-befuddled brain, I found myself losing interest in both her and her lips. After about the fifth time she said 'I', I realised how completely self-centred she was. The whole experience had been about her, and while I didn't have a problem with that in itself, I couldn't help feeling I'd been used. At least to a certain extent... for the purposes of fulfilling a fantasy.

"I'm not going to be weird," I murmured, answering her original question.

"Good." She smiled.

"But can I give you a piece of advice?" I paused, but not long enough for her to interrupt, and then said, "I think you should invest in some condoms of your own, and carry them with you. I'm all for having a good time, but at least be safe."

She stared at me for a moment, and then she laughed, and I laughed too, before she leant up and kissed me on the cheek.

"Thank you," she whispered and then turned, grabbing her bag and heading up the beach.

I wasn't sure if she was thanking me for the advice, for the sex, or for not being weird. And, in all honesty, it didn't matter.

*

It was a couple of months later, just after my nineteenth birthday, that I had my tattoo done. I wasn't drunk; I was stone cold sober, but I suppose it was something that I had done on a whim. Well, kind of. I was in Newquay, attempting to buy Christmas presents, when I walked past the tattoo parlour and saw the picture in the window. It was of an eagle, and was done in a Celtic design, and I thought it looked fantastic. Without even thinking, I went inside and asked about it, and the man started to explain that it was a design he'd just done for another customer. I nodded my head, taking an interest, but thinking to myself that, if I ever had a tattoo, I'd want something unique, not something that had been designed for someone else, and that I was just copying. Getting into his stride and, I presume, sensing my interest – as well as a potential customer – the man went on to explain that the knots within the design were all symbolic, as was the eagle itself. I asked about that and he told me that the eagle represented maturity and fearlessness. I chuckled.

"What's wrong?" the man asked, introducing himself as Dave, at that point.

"I'm not sure either of those traits exactly suits me," I replied.

"Then what does?" he asked, looking at me in an inquisitive way.

"Well…" I wracked my brain, trying to think of what words best described my character. "I'm a bit of a loner, I suppose."

"You don't have many friends?" he asked.

"Yes, but they've all gone to uni, and even when they were here, I often used to spend time by myself… I suppose I was always a bit like that, ever since my parents divorced—" I stopped talking suddenly. "Sorry," I murmured. "I didn't mean…"

"It's alright," he interrupted, smiling. "People tell you all kinds of things in this job."

I felt embarrassed then and wondered how I could get out of his shop without being rude.

"What about a wolf?" he said.

"A wolf?"

"Yes." He nodded his head. "A lone wolf."

I liked the sound of that.

It took Dave a couple of weeks to come up with the design, during which time my feet got colder and colder, to the point where I'd prepared a speech, explaining that I no longer wanted the tattoo, but would happily pay him for the design, thinking to myself that I'd just have it as a poster on my bedroom wall, or something. But when I went back, when I saw what he'd done, I knew I had to have it – on my skin, not on the wall.

He'd incorporated all the knots we'd talked about; the ones that represented inner strength, the eternity of nature, luck and love – not because I felt I had those traits, but because they were the ones I aspired to, or that I admired. I drew the line at anything to do with sexuality and relationships… and as for wisdom, well, I felt I'd already displayed a distinct lack of that, so we agreed to leave those out.

I'm not going to say it was a painless experience, but Dave kept me talking and because the design was in a single colour, it didn't take as long as I'd expected.

My parents' reactions were exactly what I'd anticipated. My mum freaked out, asking me why I'd 'ruined' my 'beautiful body', while my dad raised an eyebrow and then frowned at Michelle when she started to admire the artistry.

I didn't care though.

My lone wolf was me… and I loved it.

I had a nice life, even after all my friends had gone away. I enjoyed my job, and I spent most of my evenings and weekends at the beach, sometimes by myself, but quite often with Dean… and in the holidays, most of the other guys would come home and we'd hang out together, just like we always had. Fiona, however, never came back, and I heard on the grapevine that she'd met a guy at uni and had moved in with him. So much for spreading her wings…

I'd like to say I spread mine instead, but after my experience with Fiona, I'd changed my outlook; or I suppose you could say I'd had it changed for me. Yes, I was still fascinated with girls – naturally – but

I couldn't forget that feeling of being used, and I'd decided that I didn't want to be the kind of guy who could make a girl feel like that. Despite the ample opportunities, I didn't want to have a series of holiday romances, with girls who came to the bay for a week or two in the summer, and then left again, taking any notion of my responsibility towards them back home to wherever they lived, and leaving me to move on to my next conquest. I wanted something a bit more than that. The problem was that I wasn't entirely sure what the 'more' was, or how I was going to find it. And until I worked that out, I decided I'd rather be single. After all, compared to a lot of people, I had a pretty amazing life.

It was a warm afternoon at the beginning of September, and I'd finished work a little earlier than usual because the supplies we'd needed had been delayed until the following morning, and there was no point in us all standing around on the site, doing nothing. Being as it was a beautiful day, I headed home to change and then went straight down to the beach, not surprised to find a lot of the guys already there, enjoying a supposed well-earned break from university. They'd all finished their second year, and unlike the previous summer when they'd come home, the differences between us seemed more marked. Dean and I were working and earning a living, budgeting and – to a certain extent – thinking about the future. I was saving for a deposit on a flat of my own, and Dean had already left home and was living in a rented studio apartment just down the coast. In our conversations with our student friends, it felt to both of us as though they'd never left school. They gossiped, just like we'd all done in our youth, about who was cheating on who, with whom, who'd got too drunk to make it home and had ended up sleeping in a gutter, or a bush, or a complete stranger's bed, and which lecturers they liked and didn't, and why… it felt like stepping back in time, by about five years, which wasn't bad, considering we were all only twenty.

Even so, there was still the underlying friendship, bound by the beach, and by our boards.

On that particular afternoon, it was really quite warm – too warm for wetsuits – the waves were pretty good, considering it was still only early September, and we all surfed for a while, before walking up the beach together, talking and laughing – especially at Rick, who made an easy target at the best of times.

We were still quite a long way from the place where we'd left our things when, out of the corner of my eye, I saw a girl coming down the pathway onto the beach, and I felt the strangest sensation surge through my body, like a flood of heat sweeping from my head to my toes. Even from that distance, I could see that she was absolutely stunning… and I was used to hanging around with half naked women, so I knew a stunning girl when I saw one. This girl wasn't half naked though; she was wearing cut-off denim shorts, which accentuated her long legs, and a tie-dyed t-shirt, and as I continued to walk, amazed that I was still able to put one foot in front of the other, the sea breeze caught her top, pasting it to her, and revealing perfectly shaped breasts. I shook my head, wanting to slap myself for being so superficial, so obvious in my appraisal of her, but even as I mentally scolded myself, I couldn't get away from the fact that she was the most beautiful girl I'd ever seen in my life.

I somehow snapped out of my dreams, and focused on the sand in front of me, determined not to ogle her anymore… that was, until I reached our spot and glanced up again, to find that she'd clambered up onto the rock that was about a third of the way down the beach, and that she seemed to be looking in our direction. I couldn't make out if she was interested in us in general, or in one of us in particular, although I hoped it was the latter, and that the 'one in particular' might be me. And while I contemplated that, I picked up my towel and started to dry off, turning my back to her, just to compose myself for a moment.

When I turned around again, she was staring directly at me, and I had to smile. It was completely involuntary – a natural reaction, as though my face just responded to her gaze, without me having any control over it. To my utter amazement, she smiled back, and although she was still a fair distance away, I noticed a flush creeping up her cheeks, and in that instant, I instinctively knew she was the 'more' I'd been looking for.

Acting on impulse and without giving myself time to think – or to chicken out – I draped my towel around my shoulders, just so my hair didn't drip everywhere really, and started walking towards her. With every step, I convinced myself that I could do this. She may have been the girl of my dreams – the girl of my fantasies, really – but I could talk to her. Of course I could. As I got closer, I could see her better, and I saw that 'beautiful' wasn't a descriptive enough word for her. With my limited academic abilities, I didn't know what the word was, but she was 'it'. She had long, straight, light brown hair that caught in the wind every so often, and her lips were full, and pink and, as she captured the lower one between her teeth I felt a strong urge to capture her face in my hands and kiss her deeply. She glanced away for a second, as though looking for something, but then turned back to me, and I did my best to hold her gaze until I arrived in front of her and smiled, feeling as though I'd fallen, just slightly, into her pale hazel eyes. I'd never reacted to anyone like that before, but I was increasingly aware that I couldn't just stand there. I had to say something.

"Are you okay up there?" I asked. It was a lame beginning, but it was the best I could do, considering the effect she'd had on me.

"Um… yes thanks." Her voice matched her perfectly. It was soft, pretty, delicate, and yet she seemed uncertain of herself and I realised there and then that the 'more' wasn't a person at all. It wasn't a 'who', it was a 'what'. And the 'what' was an overwhelming, protective urge, which was aimed directly at her. It was a need in me to make this girl feel safe, to make her smile every single day, to make her feel comfortable and contented every moment of her life, to make her feel needed, and wanted… and loved.

Loved? What the…

I reminded myself to speak again. "You can join us if you want, rather than sitting here by yourself." I wasn't sure why I'd said that, except that she looked sort of lonely, and I had an urgent, desperate need to take care of her, to spend time with her… starting right at that moment.

She stared directly at me and I wondered what she was thinking. There was a hint of doubt in her eyes and it occurred to me that she might be scared. After all, she didn't know me from the man on the moon, and I'd just suggested she should come and sit with my friends and me. What could I say to reassure her? Perhaps if I told her she'd be safe with me… that there was nowhere safer in the world than with me, because I'd never let anything happen to her… might that work?

"Um… okay," she said suddenly, interrupting my train of thought, and making my reassurances unnecessary, which was probably a good thing, because with hindsight, I realised they'd probably have scared her even more.

I smiled at her as she started to slide down the rock, her sandals clutched in her hand, and instinctively, I reached out, placing my hands on her slim waist and lifting her down to the ground. She felt feather-light in my arms, and despite the temptation to keep hold of her, I didn't. I let her go, and turned back, leading her towards my friends, knowing she'd probably feel safer with them, than alone with me. At least a few of the girls were there, and I reasoned that was probably why she'd accepted my invitation. It made sense, and I didn't mind at all. I was going to get to sit with her for a while – and that was all I wanted.

As we got back to where everyone else was sitting, I realised they were all looking up at us, confused, I think, by the fact that I'd brought a complete stranger into our group. I glanced at Dean, who raised his eyebrows, and then at Rick, who had a lecherous grin on his face, which made me doubly protective of the girl, and enabled me to reach a very quick and easy decision. There was no way I was letting him anywhere near her. "I'd make the introductions," I said, looking down at her, "but you won't remember their names anyway." She smiled up at me and I suggested she take a seat on the beach mat, which she did, crossing her legs and putting her sandals down beside her.

Within seconds, Sara came over, giving me a glare, before she sat down beside the girl, leaning into her in a friendly, girly kind of way, which was fairly typical of her.

"You're not from round here, are you?" she asked. I supposed it was as good an opening to a conversation as any – and it was certainly no worse than my pathetic attempt.

"No," the girl replied.

"So where are you from?"

"I'm from Surrey."

Sara smiled and nodded her head, and I decided to sit down myself, feeling suddenly self conscious about standing there in front of them both, and doing nothing other than staring.

"Would you like a coke?" I offered the girl and she smiled her acceptance as I reached over to the cool box and handed her a bottle, which she took, thanking me, with yet another cute smile.

"Did I hear you say you're from Surrey?" I asked, joining in their conversation, and hoping I didn't sound too desperate not to be left out.

"Yes."

"Well, that explains your accent," I replied and Sara laughed, possibly at my dumb answer, although I joined in, and within seconds the girl did too, which was a huge relief, being as I wondered for a second if I'd insulted her.

"I suppose I do sound odd to you," she said, struggling to open the bottle of coke, which I took from her, opening it, and handing it back.

"No more odd than we sound to you."

"Yes, but your accents are softer," she said, and put the bottle to her perfect lips, taking a long sip, before looking back at me. "I like them." *Nowhere near as much as I like you.* Was 'like' the right word? I wasn't sure...

"I take it that, being from Surrey, you've probably never surfed before?" Sara asked and I wanted to kick myself for not thinking of asking that. It would have been so much better than any of the things I'd said so far.

"No," the girl said, shaking her head. "Never."

"And would you like to?" I asked, getting in my question before Sara had a chance.

The girl's eyes lit up and she breathed, "I'd love to," her response – and the manner of it – making my heart flip in my chest.

"Then why don't I teach you?" The thought of seeing her in a swimming costume, let alone touching her, holding her while I showed her the techniques required to surf, made my whole body harden with need, but I swallowed all of that down and focused on her, as the doubt

32

spread across her face again, and I wondered if I'd overstepped the mark.

"Well, because I don't have a board," she said, "or a swimming costume."

Was she kidding? "You don't own a swimming costume?" Was that what she meant? Or was she saying that she'd come on holiday to a seaside resort, and hadn't brought one with her, which was almost as nonsensical. "Not at all?"

She smiled and shook her head. "No, I mean, I do own one, but I haven't got it on me right now."

I chuckled to disguise my sigh of relief. "Oh, I see. Well, why not come back tomorrow and I'll teach you then?"

"Because I still won't have a board?"

"You can borrow one of mine," I offered, hoping that I didn't sound desperate. Again.

"Really?" Her excitement had returned, and I nodded my head, unable to stop staring at her. "I probably won't be any good," she said, sounding kind of sad, and I shrugged my shoulders.

"If you don't try, you'll never know, will you?"

In any case, I had a feeling she'd be just fine. Well, she would if I kept hold of her, anyway.

"No, I won't," she replied.

"So, you'll come back tomorrow?"

She tilted her head and then nodded, before taking another sip of her drink, as Sara leant forward and started asking about her t-shirt. I zoned out a bit at that point – they were talking about clothes, after all – but their brief conversation gave me the chance to just sit and admire… and that was all I needed to do.

I suppose it was about half an hour later that the girl checked her watch and announced that she needed to be going. I got up with her and told her I'd see her the next day, and she smiled up at me, before turning to go, saying goodbye to Sara.

I watched her until she'd disappeared around the bend in the path, at which point the questions and comments started.

"You're a dark horse, Barclay."

"Where have you kept her hidden all this time?"

"Please tell me you're going to introduce us properly tomorrow… she's going to haunt my dreams forever…"

That last remark came from Rick and I just glared at him until he looked away, and I became aware of Sara standing beside me.

"What was that about?" she asked, a little more quietly than the others.

"What do you mean?" We both sat down together, a little way away from everyone else, although we still kept our voices lowered, so no-one would hear what we were saying.

"I mean, it's not like you to just pick up girls on the beach. That's Rick's speciality."

"I know… but I saw her and…"

"You couldn't resist?"

"Something like that."

I turned to her, noting how much blonder she looked than usual – probably because we'd had such a good summer. Her blue eyes seemed more serious than usual though. "You need to be careful," she murmured.

"Careful?" What was she suggesting?

"Yes. Surely you noticed?"

"Noticed what?" I wished she'd stop speaking in riddles and just come out with whatever it was that was bothering her.

"She's young, Adam."

"I know she's young." None of us was exactly what could be termed 'old'.

She shook her head. "No. I mean, she's *really* young."

I frowned, thinking, recalling the girl's beautiful face and perfect figure. "She had to be eighteen, surely?" I reasoned, and Sara stared at me, before shaking her head again.

"I'd say she was nearer sixteen."

"Sixteen?" *Really?*

"Yes."

I took a deep breath. "Okay… but even if you're right, it doesn't make any difference."

"Yes, it does," she said, raising her voice just slightly.

I shook my head. "I'm not Rick," I pointed out, feeling a little aggrieved, and she put her hand on my arm.

"I know you're not. But you need to bear in mind that she'll probably have different expectations of a holiday romance to someone who's our age."

"Who said anything about a holiday romance?" I replied dismissively, as though I'd even contemplate such a thing, and Sara narrowed her eyes.

"What did you have in mind then?"

I hesitated, wondering whether to bluff, or be honest. I chose honestly… sort of. "Something very different."

She clearly understood, because she smiled and leant into me, nodding. "In that case, it might have been a good idea if you'd bothered to find out her name…"

I felt my shoulders drop. How could I have been such an idiot? I'd been so busy admiring her, thinking about teaching her to surf, about spending time with her, I'd let her go, without getting her phone number, without any idea of where she was staying, or how long she was going to be here, and to cap it all, I hadn't even remembered to ask her name. I felt like such a fool.

"Don't worry," Sara whispered. "You'll be seeing her again tomorrow. You can ask her then."

I nodded and resolved to find out as much as I could about the girl when she came back the following afternoon. I wanted to know everything. I didn't just want her name and number; I wanted to know what music she liked, what her favourite food was, what made her happy, and what made her sad. I wanted to know what it would feel like to hold her in my arms, to kiss those sweet, tender lips, and to watch the sunset with her beside me. I also wanted to know where she lived in Surrey, so that when she went home again, I could go and visit her, because the very last thing I wanted with her was a holiday romance.

I wanted so much more.

For the first time in my life, I wanted everything. Because in the space of less than an hour, the girl had stolen my heart, and I didn't care if she never gave it back.

The following evening, I raced home from the site we were working on, cursing the fact that I was running a little later than usual, because the supplies we'd been waiting on hadn't arrived until nearly lunchtime in the end, and we'd been put back. After a super fast shower, and a change of clothes, into board shorts and a t-shirt, I headed off to the beach, making sure to take a spare board with me in the back of the Land Cruiser.

By the time I arrived in Carven Bay, it was nearly six o'clock, but I hoped she'd still be there and couldn't disguise my sense of disappointment when I walked down the path onto the beach and saw there was no sign of her. In fact, there was no sign of anyone – well no-one I knew, anyway. There were a few stray holidaymakers; families with small children and dogs, scattered around the beach, making the most of the last few days of the summer, but none of my friends were there that evening, and I didn't mind in the slightest. In fact, I preferred it that way, because it meant I could sit by myself and wait. And I did wait. I waited until it was nearly dark before I accepted the reality that she wasn't going to come, and I got up again, returning to my car, my boards tucked under my arm, my head bowed, grateful that I'd been alone in my humiliation.

I went back again the next night. And the night after that. And it was on that third evening that I met up with Rick, Terry, Christina, Claire and Sara, who'd all gathered there earlier in the afternoon, evidently.

No-one questioned why I'd brought two boards with me, and I joined them, sitting down and keeping an eye on the pathway that led down to the beach.

I suppose I'd been there for around an hour and a half, when Sara came over and sat beside me.

"What's wrong?" she asked, keeping her voice low.

I wondered about saying 'nothing', but what would have been the point in that? I assumed my expression, or my body language had given away that something wasn't right, or she wouldn't have asked the question.

"That girl…" I replied quietly, "… the one I met on the beach the other day… the one who said she wanted me to teach her to surf…"

"What about her?"

"She didn't come back."

Sara sighed and nodded her head. "Maybe she was…"

"Lying?" I suggested.

"No."

"Just being kind?"

She looked at me, her narrowed eyes telling me to just shut up and listen. So I did. "I don't think she was lying, or just being kind. She seemed to like you, and she seemed keen to learn to surf. I was going to say that maybe she was held up."

"Three days in a row?" I said, unable to lift my mood.

"Well, maybe something happened at home… she said she was from Surrey, so perhaps her family had to cut short their holiday and go back there."

I nodded my head, although I wasn't convinced.

I was so unconvinced that for the next three weeks, I spent every evening and all my weekends at the beach, just watching and waiting… and hoping.

She never came back. In fact, I never even saw anyone who looked remotely like her – although that would have been impossible, being as there was no-one in the world who looked like she did. There was no-one with a face as beautiful as hers, or a body as perfect, or a smile that lit up my life and made my heart burst.

She filled my dreams though. Every night, I pictured her, tempting me, torturing me, teasing me. But whenever I tried to touch her, she was always just out of reach.

By the end of the month, everyone was due to return to uni, and I'd almost given up hope. No-one came on holiday to Carven Bay for that length of time, and I knew in my heart of hearts that the girl was long gone, and for whatever reason, she'd decided against coming back to the beach. We'd all decided to meet up on that Saturday afternoon, and although I wasn't in the mood, I did my best to join in with the festive atmosphere that everyone else was creating.

"You're still thinking about her, aren't you?" Sara's voice shook me out of my daydreams, which had, indeed, been about the girl. She sat down beside me and I glanced at her, nodding my head. "Hurts, doesn't it?"

I frowned, turning to face her. "What?"

"Love."

"Who said anything about love?"

She smiled. "I did."

"Well, that's just ridiculous," I blustered, trying not to let her see how close to the mark she was. "I mean, I don't think I even spent an hour with her, so how can I be in love with her?"

"Because it happens that way sometimes," she murmured, running her fingers through the sand between us. "It did with me."

I sat back slightly, looking down at her. "Really?"

"Yes. It—It was someone I met years ago, when I was much younger, and the moment I set my eyes on them, I knew I'd never feel the same way about anyone else."

I had to admit – although only to myself – that I felt exactly the same way about the girl. She'd changed my life. I thought she'd probably changed me too, but I wasn't ready to say that out loud. "Is it someone I know?" I asked Sara, diverting her attention – and my own – away from me.

"Yes," she whispered, although she turned away slightly, making it hard to hear her.

We had only a few friends in common, all of whom were sitting nearby, and I glanced around at them. "Tell me it's not Rick," I murmured and she turned back again, smiling.

"It's not Rick."

"Thank God for that." I smiled back at her. "And I hope it's not Terry, because Christina will scratch your eyes out."

She pulled a face. "No, it's not Terry either."

"Dean?" I suggested, wondering how he'd feel about that. Sara was very pretty, so I didn't imagine he'd have too much to complain about. She shook her head. "Then it has to be Connor."

"Does it?" she said softly and I felt my skin tingle with shocked realisation.

"Oh God," I whispered. "I'm so sorry." Sara's head tilted to one side, but before she could say anything, I carried on, "Here I am going on about this other girl, and all the time you're…"

"I'm what?" She looked and sounded confused, but then suddenly her face cleared and I could tell she was trying not to smile – well, to laugh actually. "You thought was I talking about you?" she said.

"Well, yes. I mean, there's no-one else here, is there?"

"Yes, there is."

"No, there isn't. If it's not Rick, or Dean, or Terry or Connor… and it's not me… I don't…"

"It's Claire," she whispered and, as she spoke, her gaze settled on our friend, whose dark hair cascaded over her shoulders, her long legs curled up beneath her as she sat beside Connor, talking avidly, her face animated, her eyes sparkling.

"Oh." It was all I could think of to say.

"I'm sorry if I've shocked you."

"You haven't. Does… does she know?"

"Good God no." She shook her head vehemently, and then reached out, clutching my arm. "And you can't tell her, Adam. Please."

I heard the desperation in her voice. "I won't." She sighed out her relief, before I added, "But maybe you should?"

She shook her head. "No. I think she's met someone at uni… a guy called Ewan, I believe. She seems fairly keen on him, so I doubt she'd be interested in me."

"Love sucks, doesn't it?" I murmured, and she looked up and smiled.

"You're admitting to it then, are you?"

"Yes." It seemed only fair, considering she'd poured her heart out to me. "I guess this is the moment where I should probably say that, if we're both still single when we get to thirty, we'll marry each other… but I'm going to assume you wouldn't be overly keen on that idea?"

She chuckled and leant a little closer. "No, I wouldn't," she replied. "But thanks for the offer."

We sat together, shoulder to shoulder, and stared out at the setting sun, both wishing things could have been different.

Chapter Two

If I'm being completely honest, I would have to admit that I spent the next few years doing my very best not to grow up too much.

I still went surfing, even though most of my friends fell by the wayside. Rick amazed us all by settling down just a year or so after he finished at university, and he and his partner moved to Hereford to be nearer to her family. Connor moved to Scotland and became a marine biologist, and although we kept in touch for a while, it petered out as he developed new interests up there. Terry and Christina stayed up in Durham in the end, both finding good jobs, and presumably enjoying their freedom too much to consider coming back. Claire ended up marrying the guy she'd met at uni. Sara had been quite right; his name was Ewan, and it transpired he was from Cheshire, but he didn't have much family, so they decided they were going to live in Carven Bay. As for Sara, well, she moved away about a month or two before Claire's wedding. Everyone was surprised by that – especially Claire – although I wasn't. I didn't say anything though, and attended the wedding ceremony at the local church, and at the reception afterwards, I raised a glass in Sara's name, and hoped she'd find happiness with someone else. Whoever she might be.

As for my own heart… well, I recovered from my infatuation with the girl. I called it an infatuation, because I persuaded myself after a while that I couldn't possibly have fallen in love with someone, based on less than an hour's acquaintance. You had to at least know a person before you could fall in love… in any case, that was what I kept trying to tell myself for the next couple of years, because it took me that long to get over her. And then, not long before my twenty-third birthday, I started seeing Faith. I met her on a night out with Dean and she was fun, lively, gregarious and probably just what I needed at the time to bring me out of my shell. We dated for six months or so – a record for me – until I think we both realised that it wasn't working, and we parted. That feeling of relief I'd felt when I'd split up with Shelley all those years earlier was still there, and I knew I had nothing to regret.

When I was twenty-six, my dad made me a partner in the business and I finally managed to buy my own flat – a beautiful one bedroomed place right on the seafront, just around the corner from my mum's house in Carven Bay. I took my time, saving up and buying furniture that I liked, and although my mortgage sometimes scared the living daylights out of me at the beginning, I was earning enough to afford it. And it certainly made my short-lived relationships easier to manage. At least I wasn't having to explain my constantly changing girlfriends to my dad, or to Michelle, or – worst of all – to Amy, who was a teenager by that stage, and looked at the world through rose-tinted glasses, tending to frown at me when each and every relationship came to an end, not understanding, I think, that I didn't sleep with every woman I dated. And that wasn't something I was about to explain to her either… even if only because I wasn't willing to admit to anyone that I was still looking for something 'more'.

Of course, I'd found it once, but I'd been too stupid to keep hold of it. And while I may have tried to convince myself that my feelings for the girl were in the past, as the years went by, I still thought about her. I thought about her a lot, and eventually I came to realise that the only time I'd ever actually felt truly contented in the company of another human being, was that brief time I'd shared with her on the beach.

My thirtieth birthday came and went, and I suppose it was then that I started to wonder whether my one chance of lasting happiness had come and gone; whether in letting the girl get away, I'd lost any hope of ever really feeling alive. No-one else had ever made me lost for words, made my body ache or my heart soar like she had, and the only time I came anywhere close to a similar feeling was when I went surfing. But that wasn't quite the same. I couldn't hold my surfboard in my arms at night; I couldn't devote my life to making it feel happy, and wanted and loved. Because ten years down the line, that was how I still felt about the girl. I didn't even know her name, and in spite of all my attempts to convince myself otherwise, she was still 'it' for me. She was still the one.

I'd just got back from work when my mum called. Our relationship had never really suffered from my moving out – not in any proper sense of the word – but after I'd moved back to Carven Bay we'd become much closer again, and then once Nathan went to university in Kent, things were better still. We talked regularly and I went round there a couple of times a week, so I wasn't that surprised by her phone call.

"I'm just ringing to remind you about Friday night," she said and I felt my heart sink to my shoes. "I know you don't want to come, but please say you'll put in an appearance."

I took a deep breath. "Nathan and I don't get on, Mum…" I reasoned. It wasn't an excuse; Nathan and I hated each other – with a passion.

"I know, but it's his twenty-first."

"And I'm sure he won't even notice whether I'm there or not."

"Maybe… but I will."

She knew how to get round me. Every time. "Okay. I'll come. But I'm only going to stay for half an hour."

"Thank you," she replied. "He's got some of his university friends coming down for the weekend. Evidently one of them is his girlfriend."

"He's got a girlfriend?" I was surprised by that.

"Yes. Her name's Amanda."

"What's she like?" I asked, my imagination going into overdrive.

"I don't know. This is the first we've heard of her. But she seems to be good for him. He's a lot calmer than he was…"

I wasn't so sure of that. I couldn't imagine anyone calming Nathan. He'd been home for the best part of three months already, during the long summer holidays, and I'd managed to avoid any contact with him. Still, I only had a couple of days to go, and I could see for myself…

By the time I arrived at Nathan's party, it had been going for well over an hour, but my tardiness was intentional. I wanted to slide in, show my face, and then slip away again, with as little fuss as possible.

Arriving early was a sure-fire way to scupper that plan. As I went around the back of the house, through the open gate, I couldn't help but smile. Despite the problems during my teenage years, my parents – all four of them – still got on really well. My dad and Derek were, at that moment, presiding over a large barbecue, while Michelle was carrying two bowls of salad from the house to the table that had been set out on the patio. There were a few local friends and neighbours gathered around, and near the bottom of the garden, was a gaggle of twenty-somethings, behaving more like errant teenagers, in the centre of which was my half-brother.

Ignoring him and his friends, I turned to Amy, who was standing by herself, leaning against the wall near the patio doors, a glass of white wine in her hand.

"Hello," I said, going to stand beside her.

"Hi." She looked up at me.

"Is it me, or is this music really loud."

"It's not that loud, but it's the reason your mum and Derek decided to invite the neighbours. It saved annoying them…"

"I feel old," I murmured, nodding my head towards Nathan and his friends.

She chuckled. "That's because you are old."

"Thanks. Have you met his girlfriend yet?" I asked.

"Yes. She's far too good for him."

I laughed. "That wouldn't be hard though, would it?"

She shook her head, smiling. "No, I don't suppose it would."

At that moment, my mother came out through the patio doors and caught sight of me. "You're here," she said, as though she'd half expected me not to turn up.

"I said I'd come," I replied, and she came and stood in front of me, giving me a look that told me she hadn't believed me.

"Have you spoken to Nathan?" she asked.

"No. I didn't want to spoil the evening… for either of us."

She frowned and shook her head. "Don't be like that," she murmured. "Come and say hello."

"Mum, I don't need to say hello to him."

"It's his birthday, Adam. Just say hello."

I sighed deeply and followed her down the garden. It seemed easier than arguing and making a scene.

Nathan and his friends were still grouped together, and I wondered how Mum was going to execute this tricky reconciliation, but as we approached, they all seemed to move, leaving Nathan and I facing each other.

"Happy birthday," I said, because it seemed like an appropriate greeting.

"Thanks," he replied. There was still that grudging, argumentative tone to his voice, and the sneer on his lips and scowl in his deep blue eyes hadn't changed one bit. He'd cut his dark brown hair shorter than I remembered, but was still as gangly as ever... and other than our shared height, we looked nothing like each other.

"This is Nathan's girlfriend," my mother said, indicating the girl who was standing to his right.

She was – as Amy had pointed out – far too good for Nathan. Pretty and with blondish-red hair, she leant into him and sighed out a, "Hi," to me, a smile forming on her lips.

"Hello," I nodded back.

"Now," my mother said, as she continued with the introductions, "you'll have to stop me if I get the names muddled," and I wondered why I needed to meet these people, and if it was really necessary, why Nathan couldn't introduce them himself. "This is Nick," she said, and a blond haired youth of medium height held up his hand, as though his name had been called in the class register. I nodded to him, but kept my hands still. "And this is Jordan." A girl with shocking blue hair and far too many piercings on her face frowned at me, so I frowned back. "And... where's Jade?" Mum asked, looking around.

"She went to the loo," Nathan replied, then looked over Mum's shoulder. "Oh, here she is."

I turned and couldn't help staring at the beautiful blonde girl who was approaching us, a gorgeous smile on her face, her eyes sparkling.

"Did I hear my name?" she said, her voice much lower and sexier than I was expecting, considering her age.

45

"Yes," Mum replied. "I was just introducing everyone to Nathan's brother, Adam."

"Half-brother," Nathan corrected, but no-one paid him any attention. Well, Jade and I didn't anyway.

She turned to me, and I turned to her, and we both smiled and said, "Hello," at exactly the same time.

I felt her eyes wandering over me, and allowed mine to do the same, absorbing the sight of her long slim legs encased in skin-tight jeans, her tight, low-cut top that left little to the imagination, including the fact that she wasn't wearing a bra, and her generous lips, and wide blue eyes, set in a captivating face. My attraction to her was purely physical, and judging from the look in her eyes, the feeling was mutual, which I found puzzling, I'll be honest. After all, why would a girl – and she was little more than a girl, really – as beautiful as she was, be interested in someone like me? She should have been flirting with someone my brother's age, and yet her eyes were definitely twinkling in my direction… and I wasn't about to say 'no'.

"Can I get you a drink?" I offered, noticing that her hands were empty.

"Thanks," she replied. "Why don't I come with you?"

I smiled, and together we walked back towards the house. "So, you know my brother?" I said, in typically lame style.

"Yes," she replied. "We all live together."

"All of you?" I glanced over my shoulder to the group of them. "All five of you?"

"Well, there were four of us… Nathan and Nick, and me and Jordan. Amanda and Nathan got together right at the end of last semester, and from what I've gathered, she'll be living at the house with us when we go back."

"I see." I wasn't overly concerned about what Nathan and Amanda were getting up to. I was far more interested in Jade.

She stood right beside me, her hand on my shoulder and her body literally draped against mine as I poured us both a glass of wine, and then I turned and reluctantly broke the contact to offer her the glass.

"Cheers," I murmured.

She clinked her glass against mine and took a sip, maintaining eye contact as she licked her lips. Part of me wanted to hope that, at her age, she didn't really know what she was doing, but deep down, I thought she probably did. The problem was, I didn't care. She was mesmerising, and we both knew it.

"Are you here for the weekend?" I asked, partly to break the strained silence, but also because I wanted to know. I *needed* to know.

"Yes," she replied. "We came down together by train this morning, and we're staying here at your mum's and then Nathan's driving us all back to Kent on Sunday morning."

"Sunday morning?" I queried, working out that I had less than two days... two short days, until she was due to leave again. She nodded, and for the second time in my life, I acted on instinct, and took my courage in both hands. "I'm not a great one for parties," I said, leaning closer to her. "Would you like to come for a walk with me?"

She licked her lips again, and then nodded her head, and placing both of our glasses on the table, I took her hand and led her out through the front door.

"Where are we going?" she said, pulling her hand from mine and linking our arms together instead.

"Well, we can go down onto the beach, or it's still light enough to go up onto the headland... we can go wherever you want."

She stopped, pulling me back with her and I turned to face her as she looked up at me. "Wherever I want?" she whispered.

"Yes."

"Where do you live?" she asked.

"Just around the corner." I pointed. "On the seafront."

She nodded. "Can we go there then?"

"You want to go to my place?"

"Yes."

I hesitated for probably less than a second, and then took her hand again.

My flat was about a five minute walk away, and during all of that time, we didn't say a word to each other. For myself, I was too busy wondering whether Jade and I both had the same thing in mind. I thought we did, and the look in her eyes seemed to imply it, but I didn't want to take anything for granted, and was trying to take advantage of those few moments to work out how to play things when we got home, just in case I'd read the situation wrong, and she'd only wanted to get away from the party, to somewhere quieter. If I'm being honest, I was also growing more and more nervous with every step. It had been quite a long time since I'd had sex, and never on such a short acquaintance, and I had a feeling I might not live up to her expectations.

As I opened the door and let us in, all of my doubts disappeared. I needn't have worried about taking things for granted, or what to say to her, because before I'd even closed the door, Jade was all over me. Her lips were on mine, her tongue in my mouth, as her hands grappled with my belt, and I let her push me back against the wall beside the door. She worked fast, with expert hands and, within less than two minutes of us walking through the door, she was kneeling in front of me, my jeans and trunks around my ankles, her blue eyes gazing directly into mine.

"I knew you wouldn't be disappointing," she murmured, smiling, as she took me in her mouth.

A few minutes of that was all I could stand and, before I completely embarrassed myself, I lifted her to her feet, and kicking off my jeans and underwear, I carried her into the living room and straight over to the sofa, lowering her and quickly removing her clothes, while she squirmed and squealed in breathless anticipation – or so it seemed to me.

"Take me," she murmured, lying there, raising her hips and letting her fingers play across her stomach, wandering lower, as I pulled my shirt off over my head, remembering at the last minute to run back to the hall to retrieve a condom from my wallet, which was still in my back pocket – a lesson learned from my brief interlude with Fiona, and not one easily forgotten.

"Take me," she urged again, as I re-crossed the living room. And I did. She welcomed me with ease and sighed deeply as I entered her, wrapping her arms and legs around me. "Harder," she whispered, and I obliged. It seemed to be what she wanted, and she climaxed quickly and noisily, as I did likewise.

"Are you okay?" I asked, leaning back eventually and looking down at her.

"Hmm…" she sighed, opening her eyes and staring up at me. "I needed that." She rested her hand on my chest and smiled. "Definitely not disappointing."

I couldn't help smiling myself, because that was rather gratifying, considering my worries beforehand.

"Where's your bedroom?" she asked.

"Through there." I nodded my head over my shoulder, in vaguely the right direction.

She grinned. "Well, we seem to have christened your sofa… so why don't we try your bed next?"

Over the next four or five hours, before sleep finally claimed me, I discovered that, thanks to Jade's expertise, I had more staying power and stamina than I'd ever imagined possible, which was just as well, because it seemed she was insatiable.

During one of our necessary breaks, while I caught my breath, and fetched us some ice cold water from the fridge, I suggested to Jade that she should text one of her friends to tell them where she was. It had already become clear that she intended to stay the night, which was fine with me, but I didn't want anyone to worry about her, or – more importantly, perhaps – to come looking for her.

The next morning, we were woken by Jade's phone buzzing. She sat up, bleary eyed, and informed me over her shoulder, that the message she'd received was from Nathan. I half expected him to be berating her for spending the night with me, but as she lay down and turned towards me, she informed me that he'd merely said that he and the rest of their group were planning to spend the day surfing, and if she wanted to join them, she was more than welcome.

"Do you want to go?" I asked, as she allowed her hand to wander down my chest, across my stomach and continue southwards, until I sucked in a breath at the intimate contact.

"I would," she replied. "Although I can't surf."

"Nathan can," I told her. "I'm sure he'll teach you."

He'd learned in his teens, having insisted on having lessons. He wasn't that good, but he thought he was, and whenever we surfed together, he tried to turn it into a competition, which he'd always lose. As a result, we rarely surfed together.

Jade glanced up at me and then changed position, twisting around and straddling me. She was about to lower herself onto me, when I stopped her.

"Condom," I reminded her, and she huffed out a sigh, leaning over and pulling one from the box which I'd left on the bedside table. Rather than handing it to me, she ripped into the foil packet with her teeth and removed the condom, rolling it over me with an expert touch, before she resumed her earlier position.

"Can't you teach me?" she asked, settling onto me and grinding her hips in a circular motion.

I was tempted to point out that I didn't think there was anything I could teach her, but I didn't and instead I clarified that she was talking about surfing.

"Of course," she said, grinning and clearly understanding my unspoken implication.

"I'd love to," I replied, as she started to move, "but I'm not sure Nathan will appreciate having me there."

"Why not?"

"In case you didn't notice last night, we don't get on."

"You don't?" She seemed surprised, although not enough to put her off the rhythm she was building.

"No." I clutched her thighs.

She shuddered slightly. "Well, I'm going to assume that learning to surf involves an element of touching?"

"Usually, yes."

She leant forward, resting her hands on my chest and staring into my eyes. "In that case, I definitely want you to teach me. I want to feel your hands on me…"

"Hmm… so do I."

I put my actions into words and placed my hands on her breasts, which seemed to be all it took to push her over the edge, and for me to follow closely behind her.

*

Once we were dressed and had eaten breakfast, over which I managed to discover, by some direct questioning, that she was studying History and that she came from Suffolk, Jade returned to my mum's house to meet up with Nathan and their friends, and to put on a swimming costume – which she'd luckily brought with her – and a change of clothes on top. She didn't need to worry about showering, being as we'd done that together at my place.

By the time I arrived at the beach, bringing an extra board for Jade, everyone else was already there, and as I approached, I wondered if there would be any awkwardness – other than that which usually existed between Nathan and myself – about the fact that Jade and I had left the party so early, and that she hadn't returned. I needn't have worried though, because everyone greeted me perfectly normally, other than Nathan, of course, who had to get in a jibe.

"Hey, bro'," he called. "Good night?"

I hated him calling me 'bro'; it implied a familiarity between us that didn't exist. I also wasn't about to answer his question. I'd had a very good night, as it happened, but that wasn't for public consumption. So I ignored him and went over to Jade, putting down the boards, and sitting beside her.

"It was a good night, wasn't it?" she asked, loudly enough for everyone else to hear, but in a voice that carried sufficient doubt for me to be forced to respond and put her mind at rest.

"Yes," I whispered, leaning into her and giving her a gentle, brief kiss.

She smiled, just as I heard Nathan laughing behind me. "Grow up, Nathan," I growled, without bothering to turn around, and Jade giggled, as did everyone else. I could only imagine my brother's reaction to that, but I wasn't going to give him the satisfaction of looking.

"So, how does this surfing thing work?" Jade asked.

"'Surfing thing'?" I replied, grinning down at her.

"Yes." She was so obviously flirting with me, and I decided I may as well join in.

"Take your clothes off and I'll show you."

"All of them?" Her eyes widened, but with excitement, not shock, and I knew I had to rein her in.

"No." I leant in closer. "Save that for later."

I heard her moan slightly and for a second I wondered if that was anticipation or disappointment. I hoped it was the former, but as she slowly stood and undressed, I became less sure, being as she was wearing the skimpiest bikini I'd ever seen. It barely covered her, and when she turned and bent down, very deliberately taking her time in folding her clothes, and demonstrating to everyone present that the bottom part of her bikini was a thong, I started to wonder what on earth I'd got myself into.

Part of me wanted to cover her up, or even to scold her for exposing herself like that in a public place, but then what right did I have? None at all. We'd spent the night together, nothing more. That didn't make her 'mine', and I wasn't even sure I wanted her to be. In any case, I wasn't entitled to tell her how to dress. If she was comfortable wearing something so revealing, then so be it. The fact that it made me uncomfortable was my problem, not hers.

She turned back to face me and smiled. "You like what you see?" she said, tilting her hip.

"Of course."

And with that, she knelt down in front of me, kissing me deeply. I let her, until I felt her hand on the front of my shorts, at which point, I pulled back, grabbing her wrist.

"Not here," I muttered.

She pouted and got back to her feet again. "Don't you want me?"

"Of course I want you, but not here. That can wait until later."

"I'm not very good at waiting," she replied petulantly, for the first time reminding me of the age gap between us. I sighed and stood up, facing her.

"I thought you wanted to learn to surf?"

Her lips twitched upwards. "Does that mean you'll touch me?"

"Yes."

She grabbed my hand. "In that case…"

*

I'd taught a few people to surf over the years, but Jade was a tough student; not because she was no good at it, but because she had absolutely no focus whatsoever. Every time I touched her, to help her balance, or place her feet or body correctly, she'd get distracted and throw her arms around me, kissing me, even a couple of times leaping up into my arms and wrapping her legs around me, which I had to admit was very diverting, especially given the non-existent nature of her bikini bottoms. I wasn't complaining about that – not really – but it meant that we didn't hit the water until late afternoon, by which time everyone else was already sitting back on the beach mats, watching us.

Nathan had been 'teaching' Amanda – which basically meant he'd been using the surf lesson as an excuse to feel her up all day. I know I wasn't a great deal better, and that I enjoyed having Jade in my arms, but Nathan was taking it a lot further – and I mean a lot further. Nick and Jordan, on the other hand, hadn't even tried to surf. I'd offered to lend them a couple of boards and show them the basics, but they'd shrugged and said they'd rather just swim, so I let them be. I had my hands full with Jade – quite literally.

After about half an hour in the water, it became clear to me that Jade wasn't that interested in surfing, and that she'd far rather fool around with me, so I gave up and suggested we call it a day. She smiled her agreement and held my hand as we started up the beach, my board tucked under my other arm.

"Thanks for today," she said quietly, "it's been fun."

I looked down at her smiling face. "You're a shocking liar."

"I'm not lying," she replied. "I have enjoyed the day…"

"Just not necessarily the surfing aspects of it?" I suggested and she broke into a broad grin.

"I guess I'm busted."

"I guess you are." I tried to sound stern and she licked her lips, slowly, seductively, knowing exactly what she was doing.

"Am I forgiven?" she murmured, lowering her voice.

I leant down, my mouth close to her ear. "I'll tell you later."

She shuddered and I couldn't help smiling, recalling all the things we'd already done and wondering what else was to come with my daring new lover. I had no idea how long our adventures would last, but I had every intention of enjoying them while they did – for as long as I could keep up with her, anyway.

As we approached the group, I noticed Nathan was behaving oddly. That's to say, he was behaving more oddly than usual. He seemed to be trying to hide something, which was confirmed when Amanda shifted her position to block my view of my brother. Something was definitely going on and, knowing Nathan's capacity for stupidity, I intended to find out what.

"What are you doing, Nathan?" I said, as we got within a few feet of them.

"Nothing."

That was a sure sign he was up to something.

"Yeah, right." I let go of Jade's hand, put my board down and walked over to where he was sitting, with one hand behind his back. "What's in your hand?"

"Nothing," he repeated.

"Then show me."

I saw the moment his temper flared, right before he jumped to his feet, doing his best to get in my face, which he could, because we were the same height, even if I wasn't remotely intimidated by him.

"It's none of your fucking business, pretty boy," he goaded.

I shook my head. "Still got a foul mouth on you then?" I replied.

"What if I have? What's it got to do with you?"

"Everything. Now, what have you got in your hand?"

I reached forward, trying to grab his arm, but he pulled back, taking a half step, which gave me the opportunity trip him, placing my foot between both of his and watching as he tumbled onto the sand, landing on his backside, and revealing the spliff he was holding between his thumb and forefinger, tucked up in his hand.

"You idiot, Nathan." I bent down and ripped it from his grasp. "You never change, do you?"

He glared up at me, then clambered to his feet again. "Give that back."

"No."

He raised a fist, but I caught it in my free hand and pushed him backwards again, with just sufficient force to ensure that he hit the sand for a second time.

"You need to grow up," I said quietly, leaning over him to stop him from getting up again. "I mean it…"

"Or what?" His eyes narrowed, his hatred of me obvious.

"Or you're going to wind up dead, that's what. And while I don't particularly care, I think Mum and Derek might be upset."

"Stop being so dramatic. It's just fucking grass, bro'…"

"For today, yes. But what about tomorrow? What about when it's cocaine, or heroin?"

He smiled, but there was no friendship there, no warmth. "I know what I'm doing," he sneered.

"They all say that."

"Know many junkies then, do you?"

"No, but unlike you, I'm not stupid."

I stood upright, and turned, looking at his friends, who were staring at the two of us. Jade was standing slightly apart from them, her eyes fixed on mine, before she lowered them to my brother's prone figure.

"I'm sorry," I said to her and she looked back at me, smiling slightly, although she stayed rooted to the spot. "I'm going home." She nodded, but didn't move and I knew she wouldn't be coming with me, and not waiting to find out why, I grabbed my boards and headed up the beach.

I heard Nathan shouting something, but I ignored him and kept going, dumping my boards on the rack in the garage block opposite my apartment, before going straight upstairs and letting myself in. I was still holding the spliff in my hand and went through to the kitchen, putting it in the sink and running the tap for a couple of minutes, to drown it, before throwing it in the bin.

Then I showered and changed, and sat in the living room, staring into space and trying very hard not to think too much. It didn't work all that well, and while I wasn't really bothered, or even that surprised, about Nathan's behaviour, I was concerned about Jade. I couldn't help wondering whether she shared Nathan's perspective – and his habits –

and I knew that if she did, then I *would* be bothered. I'd be very bothered indeed.

The knocking on my door brought me out of my thoughts, and I answered it, not overly surprised to find Jade standing on the other side, her hands buried in the pockets of her shorts.

"Hi," she said softly, looking up at me through her eyelashes.

"Hi."

"Can I come in?" I stood to one side and let her enter, closing the door behind us. "I'm sorry I didn't come back with you," she said as we wandered into the living room. "I—I just felt like I should stay with Nathan for a while."

"Why?" I asked.

"Because he's my friend," she replied, tilting her head to one side. "Because I share a house with him – and all the others – I have to live with them. I didn't want there to be any awkwardness between us when we go back to uni."

I nodded my head. It made sense, after all.

She took a step closer, but I held up my hands and moved away, keeping my eyes fixed on her. "Can I ask you something?"

She nodded her head, but before I could speak, she said, "You want to know if I'm into skunk too?"

"Yes."

She sighed. "I've tried it a few times," she replied. "But it's not really my thing."

"What is?" I asked, worried that she was going to tell me she'd graduated to crystal meth, or something.

She took a couple of steps closer. "You."

That blew me away and it took me a moment to reply, "You can't say that. You don't even know me."

She smiled at that. "I know the bits of you that matter. And, believe me, I'm impressed."

I wasn't sure what to say, and when I didn't reply, she closed the gap between us, pressing her body against mine, although I didn't put my arms around her and she clearly noticed. "Don't be grumpy," she muttered, through pouting lips.

"I'm not."

"Yes, you are." She took my hands in hers. "Take me to bed," she whispered. "I want to get high on you."

I was easily persuaded and we spent the rest of the afternoon, and the evening, in bed, only getting up when the Chinese take-away that we ordered was delivered. Exhausted from the day's activities, Jade slept in my arms and I felt relieved by that, being as I was running out of steam by then. She was fun, confident, and more than diverting… but she was also exhausting, and I was glad of a few hours' sleep.

She was leaving the following morning, but we made the most of the couple of hours before she was due to meet with Nathan and the others at my mum's house.

Before we left the flat, she asked for my number, which made me smile. I'd been going to ask for hers, and I felt kind of gratified that she'd made the first move – although, in reality, that was par for the course with Jade, so I don't know why I was surprised at all.

Then, after we'd exchanged numbers and made sure she'd gathered up all her things, I walked her round the corner to Mum's house, where Nathan and his friends were packing up the car. He glanced at me as we approached, his look dark and presumably intended to threaten. I held his gaze until he looked away again, while Jade ran into the house to pick up the remainder of her belongings that she'd left there. While everyone was saying goodbye to my mum and Derek, Nathan sidled over to me.

"I presume you're going to tell on me," he said, standing beside me, neither of us looking at the other.

"Tell on you? We're not in school, Nathan."

He turned, staring at me now. "You know what I mean. Are you going to tell Mum about the grass?"

"No." I saw his shoulders drop and heard him sigh with relief. "But you need to stop. If… if you need some help, then maybe you should see someone. I'll pay for it, if—"

"Stop it," he hissed, and I knew he was desperate to raise his voice.

"Stop what? Stop trying to help you, even though you don't deserve it?"

"No. Stop acting like your dad."

I leant back slightly, looking at him, confusion and lack of sleep muddling my brain. "What do you mean?"

He glowered at me. "Ever since you moved out, Geoff's been hounding me, handing out unwanted advice, telling me how to live my life."

"Then it's a shame you didn't listen to him."

"Why would I? I already have a dad. I don't need another one."

I wanted to argue that he clearly did, but I couldn't. Derek had always been fair with me, and I couldn't say anything against him – even if I did feel that his absences from home, and his weakness when it came to Nathan, had contributed to the creation of the pathetic individual who was standing in front of me.

"Do what you like, Nathan," I whispered. "You will anyway."

"Too fucking right, I will."

I shook my head and he walked away, going over to my mother, who smiled at him benignly, blissfully unaware of her son's misdemeanours.

"Are you alright?" Jade came over and put her arms around my waist, leaning into me.

"I'm fine."

"Will you miss me?" she asked, smiling.

"I might do."

Her brow creased, although she was still smiling. "You'd better," she muttered.

"Well, at least I'll get some sleep at night now you're going," I replied, trying to make light of things. We hadn't discussed the future at all, and although we'd exchanged phone numbers, that didn't mean a thing. For all I knew, I might never see her again.

"I hope you'll be sleeping at night… and only sleeping," she murmured, staring into my eyes, making her meaning clear and showing a chink of insecurity. "And I hope you'll dream about me too."

I leant closer, surprised by her comment. "Does that mean you want us to keep seeing each other?" I asked and she nodded her head with disarming enthusiasm.

"I know it won't be easy," she said, "with me being in Kent, and you being here, but please promise me you won't…"

I put my fingers over her lips, silencing her. "I'm not a cheat, Jade, if that's what you're thinking. If we're together, then we're together. It doesn't matter how far away you are."

She sighed and, placing her arms around my neck, pulled me down and kissed me fiercely, passionately, regardless of the eyes that I knew would be on us.

It was Nathan tooting the horn that broke us apart, and Jade giggled, smiling up at me, then turned and ran towards the car.

"I'll text you," she called over her shoulder as she climbed into the back seat, closing the door behind her, before she leant out of the window, adding, "Or you can text me."

"Okay."

Nathan drove away amid squeals and waving arms, and I turned and faced my mother and Derek.

She raised her eyebrows, before letting go of Derek and wandering down the path to me, where she linked her arm through mine and gazed up at me.

"Can I assume the party wasn't as much of a waste of time as you thought it would be?" She was barely managing not to laugh.

I looked down at her and couldn't help smiling. "You can."

I sent the first text, typing it out it as soon as I arrived back at the flat, telling Jade I'd had a really great weekend and couldn't wait to see her again. And then wished I hadn't, being as her response came in the form of a series of abbreviations and emojis, and took me nearly ten minutes to translate into vague English. I replied and asked her to use actual words, and she sent me back a laughing face emoji, which did actually make me laugh.

After that, her messages were written mostly in proper English, which was a relief, as work got really busy at the beginning of October, and I didn't have time to spend deciphering what she was trying to tell me.

We called each other too, usually late at night, once she'd finished studying, or had come home from an evening out with her friends. We didn't speak every day, but it was fairly frequent, usually three or four times a week, and every single time, perhaps because it was late at night, the conversation would turn to sex. I missed her – there was no doubt about it – and she made it very clear that she missed me too… or at least she missed what I did to her, and at the time that felt like the same thing.

One Wednesday in the middle of November, she surprised me by calling much earlier in the evening, literally just after I'd walked in the door from work.

"Is something wrong?" I asked.

"Yes." I could hear the sadness in her voice.

"What is it?"

"I need you."

I laughed, just gently, and sat down on the sofa, looking out over the bay, or the least the shadow of the bay, being as it was dark outside. "I need you too."

"No, Adam… I mean, I *really* need you." I wasn't sure what she expected me to do from over three hundred miles away, but before I could reply, she continued, "Can you come and see me?"

"When?"

"At the weekend?" She sounded really desperate and I shook my head, smiling to myself, and tried not to think about the five hour drive.

"If you want me to."

"Yes… Oh God, yes." I laughed out loud at that point. "Can you come on Friday? Then we can have Saturday and most of Sunday together."

"I suppose, but it'll be nearly midnight by the time I get to you."

"I don't care."

"You might," I warned her. "I'll be tired after a drive like that."

There was a moment's pause, and then she said, "I'll revive you," and I laughed again.

The drive to Canterbury was every bit as exhausting as I'd expected and I didn't pull up outside Jade's student house until gone midnight in the end, having been held up by an accident on the M23.

She opened the door before I'd even slung my messenger bag over my shoulder, and ran down the short pathway, throwing herself into my arms and wrapping her legs around my waist, kissing me deeply.

"Can I assume you've missed me?" I asked, when she eventually came up for air.

"Stop talking and come inside," she replied, and I smiled and carried her back up the path and through the front door of the surprisingly neat semi-detached house. "Take me upstairs," she whispered, and I obliged, following her directions to the room at the front of the house, the door of which was ajar.

Inside, I quickly took in my surroundings, which were basic, consisting of a wardrobe, chest of drawers and – thank goodness – a double bed. On the long, interminable drive, I'd suddenly realised, with a certain amount of dread, that she might only have a single, and at six foot four, I wasn't sure how well I'd sleep in such narrow confines. Still, I needn't have worried. As I lowered her to the floor, dropping my bag at the same time, I looked down into her eyes, and recognised the glint in hers… and wondered if I'd get any sleep at all in the next two days.

Jade was even more eager than I'd recalled and, when I woke the next morning, after just a couple of hours' sleep, I was relieved when, following the briefest of kisses, she offered to go and make us a coffee. She pulled on a robe and went out onto the landing, leaving the door slightly open, which meant I could hear my brother's voice, coming from downstairs. I couldn't make out his words, but I knew it was him and wondered about the wisdom of my visit. Obviously, it was great to see Jade again, and to have spent the night with her, but the prospect of another confrontation with Nathan really didn't appeal.

When Jade returned, carrying two steaming mugs of coffee, which she put down on the bedside table, I turned over in bed to face her, admiring her as she slipped off the robe and clambered in beside me.

"I heard my brother," I remarked and she looked up at me. "Was he making trouble?"

She smiled. "No."

"Does he even know I'm here?"

"Well, he didn't, but he does now."

"How? Did you tell him?"

"No. He saw your car outside."

I nodded my head. "Okay…" I reached over and pulled her into my arms, turning onto my back as she nestled into me. "Look, I don't want another fight with him. I didn't drive all the way down here for that…"

"Why did you drive down here?" she asked, teasing.

"To see you, of course." She rested her head on my chest. "The point is, I think it's probably best, for everyone's sake, if you and I maybe go out for the day?"

She sat up, staring at me. "Go out?"

"Yes. If Nathan and I are in the same room, then it'll only end badly, trust me."

She frowned. "But why does that mean we have to go out?"

"Well, we can hardly expect him to leave the house, just because I'm here," I reasoned, and she shook her head.

"No, you don't understand. What I mean is, why do we have to go anywhere? Why can't we stay here… in bed."

"All weekend?"

She smiled, her fingertips walking slowly down my chest and stomach, as she nodded her head. "Hmm…" she moaned. "When a man looks as good as you do, and has a rock hard six pack like this…" She let her fingers roam tantalisingly lower. "And a perfectly formed, rock hard…" she grinned, licking her lips, trying to tempt me. "What more could a girl want?"

I was tempted to say 'some self control', but I figured it was too late for that.

"You do know I'm thirty years old, don't you? 'Rock hard' isn't always guaranteed at my age."

She halted her little meander down my body. "What difference does age make?"

"Well, it takes a bit longer to recover… in between…"

"Really?" She seemed genuinely surprised and pulled back the duvet, a smile forming on her lips. "Looks pretty *rock hard* to me," she whispered and moved down the bed, proving the point with her mouth.

*

As Jade had suggested, we spent the whole weekend in bed, although we did shower together a couple of times, and we ordered in food, which Jade collected from the delivery guys, as and when required. I therefore managed to avoid seeing Nathan at all, but when I loaded my bag onto the passenger seat of my car on the Sunday afternoon, I had to admit to myself that, in spite of having been horizontal for almost forty-eight hours, I'd never been so tired in my life.

"Can you come back next weekend?" she asked as I closed the door and turned to face her.

"No." Her face fell and I moved closer, cupping her chin in my hand. "I'm sorry, but we've just taken on a really big job, and I'm going to be working flat out between now and Christmas."

"Even weekends?"

"Probably Saturdays, yes."

She paused for a moment and then shrugged her shoulders. "It's probably for the best," she mused and I wondered at the change in her.

"It is?"

"Yes."

"Why?"

She smiled. "Because I really should be getting started on my dissertation, and you'll only distract me."

"In a good way?"

"Yes, in a good way."

We parted with a deep and very intense kiss, and then I made the long, laborious journey back to Cornwall, looking forward to a good night's sleep, and feeling grateful that Jade was nearing the end of her course, and that I wouldn't have to make that trip too often.

We continued to call and text each other over the coming weeks and, as Christmas approached, she asked about my plans.

"I'm working for most of the time," I replied. "We're still finishing off that job I told you about."

I heard her sigh. "That's a shame," she muttered.

"Why? What did you have in mind?"

"Well, I've got to go home for Christmas, but after New Year, I've got a week all to myself before I have to come back here... and I was wondering if you felt like having a visitor?"

"You want to come down to Cornwall?"

"Yes."

"For a week?"

"If you'll have me."

I smiled. "Sounds perfect." It would give us time to really get to know each other.

"So, will you be able to get some time off work?"

"I should think so. The job we're working on is for a local business and it has to be finished by New Year, so I can't imagine it being a problem for me to take a week off afterwards."

"Fabulous." I could hear the enthusiasm in her voice. "Just think," she murmured, "a whole week in bed..."

When Christmas arrived, Nathan came with it, although he came alone, revealing that he and Amanda had broken up a couple of weeks previously. Jade hadn't mentioned Amanda's departure to me, but then we rarely spoke about Nathan; we had better things to talk about. As was usual when he came home, I managed to spend the minimum amount of time with him – just calling in on Christmas morning to visit Mum and Derek, before spending the rest of the day with Dad and Michelle. It was better that way – and much easier than sitting in an awkward silence with Nathan.

As we stood on the doorstep, saying goodbye, he nudged into me though and whispered, loudly enough for my mother and Derek to hear, "I gather you've got company after New Year?"

I kept my expression impassive, not wanting to give anything away. "Yes," I replied.

"Who's that?" Mum asked.

"Jade's coming to stay for a week," I said, and she smiled.

"You're still seeing her then?"

"Yes."

"Didn't you know?" Nathan turned to her.

"No... but then your brother is thirty-one years old now," she replied. "He's entitled to a private life."

It was the first time I'd ever heard her answer back to Nathan and I smiled at the sour look on his face as I walked down the path, pleased that she'd finally put him in his place for once, although my mother's comment only served to remind me of two things; one, that I was another year older; and the other, that Jade hadn't known about my birthday. I hadn't felt like I could tell her and so it had passed by at the beginning of December, without any acknowledgement from her, which felt kind of strange and added to my resolve that we needed to get to know each other better... and that we had seven days coming up in which we could do just that... providing I could get Jade out of bed.

It proved to be easier said than done, in the end. She arrived on the mid-afternoon train on the third of January, which was a freezing cold day, with a sharp easterly wind and grey, threatening skies. I'd managed to get the time off, arranging it with Dad, and even telling him why – which made him smile – and I met Jade at the station, taking her straight back to my flat. Letting her in, I wasn't at all surprised when she wanted to go to bed right away, even though it was only four in the afternoon; we hadn't seen each other for ages, and I'd missed her as much as it seemed she'd missed me.

Two hours later though, when I suggested we could cook something to eat, she positively sulked, and I wondered if this was going to be the tone of our whole week.

"Why don't we order in?" she suggested.

"Because if we cook, we can talk," I reasoned, getting up and holding out my hand to her.

"Don't you think talking is overrated?" She lay back on the bed, parting her legs.

"Very probably." I grabbed her ankles and pulled her towards me, then leant over, my hands either side of her. "But I want to get to know you better."

She smirked. "I think you know me well enough."

"Carnally, yes... but I don't know anything else about you." I stood up again and held out my hand for the second time of asking. "Come and help me cook."

She pouted, and then moved up the bed in the opposite direction, pulling the duvet over her. "It's too cold."

"Okay. Stay in bed. I'll bring you something to eat in a while."

I wasn't going to give in, and without bothering to dress, I went out into the kitchen and started chopping vegetables to make us a stir-fry. I didn't intend taking very long over making our meal, but as far as I was concerned, it was the principle. We needed to do something, other than have sex. I'd rather have done it together, but…

"Sorry." I turned to see her standing, naked, by the island unit that separated my kitchen from the living area, and I put down my knife and went over to her, pulling her into my arms.

"You don't have to be sorry."

"You're not cross with me?"

"No." I wasn't. I was a bit disappointed that she wouldn't just talk to me, but I wasn't cross.

"Then come back to bed," she whispered, snaking her hands around my neck.

"I will… when I've finished cooking."

She opened her mouth, as though to argue, but then thought better of it and stepped back. "Promise?" she murmured.

"Yes… you go and keep warm."

She shrugged and smiled, and scurried away, and I returned to the vegetables.

And that was basically how it went for the remainder of Jade's week with me. Whenever I suggested doing anything, whether it was going for a walk, having dinner out, drinks at the pub, or just sitting and watching a movie, she'd find a reason not to and initiate sex instead.

By the time I put her on the train back to Kent, not only was I completely exhausted – again – but I was starting to wonder if that was all she wanted from me. Sure, I liked having sex with her, but I couldn't see that as the basis for a relationship. I couldn't see it as the basis of the 'more' that I'd been searching for ever since I'd met the girl on the beach over ten years earlier and had realised that 'more' even existed. Jade and I had officially been 'together', for want of a better word, since the middle of the previous September, which made it almost four months, and while I knew her body intimately, I still felt as though she was a complete stranger to me.

Chapter Three

It was only a couple of weeks later that my doubts were set aside, when Jade called me, late one Friday night and asked what I was doing for the second weekend in February.

"As far as I know, not a thing," I replied, lying back in bed.

"Good," she said, sounding relieved and cheerful.

"Why? What did you have in mind?" I wondered if she was contemplating another weekend of sex, and whether I might be able to persuade her to at least try doing something else with me for a change.

"I've got a reading week," she replied.

"Which means you're supposed to be reading, not seeing your boyfriend, doesn't it?" There was a stoney silence on the end of the phone. "Did I say something wrong?" I asked, when it became clear she wasn't going to speak again.

"No... it's just, you called yourself my boyfriend."

"And that's a problem?"

"No."

"Are you smiling?" I asked.

"Yes." I smiled myself at that thought.

"Good... now, tell me about this reading week."

She explained that she knew she wouldn't get much done at the student house, because there was always something going on there, and that she'd decided to go home to her parents in Suffolk for the week.

"Okay," I said, wondering where I fitted into this plan.

"And I wondered if you'd like to come for a visit," she added, "just for the first weekend."

I was stunned. "You... you want me to meet your parents?"

"Yes. I mean, you are my boyfriend, after all."

There was a teasing, fun note to her voice, and I smiled again. "Do they know about me then?"

"I've told them I'm seeing someone... I had to explain where I was going after New Year. And, before you ask, I've told them that you're older than me."

"Have you told them how much older?" I asked.

"Yes. I told them you're thirty."

"Well, I'm thirty-one now."

"You are?"

"Yes."

"When was your birthday?" she asked.

"At the beginning of December."

"And you didn't tell me?" Now she sounded hurt, all thoughts of fun and teasing gone.

"No. I didn't want you to feel like you had to do anything, and anyway, it's just a birthday. Speaking of which, when's yours?"

"Not until July," she said, her voice still a little sad.

"And that's when you'll be twenty-one?"

"Yes."

She fell silent and I knew I had to say something.

"I'm sorry I didn't tell you."

"It's okay. It's not like I told you when my birthday is either."

She seemed disappointed and I supposed that was understandable in the circumstances. It was something we could talk about when we next saw each other... when I met her parents.

"What did they say?" I asked.

"Who?"

"Your parents, when you told them I'm so much older than you."

"Oh... they were fine with it. Dad is eight years older than Mum, so there wasn't really much they could say, was there?"

"No, I don't suppose there was."

"So, do you think you'll be able to come?" she asked, sounding a little more enthusiastic again.

"For you... anything," I replied and she giggled.

*

Her parents' house was huge... beyond anything I'd expected, even when my SatNav was guiding me through the outskirts of Bury St Edmunds and into the countryside, where the only buildings seemed to be large farmhouses and barn conversions. Even then, I didn't expect anything as grand as the building that came into view as I drove up the wide driveway, and for a moment, I wondered if I'd got the wrong place. That is, until Jade appeared at the doorway, waving frantically. I parked next to a brand new Range Rover, and grabbed my bag from the passenger seat, walking over to her and noting that she hadn't run to greet me this time. Instead, she hugged me and leant up, kissing me on the cheek.

"Mum and Dad are watching," she whispered.

"They are?" I glanced around.

"They're in the drawing room."

I had no idea which of the many windows represented the drawing room, but decided I'd better be on my best behaviour and put my arm around Jade's shoulder as she led me indoors, into a huge hallway, with black and white tiled flooring, an inglenook fireplace and a wide staircase.

"Leave your bag there," she said, nodding to a long table near the door and I dumped my bag beside it, letting her lead me further into the house, to the first door on the left.

This, it seemed, was the drawing room, being as standing inside it, were a man and a woman, who smiled at me as I entered.

"This is Mummy and Daddy," Jade said and in a dreadful moment of panic, I realised I didn't know her surname. I'd spent the night with her on several occasions, I'd had sex with her in some fairly imaginative positions, and yet I had absolutely no idea how to address her parents. I floundered, wondering what on earth I was going to do, as her father stepped towards me, his hand outstretched.

"Call me Christopher," he said, saving me from the ultimate humiliation, before he turned and indicated his wife. "And this is Helena."

I shook her hand as well, noting that she shared Jade's colouring, although Christopher was much darker, both in his hair and skin tone.

"Welcome to our home, Adam," Helena said. "We have some tea ready, but if you'd prefer to freshen up first, I'm sure it would wait a while…"

"Tea would be lovely," I replied, accepting the offered hospitality, and we all sat down on the deep, comfortable sofas, with Jade by my side, a decent distance away, logs burning brightly in the large fireplace, surrounded by enormous landscape paintings, and views through the windows of the open countryside.

"You have a beautiful house," I said, taking the offered cup of tea from Helena.

"Thank you." She smiled at me. "It used to belong to Christopher's parents, but we inherited when his mother died about ten years ago." She looked to her husband for confirmation and he nodded his head, taking his own cup of tea from her, before she sat down herself.

"I noticed a lot of farms on my way here," I added, making conversation. "Do you farm your own land?"

"No," Christopher replied. "My father used to, when he was alive, and Mother took over from him, with the help of an estate manager, but now we rent out the land to other farmers. I'm afraid I was always something of a disappointment to my parents, in that department. Farming is not something that interests me; it never has."

"Oh?"

"I'm sure Jade's already told you, I work in the city." He smiled at his daughter and I tried to keep a straight face and not give away the fact that she hadn't told me anything… about anyone. Including herself. Not even her surname. "It means I don't spend very much time at home," he added, "but that's the price you pay, I suppose."

I looked around at the opulent surroundings, the paintings, the smart furniture, the jewels his wife was wearing, and then glanced at Jade, noting the sadness in her eyes, and wondered if it was a price worth paying.

"You're from Cornwall, aren't you?" Helena asked.

"Yes."

"And what do you do?"

"I own a building firm, with my dad." They both nodded at the same time. "I suppose I'm the fourth generation in the business, being as it was my great-grandfather who started it – not that I remember him, or my grandfather for that matter, but we've been going longer than any other building firm in North Cornwall... if that's anything to shout about."

"These days it is," Christopher said, with a smile. "So, whereabouts in North Cornwall are you based?"

"The company is in Newquay," I explained. "But I live a bit further along the coast, in a small village that no-one's ever heard of."

"And you like living in a village?" he asked.

"Well, I like living about forty feet from the beach, so yes."

"It sounds lovely," Helena mused.

"It is," Jade replied for me, and then took my hand. "Do you want to freshen up now?" she asked.

"Okay." I quickly swallowed down the rest of my tea, putting the cup back on the tray.

"We've put Adam in the yellow bedroom," Helena said, looking up and frowning slightly as Jade and I both stood at the same time, and I felt Jade stiffen beside me for a second.

"Okay," she replied, her voice a little stilted, before she practically dragged me out of the room.

Once she'd closed the door, she let me go and stood still, in the middle of the hallway, turning this way and that, pushing her fingers back through her long hair. "How could she?" she whispered. "How could she do that?"

"Do what? What's wrong?" I stepped closer, grabbing her hands and holding them between us.

She looked up at me, her eyes dark with what appeared to be anger... bordering on fury.

"Come with me," she said, and turned. I picked up my bag from its place by the front door and followed her up the stairs and around the galleried landing, to our right, passing three doors before she opened one, which led us into a beautiful bedroom, the walls of which were, indeed, yellow. The furniture was a pale wood and the curtains and bedding were light blue and very sumptuous.

"What's wrong, Jade?" I asked, closing the door and letting my bag drop to the floor beside me. Something clearly was.

"They know I came to stay with you in January. They know you've been to stay with me in Kent. And yet they've put you in here… about as far away from my room as you can get."

I nodded my head, understanding now what the problem was. "Well, I suppose that's fair enough. I mean, they may be able to accept that we're having sex with each other, but that doesn't mean they necessarily want it to happen under their roof."

She glared at me from across the room. "Are you serious?"

"Yes. It's their house, Jade." I walked over, standing in front of her. "It's fine. I'm happy just being here with you."

"But I've missed you." There was a slightly childish whine to her voice, which grated on me.

"I know." I did my best to ignore my misgivings. "And I've missed you too. But look on the bright side…"

"There is one?" she sulked.

"Yes, at least we'll get to spend the weekend together."

She sighed deeply and leant into me, putting her arms around my waist, and I held onto her, feeling slightly guilty for my own gratitude that her parents had inadvertently gifted me an opportunity to get to know their daughter, outside of the bedroom.

That evening, Christopher and Helena took us out for dinner in Bury St Edmunds, to a very nice French restaurant, and insisted on paying. By the time we got back, however, I was completely exhausted, having been driving for nearly six hours, and I excused myself, giving Jade a chaste kiss on the cheek in front of her parents, before heading straight for bed.

My room had an ensuite shower room and I took advantage of that, before falling into bed and almost immediately, into a deep sleep.

I suppose it was because I was in a strange bed, in a strange room, in a strange house, that the sound of the door opening woke me instantly.

"Who's there?"

"It's me… who else did you think it would be?"

Jade's voice was unmistakable and I turned over, flicking on the bedside lamp, to see her standing just inside the door, wearing a short, silky robe.

"What are you doing?" I sat up.

"I've come to see you." She pulled at the tie around her waist, releasing it, and let the robe fall from her shoulders to the floor, revealing her naked body.

"You shouldn't be here," I said, even as she walked towards me.

"Don't be a spoilsport."

She pulled back the duvet and climbed into bed, pushing me back into the mattress and straddling me. I held her by the waist, preventing her from taking things further. "I'm not," I replied, "but you should respect your parents' wishes, and I don't want to fall out with them on my first visit."

She leant forward. "Don't you want me?"

"I think it's glaringly obvious that I want you."

It was. I hadn't seen her for over a month, and my body had responded to hers within seconds of her removing her robe. Even so, that didn't mean I thought it was right for her to be there.

"Well then," she said, taking my hands and holding them in hers. "Forget about my parents. They'll never know. And I need you. Now."

And with that, she raised herself up and leant forward, pushed my hands down into the pillow, beside my head, before lowering herself back down again and letting out an almost silent sigh of satisfaction as she took me deep within her. I was lost, for a moment… but it was just a moment, before the realisation hit me and I pulled my hands free, lifting her off of me.

"What?" she whispered.

"Condom," I muttered, and she stifled a giggle, rolling onto her back.

I could see that I wasn't going to win the argument about obeying her parents' rules, but at least if we were going to do this, then we'd be sensible, and I got up and went over to my bag, grabbing the box of condoms I'd brought with me.

"You came prepared then?" Jade said, kneeling up and moving to the side of the bed, to face me.

"Yes," I replied, as she took the box from me, tearing into a foil packet and rolling the condom tantalisingly slowly over my erection, before turning around, her back to me now, then leaning forward on all fours, and crawling into the centre of the bed, making her desires obvious – which, let's face it – she was prone to do.

I knelt behind her, obligingly, grateful in a way that we'd changed positions, so that when she climaxed – both times – she could smother her cries, burying her face in the soft duvet.

Afterwards, I collapsed down and rolled over onto my back, utterly spent, but rather than turning and lying beside me, she got up, flushed and still breathing hard, and without a word, she put her robe back on and walked out of the bedroom as silently as she'd entered, leaving me sprawled across the bed, wondering if it was normal to feel used by your own girlfriend.

The following day we went out together, just Jade and I, because we couldn't stay in bed as I think she would have preferred and, at least by going out, we could be alone. After the previous night's exploits, I was feeling even more uncertain than usual about our relationship, and whether it had any future.

I took her to lunch in Bury St Edmunds and, after we'd placed our order and our drinks had been brought to the table, I asked her about her plans.

"Plans?" she said, looking confused.

"Yes. What are you going to do, after university?" It seemed easier to start there, rather than asking her outright whether she intended to keep seeing me in the long-run. After all, if she announced that her goal had always been to move to the Outer Hebrides to take up crofting, then I could be fairly sure I wasn't part of the bigger picture.

"If you're talking about a career, then I've got absolutely no idea," she replied.

I stared at her. "So, you started a three year course in History, with no idea what you were going to do at the end of it?"

"Pretty much, yeah. I mean, I liked history at school, and at college, so it seemed like a good plan at the time, but I still don't have a clue about what I actually want to do. I don't think that far into the future."

"How far into the future do you think, then?" She only had a short while left on her course. Her future was pretty imminent, if you asked me.

She shrugged. "Oh, I don't know… a few weeks or months, maybe."

"So, where do you see yourself in a few months?"

She leant forward across the table. "Well, I was going to talk to you about that."

"You were?" I was intrigued, and leant in a little myself.

"Yes. I was going to ask if I could come and spend the summer with you." I think the surprise must have shown on my face, because she continued, "Don't worry. I won't sponge off you; I'll find work somewhere… I'm just not ready to think about facing the big wide world yet, and I know Mum and Dad will be nagging me to get a proper job." She rolled her eyes and smiled slightly. I smiled back, but refrained from saying that I didn't think her parents wanting her to find permanent employment after three years at uni – probably at their expense – was that surprising. "The thing is, I just want to take a few months to myself to chill." She tilted her head. "That's not so unreasonable, is it?"

"No…"

"So can I come and stay?"

"You can… but only if you tell me something." Her face darkened. "What?"

"Your surname. I nearly died yesterday when I got here and realised I didn't even know what to call your parents."

She laughed, letting her head rock back.

"It's Pearce," she said, then grinned and leant right forward, kissing me, before sitting back down and looking rather pleased with herself.

As I took a sip of water, I looked at her over the rim of the glass trying not to read too much into her request to come and stay. I thought it might mean she was serious about us, but there was still a nagging doubt in the back of my mind that, in reality, all she was looking for was somewhere to crash, and someone to sleep with – and I fitted the bill. At least for the time being.

On the drive back to Cornwall the following day, I had plenty of time to think, and I started to wonder if, maybe the age gap really was too much. Maybe that was the problem between Jade and me… because without a doubt, I knew there was a problem. I was looking for a relationship, that involved more than just sex; where conversation and companionship, a need to just be together, and perhaps the odd shared interest also featured, just as much as physical pleasure. I was looking for 'more'. I was looking for love. Jade, on the other hand, was looking for fun. And if recent experience was anything to go by, she wasn't looking for anything else. Maybe I'd been the same at her age though. Maybe I was doing her an injustice, and I thought back, trying to remember what I'd been like at twenty. And then it came to me. That was how old I'd been when I'd met 'the girl'. That was when the concept of 'more' had first occurred to me, and I realised that my issues with Jade had nothing to do with our ages. They had everything to do with finding the right person. And, yes, they had everything to do with love. And, having experienced it once – even if it had been very briefly, and over a decade ago – I knew without a doubt, that I wasn't in love. I wasn't in love with Jade, anyway.

I felt like I had a decision to make. At my age, it seemed as though I shouldn't be wasting my time on something I knew was wrong. Not only was it frustrating, it wasn't fair on Jade either. So, I wondered, should I end it with her there and then? The problem with that was, I had no idea how she felt about me – other than her obvious lust, that is, – and I didn't like the thought of hurting her, especially not with her finals looming. I may not have been in love, but I did care about her, and I remembered that disappointed sound in her voice when she realised I hadn't told her about my birthday, and that sad look in her eyes when her dad talked about being away from home, and I didn't want to be responsible for causing that again. So, my other option was to give it the summer. It was only a few more months, after all. I could let her come and stay with me for a while and see how things went. Let's face it, if you added it up, we'd actually spent less than a fortnight together, so I reasoned, there was always the chance that, if we gave our relationship a little more time, we'd find a way to accommodate each other's needs. We'd learn to compromise, and possibly even to fall in love. We'd have a summer of fun, anyway… and I could give her that much, couldn't I?

Maybe I was taking the coward's way out. Maybe I should have ended it when I had the chance. The point is, I didn't.

Over the coming weeks and months, work got really busy. Dad had turned sixty in January and it seemed like a watershed moment for him. He'd decided to take more of a back seat in the business, and was slowly but surely handing the reins over to me. That meant that, instead of my days being filled with manual labour, I was going out to see clients, studying plans, taking briefs, preparing quotes, and organising schedules, as well as overseeing the various projects we had ongoing at any one time. Dad was still very much in charge, and I always deferred to him – especially when it came to pricing and schedules – but it was clear to both of us that I was the boss in training. And, as much as I'd always enjoyed my outdoor life, I liked my new role too. I still had plenty of time for surfing, and at least no-one expected me to wear a suit to work; smart jeans and a shirt seemed to be perfectly adequate attire for my meetings, and that was just fine with me.

Jade was just as snowed under as I was, being as her final exams and the time for handing in her dissertation were drawing nearer. We still talked on the phone whenever we could, but as April turned to May, I noticed that she was becoming more and more distant, more abrupt, and that our calls were shorter than before.

It was late one Friday evening, in the middle of May, when I decided to mention the change in her. I'd phoned, and she'd sounded almost impatient when she'd picked up.

"What's wrong?" I asked.

"Nothing."

That clearly wasn't true. "Jade, something's not right. You haven't been yourself for weeks. What is it?"

"I'm stressed out, okay!" She was almost screaming down the phone.

"Okay," I said calmly. "What are you stressed about?"

"Well, probably the fact that my dissertation is due in next Friday, and I've still got two thousand words to write, and that it's only three weeks until my finals, and I haven't revised anywhere near enough…" Her voice trailed off and I heard her sob.

"Are you crying?"

She didn't reply, but I knew she was and I felt helpless, more than three hundred miles away.

"Don't cry," I said softly.

"Sorry," she whimpered.

"And don't be sorry. I'm the one who should be saying sorry."

"Why?" She sounded confused, although I could still hear her trying to catch her breath.

"Because I'm being insensitive. I should have realised how difficult things are for you, and not asked such stupid questions." I heard her let out an even louder sob. "Please don't cry, Jade."

"Then stop saying sorry," she muttered. "You haven't done anything wrong."

I wanted to disagree. After all, it hadn't been that long ago that I'd been thinking about ending our relationship, before we'd even given it a chance, and here she was crying down the phone at me and telling me I'd done nothing wrong. I didn't feel too good about myself at that moment.

"Shall we change the subject?" I suggested.

"Yes, please."

"Okay… I've been thinking about when you finish uni…"

"What about it?" she interrupted, her voice a little clearer.

"I was just wondering whether you wanted me to drive down and pick you up from Canterbury. It makes sense, when you think about how much stuff you'll have." I wasn't being entirely truthful. I hadn't been thinking about it that much, but I hoped that talking about the summer, and the time after her exams might cheer her up.

"You can't," she said quickly.

"Why not?" Her response surprised me.

"Because I'm going home."

"You are?" This was news to me.

"Yes. Just for a few days… maybe a week. I told Mum and Dad about my plan to come to you, and they weren't exactly happy."

"Oh." I wondered if it was me they weren't happy about, or the fact that Jade was so obviously postponing looking for permanent work. I didn't like to ask though, in case she got upset again.

"But they said it was okay in the end, as long as I actually got a job and didn't expect you to pay for everything, *and* I went home first, just to see them… I thought I'd told you."

"No, you hadn't."

"Oh. Sorry."

"Don't worry about it. You've got a lot on your mind." The phone went silent for a moment, and then I asked, "So what's happening at the end of your exams then? Is your dad coming to pick you up?"

"Yes, it's all arranged. My last exam is on the thirteenth of June, which is a Thursday, and he's coming to collect me on the Friday evening. It's going to take me most of Friday to pack, I think."

"I'm sure it will."

She sounded a little brighter and we talked for a few more minutes, before she started to yawn, and I suggested that, whatever she was doing, she should stop it for the evening and go to bed. She needed sleep. She agreed and we said goodnight.

As I lay in bed myself a little later on, I realised that had been the first time Jade had ever shown any real emotion with me. And while I didn't want her to cry all the time, I hoped that this new openness might be a taste of things to come…

Jade's mood stayed quite low over the coming days, not even improving once she'd handed in her dissertation, after which she wailed down the phone at me that she was convinced she was going to fail her degree and that the last three years had been a complete waste of time… and her parents' money.

I reassured her that she was amazing, that she wasn't going to fail, and that I had every faith in her. At one point, she asked what I knew about it, being as I hadn't even been to university, which kind of stung, but she apologised within seconds, and I forgave her. It was all clearly getting to her, and I knew that the sooner she got away from studying and came down to Cornwall to be with me, the better things would be.

On the Wednesday before her last exam, I called to wish her luck. She was very subdued, but I didn't query that and tried to focus our conversation on the future, telling her how much I'd missed her, and that I couldn't wait to see her again. Normally, that would have brought about a suitably coarse response, accompanied by graphic descriptions of what she intended to do with me the moment she clapped eyes on me, but on that occasion, she just said, "Me too."

"You need a break," I replied.

"Yes." She sounded so tired, I wanted to let her sleep on me for a week.

"Will you call me after your exam?" I asked.

"We're all going out for a few drinks," she replied, "so I probably won't. Sorry."

"Don't be sorry. You need to get out; it'll do you good. Just don't drink too much, will you?"

"I'm not making any promises," she said and then the line went quiet, and for a moment I wondered if we'd lost the connection, but then I heard her say, "Goodbye, Adam," and she hung up.

It seemed like an odd and slightly abrupt way to end our conversation, but at the time, I put it down to the stress she was under. Maybe I should have realised there was more to it than that. But I didn't.

I had a really busy end to the week, with several potential new clients to see, as well as a backlog of quotations to catch up on, and three site visits to make. By the time I got home on Friday, it was gone seven and I was in need of a shower.

I was still drying myself off, when I heard my phone ringing and, thinking it might be Jade, I wrapped the towel around my waist and padded out of the bathroom and into the kitchen, where I'd left my phone on the island unit.

I checked the screen and saw that it wasn't Jade after all, it was an unknown number, and I thought about leaving it, but then changed my mind and answered, "Hello?"

"Hello... Mr Barclay?"

"Yes."

"Um... This is Police Constable Morris here. I'm with your mother..."

"You are? What's happened? Is she alright?"

"It's about your brother."

I wondered what Nathan had done now. "And?" I asked, a little impatiently.

"I'm afraid I've just had to break some bad news to your mother... would it be possible for you to come round? She's asking for you."

"What bad news?" I asked.

"Would you be able to come now?" he asked, ignoring my question and sounding a little desperate. In the background, I could hear my mother crying.

"Yes. I'll come straight away."

I hung up and dashed into my room, pulling on some jeans, a t-shirt, and trainers, ignoring the fact that my hair was still wet and dripping onto my shoulders, before grabbing my phone and keys and running from the flat, wondering what on earth my brother had done now, but realising it must be bad if the police were involved and my mother was crying over it. I'd never known her to cry before, not even when Nathan had been at his worst.

It took me less than two minutes to run to my mother's house, and I was only halfway up the garden path when the door was opened by a fresh-faced policeman.

"Mr Barclay?" He looked worried.

"Yes. Where's my mother?"

"She's in there." He nodded towards the living room and I walked past him, going straight through the door, where my mother was sitting on the sofa, a handkerchief clutched to her nose, her shoulders shaking.

"Mum?"

She looked up at me. "Oh, Adam…"

I sat beside her and pulled her into my arms, holding her as she wept.

"What's happened?" I asked, but she shook her head and I glanced up, noticing that Constable Morris had followed me into the room.

"It's your brother, Nathan," he said, standing awkwardly in the middle of the room. "I—I'm afraid there's been an accident." I waited for him to continue. "I'm sorry to have to tell you, but… your brother is dead."

Mum let out a pitiful wail and I gripped her tighter. "Dead?" I whispered.

"Yes."

"Does Derek know?"

Mum looked up at me and nodded her head. "Yes. This kind young man called him before he phoned you. He… he's on his way back."

"From where?"

"He evidently had a late meeting on the other side of Newquay," Constable Morris said, taking up the story, as my mother nestled into me, sobbing again. "He won't be long now."

I nodded my head, trying to take it all in; trying to comprehend my mother's pain, which I knew must be indescribable. Her son had just been killed and, as much as I never really liked him, I loved her, and I hated seeing her like that.

We all jumped at the sound of the key turning in the lock, and again when the door slammed, and then Derek appeared, his suit dishevelled, his face pale.

I stood and let him take my place on the sofa beside my mother, holding her in his arms, while I went to stand next to Constable Morris and watched them cry together, feeling almost as awkward as him, I think.

"Do we know what happened?" Derek asked eventually, wiping his damp cheeks with the back of his hand and looking up.

The constable shook his head. "Not really, I'm afraid. We haven't been given much detail. We got a call from our colleagues in South Yorkshire…"

"South Yorkshire?" Derek and I both interrupted at the same time.

"Yes." He looked from me to Derek, and back again. "They informed us that Nathan Powell and his girlfriend had both been killed outright in a collision on the A1(M) at just after five o'clock this afternoon."

"Girlfriend?" My mother looked up now. "Nathan didn't have a girlfriend."

"Well, female companion then," the constable said, blushing.

"What was he doing in South Yorkshire?" Derek asked.

"I'm afraid I don't know," Constable Morris replied. "Do you have any family up there?"

"No."

"Well, maybe his girlfriend did. There were two suitcases found in the car – one for each of them."

"I told you, Nathan didn't have a girlfriend," Mum reiterated, ignoring the constable's last statement.

Derek tightened his grip on her shoulder. "I suppose he could have done," he reasoned. "Let's face it, we hadn't seen him since Christmas…"

"We spoke on the phone though," Mum said, choking out her words. "He'd have told me."

I wondered about that, knowing how secretive Nathan could be, but didn't say anything.

At that moment, the policeman's radio made a loud crackling sound and he pressed a button on the side of it, before murmuring something, and then saying, "Excuse me," and leaving the room. I heard the front door open, but not close and worked out that he must be standing on the doorstep, listening to something that he'd rather we didn't hear.

"My poor baby," Mum whispered, leaning into Derek, and he pulled her close and sat them back into the sofa.

"Do you want me to do anything?" I asked, feeling useless.

Derek shook his head, so I remained where I was, disconnected as ever, watching them pour their grief into each other, until Constable Morris came back into the room.

"Is everything alright?" I asked.

"We're not sure," he replied, looking puzzled. "We've got the name of the girl who was in the car now, and the local force where she lived have been to speak to her parents. They don't know anyone who lives in the north of the country either, and it seems that she already had a boyfriend herself, so there's some confusion about what she was doing travelling, so far away, in a car with your brother…"

"Well, maybe she'd broken up with her boyfriend recently, hadn't had time to tell her parents about it, and was seeing Nathan instead," I suggested. "It doesn't explain what they were doing on the A1(M), but it might explain why they were together?"

"Hmm… the odd thing about it is that the girl's parents said her boyfriend was from Cornwall too. Not your brother… the other one. The one they knew about. The parents said they didn't know exactly whereabouts he lived, but somewhere near to Newquay evidently…"

"Did they know the boy's name?" Derek asked.

"Not his full name, no… They just knew him as Adam."

My skin froze and I felt my mother and Derek staring at me. "W— Was her name Jade Pearce?" I asked, squeezing the words through my closing throat.

"Yes," the constable replied, turning to face me.

"Then I'm Adam… I'm… I mean, I *was* her boyfriend."

Constable Morris paled noticeably and his jaw slackened. "Oh Christ," he muttered under his breath.

"Adam?" Mum whispered and I looked down at her. "What's going on? What does it all mean?"

I shook my head, unable to speak, my mind in turmoil. Jade was leaving me to be with Nathan… it was the only thing that made sense. What I didn't know was, how long it had been going on for. Weeks? Months? The whole time we'd been together? That thought made my stomach churn and bile rise into my throat, and I took a deep breath, trying to calm myself, even though my skin was crawling at the thought of my brother sleeping with my girlfriend while she and I were…

"Adam?" Derek's voice brought be back into the room, and I focused on him, and my mother.

"Sorry," I whispered. "I need to go."

Mum got up and came to stand in front of me, looking up into my eyes. "Don't think too badly of him," she murmured, resting her hand on my arm. "Please. It might not be what you think. There… there could be an innocent explanation."

I smiled – well, I tried to – and I put my arms around her as she leant into me, unable to think of a single innocent explanation that fitted with the facts.

She pulled back after a minute or so, and I let her go, turning to the policeman. "I'm going home," I said and he nodded, asking for my address, which I gave him.

"Will you be alright?" Derek asked, standing beside my mother now.

"I'll be fine." I nodded and went to the front door, letting myself out.

The walk home was a daze, as I tried hard not to think. I wasn't ready to think. Not yet.

Back in my flat, I sat on the sofa, watching the sun set across the bay, my mind a confused blur of unanswered questions, whirling round in circles, driving me slowly insane. Even then though, even as I tried to work things out, I realised it was pointless. I'd never know the truth. I'd never understand what had happened between them. And somehow I was going to have to learn to live with that.

I've got no idea how long I'd been sitting there, when the knocking sounded on my door, but I ignored it, not wanting to face anyone.

"Adam?" My dad's voice echoed through the flat. "Open the door."

I waited, hoping he'd go away.

"I'm not going anywhere until you open the door," he said after a minute's silence, and I knew he meant it.

Dragging myself to the door, I pulled it open and walked away, leaving him to follow me back into the living room, which he did, sitting at the other end of the sofa.

"Derek called me," he said, explaining his presence and I looked across at him, his eyes betraying his concern. "He said you were upset… well, angry."

"And you're surprised by that?"

"No, but try not to over-react. You don't know that anything was going on between them," he said. "It could have been innocent…"

I narrowed my eyes. "I'm not an idiot, Dad. Don't treat me like one. I'll take that crap from Mum and Derek, because it makes them feel better to think that butter would melt in Nathan's mouth. But I'm not taking it from you."

He stared at me, hesitating, then said, "Sorry."

"Facts are facts," I continued, ignoring his apology. I didn't want apologies. I wanted to rant. So I did. "It's obvious to me that Jade had decided she wanted to be with Nathan, and that they were driving somewhere far away from here… well, from me, anyway… and from her family, so that they could be together. It's the only thing that makes sense. But what I'd like to know is, how long it had been going on for? Did Nathan persuade her to leave with him? Was it her choice to go? Did she talk him into it? Was she sleeping with both of us at the same time? Were they in love…?"

"Were you?" he interrupted, stopping me in my tracks.

"No." I sighed, calming slightly. "We'd made plans for the summer. Jade was going to come and stay here. We were going to get to know each other better… at least I thought we were." I leant forward, resting my elbows on my knees and letting my head fall into my hands. "I know I'll never get the answer to all my questions, but what I really don't understand is, if she didn't want to be with me, why didn't she just tell me? She could have called me. I'd never said I loved her, and she must have known I wouldn't have stood in their way. I mean, I know Nathan and I have history, but if he loved her…" It was impossible for me to say Nathan's name without the anger showing through. Dad must have noticed, and moved a little closer.

"Try not to hate him, for your mother's sake," he said softly.

"That's asking quite a lot at the moment, Dad."

"I know, but your mum's in pieces. Just try and remember the good times."

"With Nathan? I'm not sure there were any."

"I meant with Jade."

I stared out of the window, recalling her smile, her laugh, her playfulness, the sparkle in her eyes, the way she used to tease me. I didn't dwell too long on my memories of having sex with her... they just reminded me that she'd chosen Nathan over me, and that hurt too much to think about at the time. It wasn't going to help anyone either, least of all me. "She said goodbye to me," I murmured eventually, turning back to my dad, who was still staring at me. "The last time we spoke... right at the end of the call, she said 'Goodbye, Adam.' I thought it was odd at the time."

"Why? Didn't she normally say goodbye to you?" he asked.

"Not like that, no. Maybe... maybe I should have realised then. Maybe I should have seen it coming."

"You weren't to know, son."

I shrugged. "I wish I had though... at least I could have said 'goodbye' too."

Part Two

Jenna

Chapter Four

I stood on the driveway, watching the removals lorry drive away down the winding lane, and took my first deep breath of sea air.

It was easy to see why Mum and Dad had chosen Carven Bay to retire to and, glancing back at their smiling faces as they stood by the front door, why they were so happy with their decision. It had nothing to do with the small, practical, chalet-style bungalow they'd purchased, with its large, well-equipped dining-kitchen, elegant living accommodation and spacious bedrooms – at least that was what it had said on the estate agent's leaflet, anyway. It didn't even have anything to do with the fact that, having sold our six bedroomed house just outside of Camberley in Surrey, they were now mortgage free for the first time in years. It had everything to do with the panoramic view before me; a view which took in the wide sandy beach, the azure waters, their lace-edged waves lapping high on the sandy shore, and the grass-tipped rocks lunging seawards, beneath clear blue skies. It was beautiful. It was majestic. It was…

"Hello?" The voice made me spin around and I saw a couple, standing on their corresponding driveway, looking across to ours. The man appeared to be roughly the same age as my dad, so approaching sixty, while the woman beside him was maybe a year or two younger. He had more hair than my dad, this man's being a dark brown, with grey showing at the temples, while what was left of my dad's was the shade that I believe people refer to as 'salt and pepper', and the woman was more blonde than my mother, who shared my own colouring, which was essentially a rather boring light brown. Even though she was in her mid-fifties, my mum's hair hadn't greyed at all, and neither had she lost her trim figure. I lived in anticipation that, if I was going to take after her, there was hope for me yet. "You've just moved in then?" the woman continued, as my parents stepped forward, saving me from having to make conversation with these strangers, who looked pleasant enough, but who I doubted would have anything in common with me.

"Yes." My dad offered his hand in greeting. "I'm Dennis Drake, and this is my wife Carole." My mother also shook hands with both of them, as they introduced themselves as Patrick and Serena Holmes.

"Is this your granddaughter?" Mrs Holmes asked, nodding in my direction.

I could feel the blush rising up my cheeks, although I was well used to the misunderstanding by that stage.

"No," my mother said, blushing herself, just a little. "This is our daughter." She motioned for me to step forward and join them, and I did. "This is Jenna," she added.

Mrs Holmes offered me her hand and, despite my embarrassment, I took it. She had a firm handshake, as did her husband. "So, have you managed to find work down here?" he asked, and for a moment I wondered if he was talking to my dad, until I realised his pale blue eyes were fixed in my direction still, and it dawned on me that, his wife having made one faux pas, he'd walked right into another, and had assumed I was older than my years.

"No," I replied. "I've just finished my GCSEs and I'm due to start at college next week."

"Oh, I see."

"We've taken early retirement," my mother said, as though that explained everything. It didn't. Not really. To a stranger, it didn't account for the fact that my parents were rapidly approaching sixty, while I was a mere sixteen. But then strangers weren't aware of the fact that my parents hadn't met until they were in their early thirties, or that they'd spent a few years travelling and enjoying themselves before they got married, and then discovered that, at that age, having babies wasn't as easy as they might have hoped, and that my mother had been just a week away from her fortieth birthday when I'd finally put in an appearance. As my father always said, though, whenever I got embarrassed about the situation, I was the living, breathing proof that good things come to those who wait.

Mr Holmes nodded his head. "We did the same thing a couple of years ago, and it was the best decision we ever made." He put his arm around his wife and she looked up at him affectionately. "So, where are you from?" he asked.

"Camberley, in Surrey," my mother replied.

Mr Holmes nodded his head. "I know it well. I used to work in the aviation industry…"

"Ah, so you'd have gone to Farnborough?" my dad guessed.

"Yes. I visited all the air shows, and often had meetings there too."

"Are you from Cornwall?" my mother asked.

"No," Mrs Holmes replied, "we're both from Swindon, but we used to come on holiday down here, and when Pat was offered early retirement, we couldn't think of anywhere we'd rather live."

My mum looked up at my dad and smiled. "We were the same," she said. "Although our holidays were usually spent on the south coast. But then this house came up for sale, and we took one look at the view…" We all turned and took in the spectacle before us, collectively sighing, until Mr Holmes brought us back to reality.

"We'd better let you get on, but if you need anything, just knock."

"And perhaps you'd like to come over for a drink sometime, when you're more settled?" his wife suggested.

"That sounds lovely," my mother replied.

"We'll look forward to it," Dad added, and with nods and waves, we all went indoors.

"They were friendly, weren't they?" Mum said, once the door was firmly closed.

"Yes," Dad replied, looking around the living room and scratching his head before removing his glasses, breathing on each lens in turn and giving it a polish on the bottom of his check shirt, which he'd left untucked. "God, there's a lot to do."

"There is," Mum said. "But we don't have to do it all in one day." She squared her shoulders, resting her hands on her slim hips for a moment, and then moved further into the room, examining the boxes that had been piled there. "First thing's first…" She turned back to face us, a broad smile on her face. "Let's get the kettle on and make the beds."

"Make the beds?" I frowned at her. "Surely that can wait."

She shook her head. "No. Making the beds early on is the first rule of moving house, Jenna. That way, when you're exhausted later, and all you want to do is collapse into bed and sleep for eight solid hours, at least you know it's all made up, and you haven't got to open another ten boxes just to find the bedding."

I smiled and rolled my eyes slightly, although I couldn't deny the logic of her argument.

"Who's going to make the tea, and who's going to make the beds?" my dad asked.

"I think you should make the tea." Mum looked up at him. "Jenna and I can take care of the beds."

In reality, Mum only had to open one box to find the bedding, because she'd labelled everything so meticulously, and handing me a fitted sheet, duvet cover and some pillow cases, she despatched me up the stairs.

My bedroom was at the front of the house, and although that meant it overlooked the road, I wasn't even vaguely sorry about that, because it also meant I had the best view in the world, right down over the bay, and for a good few minutes, I stood and looked out, watching the late afternoon sun sparkling and twinkling on the surface of the water, like a sequin covered cloth, swaying in the gentle breeze.

I could hear my parents' laughter from downstairs, and smiled to myself, pleased that they'd made this decision. They'd both been happy in their jobs – Dad as a chartered surveyor and Mum as an accountant – but they'd worked long hours and I knew they longed to be able to spend more time together. Dad's company offering him early retirement had given them that chance and they'd grasped it with both hands, although they had stopped to ask my opinion first, being as their plan was to move us over two hundred miles away from the only home I'd ever known. I think they expected me to raise objections, to moan about missing my friends, about not wanting to start afresh at a new college, to protest about moving to a much smaller house. But I didn't. I reasoned that real friends would stay in touch, and those who didn't weren't worth worrying about; I explained that one college is pretty much like any other, and that I was looking forward to meeting new people – I'd have done that anyway, even if we hadn't moved, being as most of my friends were scattering to different colleges, or weren't staying in education at all. And as for living in a smaller house... well, I had an entire beach at my disposal, literally just yards away. The sense of freedom was like nothing I'd ever experienced. So what if the dining table had to be squeezed into the kitchen, and the sofas were a bit of a tight fit? There were more important things in life.

Having moved down on a Friday, we spent the whole of that first weekend unpacking until, by Monday afternoon, the house resembled a slightly disordered normality. My parents had both decided that fitting a six bedroomed house into one that was half that size was going to require some strict decluttering, but until they found the time and the energy for that, anything that wasn't thought 'essential' was re-boxed and stored in the garage.

"Why don't you go for a wander down to the beach?" my dad suggested as he sealed yet another box with packaging tape. "Mum and I can manage here, and you've done enough. You could do with a break."

I wasn't about to say 'no' to his suggestion and ran upstairs to find my sandals.

"Dinner will be at seven," Mum called, as I went out of the front door, pulling it closed behind me. That gave me a good hour and a half to explore for the first time, and I set off down the lane to the footpath that led to the beach. I knew it was there, because there was one of those wooden signposts, which had the words 'Carven Bay – Public Footpath' etched into it, and I followed it, the split rail fencing on either side barely holding back the reeds and grasses that grew up to beyond waist height at times. The path widened as I progressed, until eventually I came out directly into the bay itself, and my breath caught in my throat.

The broad, sandy beach was surrounded by low cliffs on both sides, but I ignored the ambling pathways that intersected the grassy knolls, leading up onto them and, kicking off my sandals, which I picked up and held by their straps, I made my way down onto the baby-soft sand. It felt warm beneath my feet; warm and strangely comforting, and I wriggled my toes, feeling the gentle caress of the sand against my skin. It was quite late in the day, but there were still a few families dotted around on the beach, shading beneath parasols, young children running around and playing with balls and frisbees, and despite the breeze coming off the sea, I was glad I hadn't changed out of my shorts and t-shirt, because the sun was very warm indeed.

I made my way over to a rock, which was set rather incongruously in the sand, all by itself, as though a giant had dropped it there by mistake, and I perched myself up on top of it, letting my head roll back, the wind catching in my hair, until the sound of a woman's laugh made me sit forward again.

Approaching up the beach, was a group of maybe eight or nine people, some male, some female, all carrying surfboards and all chatting and laughing among themselves. I felt an unwelcome pang of jealously stab at my core; not because they were, without exception, all very good looking, but because I wanted to join in with them.

Over the years, since I was about five years old, my parents had tried to introduce me to various hobbies, from country dancing, to drama, piano lessons and even a season with the local girls' football team. Nothing had appealed though. I'd tried it all, but to no avail, always giving up after a year or so, feeling downcast, not only by my own inabilities, but also because I'd failed to find something that interested me. But, looking at this group, who'd stopped walking now and were gathered no more than twenty feet away by their belongings, which they'd obviously abandoned while they went to surf, I thought that this, that surfing, was something that I'd really like to try my hand at.

Now they were closer, I could see that there were five boys and four girls, and I watched them, trying not to appear obvious about it, as they talked and laughed, some drying themselves off, others just sitting and occasionally pointing out to sea. The girls were all really pretty, tanned to perfection, with long hair, which draped damply over their shoulders, but which still seemed to look elegant, unlike my own, which always resembled rats' tails whenever it got even vaguely wet. They wore bikinis, showing off perfect figures and long, shapely legs, which made me feel even more inadequate. The boys – or men, really, because it was easy to see that they were all quite a bit older than me – were muscular and attractive, and as I sat there, admiring, but looking away occasionally, just in case they should happen to glance over and notice me staring, one of them in particular caught my eye. He was taller than his friends, by a good few inches, with broad shoulders and a narrow waist, and dark hair which almost touched his shoulders. As he turned away and bent to pick up a towel, I noticed a tattoo which covered the whole of his back, and I studied it closely, forgetting about the fear of being caught staring, and simply taking in the artistry of the design. It was in the shape of a wolf's head, looking straight at me, but it wasn't like a drawing or an illustration, it was in a Celtic form, all in black, intricately detailed in stylised lines and knots. It fascinated me and I gazed at it – at least until the man turned and caught me doing so. Just before I could look away, he smiled. He smiled directly at me, and without even thinking, I smiled back, feeling my embarrassment deepening as he draped his towel around his neck and started to walk in my direction.

I wished then that I'd brought a book with me, so I could look busy – but what would have been the point in that? He'd already noticed me staring, and even as I tried to think about ways out of the situation, he was standing there, right in front of me, and I discovered that his chin was stubbled – not like he hadn't bothered to shave, but intentionally – and his eyes were a very rich, intense brown, although they sparkled in the sunlight as he smiled at me again.

"Are you okay up there?" he asked. His voice was deep and masculine and, as I scrutinised him, I saw a few drops of water fall from the tips of his hair onto his firm chest, and then drip down over his taut abdominal muscles to the top of his board shorts, where they were consumed by the soft, navy blue material.

"Um… yes, thanks," I managed to say.

"You can join us if you want," he offered, "rather than sitting here by yourself."

I stared at him, and not just because he was the most gorgeous person I'd ever seen, but because, if I'd heard him correctly, he seemed to be seriously suggesting that I could go and sit with him and his friends. My initial instinct was to say 'no' – I didn't know any of these people, after all – but then I glanced over his shoulder to where the group were still gathered, and realised that they didn't look threatening at all. In fact, they looked really friendly.

"Um… Okay," I mumbled and he smiled broadly, showing off perfect white teeth to complete the picture.

I started to slide down the rock, but he reached out and put his hands on my waist, lifting me off and lowering me to the sand, as though I weighed nothing, before letting me go and leading the way back to his group of friends.

"I'd make the introductions," he said as we got there, "but you won't remember all their names anyway." I looked up at him and smiled, as he offered me a seat on a beach mat, which I took, crossing my legs and putting my sandals down beside me. I'd barely had time to get settled, when one of the girls – a blonde, who was wearing a red and white striped bikini – came and sat beside me.

"You're not from round here, are you?" she asked, and I wondered if I'd judged the situation badly; if she was going to be hostile for some reason.

"No."

"So where are you from?"

"I'm from Surrey."

She smiled and nodded her head, and I relaxed a little, just as the man with the tattoo came and sat on the other side of me and offered me a bottle of coke, which I accepted. "Thanks."

He nodded. "Did I hear you say you're from Surrey?" he asked.

"Yes."

"Well, that explains your accent." He and the girl both laughed, but not in an unkind way, and I joined in.

"I suppose I do sound odd to you." I struggled with the screw cap on the bottle, and the man with the tattoo took it from me, opened it with ease and handed it back again.

"No more odd than we sound to you," he replied.

"Yes, but your accents are softer," I said, taking a long sip of my drink. "I like them."

"I take it that, being from Surrey, you've probably never surfed before?" the girl asked and I turned back to her.

"No," I said, shaking my head. "Never."

"And would you like to?" the man asked.

"I'd love to." I looked back at him, to see he was still smiling.

"Then why don't I teach you?" he suggested.

"Well, because I don't have a board," I pointed out. "Or a swimming costume."

"You don't own a swimming costume?" He sounded incredulous. "Not at all?"

I shook my head. "No, I mean, I do own one, but I haven't got it on me right now."

He chuckled. "Oh, I see. Well, why not come back tomorrow and I'll teach you then?"

"Because I still won't have a board?"

"You can borrow one of mine," he said.

"Really?" He nodded, staring at me. "I probably won't be any good," I added, feeling the heat of his gaze, and he shrugged.

"If you don't try, you'll never know, will you?"

"No, I won't."

"So, you'll come back tomorrow?"

I didn't even hesitate, but accepted his offer, and then took another drink of coke as the girl started asking about my t-shirt, admiring the tie-dyed colours and asking where I'd bought it.

It was only as I was walking home, over half an hour later, that I realised I'd been having so much fun, talking about surfing, and music, and admiring the man with the tattoo, that I hadn't even asked his name.

Still, I reasoned to myself, it didn't matter, did it? I was going to be seeing him the next day, and I could ask him then. And besides, he hadn't asked my name either, had he? I stopped walking for a moment, almost at the end of the path... Did that mean he didn't care? Did that mean he wasn't interested? Because I was definitely interested in him. But then, if he hadn't been interested, why had he invited me to sit with him and his friends? Why had he suggested meeting up again? I smiled and continued on my way again, marvelling at my own inexperience.

That wasn't overly surprising really, when I actually thought about it, being as I'd never had a boyfriend. There was a good reason for that too, though, as I'd spent most of the previous two years pining after Dale Anderson. He was a boy in my year at school, and at the time I'd thought he was utterly gorgeous – essentially the only boy worth looking at in the whole world, which meant I did a lot of looking, and very little else, as a result of which, he went out with several other girls – mostly in the year below ours – and ignored me completely. By the time we got around to sitting our GCSEs, I'd resigned myself to the fact that he and I were never going to happen, which was only confirmed when I saw him kissing Abigail Watts at the bus stop on the last day of term. Oddly, I wasn't upset. I remember smiling to myself about how stupid I'd been, devoting so much time to a boy who never even knew I existed. What a waste...

When I got back home, my parents didn't enquire about my trip to the beach, because dinner was running late, and because they were full of news themselves. Unbeknownst to me, while I was out, they had been invited round to Mr and Mrs Holmes' house for drinks. They'd only stayed for an hour, but had learned in that time, that our neighbours had a son and a daughter. Their son, Matthew, still lived in Swindon, with his wife Joanna and their three year old son, Alex, who came to stay regularly with his grandparents. Their daughter, Natalie, on the other hand, had left Swindon years ago for the brighter lights of London, where she lived with her partner Caroline, or 'Caro' – as it seemed everyone called her – who was something quite important in the the music industry, although Mum and Dad didn't really understand what. Mum was quite solicitous in telling me this little snippet of information and seemed to think that I'd find the notion of two women living together a bit shocking. But then I'd never explained to her, or my dad, about Sienna Abbott and Lilly Thorpe, two girls in my year at school, who could regularly be seen holding hands, and sometimes kissing, when they thought no-one was watching, so I suppose she wasn't to know that I was beyond shocking when it came to such matters.

While they were telling me all of this, as well as complimenting Mrs Holmes' gardening abilities, Mum put some chicken breasts in the oven and started making a salad, while Dad laid the table

"I might go for a swim in the morning," I said, once they'd finished telling me about their evening, and knowing I'd need to explain my absence from the house the following day.

"That's a good idea," Mum replied as she chopped up a pepper. I felt guilty for not explaining about the man, or how I'd met him, but I wasn't sure they'd approve, being as he did seem to be a lot older than me… and I did so desperately want to see him again.

Not long after dinner, I made my excuses and went up to bed, undressing and getting into my pyjamas, but lying on top of the duvet because it was so hot. The sound of the waves lapping on the seashore drifted in through my open window and, staring at the ceiling in the moonlight, images of the perfect man flittered before my eyes…

His arms come around me, his strong muscles binding me tight to his muscular chest as he closes the gap between us, our bodies drawn together, skin against skin.

"I love you, Jenna," he murmurs, his husky voice, filled with desire, whispering across my sensitised skin, his lips brushing against mine, hard and demanding, before he lowers me down onto the sand, the waves lapping up and over us…

I woke with a start, the sun pouring in through the still-open curtains, feeling hot and bothered, flustered, breathing hard, and slightly on edge, like nothing I'd ever felt before. There was a nervous energy surrounding me and I knew I was blushing as I recalled the vivid images of my dream. My skin felt like it was on fire, my body like it was a raging inferno, and I struggled to catch my breath as I shot out of bed and sat on the edge, my mind in a whirl. I stared at the pine wardrobe doors and wondered if I dared to go to the beach after all. How could

I look at the man again, knowing the content of my dreams? Would I be able to face him, with the memory of his imagined kisses, words and touch so fresh in my mind? I took a deep breath and pursed my lips to stop the smile from spreading... of course I would.

I had a cool shower, and told myself it was because the weather outside was already warming up, and that it had nothing to do with the heat that was still burning within me. Of course it didn't. I had that under control. Completely. And as I got shampoo in my eyes and jigged around, yelping and trying to wash it out again, I giggled at the thought of what the man might make of me if he could see me now.

Back in my room, I went through my wide chest of drawers, which was set beside the wardrobe, both of them taking up the long wall opposite the window. I didn't want to put on any underwear, because I was going to have to get undressed on the beach, and there was nothing more inelegant or unbecoming than struggling to hold a towel around you, while trying to pull your knickers down. So, I decided to put my costume on under my clothes, and pulled out my simple black one-piece, throwing it onto the bed, alongside my cut-off denim shorts and a plain white t-shirt. As I dried my hair, I recalled that all of the girls at the beach had been wearing bikinis, not one-piece suits, and I kept glancing over at the bed, at my rather boring choice of swimwear. It may have been practical, but that was really the only thing it had going for it, and once I was satisfied with the way my hair looked, I put away my dryer and, without giving the matter too much thought, went back over to my chest of drawers and pulled out a navy blue and white polka dotted halter neck bikini. I owned three bikinis, as well as two one-piece costumes, and this was by far and away the nicest of them all. As I pulled on the top, fastening it behind my back, and doing up the ties at my neck, I looked in the mirror and smiled. I've always been quite well endowed, having been an early starter in that department, and this bikini – while covering everything that it was designed to – had the added bonus of showing off my assets to their best advantage. The bottom part of the bikini was brief, but not obscene, with ties at the sides and, as I did them up, I couldn't help smiling, and blushing just slightly, wondering if the man would want to undo them later on… I wouldn't have let him – obviously – but I liked the idea that he might want to.

Once I was dressed, my shorts and t-shirt covering my bikini, I went downstairs and had a quick breakfast of cornflakes, with a glass of orange juice, before dashing out of the front door, waving my goodbyes and promising to be back for lunch. This time, unlike the previous day, I'd remembered to bring a book with me, as well as a towel and beach mat, which I'd put into a large tote bag, slung over my shoulder.

I almost bounced down to the beach, the sun already beating down warm and slightly humid, and I pulled my sunglasses from my bag, putting them on and gazing up at the clear blue sky above. It was a perfect day. A perfect day to learn to surf… and, of course, to fall in love. And I had every intention of doing both.

As I came out onto the beach, I was surprised by how empty it was – in that I had the whole place to myself – and I glanced around, removing my sunglasses as I searched for my friends of the previous day. It took me just a few seconds to realise that they weren't there. They were nowhere in sight, in fact, and I felt my shoulders drop in disappointment as I made my way over to the solitary rock and clambered up onto it to await their arrival, sighing deeply to myself and wishing that we'd set a time for our rendezvous, and that I'd bothered to find out the man's name, or better still, his phone number.

I'd been sent a reading list by the local college, where I was due to start two days later, with the instruction to 'read as many books as possible', during the long summer holidays, and had been working my way through several of the titles, having saved Jane Austen's *Persuasion* until last. And so, I sat on the rock and began the sometimes humorous, sometimes sad tale of the seemingly unrequited love of Anne Elliot for Captain Wentworth. It wasn't perhaps the best of novels for me to be reading in the circumstances and, every time I looked up to see whether the man and his friends had arrived, I felt my dismay and compared it to Anne's, as my eyes settled on an empty beach.

By noon, I knew I had no choice other than to return home, and so with a heavy heart, I put away my book and – unaided this time – slid down the rock and onto the sand. Looking around once more, I walked back to the path, feeling despondent and wondering why the man had bothered to make the arrangement if he didn't intend to keep it.

I hadn't meant to go back the following day, but after another night of steamy, romantic dreams, in which he featured larger than ever, I couldn't help myself. During the previous afternoon, in between going to the supermarket with Mum and reading a little more of *Persuasion* in my bedroom, I'd wondered whether maybe something had happened to keep him away. With no way of contacting me, he'd have been unable to let me know. So, perhaps, I reasoned to myself, it would be best if I tried again... just to be on the safe side.

I didn't wait so long, not the second time. When I saw he wasn't there, and neither were his friends, I gave it half an hour and went home again, feeling upset obviously, but more angry than anything else. It seemed like such a rude and insensitive thing to do, even if I had misread the signs, and he hadn't been interested in me... not in the same way I was interested in him, anyway. Still, it was his loss. Or at least that's what I told myself, while deeply regretting the fact that I'd never see him again – and that I'd probably never get the chance to learn to surf either.

I started at college in Newquay the very next day, which proved to be an excellent distraction from my continued dreams and fantasies about my wolf man, as I'd come to think of him. The college, which was a twenty minute bus ride away, was actually part of a school, although it had its own separate campus, and almost everyone else had already been attending for years, which meant they all knew each other. They were very friendly, nonetheless, and in my first class of the day, which was Mathematics, I met Nadia and Alisa, who were quick to befriend me, intrigued by my accent, it seemed, and keen to introduce me to their friends, which they did at lunchtime in the enormous cafeteria.

So, over a cheese and salad sandwich, I met Lara, Kathy, Miles, Eric, Gary, Andy, and Scott. At first, as I looked around, I wondered how I'd ever remember all their names, but then I quickly realised they all had their own little idiosyncrasies. To start with, Lara and Miles were very clearly an item – given away by the fact that she was sitting on his lap and they kept kissing each other – so that made them a little easier to recall. I discovered that Kathy was going to be in my English Literature classes, and that she had a passion for Shakespeare. Eric had red hair. The kind of red that comes out of a bottle. Judging from his eyebrows, I think his original shade was a mid-brown, but he wore the red, and his black clothes with an air of self-assurance that didn't bear question. Gary and Andy were the comedians of the group, in a kind of slightly annoying, childish, slapstick way, which I wasn't entirely sure I would get used to... And then there was Scott. His hair was blond, short, neatly trimmed, and he had the most piercing deep blue eyes I'd ever seen, set in a perfect, handsome face, with high cheekbones and a dimpled chin. What's more, while everyone else was wearing t-shirts, or casual tops over their jeans, he was dressed in a more formal shirt, undone at the neck, with a waistcoat over the top. I'd never seen anyone quite like him, and I found my eyes constantly drawn to him while we all chatted around the long table.

"What have you got this afternoon?" he asked when our eyes met for about the fifth time.

"Design and Technology," I replied, recalling my timetable. "I'm not sure where..."

"I'll take you," he interrupted, and leant over the table slightly.

"You don't have to. I'm sure I'll find my way." I felt a little affronted that he thought I was incapable of following the map of the school I'd been given earlier that morning.

"Well, being as I'm taking DT as well, I can either show you the way, or just follow you and admire the view... it's up to you."

As he spoke, he started to smile, and I had to smile back as I accepted his offer, surprised by his compliment. After lunch, we left the cafeteria together, walking out of the double doors and along the corridor to the end, before leaving the building.

"Where are we going?" I asked, wishing I'd thought to check the map first.

"DT is in the art block," he replied, nodding towards the newly constructed glass building ahead of us.

"Oh."

He leant closer. "You see? You did need me really."

I looked up at him, and he smiled again, his eyes sparkling down at me, and I wondered what I'd ever seen in the wolf man.

By the time half term came around, the ten of us were firm friends. I'd even grown accustomed to Gary and Andy, although only in small doses. Lara and Miles spent a lot of time on their own, so I didn't see so much of them, and I suppose of all the girls, it was probably Kathy that I got on with best of all, because we had the most in common. As for Scott... I wasn't so sure. What I mean is, I was sure I liked him. I liked him a lot, in fact. He was perfect, so what wasn't there to like? I thought about him all the time, sometimes to the point of distraction. But I really wasn't sure how he felt about me. One minute he was all over me, attentive and caring, laughing, talking to me for ages – just the two of us – and looking deep into my eyes, making me feel like I was the only girl in the world; and the next, it felt like I didn't exist. I could pass him in the corridor and he'd barely acknowledge my presence. Admittedly our timetables didn't allow for many meetings because although we both studied DT and Maths, we were only together for Design and Technology, because we were in separate groups for Maths, and for our other subjects, Scott was studying Physics and I was doing English Literature. Even so, we spent a fair amount of time in each other's company, and we had lunchtimes together – when he could be bothered to remember who I was, that is.

November was about to become December and I was on the back end of a couple of days of being cold-shouldered, when Scott cornered me by the main staircase, just as I was about to go up to my English class.

"Just the person," he beamed.

"Me?" I was so surprised he seemed to be talking to me, I even glanced around, to make sure there wasn't someone else standing close by. Someone more interesting than me.

"Yes, you." He moved closer. "I'm having a party next Saturday, and I wondered if you'd like to come?" I stared at him for a moment, and it must have been a moment too long, because I heard him say my name, as though he wasn't sure whether I'd heard him.

"Yes?"

"Are you okay?"

"Yes."

"So, what do you say?"

"You want me to come to your party?" I'd moved beyond surprise to incredulity, but I had at least regained the power of speech.

"Of course," he replied, starting to walk slowly backwards towards the double doors that led to the science block, his eyes boring into mine. "It's my birthday. Wouldn't be the same without you there." My mouth dropped open. "Say you'll come," he pleaded through his grin, clasping his hands together, and holding them out in front of him, beseeching me.

I nodded my head, dumbfounded and he winked, then flipped around, and walked away, leaving me to wonder whether I was dreaming, or whether that had really just happened.

It happened. I knew that because Scott sent me a text that evening, with his address on it, and I went to the party the following Saturday. Scott's parents were there, and they seemed really nice – much younger than my own, of course – although they stayed in the background, just overseeing things and making sure no-one went too crazy. Scott was the life and soul of the event, which was only to be expected, I suppose, being as it was his party. Even so, I was starting to wonder why he'd made such a big deal about inviting me, being as he'd only managed a brief nod in my direction on my arrival, and hadn't actually said a thing to me in the two hours I'd been there. I was sitting with Kathy, wondering whether to call my dad to get him to come and collect me, when Scott suddenly appeared in front of me, leant down and took my hand, pulling me to my feet, without uttering a single word. He led me out into the hallway, which was quieter than the living room, and I found myself in a small alcove, my back against the wall, with Scott facing me. It was dark, but I could see the glint in his eyes as he leant in close.

"I'm really glad you came," he murmured.

"You are?" That didn't make sense to me, given that – until that moment – he'd barely acknowledged my existence.

"Of course I am. Like I said, it wouldn't have been the same without you."

I had to smile at that, my confusion forgotten in an instant, and he moved a little closer, our bodies almost touching as he brought his hand up and cupped my face, which made my skin tingle with anticipation. I wondered if he was going to kiss me. I really hoped so, although I tried hard not to let it show. I tried not to lean in too, or raise my face to his.

"Will you go out with me?" he said, his eyes examining mine intently.

There was a sort of masculine self-confidence about him, which was hard to resist, and standing that close to him, it was impossible not to be spellbound by his physical beauty, and before I'd even realised it, I'd said, "Yes."

He stepped back, putting some air between us, and smiled down at me.

"Come on." He pulled me away from the wall. "We'd better get back, before someone comes looking for us."

Personally, I quite liked the idea of staying where we were, and I wasn't bothered about people looking for us, but he was already dragging me back into the living room, where he let go of me and went straight over to Miles, who was standing at the other end of the room – for once, not joined at the hip to Lara. I stood for a moment, wondering what I should do. Was I meant to follow him? I wasn't sure. After a minute though, Eric joined them and, with their heads bent together, it became clear they were deep in conversation, so I went back to Kathy, feeling even more confused than before.

"What was that about?" she asked as I sat down.

"I'm not sure," I replied honestly. "I think Scott just asked me out."

She grinned. "You only *think* he did?"

"Yes."

"But you're not certain?"

"Well, he definitely asked me to go out with him… but then he brought me back in here and started talking to Miles and Eric like I don't exist."

She shook her head. "That's boys for you," she said with the extensive wisdom of a sixteen year old. "No idea how to treat a girl right."

I nodded my head and picked up my can of coke from the floor, where I'd left it. When I looked up, Scott was staring at me, a slow smile crossing his face.

My doubts proved unfounded as we had our first date the very next day.

Scott sent me a text message early on the Sunday morning, asking if I wanted to go to the pictures with him. I agreed and we met outside the cinema complex at three in the afternoon, where I discovered that he'd already bought the tickets.

"*Love Actually*?" I queried, looking at them. "Really?"

His smile faded. "You don't want to see it?"

"Yes. I've wanted to see it ever since it came out, but surely it's not your kind of film, is it?"

He shrugged his shoulders. "I shouldn't think so, but I thought it was probably yours."

I felt myself blush with satisfaction. He was doing this for me. I linked my arm through his as we went inside, and he bought me popcorn and coke, and we eventually found our seats.

The film was everything the trailers had led me to believe it would be… and more. We both laughed at Rowan Atkinson's over-zealous shop assistant, and giggled at Hugh Grant's dancing. About half way through, Scott reached over and took my hand in his, and in the scene where Emma Thompson discovered Alan Rickman had bought a necklace, but had given it to his secretary, rather than to her, he gave my fingers a light squeeze and rubbed his thumb along my knuckles, which felt reassuring and rather sensual – both at the same time.

It was dark by the time we came out and, as we waited at the bus stop, he put his arm around me, holding me close to him.

Scott lived not far from the cinema and I knew he'd have walked, so when my bus arrived, I fully expected him to say goodbye. He didn't. He stepped forward, as though to come with me.

"You don't have to see me home," I remarked, looking up at him.

"Yes, I do."

"But…"

"No arguments," he said and paid for our bus fares.

Sitting at the back, where it was quieter, he held my hand. "How will you get home?" I asked him.

"I'll catch a bus back," he replied.

I nodded and smiled, feeling rather gratified that he'd put himself out for me, and all the way home, we talked about the film, while I rested my head on his shoulder.

The walk from the bus stop to my house was less than five minutes, and when we arrived at the front door, he pulled me back.

"Come down here," he said, leading me around the side of the house to the garage, where it was darker, out of sight of the street lamp and the light that hung above our door. I followed and let him push me back against the wall beside the garage, his body crushed against mine, his hand cupping my face again as he leant forward, tipping his head to one side, and kissed me.

There was something intensely satisfying about that kiss. I think it was the combination of the darkness, and the way his thumb gently caressed my cheek, while he ruthlessly claimed me. It felt like he knew what he wanted; and he wanted me. And I wanted him too.

After nowhere near long enough, he pulled back and stared at me and, although it was dark, I could see what looked to me like longing in his eyes as he brushed his thumb along my bottom lip, making me tremble.

"See you tomorrow," he smiled, stepping away from me.

"O—Okay." I could barely speak. I wasn't sure I could stand unaided, and I continued to lean against the wall for support.

"Are you alright?" he asked.

"Y—Yes."

"Sure?"

"Yes." I pushed myself upright and discovered that my legs were, indeed, working.

Turning away, he walked back to the front of the house and I followed behind, floating, drifting in his wake, until we reached the door, where I stopped. He didn't.

"Goodnight," I called after his retreating figure.

He turned, walking backwards for a couple of steps, his hands plunged into his pockets. "Goodnight Jenna," he said. I could see his smile and matched it with my own.

The next day at college, Scott and I didn't have any classes together, but I looked forward to lunchtime, hoping perhaps for a repeat performance of his kiss from the night before. My hopes were dashed when he spent the whole hour talking quietly to Miles and Eric, only occasionally glancing over in my direction. I found myself struggling not to cry, which was most unlike me, and in the end, I took myself off to the toilets, where I sat in a cubicle for ten minutes and gave myself a good talking to about being beholden to a boy. Even if that boy did look like a god, and kiss like an angel, I was my own person, and the sooner I remembered that, the better.

I didn't bother going back to the cafeteria, but went straight to my next class – English Literature – where we were reading *Othello*. I did my best to concentrate, harnessing myself to Kathy's inordinate enthusiasm for anything Shakespearean, and made it through the two hour lesson, escaping afterwards and making my way to the bus stop before Scott had the chance to ignore me again.

We weren't allowed to take our mobile phones into college, so I didn't get Scott's message until I reached home.

— *What happened to you? I waited after college, but Kathy told me you'd already gone home. What's wrong?*

He hadn't even signed his name, which, after the way he'd behaved at lunchtime, did nothing to make me want to respond politely. So I didn't.

— *I'm surprised you even noticed I wasn't there.*

— *What does that mean?*

— *Work it out for yourself.*

111

My phone remained silent for ages – long enough for me to go back downstairs, get a coffee and a couple of biscuits, ask Mum what was for dinner, and come back up again, before it rang.

"You're going to have to explain, because I'm not getting it," he said, not bothering with a 'hello'

"I don't like being ignored, Scott." I hated that he couldn't work it out for himself.

"When was I ignoring you?"

"At lunchtime. It felt like I didn't exist."

He sighed. "For Christ's sake, Jenna… I'm right in the middle of this group project in Physics with Miles and Eric, and we're struggling with it, if you must know. But if we're going to hand it in before Christmas, then we're going to have to spend a lot of our spare time on it – lunchtimes and after school, you know? Lara's already giving Miles a hard time about how she doesn't see him anymore, but I didn't think you'd be like that. I didn't think you'd be so… well, so clingy."

Was I? Was wanting a moment's attention being clingy? I wasn't sure. Maybe it was…

"I'm not," I whispered, feeling self-conscious and embarrassed now. "I'm sorry."

"You don't have to be sorry," he replied, his voice softening. "I probably should have explained."

"You don't have to explain," I countered. "I'm not entitled to know everything about you. We've only had one date, after all."

There was a moment's pause. "Feel like a second one?" he asked and I was absolutely certain he was smiling now. My own lips twitched upwards and I felt my stomach flip over at the thought of more of his kisses.

"Yes," I replied, and he chuckled.

"Well, I can't do much during the week," he said, "not at the moment. But how about we go for a walk on Saturday afternoon?"

"Okay."

I made it through the week, surviving on the occasional wink and smile, and to be fair, he did stand at the bus stop with me on Wednesday and Friday, even though he then had to go to the library to meet Miles and Eric. I told him it was fine, that he didn't need to wait with me, but he insisted, and I didn't object again.

His Physics project kept him busy though, so it was Saturday afternoon before we really got the chance to be alone together, when he came over and we walked down to the beach, and out onto the headland. I was grateful we'd avoided the bay itself, not wanting to be reminded of the wolf man and my stupid daydreams… and the disappointment that had followed them. Instead, Scott put his arm around me and led me up on top of the low cliffs. It was cold, the wind blowing in my hair, and once the path had turned, and we were out of sight of the village, he captured me in his arms, and pulled me close to him.

"I'm sorry," I said quickly, before he had the chance to say or do anything himself.

"What for?" He seemed genuinely puzzled.

"For being clingy." I decided to use his word, because I couldn't think of another one, and I did want to apologise.

"Don't worry about it," he replied, and lowered his face to mine, kissing me deeply. The wind swirled around us, icy gusts biting at my skin and snatching at my hair, but I didn't feel a thing, because Scott was holding me, and nothing else mattered.

When he pulled back, I stared up at him, his eyes fixed on mine.

"It's kind of nice," he said, breathing hard.

"What is?"

"That you're a little bit possessive." I still wasn't sure that was the best way of describing my reaction to his behaviour, but I didn't say anything. "It means you're interested."

"Of course I'm interested. Aren't you?"

He grinned and captured my lips with his own again, his hands wandering and eventually finding their way to my bottom, where they rested, clutching me to him. For an instant, I thought about moving them up to my waist again, but then I realised that I rather liked the way it felt to be held like that. There was an intimacy to it which I didn't want to end.

"Does that answer your question?" he said leaning back at last.

I nodded my head and he turned us, taking my hand as we carried on walking.

"Was that the only reason you were ignoring me?" I asked him eventually. "Because you were busy with your project?" Despite my apology and everything he'd said, I still wasn't convinced I was being 'clingy' or 'possessive', or that I was the one who was responsible for our argument. I wanted to know for certain that there was nothing else going on.

"I wasn't ignoring you," he replied, staring out to sea, to where a bank of murky grey clouds were gathering on the horizon. He stopped walking suddenly and I did too, unsure what was coming next. "I'm not at college for the fun of it, Jenna," he said seriously. "I want to get into a good university…"

"I know. So do I."

"And then I want to get a well-paid job," he continued as though I hadn't spoken. "And that means I have to take my studies seriously.

"I agree with you," I replied. "But surely that doesn't have to be to the exclusion of everything else, does it?"

"No, of course not. But I wasn't excluding you, any more than I was ignoring you." He shook his head, calming and smiling slightly, as he moved closer. "It's all in your head, beautiful." He brushed his fingers gently down the side of my face.

"Is it?"

"Yes." He leant down and kissed me, briefly. "Just go with it," he murmured.

So I did.

I continued going with it right through Christmas, during which I didn't see Scott at all, because he and his parents went skiing in Colorado for the whole of the holidays. I sent him a text message every morning when I woke up, and every evening before I went to bed. He replied to most of them – eventually – explaining that they were skiing and the time difference made it hard to keep up. For myself, I couldn't wait for the holidays to be over, so we could get back to college and seeing each other again – even just weekends together was better than being apart the whole time. Unfortunately, by the time he and his parents returned, there was only one day before college was due to start, and Scott said he was too tired to meet up, so the first time we saw each other was in the cafeteria, surrounded by our friends, and while he put his arm around me and told me it was good to see me, it all felt a bit flat.

Things quickly returned to normal though, with Scott focusing hard on his studies during the week, and spending weekends with me, so it was a huge surprise when he invited me back to his house one Friday afternoon just after the February half term. We'd been together for about three months by then, and not once had we done anything on a weekday... not even a Friday.

"Tonight?" I asked as we walked up the school driveway.

"Yes."

"But it's Friday."

"I know."

"We don't normally see each other on Fridays," I reasoned.

"And what happened to going with it?"

I smiled up at him and he smiled back, leading me away from the bus stop.

He lived in a very smart, newly built house, on a small estate, about a ten minute walk from the college, and when we got there, we went in through the back door, to which Scott had a key, and I felt my mouth drop open at the sight of the magnificent kitchen before me. Unlike the kitchen at home, which had pine doors and was a little dated, this was gleaming and white, with almost completely empty granite worktops and a sparkling stainless steel oven and fridge.

"Do you want to call your parents?" he suggested, dumping his bag by the back door and laying his jacket over one of the high backed dining chairs that were set around the rectangular table. "You should probably let them know where you are."

I nodded, putting my bag with his, and he led me through to the hallway, leaving me by the telephone which was on a low table just inside the front door. I dialled the number and waited until my mum answered, before explaining that I'd be late home.

"You're at Scott's?" she queried, even though I'd already told her that once. She and Dad knew I was seeing him. They'd known since before Christmas. It had been impossible to keep it from them, and besides, he was my own age, so I didn't think they'd mind. They didn't... although they did insist on meeting him, which I thought was very old fashioned. Scott had smiled when I'd told him that, then he'd kissed my forehead and told me he thought it was 'sweet'. The meeting, which had happened the next weekend when Scott came to collect me to take me out into Newquay to go Christmas shopping, had gone really well, with Scott turning on the charm and my parents lapping it up, broad grins on their adoring faces.

"Yes."

"On a Friday?"

Even my mother was used to our arrangements, and that thought made me smile.

"Yes."

"Will you be home for dinner?" she asked.

"I imagine so, but I'll let you know if not."

"Okay... well, have fun," she said and we ended the call, before I replaced the phone in its holder and turned to find Scott leaning against the wall, looking at me, a glass of coke in each hand.

"Coming?" he said and I nodded, then followed him through into the living room, which I remembered from his party. It was predominantly white – or at least the walls were. The furniture, curtains and carpet were very pale grey.

Scott placed our drinks on coasters, on the low table, and then plonked himself down on one of the sofas, looking up at me.

"Okay?" he asked and I nodded again, going to sit beside him.

"Where are your parents?" I asked.

He turned to me, tilting his head, as though confused. "At work," he replied.

"Both of them?"

"Yes."

I picked up my coke and drank carefully, the thought dawning that we were alone in the house, before I looked back at him. "What do they do?"

"Dad's an engineer," he replied.

"Is that why you want to go into that field?" He'd already explained to me on one of our walks that he was looking at Aeronautical Engineering as a course at university, while I'd mentioned my interest in Architecture.

He nodded his head. "Dad works mainly in the marine business, but I suppose he's the one who's fired my enthusiasm, yes."

"And what does your mum do?"

"She's the PA to the boss of an electronics company."

"I see."

"What do your parents do?" he asked, grabbing his own drink and swallowing down half of it in one go.

"They're retired."

He choked, taking a moment or two to recover himself. "Retired?" he said. "How old are they?"

"My dad's coming up for sixty."

"Bloody hell." He stopped. "I didn't... I mean... I thought they looked older than my mum and dad when I met them, but... bloody hell."

I felt a bit insulted by his reaction, but decided to explain anyway. "They didn't get married until they were in their mid-thirties, you see... and by the time I came along, Mum was forty."

"Forty? Blimey..." He raised his eyebrows, but didn't comment further. Instead, he leant across and took my glass from me, putting it back on the table. "I think that's enough conversation for now, don't you?" he murmured and pressed his lips to mine. I'd missed his kisses all week, and wasn't about to argue, and before I knew it, he'd moved us downwards, so I was lying on my back, along the length of the soft sofa, with Scott on top of me. He wasn't heavy, and actually, the weight of him felt kind of comforting. I could hear our breathing, our sighs and moans filling the room around us, and then I felt him move slightly to one side, his hand coming between us and fiddling with the button of my jeans. Panic filled my head... *Not yet. I'm not ready*. I grabbed his wrist and he pulled back, looking down at me.

"What's wrong?" He seemed surprised that I'd stopped him.

"I'm not sure we should do that," I whispered, embarrassed at having to explain.

"You're not sure?" He smiled now, his eyes twinkling.

"No, I'm not. I mean... I like you..."

"I like you too, Jenna."

I sighed and a smile formed on my lips. It was the first time he'd said anything like that to me and, as he leant down and kissed me again, I melted into him, bringing my arms up and around his neck, and letting my fingers play in his hair.

Within a few minutes, his hand was toying with the fastening of my jeans again, and I let go of him to grasp his wrist, halting him once more.

"Scott. I'm not ready for that..."

He sighed heavily. "Okay." He paused for a moment, and then looked directly at me. "It's just that... you're so beautiful."

Had he really just said that? "I—I'm not," I replied.

"Yes, you are."

He lowered his lips to mine and I relished his evident desire, as he rested his hand over my breast. I didn't mind that. Actually, I liked it. I liked it even more when he pushed up my jumper and eased my bra to one side, touching me, skin on skin. I felt my body respond, heat pooling in the pit of my stomach, my nerves tingling with need as he pinched my nipple and I gasped into his urgent mouth.

"Are you absolutely sure you're not ready?" he said, leaning up and gazing down at me. "Only you seem pretty ready to me."

"I just want to wait a bit longer," I murmured.

"Why?"

"I—I don't know," I stuttered. "I just want to."

He shook his head and sighed again, evidently disappointed by my response, but then he kissed me again, and for a moment, as I lost myself in him once more, I contemplated changing my mind, and what that might involve... how far he might want to go. But before I could properly process that thought, or consider how far *I'd* be willing to go, he suddenly sat bolt upright.

"Shit!" He stood and started to tuck his shirt into his jeans, not that I'd even been aware he – or maybe I – had pulled it out.

"What's wrong?" I stared up at him, still lying prone, exposed.

"My dad's home. That was his car." What was? I hadn't heard anything.

I sat up myself, panicked, straightening my bra, pulling my jumper down and swinging my legs around, my feet flat on the floor. Scott resumed his seat beside me, leaving a space between us now, and handed me my glass, grabbing the remote control and switching on the TV in the same move, just as the front door opened.

"Scott?"

"In here, Dad."

I looked up as a man appeared in the doorway. I'd been vaguely aware of him at Scott's party, but now I studied him properly, in daylight, for the first time. Tall and incredibly handsome, he was like an older version of Scott, but with slightly darker hair. Wearing a suit and tie, he carried a briefcase and stared down at the two of us.

"Hello," he said, his eyes resting on me.

"This is Jenna," Scott explained and I got to my feet.

"Hello, Mr Downing." I wasn't sure whether I should offer my hand for him to shake, but luckily, he didn't seem to expect it, and just smiled.

"Call me Justin," he replied, his voice friendly.

"You're home early," Scott said from behind me, and I sat down again, feeling awkward.

"Yes." Mr Downing put his briefcase down and stepped further into the room, loosening his tie and glancing at the television. "I've got some work to do over the weekend, so I finished early to make up for it… Um… why on earth are you watching Blue Peter?" he asked. "You're a bit old for that now, aren't you?"

"We weren't watching it," Scott replied and I noticed the smile on his dad's face, as the blush rose up mine, and I wondered if he knew what we'd really been doing. "I've only just switched it on." Well, I suppose that was the truth, at least.

"I see." His dad looked from Scott, to me, and then back again. "Well, I'll leave you in peace," he said and, picking up his briefcase, he left the room.

Scott put the remote control down on the coffee table, beside his glass, before sinking back into the sofa, turning to me, and smiling. "That was close," he whispered.

"Yes."

"Still, he's gone now." He leant closer, but I pulled back.

"Scott, he's still in the house."

He shook his head. "You don't know my dad," he replied. "Once he starts work, he won't stop. He'll be in his study for hours now."

He leant in again, but for me that brief moment of heady desire had been lost.

"I can't," I said. He stopped and stared at me, his eyes narrowing, before he sat back. "Sorry." He shrugged and I reached over, putting my hand on his thigh, and then he looked down at the point of contact, and placed his hand firmly over mine.

"Don't worry about it," he whispered, and we sat together and watched Blue Peter.

Over the coming weeks and months, Scott devoted his weekends to us. Weekdays were still scrupulously assigned to college work, revision and reading and, apart from lunchtimes and DT lessons, we didn't really see each other at all. However, the weekends were entirely ours. He said he preferred it that way, because when we were together he could focus on me, and me alone, and not be distracted by thoughts of homework, or projects, or deadlines. The only difference was that he seemed to have decided that the weekend now started on Fridays. So, after college, our Friday afternoons and early evenings were spent at his place, going through a repeat performance of that first time, with him asking, pushing, cajoling, but never actually demanding that I go a little further each week. I did… of course. Because, deep down, I think I wanted him almost as much as he seemed to want me. I just needed time. So, by the summer holidays, I'd allowed him to undo my jeans and feel me through my knickers, which set my breathless body on fire every time he did it. He'd taken my hand and placed it on the bulge at the front of his trousers, telling me that was the effect I had on him, and just how much he wanted me. I knew it wouldn't be long before I'd relent completely – and not because he kept asking me to, but because I loved the way he made me feel when we were together. I loved his touch, his words, the look in his eyes. I loved his need, his desire, his urgency. But most of all, I loved him.

With the summer holidays came the realisation that our time was our own at last. We both had a few things to do for college, but nothing overly strenuous, and that meant we could be together. Scott's parents were at work all day long, and so it didn't surprise me in the slightest when Scott sent me a text message on that first Monday of the holidays, asking me to go over to his place. I think I knew what would happen, even before I left my own bedroom, but that didn't stop me going, or looking forward to it. I was ready. I really was.

When I arrived at Scott's, he let me in through the front door, and once it was closed again, he greeted me with a long, seductive kiss, walking me back to the wall and pressing me hard against it, his body holding me in place, while his hands teased through my hair.

"I want you," he whispered, when he finally released me.

"I want you too." His eyes widened and he stared down at me.

"You mean that?"

I nodded my head and, without another word passing between us, he took my hand and led me up the stairs, around the landing and in through the second door on the left.

I tried to focus on the dark blue feature wall, the mid-grey carpet and glossy white furnishings. As I say, I tried to focus on them, but in reality, my eyes were drawn to the double bed that – in my eyes, at least – dominated the room. I didn't have too long to think about the reality of what that meant though, because Scott pulled me across the room, and before I knew it, I was lying across the mattress, no longer worrying about its commanding position or stature, my mind filled instead with a multitude of unanswered questions. What would happen next? What would Scott look like with no clothes on? How would it feel to have him make love to me? Would it hurt? Did he love me?

Within the next twenty minutes, I had answers to almost all of my questions. Except, perhaps, the one that mattered the most.

What actually happened next was that Scott stripped me naked, impatiently tugging and ripping my clothes from me. I told him to take it easy, as he tore into my lace knickers, that I'd chosen with care that morning, right after I'd received his text message inviting me over, but he just told me he'd waited so long for this... I think 'too long' were his words, actually. It felt like I was in a maelstrom of emotions, as I watched him undress at speed, lying naked and vulnerable on the bed before him. His body was as beautiful as his face, although I would have described it as athletic, rather than muscular... and I couldn't help but lower my eyes to his erection, gazing at it for a moment. It looked to be in proportion to the rest of him – at least to my untrained eye – even though I couldn't help thinking that it had seemed thicker when I'd stroked it through his trousers, but despite that, as I raised my eyes back to his face, I was thrilled – beyond delight – that someone like Scott could want to be with me. He put on a condom, which he retrieved from the bedside table, and the next thing I knew, he was poised above me, my legs wide apart, his body supported on his arms. I wanted a moment to focus, to absorb him and what we were about to do, to talk, to explain my fears, to tell him how I felt about him, but he had other things in mind, and within seconds, he was inside me. He didn't stop to let me digest the pain – which was, admittedly, quite brief and tolerable – or to acclimatise myself to the intrusion of having him inside me, but started to move straight away, taking me in hard, fast thrusts, his eyes closed, his silence and remoteness quite astounding, until after a few minutes, he stilled, groaned and sighed, opened his eyes, gazing at a spot above my head, and then collapsed on top of me, seemingly spent.

I waited, still wondering what would happen next and eventually, he raised himself up again, panting, his breathing heavy, as he looked down at me.

"You were incredible," he said. "Absolutely incredible."

His words were nice, the look in his eyes was comforting, but I couldn't help feeling disappointed. It hadn't been anything like I'd imagined. We'd waited for such a long time to be together and I suppose I'd hoped for fireworks, for passion, for a fierce intimacy – the type that lasts a lifetime. I'd hoped for love.

Had I aimed too high, I wondered.

After that first, frenzied connection, Scott invited me over to his place every day, taking full advantage of his parents' absence, and it was a couple of weeks later that I had my first experience of fireworks – well, a sparkler, anyway.

Every other day, Scott had taken me straight to bed upon my arrival and, while I was starting to get a little bored, I didn't know quite how to tell him that without hurting his feelings, so I was relieved when, on that particular Tuesday morning, he took me through to the kitchen. I expected him to offer me a drink, or something to eat, but instead, he stood me by the island unit and started to undress me.

"What are you doing?" I glanced around, making sure the windows weren't overlooked. Luckily they weren't, being as the kitchen was at the back of the house and the garden was very private.

"I'm undressing you," he replied, smiling and undoing my bra at the same time.

"Out here?" I queried and he nodded, silently removing my shorts and knickers, so I was standing naked in his mother's kitchen. I was about to ask why, when he put his hands on my waist and lifted me, sitting me up on the pristine work surface. Part of me wanted to giggle, but part of me was also shocked – although not as shocked as when he pulled me forward, then placed his hands on my knees and parted my legs, exposing me. "Scott…" I whispered, feeling shy, but also rather thrilled at the same time.

He looked up but didn't say a word and instead leant down and licked me, intimately. The sensation was like nothing I'd ever felt, and as he did it again, I found myself clutching to the back of his head, holding him in place and wanting more… much more. I got it too. I felt sparks fizzing through my body, saw stars behind my eyes, and then, without warning, my body seemed to explode into millions of pieces, all floating around above me, whirling and gliding in space, before falling miraculously back into place again, as I finally managed to catch my breath and open my eyes, to discover that I was still whole, I was still me, and I felt more complete than I'd ever felt before. Looking down, Scott was staring up at me, a smile etched on his lips as he stood and started to undo his jeans. Then he lifted me down onto the floor again, my unsteady legs just about supporting me. He placed his hands on my shoulders and I felt the pressure as he pushed me down.

"What?" I said, looking up into his face. "What do you want?"

"Kneel down," he murmured.

"Kneel down?" I wasn't sure what he meant, but he just nodded and I felt the pressure of his hands again.

"I did it for you," he said and it was then that I understood.

"I'm not sure." I heard his impatient sigh.

"At least give it a try?"

I wondered about saying 'no', but then realised he was right, he had just done it for me… so I knelt, coming face to face with his arousal. He moved his hands from my shoulders to behind my head, gathering my hair and holding it tight as I opened my mouth, letting him in. He didn't hold back, forcing himself down my throat until I gagged, pushing on his thighs, my eyes watering. Still he continued, back and forth, grunting and groaning, until I felt him swell. I tried to pull back, but he kept his hands firmly on the back of my head, and I felt the surge of hot liquid fill my mouth. I couldn't bear to swallow it though, so I held it there, for as long as I could, and then I finally broke free of him and got up, running to the sink, where I spat it out, retching and trying not to vomit.

"For Christ's sake, Jenna," he said from behind me. "What's wrong with you?"

I turned to him, wiping my mouth with the back of my hand. "I didn't like that."

"What?" he said putting his hands on his hips. "All of it?"

I shook my head. "No, just the last part. And…"

"And what?"

"Well, I didn't like you forcing yourself into my mouth, or pulling my hair like that, if I'm being honest."

He folded his arms now, glaring at me. "Anything else?" he barked.

"No." I shook my head, surprised by his reaction and, embarrassed, I went to pick up my clothes.

"What are you doing?" he snapped.

"Getting dressed," I replied from my crouched position on the floor. "I think I'd better go home."

He was beside me in an instant, kneeling. "Why?" he said and I glared at him, not bothering to answer, because I felt the response was obvious. "Okay… I'm sorry," he said eventually, getting to his feet once more. "I won't do that again. Not if you don't like it."

I gazed up at him. He did look genuinely contrite, and I realised that this was what couples did, didn't they? They talked, they discussed, and they compromised. It felt quite grown up; quite 'together'. "I just said… it wasn't the whole thing," I clarified, softening my voice. "Just the last bit. And the fact that you were so rough about it."

He nodded his head. "Okay. I'll bear that in mind…"

"Thank you."

"Now we've got that settled," he said, smiling, "we've still got the whole day ahead of us, so why don't you come upstairs with me?"

I hesitated, just for a moment, but he bent and took my clothes from me, then held out his other hand, a smile forming on his perfect lips, which only reminded me of what he'd done to me with his tongue a few minutes earlier, and I let him help me to my feet, leading me out of the kitchen and up to his bedroom.

We were half way through the holidays, and I was in the middle of my period, when Scott suggested I should go on the pill.

"We'll be able to be more spontaneous," he reasoned, holding me in his arms.

"*More* spontaneous?" I queried. "Aren't we spontaneous enough?"

He smiled. "Yes, but we could have even more fun if we didn't have to worry about condoms."

I felt like pointing out to him that I didn't worry about them. But then I realised that was rather a selfish point of view. He'd taken responsibility for everything until that point, and maybe it was my turn.

And besides, I quite liked the idea of removing that last barrier between us. I wondered if it might help me to enjoy it more, so I'd be able to have those firework moments more often. I didn't say any of that, of course. I'd have hated him to think I wasn't already enjoying what we were doing. I was. I just knew – somehow – that there ought to be more.

"Okay," I said quietly. "I'll look into it."

I did. I did more than look into it. I went to the clinic and arranged the whole thing. All by myself. When I came back and told Scott, he was over the moon and said he couldn't wait to feel me properly. I felt the same, but didn't say it.

That first time was something I'll never forget. Right from the moment he entered me, Scott didn't stop with his praise. His words were like balm to my aching heart and I lapped them up greedily. I may not have experienced any fireworks that afternoon, but I didn't care, because we were together. Really together. When he'd finished, his groans of pleasure still echoing around the room, he looked down at me, a different expression in his eyes, and I knew...

"I love you," I whispered.

He smiled. "I know," he replied and held me in his arms.

I stilled. *I know?* That hadn't been the answer I'd hoped for – or expected, for that matter.

"Don't you love me?" I asked, desperation almost overwhelming me.

"Of course I do," he said and I felt the relief wash over me, my moment of fear forgotten as I relaxed into his arms. We were in love, we were together, and everything was just as it should be.

After the long summer holidays, most of which had been spent in Scott's bed, or certainly at his house, anyway, it came as rather a shock to have to return to college. More particularly, it came as a shock to have to do without seeing him on weekdays again, but now more than ever, I understood his reasoning. We were in our final year, and that meant exams and revision, and studying hard, and pressure, and choosing universities...

We did some research and discovered that the best place for both of us was the University of the West of England, in Bristol. Their engineering and architecture courses were ideal, and we checked out the open day and arranged to go along. Our parents wanted to come too, and it gave them an opportunity to meet each other. Scott and I had been together for over a year by that stage, and while I'm not sure my parents knew how serious our relationship had become, Scott's dad was in no doubt about it, having nearly caught us out on at least four separate occasions.

So, we all travelled to Bristol together, in Scott's mum's people carrier. We actually had a really nice day out, stopping off at a pub on the way home, and discussing the pros and cons of the university between us. Scott and I were convinced it was the best choice, but both sets of parents wanted us to look at other options, so we knuckled down and I discovered that Cardiff had a good course, as did Nottingham. Scott found that Nottingham was a good fit for him too, but that Surrey would have to be his other choice. That made us both smile, being as the University of Surrey is at Guildford, and therefore very close to where I used to live. We visited all of them – Nottingham together and Cardiff and Guildford separately, and ultimately applied to three each.

Then we settled down to studying, working hard and spending as much time together as that would allow. I'd become more used the Scott's ways by then. I'd accepted the fact that sparks wouldn't always fly for me, but I loved him enough not to care and to derive as much satisfaction from his pleasure as I did from my own. My one wish – if I could have been allowed one – would have been that he'd have been more romantic outside of the bedroom. Whenever we were alone, curled up on his bed, naked and in each other's arms, he would touch me all the time, caressing my skin, kissing my face, my lips, my neck, my body, and he'd tell me how beautiful I was, how sexy, incredible, amazing, stunning… the adjectives were endless in fact, and I delighted in them all. However, away from the bedroom, especially in the company of others, he was cooler, more distant, sometimes going for hours without even speaking to me. He'd hold my hand and occasionally put his arm around me, but he didn't kiss me and never said anything romantic. It was like going out with two entirely different people. I asked him once, not long after our second Christmas together – a Christmas that he'd spent skiing with his family again – why he was like that, and he stared at me, as though I'd just landed from another planet, one in a whole different galaxy to ours.

"Like what?" he asked. "What are you talking about?"

"You're so different when we're in bed to when we're not," I replied, trying to explain.

"Well, of course I am. I can hardly do all the things I do to you in bed when we're in public, can I? I'd get arrested."

I smiled and leant into him. "I know. But sometimes you don't even talk to me."

"Yes, I do." He pulled back and looked down at me. "This isn't you being all clingy and possessive again, is it? I thought we were over that now."

I shook my head. "No, I'm not being clingy. Or possessive. I'm just wondering why you're so different when we're with our friends to when we're alone, that's all."

He shook his head and pulled me back into a hug again. "You're silly sometimes," he said and kissed the top of my head.

I wondered if that was true? Was I being silly – or at least unrealistic? Were my expectations too high? Or had I just been reading too much Jane Austen for my own good?

The first disaster of our relationship struck when we got our offers from universities… or rather Scott didn't. He was declined by Bristol – the one we'd both wanted. His was a really popular course and it appeared that his predicted grades simply weren't good enough. They accepted me, however, and we both got offers from Nottingham, and also from Cardiff in my case, and Surrey in his.

"It's Nottingham then," I said, once everything had been confirmed and we knew where we stood. We were in his bedroom, fully clothed for once, his laptop between us on the bed.

He turned and looked at me. "You're kidding, right?"

I twisted, facing him. "No."

He shut the laptop, shifting it down the bed and moved closer. "That would be a really dumb compromise," he said.

"We'd be together, Scott," I reasoned.

"Yes… but we both know that, out of the options we have left, Surrey is the better choice for me, and Bristol is probably best for you, although if you'd rather go to Cardiff or Nottingham, that's entirely up to you."

From the tone of his voice, and the scowl on his face, I wondered if he resented the fact that, even after all his hard work, I had more alternatives than he did. I also wondered if he blamed me. Not that it was my fault. It was just one of those things.

It seemed his mind was made up though and I had to face the fact that, no matter where I chose, we were going to be separated. I could feel tears pricking behind my eyes, and blinked them back. I'd never cried in front of him and didn't intend to start now. "But we'll be over a hundred miles apart," I said, surprised by the strength of my own voice.

"So? We're strong enough, aren't we?" he said, surprising me with his words and the light smile that accompanied them.

"What? To stay together, even though we're apart?" I asked.

He nodded his head, and reached out, undoing the buttons on my blouse. "We'll meet up as often as we can," he murmured, moving closer, his lips next to my ear. "And when we do… I guarantee, it'll be spectacular."

I giggled just slightly. "If you say we can do this, then we can."

"I say we can do this," he murmured back, his fingers caressing the tops of my breasts. "It's only three years."

I shuddered to his touch, revelling in his intimate attention. "I love you, Scott," I whispered, as he kissed me, swallowing my words.

Chapter Five

University was nothing like I'd expected it to be. I wasn't fazed by fresh starts or meeting new people. I wasn't even worried about leaving home and having to fend for myself. It was missing Scott that got to me. It got to me more than I wanted to admit – even to myself.

He'd become such an important part of my life by then that not having him there each day was really hard to handle. Over the summer holidays, while we'd been waiting to start that new phase of our lives, we'd spent more time together than ever. I think even my parents had worked out that our relationship was serious, but they were laid back about it and didn't question me. They knew I was sensible, and they liked and trusted Scott, so they left us to our own devices, as a consequence of which we spent almost every waking moment with each other during those long hot months... and then had to face the stark reality of separation at the end of September.

I used to text Scott every morning and every evening, and I'd call him whenever I could, but sometimes he'd only text back once a day, just before going to bed, and when I called, he didn't always pick up. Although I felt pathetic – and even perhaps a little 'clingy' – I phoned him one evening, in the middle of our second week and asked what was wrong, why he wasn't returning my texts. Was he trying to tell me something?

"Of course not," he replied, although I struggled to hear him over the noise in the background.

"Where are you?" I asked.

"In a bar. Hang on, I'll go outside." I waited a moment, sitting back on my single bed, and getting my pillows comfortable behind me, until the sounds disappeared. "Are you there?" he asked.

"Yes."

"I'm outside now." That much was obvious. "What were you saying?"

"I was asking why you don't always return my texts."

"Oh yeah – and I said, I'm not avoiding you, Jenna. I'm not trying to tell you anything either. I'm just busy."

"Doing what?"

"Finding my way around, meeting people, working out how to cook… just normal student stuff, that's all."

"That's all?" I echoed, feeling doubtful about his commitment to our relationship all of a sudden.

"Yes. I'm sure you've been doing the same," he said.

"Well, I've been meeting my fellow students, and finding my way around. I haven't been to any bars though."

"Why not?"

"Because you're not here" I wished he hadn't needed to ask. "It doesn't feel right."

I heard his sigh. "Three years is a long time, Jenna," he replied. "Just because we're apart, doesn't mean we can't enjoy ourselves."

"While we think about each other?" I said, phrasing it like a question, just to make sure.

He laughed and said, "Of course…"

"So what bar are you at?" I asked, trying to rally and not to feel left out of his life.

"Oh, it's just a little place in Guildford that one of the guys knew. I'm not sure of the name."

"I see."

"I'm sure Bristol has lots of great places you could go to." He paused. "We could have a look round on Saturday, if you like."

I stilled. "Did… did you just say 'we'?"

"Yes. I don't have any lectures on Friday afternoons, so why don't I get the train down there and stay with you for the weekend?"

"Seriously?" I couldn't hide my excitement.

"Yes. Seriously."

"But I'm not supposed to have anyone staying in my room." I could feel the weight of disappointed shrouding me.

"You can sneak me in," he replied.

"Sneak you in?"

"Yes. We'll work it out." There was another pause, before he asked, "You… you're not going to be on your period, are you?"

"No. It finished a couple of days ago."

"Good." I heard the smile in his voice and felt my own lips twitch upwards.

"And you'll definitely be here the day after tomorrow?"

"You sound like you're keen to see me," he said, teasing.

"I am."

"Well, I'll be there soon."

"Oh, thank God for that."

He laughed and then I heard someone call his name in the background. "I'd better go," he murmured. "I'll see you on Friday."

"I can't wait."

"Hmm… I sort of gathered that."

We ended the call rather speedily because his friends were calling him again, and I lay down on my bed, staring at the ceiling, clutching my phone to my chest, a smile etched on my face. It was probably ten minutes later that my phone buzzed in my hand and I turned it over, hoping it wasn't Scott, telling me he'd changed his mind. The message was from Scott and I opened it with shaking hands, fear welling inside me, reading:

— *Do something for me?*

I wondered what that meant and, intrigued, answered straight away.

— *What do you want me to do?*

— *Make sure you're wearing a skirt on Friday.*

That seemed like a strange request.

— *Why?*

His reply made me smile.

— *You'll find out soon enough.*

Luckily, when Scott arrived, most of the people with whom I shared my corridor in halls were in lectures, so sneaking him in was easy.

"I'm glad I went for an en-suite room," I said, closing the door. "At least we won't have to worry about trying to get you to the bathroom without…"

I turned and he grabbed me, pushing me back against the wall, his mouth covering mine, interrupting me. His hands were everywhere, all at once, and I'd barely had time to catch my breath before I felt him lift my skirt up around my waist and pull my knickers to one side, pushing himself inside me. I'd not even been aware of him undoing his jeans, but it was too late to worry about that. When he climaxed, it was as though the weeks apart had faded to nothing, and we were back where we belonged. Together.

Releasing me, he looked down into my eyes.

"Was that why you wanted me to wear a skirt?" I asked and he nodded.

"I knew I wouldn't be able to wait long enough to get you out of your jeans," he replied.

"It seems you were right."

He chuckled and leant in close to me again. "Next time, don't bother wearing any knickers either," he murmured, and I sucked in my gasp as he pulled away and led me over to the single bed, where he undressed me and then himself, and we lay down, my back to his front, curled around each other.

"I've missed you so much," I whispered, running my fingertips up and down his arms.

"I kind of noticed that from your phone call," he replied.

"Is that why you decided to come down here?" I tried not to wallow in self satisfaction, and failed miserably.

"Partly. I'd been thinking about it anyway, but then hearing how much you needed me… well, what else could I do?"

He'd done this for me. He'd come all this way, just because I needed him to…. wanted him to. I twisted in his arms, facing him, and kissed him gently. "Thank you," I whispered, and nestled down into him.

We lay like that for hours, as he told me about his course. He hadn't done much yet, obviously, but he'd been given an idea of what lay ahead, and I could tell he was worried. Scott had struggled to get two Bs and an A in his A-levels and it seemed the expectations on his course were high. I held him close and tried to reassure him that he'd be fine. I'm not sure he believed me, but I hoped my words gave him some comfort anyway.

We decided against going out that evening, partly because we didn't want to risk him being caught in my room, but mainly because we were already undressed and his fingers were straying. And I liked it. So, we ordered in a pizza, and I threw on a pair of leggings and a t-shirt to run down the stairs and pay the delivery man. Back upstairs, Scott peeled me back out of my leggings and we settled down to watch a movie and eat our pizza. Scott seemed to grow bored of both of them after a while and moved down the bed, his lips and tongue finding a better occupation and, as the TV flickered in the background, I soared above the clouds.

He didn't seem to expect me to return the favour that time, and moving the pizza box to the floor, he nestled in between my thighs and entered me more slowly than ever before. His movements were considered and careful and when he climaxed, I cupped his face in my hands and told him I loved him. He mouthed 'I love you too', and I thought I'd died and gone to heaven.

We slept together for the first time that night, tight in each other's arms, my body crushed against his. It was a joyous experience, one which I vowed I would never forget. Waking up beside him, I worried that he'd be shocked by seeing me first thing in the morning, with my hair in a mess, not even a hint of make-up, my teeth unbrushed. None of that seemed to worry him though and he rolled me over and kissed me as though his life depended on it. As I wrapped my legs around him, I felt as though I'd found fulfilment. The man I loved was right there with me and all of my doubts about his lack of romantic commitment simply vanished into thin air, like a sea mist, drifting away on the breeze.

After that first visit, we got into a routine. Once a month, for the next three years, either I would go to Surrey, or Scott would come down to Bristol. We preferred being in Guildford, because thanks to his parents, he was living in a small studio flat of his own, rather than in halls, and the moment I arrived, he would undress me and insist I stay that way until returning to Bristol, unless it was completely necessary for me to put clothes on – to answer the door, or pop to the shops for essential supplies. I had no objection to his request. After all, he wasn't dressed either, and I loved the way he looked at me, the way he touched me, caressed me, played with me, spoke to me... even if there weren't always fireworks, his attention was heavenly, and parting from him was nothing short of hell.

In between times, when we couldn't be together, we would call and text every single day. I noticed, of course, that it was always me who was doing the calling, and the texting, and every few months, I would ask him why that was; why he never phoned me.

"This course is murder," was his first response; followed by, "I'm so busy, I barely know what time of day it is." Then came, "I'm finding it a real struggle to keep up with some of the other guys." His insecurity was obvious, and I would always do my best to dispel his fears and set his mind at rest that he could do this. He was better than he thought he was.

One day, when I asked the question though, feeling fed up that I'd sent three text messages without reply and that my last call had gone straight to voicemail, he replied, "It's tough, living by myself, Jenna. I've been trying to make an effort to socialise... to go out more."

"I thought you already went out quite a lot," I said, wondering what he meant by that.

"I do, but when everyone else lives in halls, or in flat shares, I feel a bit excluded."

I wanted to understand, but I couldn't, because I still didn't really socialise with anyone. I didn't want to – not without Scott. Not that he ever asked.

"So who have you been out with?" I asked.

"Just a group of people," he replied.

"Boys or girls?" The words were out before I could stop them and the stony silence on the end of the phone told me I'd made a mistake.

"Are you going to go all possessive on me again?" His voice was distant.

"No. I'm not. Really. I'm just wondering. It's hard being apart from you."

"You think I don't know that?" There was an edge to his voice now that I hadn't heard before. "I miss you just as much as you miss me." He softened quickly. "But that's what's so good about us…"

"What is?" I was reeling, confused by the rollercoaster of his reactions.

"We're strong enough to get through this."

"We are, aren't we?" I was asking him a genuine question, although I wasn't sure he realised that.

"Yes." His voice whispered into my ear. "So stop worrying. Just remember what you said?"

"What did I say?"

"That we can stay together, even though we're apart."

"You remembered that?"

"Of course I did. And it's true."

I sat back on my bed. "Thank you," I murmured. "Thank you for saying that." It meant a lot that he'd done so, even though we weren't actually in the same room, in the same bed.

"That's alright. Just don't get so jealous."

I wanted to say I wasn't, but settled for, "I won't."

As a consolation for so much time spent apart, which included the Christmases during which Scott still went skiing with his parents, we had long summer holidays to spend together, and I lived on the memories during our time away from each other.

Graduation came soon enough – thank goodness – and after that came the search for work. For me, it seemed quite an easy process. Within two weeks of leaving university, I'd landed myself a dream job, working for a firm of architects, named Cole and Simpson, just the other side of Newquay. Their specialism was building environmentally friendly properties, which was something I'd developed a keen interest in during my time at university, and the twenty minute journey to their offices was no problem, as I'd learned to drive by that stage. Scott found things more difficult. Where I'd got a First in my degree, he'd struggled to obtain a 2:2, and it took many weeks of searching before he finally landed an interview... in Bristol, of all places.

I was disappointed that, if he got the job, he was going to be based so far away, but he'd been so sulky and difficult over the previous few weeks, while I went to work and he fought hard to find anything suited to his qualifications, that I was just relieved someone was prepared to see him.

He returned from his interview a different person; bright and breezy, as though he hadn't a care in the world, and I knew without a doubt that it had gone well, which was confirmed within a few days, when he was formally offered the job.

I was worried about the future, about how we'd cope being so far apart again, but I decided that for that one evening, I wouldn't raise the subject. Instead, we'd go out and celebrate his good fortune.

"Do you know," I joked as we sat in the pub, not far from his home, and right by the beach, "I could almost start to think that you're stalking me."

He took a sip of his red wine and stared across the table. "How do you mean?"

"Well, I'm from Surrey, and you went to university there, and then I went to uni in Bristol and now you're going to work there... it's like you're following me around."

I smiled at him, but he shook his head. "No, I'm not."

"Yes you are." I sat forward. "I only lived just a few miles from Guildford when I was growing up, and..."

He shook his head more vehemently. "No," he interrupted. "I mean I'm not going to work in Bristol." It was my turn to stare at him, confusion silencing me.

"But I thought they offered you the job," I managed to say eventually.

"They did," he replied. "But it's not in Bristol. It's in Virginia."

"V—Virginia?" I spluttered. "In America?"

He nodded, smiling. "Yes, in America."

"And you've accepted this?"

"Of course I have. It's an incredible opportunity. I'd be an idiot to turn it down."

I sat there for what seemed like a full minute, although it probably wasn't, and then got up from the table and left. I couldn't stay there any longer, not knowing I was about to cry for the first time in front of him... and not in public.

I staggered from the pub and across the road, onto the beach, my vision blurred. How could he do this to us? We'd spent so long apart, and now he was taking a job that was three thousand miles away – if not more? And he hadn't even discussed it with me first?

I sat down on the sand and sobbed, letting my head rest on my knees, my emotions completely overwhelming me, until I felt a pair of hands on my shoulders and the heat of a body, kneeling down behind mine.

"What's wrong?"

"You need to ask?" I turned and faced him, and he stared at me.

"You're crying." He wasn't asking. He was stating a fact – a fact which seemed to surprise him, despite the tears that were streaming down my face. I wanted him to hold me, to tell me everything would be okay. But he didn't. He just stared at me and I felt my anger build.

"Of course I'm crying, Scott. How do you expect me to react?"

He knelt back on his ankles, looking deflated. "I don't know, Jenna. I suppose I hoped you'd be pleased for me." He sounded sad and dejected.

"I am. I just don't understand why you didn't tell me that the job is in Virginia."

"Because I didn't expect to get it." He sighed. "I don't think you have the slightest idea how much I struggled at uni. It wasn't easy for me, like it was for you." I wanted to argue then that it hadn't been 'easy' for me either, that I'd worked damned hard, that I'd missed him so much it hurt, that just getting through each day was torture... but he didn't give me the chance. "I thought I was fairly bright," he continued, his voice dropping, although I could hear the emotion there still, "but I wasn't, not compared to the other guys on my course and it was really hard for me."

I moved closer, feeling sorry for him now. "I know it was."

"Then why the fuck are you raining on my parade?" he hissed, his demeanour changing completely.

"I'm not." I leant back. "I—I'm just going to miss you, that's all."

"And you think I'm not going to miss you? I thought it all through, Jenna, before I applied for the job and I reckoned that we'd managed to stay together for three years, even though we were apart, so we could do it again…"

"But it's a whole different country," I replied.

"I know that," he snapped, "but you're not letting me finish." I sat in silence until he continued, "It's a year's contract. That's all. One fucking year."

"Can you stop swearing at me, Scott?" He'd never done that before, and I didn't know why he'd started now, but I didn't like it.

He glared now, but didn't say anything for a minute. "Can you give me one year?" he asked eventually, his voice a little calmer.

"What happens at the end of the year?" I said. "I mean, are they likely to extend the contract?"

"Not in Virginia, no. I'm filling in for someone else, so when they get back, I'll come home again."

"To a job?"

"Providing I don't screw up, yes."

"In Bristol?" He nodded his head. "What would happen if I said 'no' to this?" I asked.

He stilled, looking hard at me. "What do you mean 'if you said no'? I've already said 'yes'."

"Exactly. I have no say in my own future, do I?"

"I already said, I did think it through first. This is a chance in a lifetime for me, and it's not like we won't see each other at all. You get holidays from work, and you can come over to Virginia and spend them with me. Just think how spectacular it will be…" He let his voice fade.

"Fabulous." I sniffled through my sarcasm. "So, either I accept what you've decided and we essentially live apart for another year, or I walk away from our relationship for good." I looked up into his eyes. "Some choice, Scott."

"It's one year, Jenna…" He reached out and touched my face with his fingertips. "Surely we're worth one more year." He put his arms around me. "I'll make it up to you," he whispered and leant down… and for the first time in five years, he kissed me in public.

I agreed. Of course I did. The thought of saying goodbye forever was so much worse than saying goodbye for a year. And it wasn't even goodbye for a year, because as he'd said, I did get holidays from work, and so we arranged that I'd go over to see him in October, February and May, spreading out my time off through the year that he'd be away. And he promised to come home for Christmas, so we worked out that the longest we'd be apart was three months – the time between February and May, and I think we both hoped that by then, with the end in sight, it wouldn't be too bad.

He left at the end of August, after a fortnight's whirl of paperwork and visas, checks and packing, visits to relatives and speedy goodbyes. Our own farewell was more private, more intimate and a lot more memorable, but then I think we knew we were going to have to live on it for a long while to come.

I got through life one day at a time, knowing that every night when I climbed into bed without him, I was one day closer to seeing him again. For me it was an agony of loneliness, of evenings and weekends spent by myself, or with my parents, missing Scott and wondering whether we really were strong enough to survive yet more separation.

Surprisingly, October came round more quickly than I'd expected. We'd managed to get by on daily text messages and weekly phone calls in between, but I'd kept myself busy at work to prevent the loneliness from becoming too overwhelming. Still, I'd looked forward to seeing Scott again and ran into his arms the moment I set eyes on him at the airport. He held me close for a moment, then bent down and picked up my bag.

"Aren't you going to kiss me?" I asked, looking up at him.

"Yes," he replied, trying not to smile. "When we get back to the apartment."

"Why not now?"

He stopped and turned to me. "Because I want to do a lot more than kiss you."

I barely stifled my giggle and we almost ran to his car.

Luckily it was only a short drive from the airport to Scott's flat, which was in a small complex, and he parked in a space near the door, coming around and helping me out, before getting my bag from the back seat.

"I'm on the second floor," he said as we walked in and he went over to the lifts, pressing the button.

"It looks like a nice place," I replied, looking around at the lobby area, the potted plants, occasional tables and marble flooring.

"It belongs to the company," he explained, letting me enter the lift ahead of him.

Once the doors closed, he looked down at me and I felt the tension crackle between us. It was good tension though, like highly charged electricity and, and for a moment, I wondered if he was going to kiss me in the lift. He didn't, because within seconds, the doors had opened again, and he was leading me along a hallway to a door marked '215'.

He went in ahead of me, and then turned, dropping my bag to the floor as I crossed the threshold, and he pulled me into his arms. He kissed me passionately, then kicked the door closed and pushed me back against it, tearing at my blouse in desperation. I matched his movements, ripping his shirt off, buttons flying around the room, my need for him just as acute. After a few seconds, he broke away and leant down, picking me up and carrying me over to the sofa, where he dumped me rather unceremoniously, before raising my skirt, undoing his jeans with his other hand, then ripping off my knickers and entering me. Hard. I yelped in surprise. It had been a long while since I'd felt him, after all, but he didn't give me any time to think about that, and within minutes, it was over.

He stood, looking down at me, then held out his hand, which I took without hesitation.

"Come with me," he whispered.

"Where are we going?"

"My bed. You belong in my bed…"

I grinned up at him and let him pull me to my feet.

We spent a really lovely week together. Admittedly, I didn't get to see as much of Virginia as I'd have liked, but Scott more than made up for it with the attention he paid me. He'd managed to take a few days off work himself, and when he did have to go in, I'll freely admit, I took advantage of the time to myself to catch up on my sleep. It wasn't so much the jet lag as the fact that Scott was completely insatiable. And I wasn't about to complain, knowing that it would be Christmas before I saw him again.

Saying goodbye at the airport was hard, but he reassured me that he'd be home again in eight weeks, and that I had my memories of our incredible seven days together to keep me warm.

He wasn't wrong there.

That became the manner of my visits to him. They were literally spent almost entirely in bed – or on the couch. We rarely went out and didn't see anyone else for the entirety of my time with him. He said he didn't want to share me, and the feeling was entirely mutual. He was mine and I was his, and we didn't need anyone else.

Work was really busy and before I knew it, August had come around again, and Scott was due to come home. His time in Virginia had gone well and his boss had sent back a glowing report, meaning that the company were happy to keep him on, with a promotion and a pay rise. He was over the moon, and rightly so, and I assured him that he'd earned their praise. He worked hard. I knew that, from all the times he'd been unable to take my calls, or answer my texts straight away, because he'd been held up in meetings, or struggling to meet deadlines.

I was relieved he was coming back, obviously, but that still left us with the problem of living apart again. He was going to be in Bristol, which was over two hours away from Carven Bay, and the thought of more time apart didn't inspire me.

It was during our last Skype call, while he was giving me his flight details, and packing up his things at the same time, that he raised the subject himself, surprising me.

"What are we going to do about our living arrangements?" he asked out of the blue. I couldn't see his face at that moment, because he was emptying his chest of drawers and filling his suitcase, and although his laptop was on the bed, he was out of sight, so all I heard was a disconnected voice.

"Our living arrangements?" I queried.

"Yes. When I come home."

"I don't know." He came back into view again, carrying what appeared to be a pile of t-shirts. "I suppose I assumed we'd go back to seeing each other at weekends."

"You'll be happy with that?" He sat down, turning his laptop around properly, so I could see him.

"No, but what choice do we have?"

"Well," he said, then paused for a moment and I could hear him typing something. "Take a look at this…"

"What?"

"I'm sending you a link."

I waited for a second and then a message appeared on my screen and I clicked on it. The browser opened and I was taken to the website of a property developer.

"What's this?" I asked.

"It's a new development in the middle of Bristol," he said. "What do you think?"

I scrolled down and looked at the glossy, manufactured pictures, the like of which, as an architect, I was very used to seeing, and which were designed to show the property to its best advantage. "It's very modern," I replied.

"Well, it would be," he said, "being as it's only just been finished."

I continued to study the pictures and then opened a document that showed the floor plans, for each of the two bedroomed luxury apartments.

"You're thinking of renting one of these?" I asked, noting that they weren't for sale, but for rental only, at a fairly high price.

"Not exactly. I've already signed the tenancy agreement," he replied.

"Well, it's very nice," I said, feeling a bit left out of his plans.

"So you won't mind living there?"

I stared at the screen, returning to the Skype app, and looking at his smiling face. "Living there?" I echoed.

"Yes." He nodded his head, although the connection meant his movements were disjointed.

"At weekends you mean?"

"No. Permanently."

"But… but how am I going to do that? I can't commute back to Newquay every day, Scott," I reasoned.

"No, I know you can't. I hoped you'd be willing to give up your job and move to Bristol to be with me. They do have architects there too, you know."

"But…"

"But what?" he interrupted, before I had the chance to form a sentence. "I thought this was what you'd want. You were the one moaning about us having to live apart when I came to the States. Now I'm coming home, I thought you'd want us to be together. You don't have to, if you don't want to…"

"I do want to… it's just a bit of shock, that's all." That was the understatement of the century as far as I was concerned. "Why didn't you talk to me about this before you chose the flat?"

"Because I wanted to surprise you."

"And what if I can't find another job?"

He smiled. "You will. And anyway, I'll be earning enough for the time being."

I glanced down at his face, a little grainy and pixellated on my screen, but still utterly adorable. "I suppose I should say yes then."

"You suppose? Can't you just be fucking grateful for once in your life?"

I startled at the harshness of his voice.

"Don't talk to me like that, Scott, and don't swear."

He moved out of shot for a moment, although I could hear him sighing deeply. "I thought you wanted us to live together," he murmured eventually, coming back into my line of sight, his eyes giving away his disappointment.

"I do. It's just that it would have been nice to be asked. It would have been nice if you'd consulted me about the place we're going to live, rather than just presenting me with it... that's all."

He sighed again. "That's all?"

"Yes."

"It's a flat, Jenna. What does it matter where we live? I wanted to do this as a surprise... I thought you'd be happy."

"I am." I was. Mostly. Sort of.

"Doesn't sound like it to me."

"I am, Scott. Honestly."

"It's just that I was sitting here a few weeks ago, thinking about coming home, and I realised how much I've missed you..." Had he really just said that? Out loud? Even though we weren't in bed together? I moved closer to the laptop, wishing I could see his eyes, touch his face, feel his arms around me. "I know we've done okay being apart," he continued, after a short pause, "but I think it would be a lot better if we could be together, don't you?" I nodded my head, smiling. "Sure?" he asked.

"Positive."

"No more silly objections?"

"No. I'm sorry."

He shrugged. "It's okay. Just remember to hand in your resignation tomorrow, and then while you work out your notice, we can start making plans."

"Together?" I asked, and he nodded, blowing me a kiss.

My parents were initially surprised by my decision but only because I didn't have another job to go to. They didn't wonder at all about my choice to move in with Scott. We'd been together for six years by then, and although we'd spent most of that time apart, we were more than ready for the next stage of our lives.

My boss – an absolutely lovely man called Trevor Cole – accepted my resignation with great reluctance. Like my parents, he understood my reasoning, and when I sat down in his office with him, he told me that if I ever needed to come back, he'd find a space for me. It was a kind and considerate thing to say. I doubted I'd need to take up his offer, but it was the thought that counted – as with most things.

Scott arrived home at the end of that week. He only had a few days in Cornwall, before he had to leave for Bristol and spent almost all of that visiting friends and family, most of whom hadn't seen him since Christmas. I wanted us to find some time to look at furniture, but he seemed to be busy, and when I did eventually corner him, he smiled and kissed me, and then explained that it wasn't necessary. He'd already ordered us a bed and a sofa while he was in the States.

"Without us even trying them?" I said. "How will we know if they're comfortable?"

"They're from a very good manufacturer," he replied. "Don't be so tiresome about this, Jenna. I'm exhausted."

"I know... but you didn't give me any choice. Again."

"It's a bed and a couch," he said, pulling back from me. "Why do you always have to be so difficult?"

I moved away from him myself at that point. "I'm not being difficult, Scott. I'd just like to have some say in how our home is furnished."

He sighed. "Yes, but you've got to understand that I'm moving in there in three days' time..I'll need somewhere to sit and sleep. And furniture takes a while to get organised. If I'd waited until I got back here, it wouldn't have been delivered in time." He stepped closer again. "Don't let's fight. I've only just got home." He put his arms around me and kissed me again. "I promise I won't buy anything else for the flat until you move in permanently... okay?"

I nodded my head and let myself believe him.

As it happened, it didn't work out that way.

Scott moved up to Bristol three days' later, as planned, and the following weekend, I went to visit. The flat was impressive, but seriously under-furnished, so we spent most of our time shopping, and by the time I left, we'd either ordered or bought almost everything we needed. Our bank balances had taken a serious hit, but I had quite a bit of money put aside, being as I'd had nothing much to spend my salary on for the previous twelve months – other than air fares – and Scott had been paid a bonus for his work in America, so it wasn't a problem.

The remaining three weeks of my notice passed quickly, and although I'd only been working at Cole and Simpson for just over a year, they threw me a lovely leaving party on the Friday afternoon, after which I had dinner with Mum and Dad, and then left straight away to drive to Bristol. I could have spent one more night at home, and gone the next day, but I was about to start a new life with Scott and we'd waited so long for it to begin, I didn't want to delay it for another second.

I arrived quite late and Scott helped me into the flat with my suitcase before kissing me. When he finally pulled back, I explained how tired I was and that I really needed a shower to freshen up before bed. He smiled and carried my case through to the bedroom, leaving me alone to shower and get into my pyjamas. As I brushed my teeth, I smiled to myself, realising that this was the first time I'd actually gone to bed properly with Scott. In the past, whether we were at uni, or in America, or even over the previous few weeks, when I'd stayed with him at the flat, he'd ripped my clothes off almost as soon as he'd set eyes on me, and insisted I stayed that way for the duration of our time together. Going to bed hadn't been required, simply because we'd rarely got out of bed.

I exited the bathroom to find Scott lying on the mattress, naked and aroused, but noticed that his face fell when he saw me.

"What's going on?" he said, sounding surprised.

"Nothing," I replied. I didn't really understand his question.

"Then why are you wearing pyjamas?"

"Because I always wear pyjamas in bed."

"Not when you're with me, you don't."

"Only because you've normally taken my clothes off already," I pointed out.

"Exactly."

He got up, his eyes locked with mine as he strode purposefully towards me. "I don't like you wearing anything in bed," he said, and pulled my t-shirt top over my head. "Understand?"

I nodded, smiling, and allowed him to lower my shorts, before leading me back to bed.

During that first weekend we rarely left the bedroom. But that wasn't surprising really; we'd missed each other, and we had a lot to celebrate.

However, on the Monday morning, Scott went to work, and I knuckled down to the serious business of finding myself a new job. It took me just over two weeks, and six interviews, but I eventually landed a pretty good position at a small firm of architects not far from the flat. They didn't have the same ecological ethos as Cole and Simpson, which didn't sit too well with me, but it was a job, and I wanted to pay my way. We went out to dinner to celebrate, and within a couple of weeks, we'd settled into a pretty good routine. Scott's hours were a bit unpredictable and could sometimes be long, but our social life was pretty hectic too. We ate out a lot, although we enjoyed cooking together as well, and often sat watching a movie on the sofa – which turned out to be very comfortable indeed. We established that there were several local pubs that we liked, and we went out to one or other of them a couple of nights a week, and at weekends we'd go on long walks, or sit in one of the cafés in the city centre and people watch for a while… And then there was the sex. That was a regular thing too. Literally. Every. Single. Day. Personally, I liked the mornings. There was something about being in that kind of semi-conscious state, sleepy and yet aware, which made his attentions much more intense than usual. Scott preferred the evenings though, when he could take his time. And he certainly did that. And as for the weekends… Scott still had a thing about me not wearing clothes around the flat, so whenever we were at home for any length of time, he'd strip me, usually in a very slow and sensuous way, and then he'd leave me that way, and we'd get on with the day. The difference was that, whereas in the past he would have taken off his own clothes, and we would have kissed and touched, letting the tension escalate, until we'd have wound up having sex somewhere… a sofa, a table, the floor… wherever… now, he chose to remain fully clothed. And he'd watch me. All the time.

To be honest, I found it a bit demeaning to be vacuuming or cooking, or unloading the washing machine with nothing on, but whenever I queried why he didn't get undressed himself anymore, he'd just say he was admiring the view, which didn't really make sense to me, because he could have got undressed and done that. Surely.

On top of that, I was still feeling a little put out that he never showed me any affection when we were out together. I'd done everything he'd asked of me, and yet, despite the amount of time we spent in restaurants and pubs, on walks and in cafés, as well as at the movies and just walking around the town, he never did anything more than hold my hand in public. He never once kissed me, held me, or told me that he loved me when we were outside the confines of our flat. And it bothered me.

I suppose we'd been living together for about four months or so when I decided to confront him about my worries. We'd spent the evening at one of our favourite Italian restaurants, and throughout the entire time, he'd been looking around at the Christmas decorations, and the other diners, passing comments on them and what they were wearing, discussing work, telling me about his parents' new conservatory, and generally avoiding any kind of intimacy.

"Can I ask you something?" I said as he climbed into bed beside me.

"As long as it's quick," he said, moving closer to me, his hand skimming over my skin, drifting downwards.

"Why are you never demonstrative when we're out?"

He stopped, pulling his hand away and leaning back. "Not this again, surely?" he said. "We've been through this before. I can hardly fondle you in the middle of a restaurant, can I?"

"No, and I'm not suggesting you should. But you could tell me you love me. I mean, you insist on me being stark naked around the flat, and yet outside, you act like I don't exist."

"I do not. We've spent the whole evening talking." We had, it was true, but before I could point out that I'd have preferred to talk about more personal things over dinner, he added, "And I don't insist on you being naked. I ask you to do it, because I like your body. I like watching you."

I felt like arguing that he'd never once 'asked' me, before he'd taken my clothes off, which felt like insistence to me. But I didn't. Instead, I smiled at him, trying to lighten the moment. "Why can't you say things like that when we're out?"

"Because it's private, Jenna. Like me telling you I love you. It's the kind of thing a man says in the privacy of his own bedroom."

"Really?"

"Yes." He sidled a little closer again. "It's between us, not for public consumption."

"But you could whisper it, couldn't you?"

He let out a long breath. "I could, but I'd rather save my demonstrations of affection for when we can be together, and I can show you how I feel…"

He shifted, pushing me over, onto my back and lying on top of me. "Oh?" I said, unable to keep the smile from my lips.

"Yes," he said. "And anyway, I'm a lot more demonstrative than you think."

"Is that so?" I teased, feeling his arousal right against my entrance.

"Yes." He took my hands in his and held them beside my head. "Want me to prove it?"

I parted my legs wider and raised my hips expectantly. "Yes," I whispered.

"Then marry me."

Chapter Six

Once I'd recovered from the shock of Scott's proposal, and had accepted him – well, I was in love with him, so saying 'yes' was the natural thing to do – it didn't take us long to establish that marriage was what we both wanted, and we didn't see the point in wasting time with being engaged. Breaking the news to our parents that we were getting married was quite easy and the Christmas festivities, which were only a few days away, gave us the perfect excuse. To be honest, I'm pretty sure they expected it. They certainly didn't seem very surprised, although they were pleased. Telling them that we'd decided to set the date for the first weekend in June came as a bit of a shock, I think, but they accepted it and, between them, they helped out with the planning and preparations, and made friends with each other in the process.

Scott didn't want a flashy wedding, so we went for a quiet registry office ceremony, with the reception being held at a local hotel, where we spent our first night as a married couple, before flying off to the Seychelles for two weeks of luxury at an exclusive resort, in our own beach-side hut, with a huge bed, wet room, and two separate restaurants on site, not to mention 24-hour room service. The honeymoon was a surprise, planned entirely by Scott, who'd even done the packing, telling me that if I knew what I had to take, I might guess where we were going. At the time, I'd thought it was romantic – surprisingly so for him – but when we arrived and I was unpacking my suitcase, I discovered that he'd neglected to pack my usual bikinis, of which I had three, and had replaced them with some new ones, which he'd purchased himself. To say they were revealing was an understatement.

"I can't possibly wear these," I remarked, holding one up. The top half consisted of a clear under-bust strap, to which there were attached two vertical strips of black material, which narrowed and tied around the neck, and I imagined, even at their widest point, would barely cover my nipples, leaving the rest of my breasts exposed, while the bottom half was an almost non-existent thong.

"Why not?" he asked, walking over and looking down at me.

"Scott… I'll be completely exposed," I whispered.

"I know." He grinned.

"But that means other people – other men – will be able to see me," I reasoned, and his grin widened.

"Precisely." He took my left hand in his "You wanted public displays of affection, and you're going to get them. Other men can look," he said, kissing my ring finger and gazing into my eyes, "but they can't touch. Because you're mine now…"

He took the bikini – or the excuse for a bikini – from me and threw it to the floor, then pushed me back on the bed, climbing on top of me.

"I was always yours," I whispered and he smiled as he kissed me.

Although I was shy at first, I soon got used to the bikinis, bolstered I think by the fact that our stretch of beach was actually quite private, being as the huts to either side of us were empty, and the other women who were there, and who occasionally came into view, walking along the wide stretch of sand, seemed to be wearing similar, if not smaller, outfits… and occasionally, nothing at all, at least on their top half. Every so often, I'd surreptitiously glance at Scott, to see if he was watching, but he wore those reflective sunglasses which made it impossible to tell, and in any case, what did it matter? We were married and he told me every day how much he loved me.

We'd been there for five days, I think, when Scott surprised me by raising the subject of children. It was something we'd talked about before, quite briefly, a few weeks after his surprise proposal, and had agreed that, while be both wanted to have them, we were only twenty-three; there was no rush. On that particular afternoon, however, sitting on sun loungers, beneath the shade of a couple of palm trees, gazing out onto a perfect bright blue, calm sea, the white sandy beach stretching before us, Scott turned to me, removed his sunglasses, and said, "Do you remember us talking about having kids?"

I looked over at him, feeling a frown settle on my face. "Yes. Why?"

He twisted around, moving slightly closer and lowering his voice, even though there wasn't anyone near us at the time. "Remember we said we'd wait?"

"Yes…"

"Well… are you sure about that?"

I was surprised. No, actually, I was stunned. "I—I thought we'd agreed that we wanted to travel together first, and that I should get more settled at work," I replied, unsure why I was stammering.

"I know, but does any of that matter?" he said. "We can travel with a baby, can't we? And it makes no difference whether you're settled at work or not, does it?"

"What's the hurry?" I took off my own sunglasses now, and turned onto my side to face him.

He shrugged, although he was smiling. "I'm not saying there is a hurry," he replied and let his eyes drop, raking them down my body. "But I was just watching you, and thinking how hot you look, compared to just about every other woman here… and that I want you to have my child."

It seemed to me that it would be more sensible to wait. There were practicalities like finances and childcare to consider, but also, Scott had been noticeably more attentive since our arrival in the Seychelles, and I really hoped this was how our lives were going to be now that we were married. I wasn't so sure that bringing a child into the equation at that precise moment was the right thing to do. We needed some time together first. By ourselves. "Right now?" I queried.

"Well, I believe it takes nine months," he quipped, then he lowered his shorts. "Come here," he whispered, his eyes darkening.

"I can't. Someone might see us." I glanced down the deserted beach.

"They won't." He held out his hand and I took it, letting him pull me over to his lounger, settling astride him, my knees either side of his hips. "I think you should stop taking the pill," he murmured into me, pulling me closer to him. "And in the meantime, I think we should start getting in some practice, don't you?"

We spent our entire honeymoon 'practising', and when we got home, I did as he'd said and stopped taking my birth control pills. And then we practised some more.

Needless to say, I got pregnant. I bought a test, just to make sure, doing it in the privacy of our ensuite bathroom on a Saturday morning, while Scott was still asleep. When the result showed as positive, I stared at myself in the mirror and took a deep breath. I was going to become a mother. Looking into my own eyes, I wondered if I was really ready for that.

"Are you alright in there?" Scott knocked on the door sharply, interrupting my thoughts, which was probably a good thing.

"Yes," I replied and cleared away the packaging from the pregnancy test, hiding the white stick behind my back as I unlocked the door to find him standing on the other side.

"You've been ages," he said.

"I didn't think you were awake." I looked up at him.

"I was waiting for you to come back to bed." He leant down and kissed me, pushing me backwards against the wall. As his hands started to wander, I grabbed his wrist and halted him, knowing I needed to tell him my news before anything else happened. He leant back, frowning. "What's wrong?"

"I—I've got something I need to tell you."

"Oh?"

I held out my other hand, the one with the white stick still clasped firmly in it, and showed it to him. He glanced down, focusing on the little window, and then back at me.

"You're pregnant?" he said, sounding surprised, although I wasn't sure why, considering how much sex we'd had.

"Yes." I nodded my head.

"Already?" He sounded almost disappointed.

I nodded again, feeling unsure of myself, just like I had in the bathroom.

There was a pause, which seemed to go on for a lifetime, but then he swept me up into his arms and twirled me around, kissing me deeply.

"You're pleased?" I asked, just to make sure.

"Of course. It's what we wanted." He led me back over to the bed, and laid me down, my head on the pillows, as he nestled between my legs. "I suppose the practising's over," he murmured, "but that's no reason not to keep enjoying ourselves."

I giggled, and allowed him to prove the point.

Morning sickness was a bitch. There's no other word for it. Gone were the days of early morning sex, and wandering around the flat naked all day, much to Scott's disappointment. He huffed and puffed about it, but what could I do? Literally, as soon as I turned over in bed, I needed to throw up, and it didn't stop for a good couple of hours. The very last thing I felt like doing was having sex, and I rarely hung around long enough for him to admire me, naked, or otherwise. On one particularly bad Sunday morning, Scott asked how long it would go on for, but I didn't have an answer to that. So, I checked the pregnancy books I'd bought, and they said somewhere between twelve and sixteen weeks. Unfortunately, when I told him that, he glared at me and stormed out of the bedroom, like it was my fault. I'd have gone after him to protest that the pregnancy hadn't been my idea, that he'd suggested it, and that we were still having sex in the evenings, but I needed to be sick again, and had to make a dash for the bathroom instead.

Apart from that, Scott was generally quite good. He helped a little more around the flat, did most of the cooking and let me put my feet up when I was tired, which seemed to be most of the time.

Luckily, my boss in my new job was a woman, and she'd had two children herself, her experience of morning sickness being far worse than mine evidently, so she was understanding about hospital appointments, and on the occasions when I was late in to work because I simply couldn't stop vomiting.

The office was probably seventy percent women, and roughly half of them had at least one child, and they weren't short of support, or stories. I heard about stretch marks, cravings, sleepless nights, stitches… and – perhaps most scarily of all – how having children had impacted on their relationships.

"Mike prefers playing golf to doing anything with me and the kids," Angie said while we sat over lunch one day with Rebecca and Monica. "Sometimes I think I might be better off as a single parent. At least I wouldn't have to pretend to enjoy having sex with him."

"Don't start," Rebecca replied, rolling her eyes and smiling. "John took up residence at the pub within a few days of Toby being born. I've even got the landlord on speed dial now, because my darling husband turns his phone off to make sure I can't find out where he is."

They all laughed, but I could see the sadness in Rebecca's eyes as she was speaking, and felt guilty. By comparison, Scott was positively angelic and, when he came home from work that night, I greeted him with a kiss and led him directly into the bedroom, where I showed my appreciation of how considerate he was, and how lucky I felt to have him. Okay, so he may not have been the most demonstrative of men, but he was there, he was with me, and now I knew what my friends and colleagues were putting up with from their husbands and partners, I felt guilty for all the times I'd questioned our relationship and his loyalty to it, and to me.

Slowly but surely, the morning sickness improved, and by my fourth month, we'd reverted to normal in terms of our sex life. Scott seemed pleased about that and, I wasn't complaining myself. After all, those were the times I treasured, because that was when he spoke to me from the heart, making me feel loved and wanted, and as my body changed, I needed to hear his words of love more than ever.

Although he'd been busy at work over the previous few weeks, often coming home an hour or so later than usual, Scott managed to get some time off to come to the second ultrasound with me. He'd missed the first one, but I really wanted him there for my eighteen-week scan. The night before my appointment, after we'd had sex, we lay together in bed, both staring up at the ceiling and, as he got his breath back, I asked him whether or not he wanted to know the sex of the baby.

"Do you want to?" he asked, sounding unsure.

"I don't know."

He looked at me for a moment, and then turned away, gazing up at the ceiling again. "I—I don't think I do," he said, after a moment's pause.

I didn't answer, and I didn't ask why. I didn't need to. Scott always referred to our unborn child as 'he', never 'she', or even 'it', so I knew that deep down, he wanted a boy. For myself, I didn't mind either way, but as I lay there I had to admit that I didn't want to know in advance, for the very simple reason that, if it turned out we were having a girl, I knew Scott would be disappointed, and that I'd have to live with that. I reasoned to myself that, being presented with a beautiful baby girl, holding her in his arms and looking down at her, knowing she was his, would be a completely different experience for him, to being told about it while looking at an anonymous grainy picture on a screen. At least, I hoped it would. Although from that moment on, I will confess that I kept my fingers crossed that I was having a boy.

And so, everything went along smoothly. We decorated the spare bedroom, bought furniture, and a few basic items of baby clothing… and argued. We argued mostly about the fact the Scott had assumed I would be giving up work after the baby was born, and I'd assumed the polar opposite. I had no intention of being a stay at home mum. My mother had worked, and I wanted to do the same. And in any case, I loved my job. I got fulfilment and enjoyment from it. And I knew I wouldn't feel satisfied in myself, if I gave it up. Besides which, my boss had been very generous. I hadn't been working there long enough to qualify for maternity benefits, but she'd agreed to at least keep my job open, which she didn't have to do. Scott's argument was that his mother had given up her career to raise him, only going back to work when he was fourteen, that she'd always been there for him, and he'd liked it that way, and that I could easily return to my job at a later stage. He didn't think I owed my boss any great loyalty either… she wouldn't be paying me while I wasn't working – no-one would… Scott would be supporting us – so he couldn't understand why I felt so grateful to her.

It was something we couldn't see eye to eye on, and no matter how long, or how hard we fought over it, we always ended up in the same place… stalemate.

Things changed, however, when I hit my thirtieth week.

I'd been working on a huge project for a few weeks, and exhaustion had started to get the better of me, and then my blood pressure went up a bit, so on doctor's orders, I was forced to stop work altogether, a good six weeks ahead of when I'd intended to. I wasn't happy about it, but I had to put the baby first.

I found it odd, being at the flat by myself all day. Odd, and boring. I tried to keep busy with making the finishing touches to the nursery, and with cooking nice meals for Scott, when he came in from work, but I was also under strict instructions to rest and put my feet up as much as possible. So, I read a lot, and slept a lot, and found myself gaining more weight than I had done earlier in the pregnancy. I struggled to move around, my ankles swollen and uncomfortable, and getting out of a chair felt like it would have been easier with the use of a winch, or some kind of pulley system. We also weren't short of mirrors and I could see for myself that I resembled a beached whale, having a bad day.

Despite his triumph that I'd been forced to give up work ahead of schedule, Scott had obviously noticed the changes in me too, and his attentions to me had cooled considerably, to the point where we stopped having sex altogether. After about two weeks of that, I asked him what was wrong, why he wasn't interested in me anymore. He was getting undressed for bed at the time and he stopped and looked down at me.

"Why do you think?" he said, and I shrugged.

"I have no idea. Is it because of how I look?"

He sat on the edge of the bed, his back to me. "No," he said. "It's because I don't want to harm the baby, silly."

I chuckled and, with no little effort, moved across the bed. "I'm nearly eight months pregnant," I said softly. "It's never bothered you before… and, in any case, I'm not sure you can harm the baby."

He turned, moving further away, towards the foot of the bed. "I'm also tired," he mumbled. "Things are really crazy at work."

"I know," I replied. "But I thought…"

"Why do you have to keep on?" he interrupted harshly, getting to his feet.

"I—I wasn't aware that I was." I could feel tears pricking my eyes, but I wasn't going to cry, not in front of him.

"I'm going for a bath," he said, walking out of the room.

I felt rebuffed by that and moved back to my own side of the bed, resting my head on the pillows and feeling a tear fall onto my cheek.

I hoped he wouldn't be too long, that he'd come back and apologise, that we could talk it through and work things out. Unfortunately, exhaustion overcame everything, as usual, and I fell asleep.

When I woke the next morning, he'd already left for work.

Like a glutton for punishment, I wasn't prepared to let it go and, the next evening, when he came home, I raised the subject again. This time, he turned on me.

"Will you stop fucking nagging me for sex," he barked, throwing his briefcase down on the floor.

"I'm not nagging, I'm asking. And please don't swear at me."

"What's your fucking problem with swearing, Jenna?" He took a step closer.

"I don't like it. It's not necessary," I replied, holding my ground. "But you're changing the subject. I'm just asking – not nagging – why you don't want to have sex with me anymore. You used to want me all the time."

"Yes, I did, before you…" He stopped talking suddenly and turned away.

"Before I what?"

"Nothing."

I moved closer to him now. "Before I what, Scott?"

He turned back. "Before you got so fat. No-one in their right mind would want to fuck you now." His words rang through my head as my vision blurred and, despite my size, I ran from the living room, into the bedroom, slamming the door behind me.

I lay on my side on the bed, my back to the door, crying my eyes out. I couldn't in all honesty deny the truth of what he'd said. I had put on a lot of weight, I had stretch marks crisscrossing their way over what had once been smooth skin, and I was sure that made me unattractive in his eyes – and probably in most men's eyes – but I was carrying his child, the child he'd wanted, and for him to have actually said those words to me, in such a cold, heartless way...

The door opened behind me and I tried to curl myself up, protecting myself against him, against another onslaught. God knows how I thought I could do that, with my enormous bump in the way, but I tried nonetheless.

"Jenna?" He came around the bed and into my line of sight, although he didn't lie beside me and hold me in his arms; he sat down at the end of the bed, looking at me. "Say something."

"What do you want me to say?" I saw red, leaning up and glaring at him. "You want me to say that it's okay that you lied to me last night, when you said you didn't want to hurt the baby? You want me to tell you it's okay for you to speak to me like you did just now? Because it's not, Scott... it's not okay. You're supposed to love me—"

"I do," he interrupted.

"Really? It doesn't feel like it."

"I don't see what the problem is," he said and I felt my blood boiling. "Are you serious?"

"What I mean is, you didn't want to have sex at the beginning of your pregnancy, and I don't want to now. So we're kind of even, really. And anyway, you'll have the baby soon, and everything will go back to normal again."

I sat up now, even though it took me a couple of attempts to get there. "Even? For your information, it wasn't that I didn't want to have sex at the beginning, it was that I wasn't physically capable. I was being sick every morning, if you remember. And we did still have sex in the evenings, so it wasn't like I was rejecting you. Not in the way you're rejecting me..." I felt my voice crack slightly, but swallowed it down and continued, "And if you think, for one second, that everything will go back to normal after I've had the baby, then you can think again."

He blanched, noticeably. "What does that mean?" he whispered.

"It means that you don't get to say something like that to me, and then just expect everything to be fine, Scott."

He sighed, pushing his fingers back through his hair and messing it up, unusually for him. "Okay, so I said the wrong thing, but I don't think you've got any idea how much stress I'm under at the moment… what with this new promotion."

"What new promotion?" I frowned. He hadn't mentioned a promotion and I had no idea what he was talking about.

He tilted his head to one side and let out a long breath. "One of the managers is leaving at work," he explained. "And I've applied for the position. That's why I've been putting in so many extra hours."

"But I don't understand why?"

"Why what?"

"Why you've applied…"

"Because you've made it fairly clear over the last few months that one of your main reasons for wanting to go back to work after the baby is born, is to do with money. And I know you're not convinced that I already earn more than enough, no matter how many times I've said it." It was true. We'd argued, long and loud about money, amongst other things, all of which he seemed to have forgotten, for the moment. "But I thought it might set your mind at rest if I was earning more. I have been listening, you see… I get it that babies aren't cheap. Let's face it, you've said it often enough. And this new job comes with quite a big pay rise – certainly more than enough to allow you to be a full-time mum."

I stared at him. "So you're trying to force my hand? Even though you know it's not just about money? Even though you know it's not what I want?"

"For fuck's sake, Jenna. It can't always be about what you want. You've made yourself ill working so hard when you're pregnant. I'm just trying to provide for you… you and our baby…"

I could hear the hurt in his voice, and it struck me that maybe I was being unfair. He was just trying to be considerate, after all. "Why didn't you tell me?" I asked, calming down. "About the promotion, I mean? Why didn't you talk it through with me?"

"Because I wanted it to be a surprise. And anyway, I can't be sure I'll get it, and if I don't, then I didn't want to raise your hopes…"

As he finished speaking, he moved a little closer, and I met him half way, letting him put his arms around me. I still felt a bit manipulated, but I could appreciate that he just wanted what was best for us. We didn't say anything else but he held me for a while and then suggested we get a take-away, so neither of us would have to cook. After we'd eaten, we went to bed and although we didn't have sex, he did hold me until I fell asleep.

When the first pain started, I assumed it was a false alarm. It was nearly three weeks until the baby's due date of April tenth, although admittedly there had been some confusion about that, being as I'd fallen pregnant so quickly after coming off the pill. In fact, my midwife had only joked with me the previous week that she'd be surprised if I made it to the end of March and I'd felt quite relieved about that. I was getting really fed up with being pregnant. The thing was though, it was only the twenty-third of March. And I was in agony. So, I convinced myself that I couldn't possibly be in labour and that it had to be those Braxton Hicks contractions my midwife had warned me about. I stayed in that state of denial for over three hours, feeling irregular but sharp pains, right up until my waters broke, all over the kitchen floor, and then I panicked. I toyed with calling an ambulance, but Scott's office was only a ten minute drive away and, despite our recent differences, I wanted him with me. I didn't want a complete stranger.

I never usually phoned him during the day, and I knew he was still stressed about the promotion, being as he'd been interviewed quite a few weeks beforehand, but his bosses had evidently decided to put the position out to external candidates, which I think Scott took as a bad sign. I'd tried to reassure him that it was probably just company policy, but I didn't think he'd paid much attention to what I'd said. Even so, we'd agreed that because the baby was due soon, I could call him if I needed him, so I wasn't surprised when he answered quite promptly, on only the third ring. His voice was abrupt though.

"What is it, Jenna?"

"Sorry, am I interrupting something? I can call an ambulance if you're busy."

"Ambulance?" His voice changed, to something approaching the panic I was feeling.

"Yes."

"It's started?"

"Yes. My waters broke…"

"Already? But… but it's early. I mean…"

"Scott," I reasoned, trying to sound more calm than I felt. "Can you stop talking and come home, please?"

"Yes. Yes, of course. I'll be ten minutes. Can you wait that long?"

I smiled to myself. "I'll do my best."

He arrived in less than ten minutes, but I'd taken advantage of that time to put some towels down in the kitchen, cleaning up the mess I'd made earlier, and to get my bag from the bedroom, so that when he walked in the door, I was ready to go.

Attentive and considerate, Scott took me to the hospital and stayed with me throughout my very short labour, which lasted less than two hours.

Our son was born just before three o'clock in the afternoon, and I was aware of heaving a sigh of relief when the midwife announced, "It's a boy." And that wasn't simply because I was no longer in pain, having delivered him safely, but because the look on Scott's face told me I'd been right; this was what he'd wanted.

I'd like to say I took to motherhood like a duck to water, but that would be a lie. The reality was that I felt like I had no idea what to do with this little person, who seemed so heavily dependent on me. I never seemed to feel like I was on top of things, or even like I might be able to catch up, but I think the worst thing of all for me was that I was struggling to breastfeed. I was determined to persevere though, despite Scott telling me not to bother if it was that hard, which didn't help he situation, and led to much bickering, fuelled by the ever-present tiredness.

At the end of that first week at home, both sets of parents came to visit, and it was through them that we really started to see the light, and the error of our ways. We put Jacob into his pram and went for a walk to the park, and while my dad wheeled Jacob around, my mother and Scott's took turns explaining to me that I shouldn't set myself such high standards, that it didn't matter if the ironing didn't get done, or the flat was a mess, or the sheets didn't get changed for an extra couple of days. I had to take care of Jacob and myself, and everything else could wait. I was grateful to them. It felt like I was being given permission to take a breath – and I needed it. As for Scott, I overheard his dad telling him that he needed to give me time. I had no idea what Scott had said to illicit that response, but his dad was firm in his reply, explaining that giving birth is a traumatic experience and that he had to be patient and understanding. I wasn't sure how Scott would respond to his dad's words, especially given how things had been between the two of us during the previous few days, and in the last weeks of my pregnancy, but he surprised me by being a lot more attentive after our parents' visit.

Scott had taken two weeks off work, and soon it was time for him to go back. I'd been dreading it, fearful of having to cope by myself, but in reality, it was actually easier. Scott seemed a lot happier for getting out of the house, welcoming the distraction of work, despite the broken nights; and I soon got myself into a routine with Jacob, which I found much more straightforward because I wasn't having to worry about Scott and what he was doing all the time. In the evenings, after Scott got home, we'd sit together, by ourselves if Jacob was asleep, or with him cradled between us if he was awake, and I would sometimes smile to myself, remembering those first few days, and vowing never to go back to them again.

We didn't go back. We moved forward, and things quickly settled down, especially when, about five weeks after Jacob was born, Scott instigated sex for the first time. I had to admit, I'd missed the emotional connection that was always lacking between us when we weren't having sex. It had been a long time since I'd felt anything like that, being as Scott hadn't been near me for the last six weeks or so of my pregnancy, so when he started dropping hints that evening, I really wasn't averse to the idea.

Jacob's routine at that point meant he was asleep by nine, and we knew he'd stay that way until around one in the morning, so we went straight to bed. I'd lost about half a stone of my baby weight, but still had a long way to go and felt self-conscious about my appearance, especially after the things Scott had said. Because of that, I insisted that we leave the lights off, but he was clearly keen, and didn't seem to notice – either my excess weight, or my nervousness – although he did remark on the fact that he didn't like me wearing pyjamas to bed, which I'd done since Jacob was born. I pointed out that it was easier, considering I was getting up in the night to breastfeed, but as he started undressing me, he suggested I could wear my robe to go into Jacob, and told me that he wanted me, and that he didn't want any barriers between us. I gloried in his words, which made the disappointment much more profound when he took so little time over everything, and clearly wasn't going to give me any release before satisfying himself. Even so, I think at that time, I craved his attention more than anything else, and I gazed into his eyes in the moonlight as he raised himself above me and entered me, surprised that it didn't hurt at all.

"Wait!" I whispered loudly, stopping him with my hand on his chest.

"What?" He looked down at me.

"You need a condom."

He shook his head. "No I don't. You're breastfeeding."

I giggled. "Yes, and that's not a reliable form of contraception." I moved my hand away, letting it fall down by my head. "At least, it's not reliable enough for me. I don't know about you, but I'm not ready for Jacob to have a little brother or sister just yet."

"Well, in that case, you need to go back on the pill," he huffed a little moodily and then pulled out of me and got up, leaving the bedroom.

I wondered where he'd gone, whether he'd gone off the idea and wouldn't be coming back, and was just thinking about going after him, when he returned, holding a small cardboard box in his hand, which he put on the bedside table, pulling a foil pack from it, tearing into it and pulling out a condom. I wasn't sure where he'd got them from, but assumed he must have kept them in the bathroom cabinet, or something. I didn't get the chance to ask though, as within seconds, he was back inside me. He climaxed quickly, which wasn't surprising, being as it had been so long and, as he rolled off of me, onto his back, I looked over at him.

"Did it feel different?" I asked him, feeling slightly scared of his answer.

"No," he replied, turning to face me. "Just do something for me?"

I nodded my head. "What?"

"Go back on the pill, will you? I really hate condoms."

We both laughed and he pulled me into his arms, where I promptly fell asleep.

Scott wanted me to make an appointment with the doctor straight away, but I reasoned with him that I was due to see the midwife for my six week check-up, and could raise the subject of contraception then – along with my continued struggles with breastfeeding, which I still didn't seem to have overcome. We had sex a couple of times in the next week or so, before my appointment, but Jacob had altered his sleep pattern again, and I was tired, so there was no way I could consider going back to our old routine of every night and every morning, like it had been before he was born. Scott didn't seem to mind that; he said he understood, and I was thankful for that.

My six week check up was booked for a Friday, and was late in the afternoon, but even so, I was surprised that Scott was already at home when I got back.

"How did it go?" he asked, getting up from the sofa and coming over to take Jacob from me while I took off my jacket.

"Um... it was fine," I replied, still a bit taken aback to see him there. "Is everything okay?"

"Yes. Why?"

"Well, you don't normally come home this early."

He smiled at me. "I just wanted to see how you got on, that's all."

"It was just a check-up, Scott," I explained, feeling kind of gratified that he cared so much about us to take time off work. "There's nothing to worry about."

He took my hand and led me over to the sofa, sitting us down, with Jacob on his lap and me beside him. "I know, but how did it go?"

"It went fine. Jacob is putting on weight, and the midwife says he's doing really well."

"And?"

"And what?"

"Don't tell me you forgot…" He sounded a bit put out, but then the penny dropped.

"Oh, you mean about the pill?"

"Yes."

"We discussed it," I explained, turning to face him. "And the midwife explained that I can go back on the pill, but all the while I'm breastfeeding, it would have to be the mini-pill, because the combined one could reduce my milk production, but considering all the problems I've been having, I don't think it's a good idea…" My voice faded as I noticed the expression on his face, the hard line of his mouth and the darkness of his eyes. "What's wrong?"

"So, what does all that mean? Are you taking the mini-pill?"

"No."

"Why not? You said the midwife explained it was only the combined pill that would cause a problem." He sounded almost angry and instinctively I reached over and took Jacob from him.

"You know how hard I find breastfeeding, Scott. I'm not going to risk doing anything that might make it worse," I replied firmly.

"And what about me?" Scott replied, getting to his feet. "What about my needs?"

"For heaven's sake, we can still have sex; you'll just need to use a condom for a few months."

"A few months?" He stared down at me, incredulous. "A few fucking months?"

"Scott, please…"

"Yeah, I know… don't swear." He put on a mocking voice as he spoke the last two words, and at that moment, Jacob started to cry, possibly sensing the tension between us. "When are you planning on stopping breastfeeding?" Scott asked as I tried to comfort our son.

"I don't know. Probably when Jacob's four to six months old. Why?" I glared at him.

He didn't reply, but glared back, shook his head and huffed out a sigh, then turned away and, grabbing his jacket from the hook, he slammed out of the flat.

Jacob cried even louder then and I bit back my own tears as I held him in my arms and swayed from side to side, singing him a gentle lullaby until he quietened. He seemed hungry, so I fed him, and then, after a short while I bathed him – which was something he always enjoyed – and then took him into the nursery to get him ready for bed.

Once he'd settled, I went back out into the living room, feeling worn out and uncertain, surprised to find that Scott had returned and was sitting on the couch.

"You're back then," I said, pausing a few feet away from him, keeping my distance.

"So it would seem."

"Have you decided to apologise?"

He looked up at me. "What for?"

"For the things you said, Scott," I reasoned. "And for the way you said them."

"What have I got to apologise for?" he said, getting up now and moving closer to me. "You're the one who's being selfish."

"Selfish?" I tried desperately not to raise my voice, despite the temptation. I didn't want to wake Jacob, not after he'd been so upset earlier. "I'm not being selfish. I'm putting our son first. And it won't be forever."

"Four to six months feels like forever to me," he said.

"Well, it isn't. And you need to grow up."

His eyes darkened. "I thought if I came back we could talk and…"

"And what? And go to bed?" I spat at him, still speaking in whispers.

"Yes, if you must know. But what's the point? You're not interested anymore, are you?" He didn't wait for my response, but stormed out of the flat for the second time in one evening.

I was breathing hard and managed to make it to the sofa before I collapsed, out of sheer emotional exhaustion. How could he speak to me like that? Again…

It was Jacob's crying that woke me in the early hours and, to start with, I was disoriented, until I realised I was still in the living room, lying on the sofa, and as I clambered slowly to my feet and went in to him,

I noticed that the flat was silent and in darkness, the door to our room open, and our bed empty.

According to the clock on the nightstand, it was one thirty-seven in the morning, and Scott hadn't come home.

I heard his key in the lock, quite by chance, just as I was closing the nursery door, having fed Jacob and got him back off to sleep again.

"You remembered where you live then?" I said sarcastically, going into the living room and confronting him.

He stared right into my eyes, and without a word, by-passed me and went down the hallway towards our bedroom.

"Come back here," I whispered, re-tracing my steps and going after him.

"I'm tired." He turned to face me, standing by our bedroom door.

"Why? Where have you been for the last six hours? Or should I be asking who have you been with?"

He shook his head, like he felt sorry for me. "I haven't been with anyone for the last six hours, Jenna. Although God knows why not."

"You're being such a child, Scott. Just because I won't go back on the pill…"

"It's not just about that," he said, lowering his voice considerably. "It's about always coming second…"

"We have a child now," I reasoned. "I have to take care of him."

"Yes, to the exclusion of everyone else, it seems."

"You're being unreasonable, Scott. Jacob is a baby. He's six weeks old. What do you want of me?"

"I want you to be my wife. But you've made your position very clear. I come second now…"

"No you don't. Please don't be like that."

"Like what?" He was glaring down at me. "Oh… like I don't matter, you mean? Well, did it even occur to you that I had another reason for coming home early this evening… other than finding out about your appointment? Did you even consider that this isn't all about you?"

"What are you talking about? You said you were here because you wanted to see how I'd got on with the midwife." I remembered him saying it. Clearly. I remembered how pleased I'd felt too.

"Yes, well, I just said that at the time."

"Then why did you come home?" I asked.

"Because I heard today that I didn't get the promotion," he murmured, looking down at the small space between us. "I thought the delay in making the announcement meant they'd given the job to an external candidate, but it turns out I was wrong. They gave it to Chris fucking Nicholson. And I didn't feel like staying there and watching everyone congratulating him… so I thought I'd come home. I suppose I stupidly thought you'd be interested."

"Oh, Scott. I am interested." I couldn't help but feel sorry for him. I knew how much he'd wanted that job and hearing that someone else from his department had got it instead must have been hard for him.

He shrugged. "Really? What does it matter to you?" he said. "As long as you're alright."

I sighed and moved closer to him, resting my hand on his arm. "That's not true," I reasoned. "I just didn't realise." He raised his face, looking at me now and, even though it was fairly dark in the hallway, there was enough moonlight coming from our open bedroom windows for me to see the hurt in his eyes. It tugged at my heartstrings and, before I knew it, I found myself apologising. "I'm sorry," I whispered, putting my arms around him. "I haven't been a very good wife to you of late, have I?"

He shook his head, and I let mine rest on his chest, feeling ashamed of myself for not thinking about his problems and worries. But then his arms came around me and I nestled into him.

"Forgive me?" I murmured.

He held me tighter and, despite the fact that he didn't say anything, I took that as a 'yes'.

Although we went to bed together, we didn't have sex. He said he didn't want to and I didn't mind that. I wasn't sure I wanted to either. It felt like we would have been papering over the cracks, making light of the problems in our relationship. And there clearly were problems. I hated the way he spoke to me sometimes, but I could see how much stress he was under and, as I lay there watching him sleep, I resolved to make more of an effort. I knew it couldn't all come from me, and that Scott needed to change too, but I thought that if I could try to see things from his perspective, to understand his needs a bit better, then maybe we could work it out. I hoped so anyway, for our sakes as well as for Jacob's.

I suppose it was about two months later when everything really changed. Despite my best efforts, things had still been rather awkward between Scott and I. He'd been working long hours, trying to impress his bosses – or maybe make them regret their decision not to promote him, and as a result of that, I'd often been in bed by the time he came in from work at night. Our weekends seemed to revolve around Jacob, catching up at home, and sleeping, so we had little time for each other. But on that particular Friday, I was feeling quite cheerful, probably because, although Jacob still wasn't sleeping through the night, he had just mastered the art of stretching his sleep from about eleven at night, until five in the morning – and that felt like a whole night to me. I suppose I was hoping Jacob's new-found habit would give Scott and I the chance to actually feel like human beings again, for the first time in ages.

I'd just put Jacob down for the night and, rather than rushing to bed as usual, desperate to grab as much sleep as possible, I decided to have a bath, and spent the next half hour luxuriating in deep, soft bubbles, surrounded by scented candles. Climbing out, I wrapped myself in a large fluffy towel and crossed the hallway from the main bathroom to our bedroom, almost jumping out of my skin when Scott appeared from Jacob's nursery.

"You're home?" I said.

"Yes," he replied, looking down at me. "I got home about ten minutes ago and thought I'd check on Jacob. I assumed you'd be asleep."

"I—I was in the bath." I knew I was stammering. I also knew why. I was nervous. By some judicious timing, I'd scrupulously avoided letting Scott see me naked since Jacob's birth. We'd always had sex in the dark – when we'd had the time and energy, and when we weren't fighting – so while his hands may have been familiar with me, his eyes were not. And while I'd lost almost all of the weight that I'd gained during my pregnancy, I wasn't sure if I was ready to face him yet. I knew that if he was disappointed or critical, it was going to hurt.

"So I gathered." His voice was deeper than usual and he moved closer, then reached out and put his hand in the top of my towel, between my breasts. "You look good," he whispered.

I felt myself blush and then yelped as he yanked the towel away, exposing me completely.

"Oh God," he murmured. "You look *really* good. I'd forgotten…"

"You'd forgotten what?" I felt his eyes on me, consuming me; felt the heat rise within me.

"How sexy you are…"

He closed the final gap between us, melding my body to his and kissed me deeply, walking me backwards across the hallway and into our bedroom, kicking the door closed behind him.

Life very much returned to normal after that night. Scott somehow managed to cut his hours, returning home much earlier in the evening and making time for me – and for Jacob. He seemed to want me more than ever and didn't even argue about using a condom, although that too changed within a few weeks, when I reached the decision to stop breastfeeding. I'd done it for over four months and had never really settled to it. It was time to reclaim my life – well my breasts, anyway. I was almost offended by how much Jacob seemed to prefer formula milk from a bottle, but I reasoned that it did make life so much easier. Scott could feed him for one thing, and that meant I could go out more at the weekends and leave them by themselves, which was a godsend, even if only from the perspective of getting my hair cut, or buying shoes or underwear, being as I'd never mastered the art of expressing my milk either, and had taken Jacob everywhere with me since the day he was born. I loved watching the two of them bond though, and there were times when I wondered why I'd bothered to persevere with breastfeeding for so long.

The other advantage, of course, was that I could go back on the pill. And I did. I went to see my GP, and when I told Scott what I'd done, he showed his appreciation in more ways than one.

That first weekend, whenever Jacob was asleep, Scott took me to bed. Well, we didn't always make it to bed, and made use of the sofa, the dining table and the kitchen worktop as well. The point was that he was relentless in both his actions and his words and I loved every moment of it. On the Monday morning, when he left for work, kissing me softly on the forehead and thanking me, in gentle whispers, for a spectacular weekend, I lay in bed, waiting for Jacob to wake and stretched my sore muscles, unable to keep the smile from my lips.

As with most young families, I suppose, we settled into a routine – which was by and large dictated by Jacob. Things were still a little up and down, because I think we were taking a while to adjust to our new lives, but our weekends were the best times of all. We didn't spend them all in bed – or on the sofa, the dining table and the kitchen worktop. We went out as well and did 'family' things together. We went to the zoo, to the park, and on picnics. Every so often our parents would come to visit, or we'd go down to Cornwall to see them. But the weekends were definitely when we had most sex. During the week, I found looking after Jacob by myself more tiring than I would have thought possible, considering he was a baby, and essentially inanimate, and Scott's hours continued to be flexible, at best, so the time he and I spent together between Monday and Friday was limited. To a certain extent, it was a little bit like being at college again and, I'll be honest and admit that there were times when I used to wonder whether I'd been right, whether we should have waited before having Jacob and given ourselves a few years to get to know each other properly. But then I'd just have to look at our gorgeous little boy and know that I wouldn't have changed a thing… not a single a thing.

I surprised myself in the end, and when the time came for me to decide whether or not to return to work, I chose not to. I knew I might be letting my boss down, but she took the news well, and said she understood. I half expected Scott to crow, or at least to be a bit smug, but he just said he thought I'd made the right decision, and I couldn't disagree with him. I was enjoying being a mum, and I wanted to see my son grow, without missing out on any of those landmark moments. But also, when I really thought it through, I realised that the job I'd had in

Bristol had never been the 'dream' job for me. I'd left that behind in Newquay. And, in any case, Scott was earning enough money to keep us comfortably – especially when Chris Nicholson resigned, after only a few months in the job, and the position was immediately offered to Scott. He didn't even have to go through an interview or anything, and when he came home and told me, I could tell how pleased he was. Not only would he be getting a big pay rise, but he felt the satisfaction of knowing he was appreciated. And quite rightly so.

Of course the fact that I was no longer earning meant I had no money of my own. Scott and I had always kept separate bank accounts, with me transferring funds into his to cover my share of the bills, but now he paid for everything. Of course, that meant I had to ask him for money to buy things for myself and Jacob. He never quibbled or even asked what it was for, and just transferred whatever I needed into my account straight away, but I hated doing it and sometimes wished that he would just give me an allowance to make it a little less demeaning. I never asked about that though. Talking about money with Scott was a bit like talking about sex, or his work, or moving into a house with a garden. Invariably it would lead to a disagreement, or even an argument, and for the sake of a little humiliation, it simply wasn't worth it.

Jacob grew quickly and, before we knew it, he was walking and had turned one. As we climbed into bed on the evening of his small party, having wished goodnight to our parents, who'd spoiled him rotten with far too many presents for a one year old, we both wondered where that year had gone. I wanted to be able to say it had been fun, that the memories were all good, but I couldn't, because I could still remember the arguments, the harsh words, and the fear of our marriage disintegrating, which had been all too real on more than one occasion.

"Don't get me wrong," Scott said, settling back on his pillows, "I wouldn't change a hair on Jacob's head, but I'm not in any hurry to do that again."

"What? Have another baby?" I clarified, turning onto my side to face him.

"Hmm," he nodded his head and looked over at me. "You're not getting broody again, are you?"

"No. And in any case, if I remember rightly, I wasn't the one who got broody in the first place. It was you that wanted us to start a family so quickly, not me."

He sighed. "Yes, I suppose it was." I heard the regret in his voice and felt it stab at my heart.

"Well, I'm not ready to have another baby yet," I said, turning onto my back and staring at the ceiling.

"Good," he whispered, and I felt him shift closer, his arm snaking across my waist and his hand moving lower. "I've just got used to having you to myself again… at least for some of the time." He nuzzled into me, his lips grazing over that delicate area of skin beneath my ear. "Why don't we start going out by ourselves a bit more?" he suggested. "Like we used to…"

"How?" I twisted, looking at him.

"We can get a babysitter, can't we?"

I thought about it for a moment. Jacob was sleeping through at night now, going to bed at around eight and not waking up until six or seven the next morning. Going out in the evenings was definitely an option, and maybe it would do us good to be a couple again. I could still recall those first few months after I moved to Bristol when we used to have an active social life. We'd been happy then… really happy.

"I don't see why not," I replied, smiling slightly. "We'd just need to find someone."

"Well," he replied, "I might have the ideal solution for us."

"You might? How?"

"There's a guy at work," he began, "and he's got a daughter."

"How old is she?" I questioned, tensing. I was nervous about leaving Jacob with anyone, but the idea of leaving him with a young stranger was daunting, to put it mildly.

"I think she's eighteen," he said. "She's just started at uni, anyway, and she's evidently looking for something to do with her time…" He left the sentence hanging between us and I looked into his eyes.

"I suppose we could meet her," I allowed, and he smiled and moved on top of me.

Ella turned out to be a huge success. It transpired she was at the University of the West of England, where I'd also studied, and was reading English Literature. Her parents were local, and she'd decided that, rather than wasting her money on accommodation, she'd live at home and study close by. She was a quiet, shy sort of girl and I took to her immediately, as did Jacob, and over the following months, she became a regular feature in our lives, coming over at least once a week to babysit. She didn't mind if we were late home and usually brought some work to do, which kept her occupied. Not once did she call us and interrupt our evenings out, she always seemed to cope, even if Jacob did wake up – which was very unusual indeed – and at the end of the night, after Scott had paid her, he'd drive her home, while I undressed and clambered into bed.

One evening, I got talking to her while Scott was getting ready to take me out, and discovered that she really did love her course, and had a seemingly boundless enthusiasm for Shakespeare, which reminded me of my old friend, Kathy, who I'd lost touch with after college, when she'd gone to university in Edinburgh. There was a sadness about Ella that evening though, and eventually she confided that she was missing her boyfriend. He'd gone to Leeds University, and they were finding the separation difficult to handle – at least Ella was anyway. From what she said, her boyfriend was having a whale of a time in her absence and I noticed the tears in her eyes as she spoke. I didn't want to rub salt into her wounds by telling her that Scott and I had managed to keep our relationship going throughout our time apart at uni, so I made sympathetic noises, and moved the subject on to the book she'd brought with her – which turned out to be Austen's Persuasion, a novel that had remained one of my personal favourites ever since I'd studied it at college, all those years ago. We discussed the ins and outs of the Elliot family until Scott appeared from our bedroom, looking incredibly handsome, even by his high standards, in dark blue jeans and a white casual shirt.

He and I left quite quickly, running a little late for our reservation at the restaurant, and it wasn't long after we'd placed our order that Scott queried Ella's decision to remain at home during her studies.

"I can't understand why she'd do that," he remarked. It seemed like an odd thing for us to be talking about, but I went along with it, always slightly fearful of veering towards any of our more 'dangerous' topics of conversation, like the fact that I desperately wanted us to move to a bigger place, now Jacob was walking.

"Why not?" I countered. "Aside from the costs involved, she's shy. I can see why she'd want to carry on living with her parents."

He smiled, a little pompously perhaps. "She's going to carry on being shy, if she doesn't learn to get out a bit more."

"Maybe she's not the 'getting out' type," I replied, feeling the need to defend my fellow Austen lover.

"Well, I don't know about you," he said, almost ignoring me, "but I felt that moving away from home to go to uni was an important part of growing up."

I wondered about that. I wondered about how grown up Scott really was – even then – but I didn't say anything and, after a moment or two of silence, he continued, "I learned a lot, living by myself."

"You did?" The words were out of my mouth before I could stop them, but I couldn't fail to notice the hesitation before he responded.

"Yes. I learned to cook, to take care of myself…"

"I suppose…"

He could cook, although he didn't do it very often anymore. And as for taking care of himself… I hadn't seen much evidence of that. But then, I supposed he had me to do things for him, so he didn't need to worry. And, in reality, that was fair enough. After all, he was working long hours to earn the money that kept us in a very nice lifestyle. The least I could do was to take care of him.

"Didn't you feel like that?" he asked suddenly, pulling me back to reality.

"No," I replied honestly.

"Seriously?"

"No. I was really nervous about it, and I hated living away from home. I was incredibly lonely at university."

"You were?" He seemed genuinely surprised by that.

"Yes." I looked down at my empty place setting and took a deep breath, trying to pretend that it didn't hurt that he hadn't noticed how difficult I'd found those three years. "I missed you," I added and he smiled, then reached across the table and took my hand in his, giving it a brief, light squeeze before releasing me. "Ella feels the same," I added.

"She misses me?" he joked and I slapped his hand playfully, then let mine rest on his, before he had the chance to pull it away again.

"No, you fool. She misses her boyfriend. She was telling me tonight that he's at uni in Leeds. They're not coping well with the separation."

He smiled again. "Hmm... I guess not everyone can do it. Not everyone knows the secret to long distance relationships, do they?"

I nodded. "I know, but I didn't tell her that. She seemed upset because her boyfriend is having far too much fun without her."

"Too much fun?" Scott frowned, and using the excuse of taking a sip of his drink, extricated his hand from mine. It seemed a few minutes of hand-holding was enough for him. "What does that mean?"

"I'm not sure. Those were Ella's words, but I think she's got it into her head that he's seeing other girls."

"Well, maybe she should take a leaf out of his book," he suggested, like he was giving the matter some serious thought, which surprised me.

"To teach him a lesson?" I asked, wondering if that was such a good idea. It might just make things worse. "Because surely that could end badly. She might be wrong, and if she is..."

He shook his head. "That wasn't what I meant," he said. "What I was trying to say was that they're too young to be in a serious relationship. They should be out enjoying themselves."

"They're the same age we were," I reasoned.

"Yes, but we were different."

I felt myself smiling. "Would you have minded if I'd been out enjoying myself?" I teased, looking into his eyes.

"Too fucking right, I would." His voice was suddenly harsh.

"Scott, please…"

"I know. Don't swear." He sighed, softening again. "Yes, I'd have minded. You're mine."

I felt myself glow with pride as the smile formed on my lips once more. That was the most romantic thing he'd said to me outside of our bedroom, and I leant forward, whispering, "Entirely yours."

He grinned, and then he winked. "I'll make you prove it later." His words brushed across my skin and I shuddered. I actually shuddered.

It was a few months after Jacob's second birthday that I arranged for us all to go down to stay with my parents for the weekend. It was unusually hot, and I felt like a few days by the sea. We'd have a chance to spend some time with Scott's mum and dad as well, and Jacob really loved the beach. Not only that, but being cooped up in the flat was starting to drive me insane. I needed to get out, before I broke out.

I sensed that Scott needed a break too. He'd been working ludicrous hours for the last few months, his role as manager taking its toll, although our personal relationship hadn't suffered that much. Yes, we still bickered from time to time, but I honestly felt that getting out and having some time together in the evenings, away from Jacob and the flat, had been good for us, and Ella had made a real difference to our lives.

On the Thursday evening, after Jacob had gone to bed, I packed our bag for the weekend, looking forward to a few days of relaxation, of feeling the wind in my hair and the sun on my face. We'd planned to leave on the Friday morning, to make a real break of it, and Scott had even booked the day off, which just showed how much he needed to get away, because getting him to take time off work was like getting blood out of a stone.

After I'd packed Jacob's swimming trunks, I went over to my chest of drawers and searched through my own swimwear, wondering if I should take any. I didn't own a one-piece costume anymore, and my bikinis consisted of the three vaguely presentable ones that I'd bought before marrying Scott, and the ones he'd purchased for our honeymoon. I smiled to myself as I remembered the way his eyes had raked over my body when I'd worn them, and how passionately he'd made love to me every night in our beach-side hut, telling me how he'd occasionally caught other men looking at me – even men who had their wives or girlfriends with them – and how he'd liked knowing that I was his… and no-one else's. I shook my head, still smiling, although my smile quickly faded, as I suddenly recalled the way Scott sometimes frowned at my stretch marks. They'd faded, but they were still there, and he clearly didn't approve. He never actually said anything, but the frown was enough. So I closed the drawer, deciding that I probably wouldn't need a swimming costume anyway. After all, I could just paddle with Jacob, in my shorts, couldn't I? It would still be fun. As I zipped up our bag, it dawned on me that I'd never been swimming in the sea at Carven Bay at all, and then, out of nowhere, a distant memory filtered through my mind, of a tall muscular surfer, with dark hair, broad shoulders, and a tattoo on his back, and for a minute or two, I stood and recalled my dreams… my wild fantasies about that man – the wolf man, as I'd come to think of him – and what he'd do to me, or with me. I remembered the feeling of heat, whenever I thought of him. It was a feeling I'd never really experienced with Scott… but then the wolf man was only a fantasy, so none of that counted, did it? And of course, I couldn't forget the overwhelming disappointment when he hadn't arrived at the beach, and how let down I'd felt. I sat on the edge of the bed then and allowed myself to wonder how different my life might have been if the wolf man had been there. Would he have kissed me? Would he have wanted me? I shivered as I thought of him, but then I quickly banished those thoughts and got up again, taking a deep breath. Things may not always have been perfect with Scott, and we may have had our differences over the years, but he was there. He was reliable. More reliable than the wolf man, anyway.

Smiling to myself again, I put the bag down on the floor by the bedroom door, and started to look forward to our long weekend together, putting all thoughts of wild surfers out of my mind, once and for all.

Scott was really late home that Thursday, but I'd expected that, knowing he'd have things to finish before taking the day off, and I was just getting ready for bed when he came in. I knew at once, though, just from the look on his face, that something was wrong.

"What is it?" I asked, as he stood in the doorway to our bedroom, looking over at me.

"I'm so sorry," he murmured.

"Why? What's happened?"

"I'm not going to be able to make it this weekend."

I flopped down onto the bed, overcome with disappointment. "Why?"

He came over, pushing his fingers back through his hair, and sat beside me. "There's been a major cock up at work, and I'm going to have to work the weekend to fix it." He sighed deeply. "If I don't, it'll cost the company thousands, maybe millions of pounds... and I'll probably lose my job."

"Seriously?"

He nodded. "Yep. The mistake isn't mine exactly, but it happened within my department, and that makes it my responsibility." I could hear the worry in his voice, and leant into him.

"Oh, Scott. Look, I'll cancel the weekend, and we'll stay here."

"No." He turned to face me. "You've been looking forward to this for ages, and I know Mum and Dad can't wait to see Jacob. And there's no point in you staying here. I'll be at work anyway."

I saw the sense in what he was saying and nodded my head as he puts his arm around me. "I'll miss you," I said softly.

"I'll miss you too. And I was thinking that, maybe, when you get back, we could start looking at houses."

"Houses?" I leant back, staring into his face.

"Yes, ones with gardens." He smiled down at me, and I smiled back, right before he kissed me.

The next day, Scott left for work very early, kissing me goodbye, even though I wasn't properly awake, and telling me he'd see me on Sunday evening. He suggested I send him a text message when I arrived at my parents' house, because he wasn't sure he'd be able to take phone calls, although he promised he'd make up for missing out on our weekend when I got back. And then he was gone.

I decided there was no point in lounging around in bed. We were due to leave at ten, and even though Scott was no longer going with us, I saw no reason to change our plans. And if there was one thing that having a baby had taught me, it was that time went nowhere, so I got up and showered before Jacob woke, and then, after breakfast, I spent a few minutes removing all of Scott's things from our holdall, before getting Jacob dressed.

I quickly tidied the flat, putting Jacob's toys away, and cleaning the kitchen, so Scott didn't have to worry about any of that when he came home, and then at ten on the dot, we set off. It was a really warm day and I was grateful for the air conditioning in the car as I was certain Jacob would have been complaining about being hot otherwise.

The journey was going well, and we'd been on the road for nearly half an hour, when he piped up from the back seat, asking where 'Whisper' was. 'Whisper' was his favourite teddy bear, dark brown in colour, with a growler inside that made a sort of whispering sound when you tilted him – which was how he'd got his name.

"He's beside you, Jacob," I replied. "On the back seat."

There was a short pause, before he said, "No, Mummy."

"Yes, darling. You just need to look."

"No."

I wondered if that meant he wasn't going to look, or that Whisper wasn't there, but I'd just passed a sign that said there was a parking lay-by half a mile ahead, so I slowed and indicated, pulling in.

"Let me come and find him," I said, getting out of the car and opening the back door. I searched the seat, and then the floor, and under the seats, in the front footwell, and finally in the boot, before I reached the conclusion that Whisper wasn't anywhere in the car.

"When did you last have him?" I asked, closing the boot and going back to Jacob, leaning in to him. His bottom lip was trembling and he shook his head. "Don't worry." I did my best to hug him, even though he was strapped into his car seat. "We'll find him."

"Where?" he whimpered.

"We'll... we'll go home and find him."

"Now?" he said and I nodded, because I knew it was pointless trying to explain that Whisper really was just a teddy bear, and that he had two others in the car, and several at my mum and dad's, that were just as good. The point was, they weren't Whisper, and without him, the weekend was going to be a disaster.

I climbed back in behind the wheel, but before setting off, I called my mother. I'd already sent her a text earlier in the morning, telling her that Scott wasn't going to be able to come with us, and I didn't want her to worry about any more changes of plans. She answered promptly, sounding concerned.

"Is everything alright?" she asked.

"Yes. We got away on time, but we've just realised we've forgotten Whisper."

"Oh dear..." I could hear the smile in her voice and knew she'd understand.

"It'll only take us about thirty minutes to get home and pick him up, but we'll be a bit later than expected. I thought I'd let you know so you don't worry."

"Thank you, sweetheart," she said. "Take care, won't you?"

"Of course."

We ended our call, and I pulled out of the parking bay, driving along to the next exit on the dual carriageway, before turning back, cursing myself for being so keen to leave that morning, I hadn't thought to check the car more carefully.

Luckily, the drive back to Bristol didn't take very long at all, but rather than bothering to park in our designated space beneath the block, I used one of the visitor's ones at the front, and taking Jacob from his seat, carried him in through the front entrance.

He didn't normally like to be carried very much by that stage, having become accustomed to walking, but I think the upset of not being able to find Whisper was too much for him and he let me take him to the front door, before I put him down so I could let us into the flat.

Once inside, we discovered Whisper straight away, lying on his back on the sofa, looking rather neglected, and Jacob ran straight over and picked him up, hugging him tight.

"Just sit down for a moment," I murmured to him. "Mummy needs to go to the toilet. I'll only be a minute." It was one of those situations where I knew if I didn't go, I'd end up having to stop within the hour, and I really just wanted to get back on the road, our weekend already ebbing away.

Jacob nodded and clambered up onto the sofa, Whisper still held firmly in his grip, not about to be left behind again, as I went down the hallway to the bathroom. It was just as I put my hand on the bathroom door handle, that I heard the noise coming from behind me... from our bedroom, and I flipped around, my heart filled with fear. Jacob and I were alone in the flat, and it sounded like there was an intruder. What should I do? Call the police? Call Scott? My phone was in the living room, in my bag, along with my son... and I was frozen to the spot, until I heard a familiar grunting noise, and then a female whimper and I realised exactly what I was hearing, and that it had nothing to do with an intruder.

Slowly, gingerly, my heart pounding, I took the two paces to cross the hallway and, as quietly as I possibly could, I opened the bedroom door, my heart stopping and then breaking, as I looked at the sight of my husband thrusting in and out of the lithe female figure, lying on the bed, her legs raised high and wide. As I took another step into the room, she became more visible, her face coming into sight, and I saw who she was, letting out an involuntary gasp.

The sound alerted Scott, but even so, he took a moment to react, to turn away from Ella and look at me, the shock on his face obvious, the colour draining, even in that split second before I turned and ran from the room.

I didn't hesitate, not even for a moment, but I grabbed my bag, and Jacob, and fled, leaving the front door wide open as we ran down the corridor, ignoring the lifts and taking the stairs, my footsteps echoing in my own ears.

I unlocked the car as I approached and strapped Jacob into his seat, my hands shaking as I struggled to fit the buckles, until I forced myself to take a deep breath, calmed and then completed my task, kissing his forehead, before jumping into the driver's seat and setting off again.

How I drove to Carven Bay, I don't really know. But I did. My memories of the journey are hazy though, mingled with images of Scott and Ella writhing on our bed, the noises of their love-making surrounding me, even as we pulled up on my parents' driveway.

Mum and Dad came out to greet us, smiling and happy, and I knew I'd have to put on the performance of a lifetime. I couldn't possibly tell them what was wrong, what I'd just witnessed, only a couple of hours earlier. My dad would probably want to jump in his own car and drive straight back to Bristol to give Scott a piece of his mind, and being as he was in his late sixties by that stage, I didn't think it would be a very sensible idea. So, I plastered a smile on my face and climbed out of the car.

"What's wrong?" my mother asked, pulling me into a hug.

"Nothing. I'm just tired."

She leant back and looked at me, and I wondered if she believed me. Whether she did or not, I never found out, because Dad had released Jacob from his seat, and he came running over, wanting a hug from Granny, and she wasn't about to make him wait.

Mum had made a salad for lunch, knowing we were going to be delayed and while she cut up some cold meat for Jacob and Dad helped him to tomatoes and cucumber, I sat and stared into space, wondering what had become of my life… and what the hell I was going to do about my future.

After lunch, we cleared away and, as much as I longed to be alone, to have some time to think, I was scared of where my thoughts might lead me, so when Mum and Dad suggested a walk, I went along with the idea, and we put Jacob into his pushchair and headed out.

Although it was warm, the wind was blowing hard and we set off along the cliff path, chatting along the way about this and that. Mum asked after Scott, but I batted aside her enquiry, saying he was busy, and letting the subject drop, before Dad, who was pushing Jacob, turned the conversation around to the fact that they'd recently had solar panels installed on their roof, and how energy efficient they were proving. I wanted to pay attention, and I honestly tried to, because ordinarily anything that helped the environment would have been something that interested me, but my mind was racing and my heart was broken. My marriage was disintegrating; the man I thought I knew, the man I thought I loved, was a complete stranger to me, and there was nothing I could do about it.

After an hour or so, we decided to head back to the house where, Mum informed Jacob, she'd got a chocolate cake waiting for us. He was overjoyed and I managed a smile at his reaction as we walked back.

I was in such a daze, that we were almost at the driveway before I noticed Scott's car, parked at the front of the house.

"Oh, look," Mum said, sounding surprised, and I raised my head, my heart stopping before she'd finished her sentence. "It's Scott."

He got out of the car as we approached, his eyes fixed on mine. I could see the worry – bordering on fear – ingrained there and I looked down, unwilling to even acknowledge him.

"We weren't expecting you," my dad said, greeting him, and Scott smiled, although how he managed that was beyond me.

"Yes, I got finished earlier than expected, so I decided I'd come down and see you all." Even though I was still staring at the footpath, I could feel his eyes on me as we turned onto the driveway.

"Well, that's a lovely surprise," Mum added, opening the door to let us all in, my dad entering first with the pushchair, and Mum following, leaving me at the rear.

As I went to climb up the doorstep, Scott grabbed my arm, but I glared at him and pulled away.

"Don't touch me," I hissed as quietly as I could.

"We need to talk," he murmured.

"No, we don't."

"At least listen to what I've got to say."

I shook my head and went inside, leaving him to follow if he wanted to. Frankly, I couldn't have cared less what he did.

In the hallway, Dad was struggling to fold Jacob's pushchair, so I took over, grateful for something to do, even though I was aware of Scott's presence right behind me, and as I stood, he grabbed me again.

"Come for a walk with me," he whispered, although it was more by way of an instruction than an invitation.

"No." I pulled away and went into the living room.

"Shall I make the tea?" Mum suggested.

"Actually, do you mind if Jenna and I go for a walk?" Scott said, and I felt like I wanted to scream. How dare he manipulate me?

"We've only just got back from one," Dad pointed out.

"Precisely," I said and both of my parents looked at me, no doubt as surprised by my reluctance as they were by the tone of my voice.

"I know," Scott replied. "But something cropped up at work today and Jenna and I need to discuss it."

"Oh? Nothing serious, I hope?" Dad said.

"Hopefully not." Scott managed another smile. "But we do need to talk."

"Well, why don't you just go down to the beach?" Mum suggested. "It should be fairly quiet down there now."

Scott nodded and held out his hand to me. I looked at it, and then at him, and realised I wasn't going to be able to say 'no' to him, not in front of my parents, anyway.

"Will you be alright with Jacob?" I asked my mother.

"Of course we will." She smiled.

"Don't give him too much chocolate cake," I said. "He'll be bouncing off the walls."

She grinned. "I promise."

With that, I turned and left the room, ignoring Scott and going straight out of the front door. He followed closely behind me, catching me up and walking by my side. Neither of us said a word though, and although Scott went to take the path that led down to the beach, I turned the other way and went onto the clifftop again, stopping at a fairly secluded spot and turning to face him.

"Well?" I said, folding my arms and looking up at him.

"I'm sorry," he said.

"Is that it? You're sorry? I catch you in bed with our babysitter and you're sorry?"

I could feel my anger rising and took a breath, struggling to control myself.

"Yes," he said. "Can you forgive me?"

"No, of course I can't. I—I thought I could trust you." Tears welled in my eyes and I blinked them away, refusing to give him the satisfaction of showing him how much he'd hurt me. "I thought you loved me."

"I do."

"Oh, shut up, Scott. The only person you love is yourself."

"That's not true. I made a mistake, Jenna. It was a one-off. Ella came round because she thought she'd left a book at the flat, and she came onto me…"

"And you forgot the minor detail that you're married, did you? Don't treat me like an idiot, Scott."

"I'm not."

"Yes, you are. Ella knew we were going away today. She knew we wouldn't be at home, which means she had no reason to come to the flat, unless you'd already arranged to meet her there. You didn't have to work the weekend at all, did you? You were going to spend it with her."

He stared at me for what seemed like forever, and then blinked a couple of times and let out a long sigh. "Okay," he said, "it wasn't a one-off."

"How long has it been going on for?" I asked.

"About six or seven months, I suppose."

"Are you kidding me?" I took a step away and turned my back on him, looking up at the sky, until I felt his hands on my shoulders and flipped around. "Don't touch me!" I yelled.

"Sorry." He held up his hands. "It was a mistake though. I don't want to lose you."

"Then maybe you should have thought about that before you took our teenage babysitter to bed."

I huffed out a sigh and turned away again, unable to bear the sight of him. I thought about all the nights he'd told me he'd been working late, all the lies… and months of deceit…

"Wait a minute…" I turned back to face him. "You say it's been going on for six or seven months?"

"Yes." He nodded his head.

"And is that why you've been working late?"

He nodded again. "I… I used to meet her at hotels after work some evenings, just for a few hours. But we'd decided we wanted to spend some more time together, so this weekend seemed like a good opportunity."

"Oh, did it now?" He'd missed the point completely, and I wasn't about to let him get away with that. "What you seem to have forgotten, Scott, is that you've been working long hours, on and off, for years… certainly a lot longer than six or seven months, so my question to you is… Is Ella your first mistress? Or have there been others?"

He blushed and bit his bottom lip, and I knew I'd hit on the truth.

Folding my arms again, in an attempt to protect myself, I squared up to him. "If you want my forgiveness," I said, trying to sound sincere. "If you want even a chance for our marriage to survive, then you have to tell me the truth. And I mean all of it."

"All of it?" he murmured.

"Yes. I want to know everything. If you lie to me, you won't see me, or Jacob, ever again."

His eyes widened and he took a step back, turning away and focusing on something in the distance, before he looked back at me, his face serious and unreadable. "Okay," he said. "I'll tell you. But only because you've asked me to."

I nodded my head, mentally bracing myself for what was to come, because as much as I wanted to know the depth of his deceit, something told me it was going to be bad.

"So, there have been others, before Ella?" I asked, although I already knew the answer to my question.

"Yes," he replied.

"When was the first?"

He paused and then looked down at his feet. "When we were at college, when you were holding out on me."

I was stunned. So long ago… "H—Holding out on you? I don't understand. What are you talking about?"

He looked up again, gazing at me. "Don't you remember?" He seemed surprised. "You only used to let me go so far and then you'd stop me. Do you have any idea how frustrating that was? I needed you, and you kept saying 'no'."

"Yes, because I wasn't ready."

"Maybe you weren't. But I was."

"So you went with someone else?" I could hear the crack in my voice and I coughed to try and cover it.

"Yes."

"When? I—I mean when did you find the time? We were together every weekend."

"There are seven days in a week, Jenna." His voice was so patronising.

"But you were so serious about studying…"

"Yes. But wanting you and not being able to have you was driving me insane. I couldn't concentrate on anything. So Lois used to come round a couple of afternoons a week. It was enough. Just to take the edge off. It wasn't easy, waiting for you, you know."

Lois? I didn't recognise the name. Not that I cared. "But you didn't wait, did you?" I pointed out the obvious.

He shrugged his shoulders and looked away again. "I don't know what you're worrying about. She didn't mean anything. And if you hadn't made me wait in the first place, it wouldn't have happened, would it?"

I wanted to yell at him that I hadn't been 'making' him do anything. I'd been asking him to wait for me, because I thought he loved me, and that's what people do.

"I'm going to assume that once we started having sex, you stopped seeing this Lois?" He blinked rapidly but didn't reply. "Scott?"

"I stopped seeing her, yes. But…"

He left his sentence hanging, but it didn't take a genius to work out what he wasn't saying. "You started seeing someone else?"

"I didn't actually have sex with her," he said quickly, as though that justified what he'd done. "But she was… well, a bit more accommodating than you."

"Excuse me? When was I ever not accommodating? What the hell did this girl do for you that I didn't?"

"She swallowed, Jenna." He shrugged his shoulders, staring at me. "And that was all we did."

"You mean she did that for you, and you didn't do anything for her?" I knew Scott could be selfish, but…

"No," he replied, sounding a bit condescending. "I mean, I reciprocated. Obviously."

Obviously. It took me a few moments to recover from hearing that, knowing that using his tongue was the only way he'd ever been able to pleasure me, and I stared out to sea, trying not to picture the scene he'd just painted and the intimacy it implied… between him and someone else,

"So, was that it?" I asked, eventually. "A couple of girls at college?" He shook his head slowly. "Are you saying there were more?"

"Yes."

"When?"

"While we were at uni."

"You mean the three years when we told each other that we were strong enough to stay together, even though we were apart?"

He lowered his gaze again. "I found it harder than I thought, being away from you," he mumbled, his voice barely audible.

"And you think I didn't? I told you how lonely I got… but I didn't sleep with anyone else," I fumed.

"I tried to stay faithful, Jenna." He sounded whiney, pleading, and pathetic. Just like he always had done, really. Only I'd ignored it… until now. "I did… honestly. But there were a lot of temptations. Most of the guys I knew were sleeping around, and I didn't like being the only one who went home on his own every night. In the end, I decided that, if you didn't know about it, then it didn't count."

"How many were there then?" I asked.

"I can't remember. And anyway, what does it matter? It's in the past… ancient history."

"How many?" I raised my voice.

"I don't know… half a dozen." I felt like the ground was shifting, falling from under me. "Maybe eight… ten."

"Ten?" I whispered.

"We were apart for three years. And none of them meant anything, Jenna. Not like being with you."

"And what happened in America?" I asked, wanting to get it over with, now, so I could crawl away and lick my wounds. The wounds I was vowing, even then, that I'd never let him see. "We were apart for much longer periods then," I added. "So how many women did you have while you were there?"

"Just the one," he said.

"Don't lie to me."

He shook his head. "I'm not. Her name was Mandy…"

"You mean… you had a relationship?"

"I suppose you could call it that, yes. We didn't live together or anything, but she used to stay over at weekends sometimes and I didn't see anyone else but her, so I suppose if that qualifies as a relationship…" His voice faded and he looked at me, seemingly unashamed.

"So you were actually faithful – to her, if not to me?"

"Don't be like that, Jenna. It wasn't like there was any emotion involved. Well, not for me, anyway."

"Was there any emotion involved for her?" I asked.

"She said she loved me a couple of times… you know, in the heat of the moment," he muttered. "But I never said it back… I promise." He seemed to think his promises counted for something, which they didn't. Not anymore.

"Did she know about me?" I managed to ask, reeling.

"Of course she bloody didn't," he said, as though that was the stupidest question in the world.

"And is that why we never went anywhere when I came to stay with you?" He had the decency to look away now. "I see…" I muttered. "And what did she think you were doing while I was there?"

"I told her I was busy at work," he explained.

"Sounds familiar," I mumbled, almost to myself.

"Look… there's no need to be like that about it. I ended it with her about six weeks before I came home," he said eventually. "That's when I started looking into renting the flat, so we could move in together. I didn't want to be with her, Jenna… or anyone else. I wanted to be with you."

"Really? You expect me to believe that?" I snapped. "Given that you've spent our entire relationship cheating on me?"

He narrowed his eyes. "I know none of this is going to be easy for you to accept, but like I said, you wanted to know the details, so don't act so surprised when you hear them… and don't be so bloody judgemental. It doesn't suit you."

"I'll be whatever I please. I'll act however I please. You don't get to tell me what to do. Ever again." He went to speak, but I held up my hand and, much to my surprise, he stopped. "So, after Mandy – after you came home – then what happened?"

"You moved into the flat with me and everything was fine."

I could tell from the tone of his voice that he was still hiding something, so I persevered. "Until…?"

"Do we really have to keep doing this?" he asked. "Haven't we gone through enough? Why don't we just stop now, and…"

"No!" I shouted. "I told you. You either tell me everything, or forget it."

He sucked in a breath. "Okay. There was one more, before Ella."

"When?" I already knew the answer, but I wanted him to tell me. I don't know why, because I knew it was going to hurt – maybe more than all the rest. Even so, I had to hear it.

"When you were pregnant."

I'd been right, but hearing him say it cut through me like a knife.

"When I was pregnant…" I whispered.

"Yeah. Once you got really fat, I… I just found that such a turn off, but I still needed sex. I can't help that, Jenna. It's part of who I am. You know that."

"So what happened?"

"I had an affair with someone from the office. Juliet in marketing…" Did he think I cared what she did for a living?

"Are you still seeing her as well?" I asked, the bitterness rising in my throat and almost choking me.

"No. I ended it with her a few months after Jacob was born."

"Were you with her, that night when you stayed out?" I asked him, remembering our argument.

"No," he said.

"So you'd ended it by then?"

"Well… no. But when I called her to see if I could go to her place, she was busy, so I just drove around, thinking," he admitted and I shook my head, unable to even bring myself to get angry anymore.

"Thinking," I repeated, finding that a little hard to believe.

"Yes," he replied. "You were being really difficult at the time, Jenna. I'm not sure you appreciate how hard it was living with you back then." I swallowed down his insult. "But then after that night… the night when you came out of the bathroom looking so damn sexy… well, I knew I had to end it with Juliet. I think I'd kind of forgotten how hot you actually are, what with all the pregnancy bullshit, and all the nappies, and breastfeeding, and tiredness, and the arguments, and everything… but seeing how incredible you looked… well, you were like all my dreams come true, all over again. I wasn't willing to risk losing you."

"Oh, I see. And that's why you ended up in bed with Ella, is it?"

"That wasn't supposed to happen," he said, sounding harsher than I'd expected; as though somehow the situation was my fault. "We were thrown together…"

"You and Ella?"

He nodded. "I used to take her home each time she babysat for Jacob, remember?"

"Of course I do."

"Well, I don't know if you recall the trouble she was having with her boyfriend, but one night, on the way home, she told me that they'd split up. She was upset and I was just comforting her, trying to make her feel better."

"I'm sure you were."

He glared at me. "I wasn't doing anything wrong. I'd just put my arm around her, that's all. And then she looked up at me and told me that she liked me. And before I knew what had happened, we were kissing… and one thing led to another…"

"In our car? You had sex with her in our car?"

"In *my* car, yes."

"Scott, we use your car for family outings, for taking Jacob out. It's our car… and you had sex with the babysitter in there?"

"Yes. Obviously it wasn't very practical – or comfortable for that matter – so once it became a more regular thing, we started using hotel rooms instead."

"And you've been seeing her ever since, while I've welcomed her into our home and let her care for our son?"

He didn't reply for a moment, but then he looked away, staring up the path, even though there was nothing to see there, other than the ending of my life, as I knew it. "Yes. I'll admit that I did try to give her up a couple of months back, but she got really upset about it."

"Oh, that's sad. I mean, we can't have Ella getting upset, can we?" He stared at me, but wisely kept quiet, and eventually I continued, "Can I get this straight? Since we got together, when I was sixteen, you've been with at least fifteen other women? Is that right?"

I could see him doing the calculation in his head, even though I'd been adding them up as we went along. "Yes, but none of them meant anything. I didn't love them."

"Not even Ella?"

"No. It's just sex. Nothing more. It's you I really want. You must know that by now. I mean… you might not always give me what I need, but sex with you is still better than with any of the others. You've always been the best, and the fact that I've stuck by you, just goes to show how much I love you."

His voice had softened and he moved closer. I took a step back.

"I'm sorry."

He smiled. "Hey… it's okay. You don't have to be sorry. Like I just said, I know this isn't easy for you, but maybe it's a good thing that it's all come out. Maybe now you know, we can work out the problems… build a new future together. And I'll stop seeing Ella too."

"Will you?" I laced my response with sarcasm. "You'll do that for me?"

"If you'll agree to put this behind us, and not be silly about it, then of course I will."

I shook my head. "You're bargaining with me?"

"No…" He looked confused.

"I think you misunderstood me when I said sorry." I stood firm, glaring at him. "I wasn't apologising. I was saying that I feel sorry for you. I'm sorry that you're such a shallow, insecure, pathetic excuse of a man, and I'm especially sorry that I've wasted the last ten years of my life on you."

He grabbed my arm, but I wrenched free of him in an instant, then glared even harder at him. "You don't get to touch me," I hissed. "Not now. Not ever. I'm not yours. And very soon, I'll make sure of that… legally."

"What do you mean?" he whispered, paling.

"I mean that I'll be consulting a solicitor on Monday morning and filing for divorce as soon as I can. And now, I suggest you go home to Bristol, or to your parents' house. Either way, you're not coming back with me. You're not welcome."

"Wait a minute," he said, going to reach out for me again, even though I pulled back quickly enough to stop him. "You said if I told you everything, then our marriage would be okay."

"Yes. I lied. It's a concept you should be familiar with by now. You've been doing it for years. I wanted to know what you'd done, Scott. I wanted you to tell me the truth for once in your life and I thought that might just work. It did. And now I know the sort of man you are, I have no interest in seeing you… ever again."

"Listen," he said, raising his voice, "just because I have different sexual needs from you doesn't give you the right to judge me."

"It's got nothing to do with sexual needs. Nothing at all. The problem here, Scott – apart from your spectacular selfishness – is that you have no moral compass. None whatsoever. Just think about it… you said you'd end things with Ella, if I agreed not to be silly over your multiple affairs. But hasn't it occurred to you that, if you really wanted to make things work with me, you'd have ended it with her already? I mean, obviously, if you really loved me and wanted me, you'd never have started any of the affairs in the first place, but the very least you should have done is to end your relationship with her before coming to see me today… which you clearly haven't done. And that, Scott, just goes to prove how completely selfish and amoral you really are. You think you can just take whatever you want, from whoever you want, regardless of the consequences." I swallowed down my threatening tears, and continued, "You've wasted ten years of my life and I'm just sorry that I let you do that to me. But I did, because I loved you. And I was stupid enough to think you loved me too."

"I did. I do."

"No you don't," I yelled, exasperated. "Because if you did, you'd have put me first. That's what people do when they're in love."

He was staring at me, but I could tell he was lost for words, floundering; and I had no intention of helping him. Not this time.

"Oh my God…" Another truth of the situation suddenly dawned on me. "How many of these women have you had unprotected sex with? How much danger have you put me in?"

"None," he shouted. "I'm not an idiot. The only woman I've done that with is you – when you've been on the pill."

I stared at him, remembering his hatred of condoms, and wondering if he was telling the truth, resolving there and then to get myself checked over as soon as possible, just as I recalled that night… the night we first had sex after Jacob was born, and I'd had to remind him to use a condom. He'd gone to fetch one from somewhere else in the flat, and at the time, I remembered thinking it was odd. Of course… it made sense, when I thought about it. They were probably in his briefcase, or his jacket, where he kept them on hand to use with Juliet, or whatever her name was. They weren't in the bathroom cabinet at all. For a moment, I felt sick, wondering how many other signs I'd missed…

I thought about asking him, quizzing him on whether his promotions were real, whether his stress at work had been genuine, or just an excuse to browbeat me when I wanted something he wasn't willing to give – namely a piece of himself. I wondered about asking whether he'd ever really loved me at all. But I decided I wouldn't give him the satisfaction of seeing how broken I really was by what he'd done.

Turning away, I took a couple of paces back towards my parents' house, but he grabbed me, pulling me back hard, making it impossible to get away.

"Let me go!"

"No. You're mine. We're married, remember?"

"Not for much longer. Let me go, Scott. And stay away from me, and from Jacob."

He released me then, but moved closer, his body almost touching mine, anger pouring from him.

"You won't take my son away from me," he whispered, his voice more menacing than I'd ever heard it before.

"Watch me. If you think I'm letting you anywhere near him after this, you can think again."

"If you try and keep him from me, I'll fight you for custody. And I'll win."

I felt the life drain from me, my legs turning to jelly. "You'd do that?"

"If you try and keep him from me, yes."

I could see in his eyes that he meant it. "My solicitors will be in touch," I murmured and started walking back down the path.

"No man's ever going to want you," he called after me. "You'll be on your own for the rest of your life if you leave me."

I turned then, facing him once more. "But I thought I was better than all the others, Scott," I taunted, sarcastically. "You said I was the best."

"Ha! I lied," he yelled. "You were useless in bed, just like you're a useless mother… and I'll prove that when I take Jacob from you."

I stumbled away from him, the footpath blurring beneath my feet as his threats echoed around my head.

I would fight him for Jacob. Of course I would. I'd fight him until my dying breath. And as for his other words – his other insults – they meant nothing. What did I care if other men didn't want me? With every step I took away from him, I was already starting to construct a thick wall around myself, which I hoped would protect me from ever having to feel like that again, and the thought of letting another man in, of trusting another man, of loving another man, was beyond my wildest imaginings. While I didn't like the idea of being alone, I welcomed the isolation, if it meant I didn't have to face feeling so foolish and lost and dejected, ever again.

Part Three

Jenna & Adam

Chapter Seven

Jenna

I sit on the soft, comfortable sofa in my small living room, the curtains drawn against the pelting rain, a half finished book resting by my side, a glass of chilled white wine in my hand, and soft music playing in the background, and for a moment, life doesn't seem too bad.

That is, until I remember the torture of the last few years, and have to take a large gulp of Pinot Grigio, just to calm my nerves and stem the tears that seem to have become my constant companions. I'm not crying over my broken marriage, or the heartache Scott put me through. I'm crying because it just never seems to end. Even now, despite the fact that it's nearly four years since I discovered that I'd wasted so much of my life on that man, his influence is still ever-present, like a dark cloud hanging over me, a permanent reminder of that terrible time...

As I watched Scott drive away from my parents' house that afternoon, tyres screeching, I realised I'd have to tell them something. They were bound to want to know why Scott had left so abruptly, without bothering to say goodbye, even to his son. And I knew I'd have to explain why Jacob and I suddenly needed somewhere to stay. So, I went back inside, and told them that Scott and I hadn't really been talking about something that had 'cropped up at work', but about his affair with our babysitter. I couldn't tell them about all the others, because I hadn't yet had time to process that myself, but I told them about Ella, and that I'd found her and Scott in bed together earlier that day. My dad was angry. My mum asked why I hadn't said anything when I'd arrived. Together, they were shocked and disappointed in Scott, but they were also supportive, which didn't surprise me in the least. Then, while Mum got on with cooking the dinner, Dad kept Jacob entertained, which left me free to search the Internet for a solicitor. There was never a doubt for any of us that I was going to divorce him. Even though they didn't know the full extent of Scott's deception, his behaviour was unacceptable, and as far as we were all concerned, if I never saw him again, it would be too soon.

It became clear by Sunday morning, however, that I was going to have to go back to Bristol fairly soon. I was going to have to collect some more clothes, and Jacob's toys, so I steeled myself on Sunday afternoon and, after lunch, I sent Scott a text message, keeping it brief and telling him I'd be there the following afternoon at two, that I'd let myself in and take what I needed, and that he needn't bother being there himself.

"I'll come with you," Dad said.

"I'll be fine."

"I'm still coming." He took a deep breath. "Just in case."

I smiled, blinking back my tears, grateful that I didn't have to make the journey alone, and looking at my parents, sitting on the sofa opposite me, I realised I didn't have to do any of it alone. They would support me, come what may.

It took Scott over two hours to reply to my message, and I was fairly sure I knew what had caused the delay – not that I cared anymore. He could do what he liked, with whoever he liked, as far as I was concerned.

— I've already changed the locks. I'll meet you here at four.

I clutched my phone tight, anger boiling inside me.

"What's wrong?" Mum asked.

I couldn't speak, so I showed her my phone.

"That man," she murmured, aware of Jacob, who was playing with his cars on the carpet in front of us. She passed the phone to Dad, who frowned, then looked over at me.

"We'll go at four," he said softly.

"Why should we?" I asked, still angry.

"Because you need to choose your battles. And this isn't one of them. It makes no difference to us what time we go there, but he thinks it does… so, let him think he's won for now."

I nodded my head. "Okay."

He came and sat beside me then, handing back my phone. "I think this is going to be a long game," he said, a little cryptically, although to me, it didn't feel like a game at all.

It felt very strange, knocking on my own front door, rather than letting myself in, but I did, and we waited, my dad standing right behind me, until it was yanked open sharply by Scott.

He glared at me, and then at my dad.

"Can we come in?" I said.

He didn't reply, but stepped aside and we entered the flat that, until just a few days ago, had been my home.

"I was hoping we could talk." His voice was gruff, and as we moved forward into the living area, he blocked the way to the bedrooms, where I needed to go to pack our clothes. "I've taken time off to be here."

"Well, you needn't have bothered. And if you hadn't changed the locks, you wouldn't have had to. We don't have anything to talk about, Scott. I've just come to pick up our things."

His eyes narrowed. "So you're really going ahead with this?"

"If you mean the divorce, then yes, I am."

He turned to my dad. "Can't you talk some sense into her?" he muttered.

"The only person with no sense around here is you," my dad replied, his voice quite calm. "Now, I suggest you move out of the way and let Jenna get on."

Scott huffed out a sigh and moved, and I made short work of packing a large suitcase with as many clothes as I could fit into it, working out that I had no intention of coming back again, and would just have to replace whatever I couldn't take with me, before moving on to Jacob's room and emptying it of all his clothes and toys, into the holdall and bags that Dad and I had brought with us.

"I'll start taking this lot down to the car," Dad said, coming into Jacob's room, where I was kneeling on the floor by his chest of drawers.

"Thanks."

He took the two largest bags and disappeared, as I continued packing.

"I see you're taking everything." Scott's voice slithered across my skin, like an oily snake.

"Of Jacob's, yes…"

"You won't take him from me," he warned, standing above me.

"Don't threaten me, Scott."

"I'm not. I'm telling you." He crouched down beside me now, his body close to mine. "I'll make your life a living hell if you fuck with me."

"Don't—"

"If I want to swear, then I'll fucking well swear. What's it got to do with you anymore? You're leaving me, remember?"

"Yes, because you cheated," I hissed, turning to face him and wondering what I'd ever seen in him, why I'd ever loved him. "You slept with every woman you ever met…"

He smirked. "Not every woman, Jenna… only the ones who I knew would be better than you… although that wasn't difficult."

"Oh, shut up, Scott."

"Truth hurts, does it? If you must know, they were all better than you… all of them."

"In that case, I wonder why you kept coming back to me, and why it was you who wanted to save our marriage," I countered, and he blinked a few times, unable to think of a suitable riposte, I assumed. "But I don't care either way, Scott; they're welcome to you."

My dad knocked on the door again at that point and Scott went to let him in, leaving me shaking with anger, and humiliation.

I packed as quickly as I could and we got out of there before he could say anything else, and I let Dad drive home, although we'd only got just over half way when the text messages started.

"Is that Scott?" Dad asked after the fourth time my phone beeped.

"Yes."

"What's he saying?"

I looked down at my phone, my hand trembling. "He says he's going to take Jacob, that he'll make me homeless, that he'll make you and Mum homeless, that he'll see to it that I can never get another job…" I turned to face Dad, my eyes filling with tears. "It goes on…"

"He can't do any of that," Dad reasoned. "But show the messages to the solicitor when you meet her tomorrow. She'll know what to do."

I nodded, relieved that I'd been able to get an appointment with the lawyer so soon, and hopeful that, despite his threats, Jacob and I would soon be free of Scott.

My hopes were ill-founded. Of course they were. Admittedly my solicitor – a lovely woman called Annabelle – was able to stop Scott from sending the text messages, by issuing a 'cease and desist' letter, which I was surprised to find he obeyed. But as for the rest, Scott did everything he could to make my life as difficult as possible. The one saving grace was that at least we didn't have a property to fight over… we just had a two year old son. A two year old son who I was desperately trying to protect from the man I'd once thought I loved, and the mess he'd created.

One of those messes was that I didn't have any money of my own. I'd gone to Scott for everything, and been completely dependent. And, with hindsight, I started to think he'd liked it that way. But those days were over. So almost as soon as I moved back to Carven Bay, I plucked up my courage and approached Trevor Cole, my old boss at Cole and Simpson, and found that – unlike Scott – he was as good as his word, and was willing to welcome me back, thank goodness. And so, I started working again, which meant that at least I had some money coming in. Mum and Dad were very generously helping to finance my legal fees, as well as providing much needed moral support, and looking after Jacob while I worked. I was tired, fed up and often cried myself to sleep, but I did appreciate, even then, that life could have been worse. Much worse.

The divorce itself was fairly straightforward, I suppose. I think Scott's ego had been bruised by me leaving him and that, coupled with his need to move on to pastures new – and evidently so much 'better' – meant he didn't hold things up. We were divorced within the year. As for Jacob though, things took a little longer… but then that really didn't surprise me. Scott had warned me, after all.

Not long after we split up, once the divorce was underway, I had a long talk with Mum and she persuaded me to allow Scott to see Jacob. His solicitors had been asking, and my solicitor was telling me it would look better if I relented. I was scared about what Scott might do, that maybe he'd take Jacob and disappear, but Mum proposed that I should make the suggestion – through the solicitors, of course – that Scott could come down to Newquay and stay with his parents, and that I would take Jacob there. Mum persuaded me that Scott's mum and dad were just as entitled to see Jacob as she and Dad were, and I couldn't disagree with that. It was Scott I had the problem with. Luckily, although I don't think his parents knew the details of what had gone on in our marriage, his mother ensured that I didn't have to see Scott when I dropped Jacob off, taking him from me at the door, and bringing him out to the car when I collected him. For all I know, Scott may not even have been there, but at least Jacob got to see his grandparents on a regular basis.

The months dragged by, but despite my initial fears, Scott's threats to take Jacob came to nothing, presumably because the realities of caring for a toddler had dawned on him, and they didn't fit in with his lifestyle. Whatever the reason, eventually it was agreed that Scott should have access to Jacob every other weekend, and that he would pay child maintenance for him. His only stipulation, which I was forced to agree to, purely for the sake of appearing reasonable, was that he wanted to be able to take Jacob back to Bristol with him, instead of coming down to Newquay and staying with his parents. At the time, it had seemed like a small sacrifice to make for Jacob to finally have some proper routine in his life.

With everything settled – or at least as settled as it was ever going to be, while Scott was still a part of my life – I took a few months just to catch my breath, and then I started looking for my own place. I'd loved living with Mum and Dad, but I didn't want to outstay my welcome. Ideally, I wanted to rent a two bedroomed house in Carven Bay, with a garden if possible, being as Jacob had become used to having the outdoor space. But Carven Bay wasn't exactly overflowing with small, affordable houses, so I'd had to cast my net slightly further afield, and had been looking at properties in Newquay. I'd seen at least a dozen houses, none of which fitted the bill, and after my latest disastrous viewings, one weekend in late September, while Jacob was staying with his father, I'd returned to my parents' house, feeling more than a little despondent.

"Come and sit down," Dad suggested almost as soon as I walked in the door.

I took his advice, kicking off my shoes and settling back on the sofa.

"Can we assume it didn't go well?" Mum asked.

"That would be one way of putting it. The first one had mould growing up the walls, and the second one turned out to only have one bedroom…"

"Then why did they say it had two?"

"Estate agents' licence, I think. The second bedroom was actually in the attic, but it transpired they hadn't got planning consent, and it was going to have to be converted back to storage space if they wanted to rent it out."

Dad shook his head and gave Mum a look, whereupon she nodded, and he promptly turned back to me, taking a breath. "We've got a suggestion," he said.

"Yes?"

"Why don't you buy somewhere instead of renting? You're earning well, and you'd be able to get a mortgage, and I think you'll find the repayments would be less than the rent on most of the places around here."

"I know that, but there's the small matter of the huge deposit I'd have to find… and which I don't have."

"And which we'd like to help you with."

I stared at them, and then shook my head. "No... you've already done enough for me. More than enough."

Dad held up his hand. "You're our daughter," he reasoned. "Everything we have will be yours one day anyway... we're just giving you some of it a bit early, that's all."

"But you've already paid my legal fees – well, most of them – and you've let us live here all this time, barely allowing me contribute to anything. *And* you look after Jacob for me." That was still true, even though Jacob, who'd turned four the previous spring, had started attending school in Newquay. When Mum first suggested enrolling him, I hadn't been sure he was ready, and had wondered about putting it off until he was a little older, but she'd said she thought it would be good for him. I argued that surely Jacob could just keep going to the local nursery he was already attending, but she reasoned that all he really did there was play with other kids, and while that was great for his social skills, it didn't stimulate him mentally. And it seemed he needed stimulating, being as he's actually really bright. On his first day at school, I finished work early, so I could meet him and he came running out, so fired up, and so alive with enthusiasm, I almost cried. Mum had been right. He needed this. So from that day on, I would drop him off at school on my way to work and Mum would pick him up every day at three, and spend the rest of her afternoons doing something with him to keep him entertained, whether it was trips to the beach, or making cookies. And when I got home, I'd bathe him and read him a story before bed... while she'd take a back seat, and let me be a mum again.

"Yes, and we do all of that because we love you," Dad said. Tears pricked my eyes and he got up, coming over to me. "Don't get upset," he murmured. "You've had an absolutely horrible few years, since you left Scott, and it'll do you good to start getting back on your feet again. And if we can help with that, then we will."

"We're not trying to get rid of you," Mum put in, from the other side of the room, leaning forward in her seat. "We've loved having you here. But your father's right; you need to start getting your life back."

I wondered if she was talking about men; whether they were thinking that I needed to start going out more, seeing people… dating. I almost shuddered at the thought, but Dad distracted me by handing me his laptop.

"Why don't you see what's available?" he said.

And that was how I came to buy my house.

We moved in on a cold Friday in late January to find that the boiler had packed up, there was no hot water and no heating. But even that wasn't enough to dampen my enthusiasm. For the first time in a long time, I felt free.

And I still do. At least most of the time, anyway.

The house isn't much; in fact it's tiny, but I fell in love with it the moment I saw it. It's really handy for Jacob's school, and it's not too far from the beach, or the park, and is only a fifteen minute drive away from Mum and Dad. It has a little patch of garden, just about big enough to kick a ball around in, and plenty of original Victorian features. There are two bedrooms upstairs, together with the bathroom, and downstairs, there's a small living room at the front, with a larger dining room, a tiny kitchen and a completely useless conservatory, which is just about big enough to hold the washing machine and tumble dryer, with the ironing board propped up against the wall, and not much else. And I knew instantly – even on my first viewing – that I could knock that down, along with the wall between the kitchen and the dining room, extend out a little and remodel the back of the house to make a large open plan space. So, when I bought the house, I took the plunge and borrowed enough money to get the work done… at least, I hope it's going to be enough.

I've taken my time, lived here for a just over a year to see the house through each season, weighed up the pros and cons, making sure that I'm doing the right thing, and now I've drawn up the plans for the work I want to have done. I don't need planning consent, which makes it easier; I just need to find a decent builder – one who isn't going to rip me off, and who'll do the work to a good standard.

"If you don't mind me asking, where did you find out about us?" The man on the end of the phone sounds pleasant enough and has listened attentively while I've explained my requirements.

"My boss recommended you," I reply.

"Your boss being...?"

"Trevor Cole, at Cole and Simpson."

I've been asking around at work all morning, and Trevor overheard me, and suggested I should try Barclay and Sons, telling me they had an excellent reputation, so I'm taking advantage of a quiet lunch break to make the call.

"So you're an architect?" he guesses; after all, I might be a secretary, or the office cleaner.

"Yes. I'm probably your worst nightmare as a client," I joke and he chuckles.

"Not at all. At least you'll know what you want... and I'm sure you'll agree, there's nothing worse than an indecisive client."

"Oh, absolutely. I couldn't agree more."

"We'll need to come and see your property," he says and I hear the clicking of a keyboard. "I'll just have to check Adam's diary."

"Adam?"

"Yes. He's my son. He basically runs this place now. I just answer the phones. I'm too old for gallivanting around these days."

"I'm sure that's not true," I say and he chuckles again.

"I'll be giving you a discount, if you're not careful."

"So, you're not too old to do the costings then?" I continue the light-hearted banter.

"I'm not too old to check them over every so often, no." He pauses. "Adam's got a slot available tomorrow morning, actually. At eleven, if you're free."

"I'm sorry. I'm not available during office hours..."

"Of course you're not," he says. "Silly me. See? I told you I was getting old... well, what about later on in the afternoon, then? What time do you get home?"

"I'm usually back by five-thirty at the very latest." In reality, I'm normally home before that, but I like to allow myself a few minutes to get in the door, kick off my shoes and get changed out of my work clothes before I actually have to do anything.

"Okay then, I'll get Adam to come by and see you at six o'clock tomorrow evening, shall I?"

"Are you sure? I mean, that's very kind of you… well, of him."

"Oh, don't worry about it. Adam won't mind." He pauses again and I hear him typing. "Now, I suppose I'd better have your name," he says.

"Oh yes… sorry. It's Ms Downing."

I can't refer to myself as 'Mrs' anymore, because I'm not married, but I feel myself cringe as I say Scott's name. When Jacob started nursery school – which feels like a lifetime ago now – Scott and I were still just about legally married and, although I'd toyed with reverting to 'Drake' many times, Jacob's name is 'Downing'. He was already so confused and upset by the whole situation that I didn't want to make things worse, and so I gave my name as Downing too, and I've stuck to it ever since. For his sake. No matter how much I hate hearing Scott's name on my lips, I can't escape the fact that Jacob needs at least some sense of stability, and for that alone, it's worth it.

"Thank you, Ms Downing," the man says. "I've got your address and postcode, and Adam will be with you at six o'clock tomorrow."

"Thank you very much," I reply and put the phone down, relieved that I've managed to set the ball rolling at last.

The moment we get home from after school club, Jacob races upstairs to change, while I put his PE kit on to wash, and then try to work out what I can make for supper that will taste good and be ready in about an hour… oh, and that will preferably cook itself while I quickly change out of my work clothes and then help Jacob with his spellings.

Since moving in here, I've given up meat altogether. I'm not vegetarian, in that I eat fish, but I decided a few months ago that I'd try and do a little more to help save the planet, and giving up meat seemed like a simple option, along with using less plastics, and changing my old car – which needed changing anyway – for a hybrid. Jacob still eats meat – at least he does when he's with his father, because Scott thinks my ideas are 'ridiculous' and a 'pointless waste of time'. But then, I don't really care what Scott thinks.

We've got a butternut squash, and some lemons and herbs, and I know there are some tinned chick peas in the cupboard – because there always are – so I decide to make a tagine. I don't make it too spicy, but it's one of my favourite dishes and there's usually enough left over for me to take into work for lunch, so there's no waste either. I'm just gathering the ingredients together, when Jacob comes running through the dining room and barges into me, knocking the squash from my hand.

"Be careful," I scold. "And don't run."

He glares at me and I wonder, not for the first time in the last few months, what's happened to my son.

"I want some water," he says, nudging me to one side and reaching into the fridge.

"I think you forgot the vital word at the end of that sentence," I remark, but he ignores me and takes the jug of cold water from the door of the fridge anyway, putting it onto the work surface. I take a deep breath and close the fridge door, depositing the lemons and herbs beside the water jug and picking up the squash from the floor, before I turn back to him. He takes a clean glass out of the dishwasher, putting it down beside the jug, and is about to pour out the water, when I grab the glass and pull it away.

"What are you doing?" he asks, stopping mid-pour and scowling at me.

"I'm trying to teach you some manners. You need to apologise."

"What for?"

"Well, among other things, for pushing me."

"Why? You were in the way… as usual."

"Don't speak to me like that, Jacob."

He ignores me and grabs the glass from my hand, pouring the water into it and putting the jug back on the work surface. Taking his glass, he heads back into the dining room.

"Come back here and put the water away," I call after him.

"You're already there… you do it."

I open my mouth to tell him off again, but I can hear his footsteps on the stairs already, and let my head fall into my hands, the tears forming in my eyes before I even have time to wonder why I let him do this to me.

This is Scott's fault, and I hate him for what he's doing to our son.

To begin with, his influence didn't show too much, probably because Jacob was too young to be affected by his father's behaviour. But as time's gone on, Scott's power over Jacob has become greater, and more damaging. He's turning our son from a lovely little boy into a five year old thug, with a mouth and an attitude to match, and I'm coming to my wits' end.

I've already altered my original plans for the house to accommodate the situation... not in a major way, not in a way that will affect the building work, just in a way that's going to affect every other aspect of my life. I decided a few weeks ago that I needed to spend more time with Jacob, to try and curb his worst excesses, but with a mortgage and bills to pay, I obviously couldn't afford to take a cut in my hours, so I went and spoke to Trevor Cole about working from home – at least for some of the time anyway. He agreed, but only on the proviso that I have a space in the house that is dedicated to work. So, I'm going to convert my beloved living room, which was one of the spaces I loved most when I first saw this house, into an office, and we'll have the open plan area at the back to live in. I'd hoped to be able to keep the quiet sitting room as a sort of sanctuary, where I could read and relax at the end of the day, enjoy the fire in the winter, and open the sash windows and let the sunshine in during the warmer months, but it seems that's not to be.

I've also started to wonder whether I should speak to my dad about Jacob. My parents aren't ignorant of what's going on. Mum may not pick him up from school anymore, being as he's just started going to the after school club, but they still see him on a regular basis. They've noticed the changes in him, even if they haven't interfered. And I really think Jacob could use the guidance of a decent, kind, gentle man, rather than just following in his father's footsteps. It was Jacob who asked to join the after school club, and I've sometimes wondered if he did that to escape my parents' influence, or whether Scott put him up to it. He seems to enjoy it though, and a few of his friends stay on too, so maybe I'm just being paranoid.

I'm not entirely sure what to do for the best though. I mean, Dad isn't getting any younger. I don't want to cause him any worry, and he and Mum have already done so much for me as it is. But I know that if I let things carry on as they are, Jacob is going to turn out just like Scott – and I can't think of anything worse.

It's odd… after what happened, I constructed a wall to protect myself from men, and it's done a good job. No-one has got anywhere near me since I left Scott and I haven't minded that in the slightest. But what I failed to take into consideration was that Jacob might be the one who could find a chink in my armour, and that he'd be the one who could hurt me most.

Chapter Eight

Adam

Today has been one of those days. You know, one of those days when you wish you'd stayed in bed and let the wind howl against the window and just pulled the duvet up over your head, and ignored it all. Except that wasn't an option, because I had to get up, go into the office and finish off some quotes, and then do three site visits, one of which turned out to be a bit of an issue, because, the property in question is fairly exposed and, although the extension we're building was fine, the roof to the main part of the house had sustained some damage in the overnight gales. It wasn't anything major and it wasn't really our problem, but we were on site, and the homeowners had a couple of young kids, so the least we could do was help to fix things up. Or, at least that's what I decided when I arrived there late this morning. As far as I'm concerned, we may have lost a day's work on their extension, but we've gained a lot more in customer relations.

I let myself into the office, at just after three-thirty to be greeted by a welcoming warm blast of heat, surprised to see that Dad is still sitting behind his desk, facing me.

"You haven't gone home yet then?" I ask, taking off my coat and hooking it up behind the door.

"No." He glances at his watch. "Although I suppose I should be."

Dad works part-time now, usually from eleven until about three, although he's been known to stretch that from time to time – like today. He's just had his sixty-fourth birthday, and although he's still clearly unwilling to completely let go, I think he and Michelle like having more time to themselves.

As a result, I now effectively run the company, although Dad still goes over my costings from time to time. He does it surreptitiously, thinking I won't notice, but I'm not blind. I know he's not doing it because he doesn't trust me, but it's just hard for him to step back. The other thing he likes to keep an eye on is the schedules – I think just so he can ensure we're busy. And we are. At the moment, we've got eleven ongoing projects, with five more scheduled to start, and it's been like that for as long as I can remember, with no sign of it letting up – thank goodness.

I sit behind my desk and check my messages, mostly from suppliers, as a flash of lightning illuminates the room and I smile to myself, grateful that I'm indoors and not out there, trying to work in this terrible weather. I don't often miss my old job, the manual labour and the working outdoors – and on days like today, I'm positively thrilled that I don't have to do that anymore – I'm thirty-five now, and I think it would probably kill me.

Apart from the change in my career, my life is pretty much what it always was. I still surf whenever I can, which helps me to stay in shape, and I suppose I'm more careful about what I eat, as much for the environment as for myself.

I haven't dated though… not since Jade, and most of the time, I don't even think about her – or Nathan. Keeping busy helps me with that. It means I don't have time to dwell on what happened, or to ask myself, over and over, why they ran away, which one of them was responsible, and why they didn't just tell me. As I said to Dad at the time, I wasn't in love with her. But I did care about her. And, if I'm being honest, what they did – and the outcome of it – still hurts.

Mum and Derek found it hard to come to terms with Nathan's death and the funeral was awful. I went, for Mum's sake, not Nathan's, relieved that by then we knew the accident had been just that. An accident. There had been no drugs or alcohol involved. Everyone else just accepted that statement from the police, but I was almost overcome with relief. I'd known about Nathan's habit, and had been haunted for a while that maybe he'd been driving under the influence, and that I could have done more to help him. As it turned out, at least I didn't have to feel responsible for their deaths. Not entirely. I still I felt that, if they'd just come and talked to me – either of them – then maybe they needn't have had to run away. But I kept those thoughts to myself and focused on trying to help my mum. I visited more often, stayed with her when Derek had to be away on business, and tried to comfort her as best I could, but she seemed to be in a kind of emotional no man's land. I suppose that's why it didn't surprise me when, a few months after Nathan's funeral, she and Derek moved to Port Isaac. It's only a forty-five minute drive away, so I'm still able to see them regularly, but I think it was too hard for Mum to stay in the house where Nathan had grown up, and know that he'd never be coming back again. She seems happier now – well, more accepting anyway – and every so often she asks when I'm going to settle down. I usually answer with a smile, and a change of subject, because I can't see that ever happening. I'll admit, although only to myself, that I'm lonely, but I've reached the conclusion that I probably had my chance fifteen years ago, when I met 'the girl', and I blew it. And maybe there just isn't anyone else out there for me.

"How's everything going?" Dad asks, getting up and pulling on his jacket, which he'd left over the back of his chair.

"Fine," I reply. I don't bother to tell him about the problems with the roof at Mr and Mrs Armstrong's property. He'll only want to stay and talk it through, and there's nothing to talk about.

"I've made you an appointment for tomorrow," he adds, coming over and standing in front of my desk. "It's a late one, I'm afraid, but the woman works during the day... and I didn't think you'd mind."

I shake my head. It's not like I have a life, after all.

"Is it in the diary?" I ask.

"Yes. She's looking to have her existing conservatory removed, and then her kitchen and dining room extended, from what I can gather."

"Sounds simple enough."

"You're due there at six tomorrow evening."

"Okay. Although I hope she's not in a hurry. We're snowed under at the moment, and the weather isn't helping."

He glances out of the window. It's raining hard again now, and he frowns.

"No, it's not. But she didn't mention a particular deadline, so I'm sure it'll be fine. We can just schedule her in."

I admire his confidence that she'll choose to use us, and I nod my head as he takes a step towards the door, before he stops and turns back.

"Are you alright, Adam?"

I look up at him. "Yes, I'm fine."

"You look tired. You haven't had a day off in ages, son."

"I know, but when we're this busy…"

"Well, you taking a day or two off wouldn't hurt, would it? You know I'll cover for you."

"I'm fine, Dad." The thought of spending time by myself at home, doing nothing but thinking, isn't inspiring. I'd rather just work, keep busy, and pretend that everything actually is alright.

"If you say so," he replies, shaking his head, although I know he doesn't believe me.

I don't believe me, so why should he?

I park up outside a very neat little Victorian terraced house, down a quiet side road at five to six, grateful that the weather has improved and at least yesterday's gale seems to have blown itself out, today having been bright and sunny, if chilly, which isn't surprising for the end of February.

I've got a few minutes to spare, so I open my folder and check the client's name. Dad's put it down as 'Ms Downing', and I smile to myself, wondering if he's done his usual trick of writing 'Ms' because she didn't make it clear whether she was married or not, or whether the title is actually accurate for once. I'd better err on the side of caution and call her 'Ms', just in case.

I gather my things together and get out of my car, noting that the one parked in front of mine is the same make – a Toyota – but a smaller model, and that they're both hybrids. I changed my car about a year ago, having stuck with Land Cruisers for years, and decided the time had come to be a bit more environmentally friendly. Dean mocks me all the time, but I don't care.

Knocking on the dark blue door, I wait for a minute before it's opened, and I feel the breath being sucked from my body, to the point where I have to cough to overcome the sensation of someone stamping on my chest. The woman standing before me is quite simply the most stunning creature I've ever seen. She's about five foot eight, I suppose, her straight, silky, light brown hair ending just below her shoulders and then curling under, very slightly, while her face is a picture of perfection, with full pink lips, soft, delicate skin and pale hazel eyes… I frown, a distant memory flitting through my brain, but it doesn't stick around for very long, because my eyes wander to the long floral dress she's wearing, topped by a pale grey cardigan. She's a woman who dresses in a style I can understand; soft and comfortable, but fitted and kind of sexy at the same time. I like it… I like her.

"Are you Mr Barclay?" she says, tilting her head and looking confused, as I realise that I've been standing and staring at her, without saying a word, for far too long.

"Yes… sorry." I hold out my hand. "Adam Barclay."

She shakes my hand and steps to one side. "Do come in."

"Thanks."

"I'm Jenna D—" she says, but then stops talking all of a sudden and blushes. "I mean… just call me Jenna." Her voice is delicate and yet uncertain and, once again, I'm reminded of something… if only I could put my finger on it.

"Only if you call me Adam." I smile down at her.

"Okay."

She stares at me for a second and then holds out her hand in the vague direction of the rear of the house. "Would you like to come through?" she suggests, and I nod my head.

"After you."

She leads the way down the narrow hallway, past a door to our right, and just before we get to the steep staircase, she turns in to a second doorway, which leads to the dining room.

"I don't know if your father explained," she says, looking up at me again, "but I'm an architect."

"No, he didn't."

She smiles and my heart flips over in my chest this time, which is almost as distracting as that stamping feeling.

"As I said to him, I suppose that makes me your worst nightmare," she adds, her smile widening.

"Far from it," I reply, wishing I could tell her she's the opposite of a nightmare; she's actually a dream come true.

She moves nearer to the long, wooden dining table, which has a bench on either side. "I've drawn up some plans," she says. "Hopefully they'll make sense."

I put my folder down on the end of the table and lean over. "They seem straightforward enough," I muse, looking at her design, and then standing up straight again to inspect the room. "You want to take down that wall?"

"Yes."

I nod. "It's load-bearing…"

"I know." She sounds offended.

"Sorry. I was talking to myself then… thinking out loud. I wasn't questioning your judgement."

She blinks a few times. "Oh… sorry."

"Don't be. It wasn't your fault. I should learn to keep my thoughts to myself." She still seems a bit uneasy, so I walk into the kitchen. "I can see why you're doing this," I look back at her. "It's going to give you a lot more space."

She smiles again, much to my relief. "Well, that's the plan. The kitchen is ludicrously small as it is, and as for the conservatory…"

I glance out at it. "Shall we be more accurate here and call it a lean-to?" I suggest, and she chuckles, the sound whispering across my skin, my nerves tingling.

"Hmm… maybe we should."

I take a breath, just to regain a little self control.

"Would you… um… would you like a coffee?" she asks, her sudden nervousness taking me by surprise.

If it means I get to spend more time with you... "That would be lovely."

She joins me in the kitchen, and at once I can see the biggest problem with the current layout. With the two of us out here, there's barely room to move and I have to step aside, right up against the worktop to give her room to fill the kettle. Part of me wonders if I should go back into the dining room to give her some space, but I don't want to. I want to stay exactly where I am... and as she moves around me, she doesn't seem to mind my presence either, smiling at me and asking about how long I've worked with my dad.

"Since I was eighteen," I reply.

"That doesn't tell me much," she says, her smile widening as she pours boiling water into the glass cafetière.

"Well, I'm thirty-five now, so I'll let you do the maths. It was never my strong point... which is probably why Dad still checks my figures every so often."

"Yes, I know. He told me."

"He did?"

"Only in jest... don't worry. He wasn't openly criticising you."

"I'm glad to hear it."

"Do you take milk?" she asks.

"Yes, please."

She squeezes past me to get to the fridge-freezer, which is by the door into the dining room, and then squeezes back again, pausing just for a moment and looking up at me. There's something captivating in her eyes, something bewitching, and I stand and stare, even after she's moved away, to the point where it takes me a second to realise that she's already added the milk to my coffee and is holding the cup out in front of me.

"Thanks," I murmur, taking it from her, before she turns back and adds a little cold water from the tap to her own cup.

"Shall we go back and look at the plans?" she suggests and, although part of me wants to say that I'm quite happy where I am, being beguiled by her, I know I'm here to do a job... and falling for her isn't part of that.

Back in the dining room, she points to a section on the drawing, which shows the corner of the kitchen. "In here," she says, "I'm wondering if it's possible to build out this cupboard."

I study the space she's pointing to, and then look over her shoulder. "Is that the cupboard under the stairs?"

"Yes. At the moment, you get to it through the kitchen, but I'm wondering if it's feasible to create a doorway in here… in this wall…" She turns, pointing. "And then whether the cupboard can be built out into the kitchen by about a metre."

"I don't see why not."

"It's just that, when the conservatory… sorry… when the lean-to is taken down, I'll lose the space I use for my washing machine and tumble dryer and I was thinking about extending that cupboard and stacking them in there."

I nod my head. "It'll mean changing the plumbing."

"Hmm… but being as the whole kitchen is being remodelled, I don't think it'll be an issue."

"No. I can't see that it would be. Are you going to use a kitchen design company for the interior work, or are you going to do it yourself?"

She looks up at me. "I was wondering if that was something you might offer."

I take a breath. "Well, I can add the cost for installing a kitchen into the quote, if you want me to. We don't normally supply the fittings, but I'm sure we can discuss that…"

She smiles. "That sounds perfect. I'm happy to source the units, but I wouldn't have a clue about fitting them."

"Okay… well, I'll work out a fitting fee and we'll take it from there."

At that moment, I'm startled by the sound of footsteps on the stairs. Until now, I'd assumed we were alone in the house, and I turn, looking towards the door, as a young boy enters. He's probably around five or possibly six years old, slim built, with dark blond hair, and is wearing jeans and a t-shirt with a dinosaur on the front.

Without stopping to say 'hello', or even acknowledge us, he runs towards the kitchen, brushing past Jenna, who is still holding her coffee in her hand, and splashing the hot dark liquid down her front. She yelps in pain and I move quickly, taking the cup from her.

"Was your coffee still hot? Is it burning?" I ask her.

"Yes." I can see in her eyes that it hurts, although she's doing a good job of hiding it, and I want to hold her in my arms… in fact, I ache to hold her, but right now, she needs help.

"Okay… we need ice."

"I don't have any."

"Anything frozen?"

She nods. "I have peas…"

I turn and see that the boy is standing by the fridge-freezer, with the lower door open, his head buried inside.

"Where are the ice-creams, Mum?" he says.

"We don't have any. You ate the last one the day before yesterday, remember?" Her voice is strained and I turn back to see she's trying to hold the material of her dress away from her.

"Excuse me," I say, going over to the small boy. "Can I just get in there, please?"

He looks up at me. "You said you'd buy some more," he says, raising his voice and clearly choosing to ignore me.

"At the weekend, yes," Jenna replies. "You know I don't go shopping during the week."

"Excuse me," I repeat, my voice a little harsher. "I need to get something from the freezer."

"So?"

I'm angry now, and fed up with his attitude, and I don't have time for this, so I bend slightly and pick him up, dumping him out of the way and open the top drawer, where there's a new packet of peas, which I grab, slamming the freezer door shut and going further into the kitchen to pick up a tea towel from the work surface. The boy is scowling at me now, but I ignore him and return to Jenna, wrapping the peas in the towel.

"You need to put this on the burn," I tell her, handing it across. "I'd offer to help, but ideally it should be next to your skin… and…"

"I'll go upstairs," she says, blushing, and turns away, heading for the hallway.

"What about the ice-cream?" the boy says from behind me.

Jenna stops and turns back. "Dinner won't be long… surely you can wait."

"I'm hungry now." His voice is demanding, insolent, but I focus on Jenna, wondering what she'll do. She bites her bottom lip, and I'm fairly sure I can see tears forming in her eyes.

"Have an apple," she says. "There are some in the bowl." She looks at me, blinking, embarrassed, I think. "I'm sorry," she murmurs. "Will you be okay for a minute or two?"

"I'll be fine… and you need to hold that ice on the burn for a lot longer than a minute or two. Don't worry about me. I'll go and take a look outside."

"I won't be long," she says quietly.

"Take as long as you need."

She smiles, just slightly, and then goes out of the door and I hear her footsteps on the stairs. Turning back into the room, I pick up my coffee and head into the kitchen, ignoring the boy, who is standing leaning against one of the cupboards, the scowl still set on his face, and I go on through to the lean-to, and out of the back door.

I wander around the tiny patch of garden, even though there's nothing much to see in the dark, taking on board the fact that Jenna evidently has a child… and a really obnoxious, rude child at that.

I'm guessing this means that Dad got Jenna's title wrong. It's not the first time he's done that, or that I've been embarrassed by his mistake, but it's the first time it's mattered. But, it makes no difference how much I like her – or even that, after less than an hour in her company, I more than like her – she's out of bounds.

I shake my head, trying to clear my thoughts, and stare up at the clear night sky, the stars twinkling brightly. I don't even feel the chill, although I'm fairly sure the temperature has dipped below freezing, and I'm not sure I care. I just can't believe this is happening to me again… Why is it that I meet a woman who's perfect, who without knowing it, in a matter of minutes, simply answers every question I could ever hope to ask, and makes me feel more alive than anything else – just like 'the girl' did, all those years ago – and I can't have her?

Taking a deep breath, I go back inside, resigned to dealing with Jenna as a client – and nothing more. Her son is nowhere to be seen and

I stand in the dining room, waiting for her to re-appear and drinking my lukewarm coffee.

When I hear footsteps on the stairs, I make a show of studying the plans again, and look up as she appears in the doorway, having changed out of her floral dress into a plain blue one, in a similar style; long, flowing, and clinging to her body in a really sexy way…

"Sorry I took so long," she says, looking up at me, and I have to remind myself not to fall into those beautiful pale amber eyes.

"Don't worry about it. Are you okay now? The burn doesn't hurt anymore?" I have to ask… despite everything, I can't help caring.

"It's much better, thank you. It hurt at the time, but luckily my coffee wasn't that hot. I always add cold water to it, because I take it black."

"Good," I reply. "I mean, it's good that your coffee wasn't too hot and didn't burn you, not that you take it black."

She chuckles and I almost hear myself groan with the disappointment of knowing we'll never be together.

"How did you get on outside?" she asks, moving further into the room.

"Fine, thanks. I couldn't see much, but if I can take the plans with me, I'll be able to cost everything up, and other than that, I think I've got everything I need." *And I really should get out of here, before I do something really stupid, like kiss you.*

Chapter Nine

Jenna

I know I told myself that I'd never look at another man again; I even built a very thick wall to protect myself from such eventualities, but it's impossible not to look at Adam Barclay. He's simply magnificent… in every sense of the word.

He's well over six feet tall, with broad shoulders and a muscular physique, and hair that's just a little on the wild side, long enough to touch the back of his collar, but not untidy… and then there's his face… my God, what a face!

His chin is angular, and I know that his stubble would be prickly to touch – unlike the man himself, who is as easy-going as anyone I've ever met. When I spilt coffee down my front, he handled the situation calmly, with care and compassion, and even when Jacob was being an embarrassing pain, showing me up as usual, Adam took it in his stride, and has been kind enough not to mention my son's behaviour since I came back downstairs.

"When do you think you'll be able to get the quotes back to me?" I ask, surprised by my own reluctance to bring his visit to an end, even though I know it must, and that to him, I'm just another client… another job to be costed and completed.

"Well," he replies, "I could probably have it ready for Friday, if that's okay."

"So soon?"

"Yes. If you want, I can bring it round in the evening."

He frowns at the end of his sentence, but I'm not sure why, and in any case, I'm momentarily distracted by the warm glow that's settled in the pit of my stomach at the thought of seeing him again. It's been years since I felt anything like that… years and years. Since before I met Scott…

"I can go through the prices with you and your husband together, if you want," he adds. "Then if either of you have got any quest—"

"I don't have a husband," I interrupt.

"Oh… your partner then."

"I don't have a partner either."

"Sorry," he says, his voice really soft, if a little bewildered. "I just assumed… what with your son…" He pauses, then adds, "He is your son, isn't he? Or have I got that wrong too?"

I smile at him. "No, Jacob's my son, I'm ashamed to say, given the way he behaves."

"Don't worry about it…"

"But I do worry about it. His behaviour is becoming a nightmare these days… It's…" I feel myself blush. "Sorry, you don't need to hear about that."

"Oh, please don't apologise," he says, moving closer to me. "I know how difficult little boys can be."

"Because you were one yourself? Or because you *have* one yourself?" I hope it doesn't sound too much like I'm fishing for information… if that's what I'm doing. I'm not sure. Am I?

"Neither," he replies. "Well… what I mean to say is that I was a little boy once – obviously – but as far as I know, I was fairly well behaved. I don't think anyone ever thought of me as difficult. And I don't have any children of my own. But my brother's behaviour when he was growing up was appalling. He made your son look like an angel."

"I doubt that."

"Only because you never met Nathan." His eyes darken slightly and his brow furrows into a frown, like he's remembering something, but then just as quickly, his face clears. "So, how about Friday evening then?"

"Oh…" I'm surprised by how disappointed I feel. "I'm afraid I can't. It's Scott's turn to have Jacob this weekend."

"Scott?" he queries.

"My ex-husband."

"You're divorced?"

"Yes. I still use my ex-husband's name…" I glance up at his face, confusion written in his eyes. "But of course you wouldn't know that, would you? How would you know that my maiden name was Drake?" What's wrong with me this evening? Why am I rambling? This poor man must think I'm mad… I'm starting to wonder myself.

"I wouldn't." He shakes his head, smiling. "But you still use his name?"

"For Jacob's sake, yes. It seemed easier when he started at nursery, being as Scott and I were still officially married at the time, even if we were living hundreds of miles apart. That's why I refer to myself as 'Ms'. It at least gives me the illusion of being free of my ex."

"But if you're divorced, then you are free of him, surely?" he asks, frowning slightly again.

"Not really. He has access to Jacob every other weekend, so unfortunately I still have to see him."

"And he'll be here on Friday evening?"

"Yes," I reply, remembering the point of this conversation. "I'm sorry. But it's always complete chaos when Scott comes over. He used to come on Saturday mornings, but because he lives in Bristol, he complained that he wasn't getting enough time with Jacob, so we changed his pick-up times to Friday nights. Now he complains about the traffic, or the weather, or the roadworks instead. By the time he's gone, I always have a headache, and the need to drown myself in a vat of wine." Adam's staring at me now. "I do apologise." I push my hair back behind my ears. "I don't know what's come over me tonight. I'm rabbiting on like a lunatic, when you don't need to know any of this, do you?"

"Don't worry," he says, giving me a smile which makes his deep brown eyes sparkle. "Why don't I come over on Saturday morning instead?"

"Really? You wouldn't mind?"

"Not at all."

"But it's the weekend. I'm sure you've got better things to do."

"Not really." He smirks. "And that makes me sound incredibly sad, doesn't it?"

"No." I smile. "When Jacob's not here, I don't do very much either."

He opens his mouth and then slams it shut again, and I wonder what he was going to say, just as he puts his hand into his back pocket and pulls out his phone, unlocking it and tapping on the screen a couple of times.

"How about ten o'clock?" he says.

"That sounds fine. But are you sure you don't mind giving up time at the weekend... for a crazy woman?"

He lowers his phone and takes a step closer, so he's maybe six inches from me, looking down into my eyes. "I don't think you're crazy," he murmurs, his voice low and slightly gravelly, making my skin tingle and my nerves shiver. "No more than I am."

I nestle into his strong, muscular chest as he holds me tight against him, closing the gap between us, our bodies entwined, skin against skin...

"I love you, Jenna..." His lips brush against mine, his tongue demands entry, which I grant willingly, and he lowers me to the sand, the waves washing over us as his hands start to wander...

I sit up in bed, startled, feeling hot, aroused, needy and let out a shuddering sigh, realising it was a dream... a dream I haven't had in years. In fact, the last time I felt like this, or dreamt like this, was when I was sixteen years old, after I'd met that man on the beach... the man with the tattoo. The wolf man. The man who never came back. Why would I be dreaming about him now?

Turning, I see that there's still fifteen minutes before the alarm is due to go off, so I lie back on the pillow, recalling the scene in my dream, still remarkably fresh in my mind; the man's voice, his words, his lips on mine... and I startle again, as I realise it wasn't the wolf man I'd dreamt about... it was Adam. It was his arms I felt around me, his bare chest I nestled into, his hands that wandered over my sensitised skin.

I cover my face with my hands. Oh God… how am I ever going to face him again?

I don't know whether my dream has put me out of sorts, or whether it's just one of those days, but nothing seems to have gone right today. I was twenty minutes late to work this morning, because of a hold up in the centre of Newquay, although there didn't seem to be any reason for it, so I'm not sure whether Trevor believed me, or whether he assumed I'd just overslept. As a result of that, I chose to sacrifice part of my lunch break, because I couldn't afford to stay late, and because I seem to be the clumsiest person in the world at the moment, I not only spilt a carton of milk in the office kitchen, but also broke my favourite mug. I had to use one of the ones which suppliers leave as promotional gifts, with their logo printed on the outside… and while I know that doesn't matter in the slightest, it bothered me.

So, the last thing I need when I pick Jacob up from after school club, is to find him in a foul mood. I haven't had a chance to look out of the office window all day, so it wasn't until I ran to my car, that I realised it was raining – yet again – and it evidently has been for most of the day. Unfortunately, that means the children have been confined to the school building, rather than being allowed to play outside and, in the world according to Jacob, that's all my fault.

"Can I phone Dad?" he mutters as soon as we get into the house.

I sigh, wishing I could say 'no', but I can't. "If you want to."

"Of course I want to," he replies. "Or I wouldn't have asked."

"Talk to me like that again, and I'll say 'no'."

He narrows his eyes. "Dad says you're not allowed to stop me from phoning him."

"Your dad says a lot of things," I mutter under my breath, and take my phone from my handbag, going to my contacts and connecting the call. Scott answers on the third ring.

"What do you want, Jenna? I'm working."

"I know you are. Jacob wants to talk to you."

"Is he okay?" he asks.

"Yes. He just asked if he could phone you, that's all."

"Okay… put him on then."

I pass the phone down to Jacob. "Hello, Dad." He sounds happy and enthusiastic and I feel my heart shrink in my chest. Why does he never sound like that with me anymore? Why is every day with me a series of complaints, arguments and pushed boundaries? I don't have time to wonder though, before Jacob disappears into the hall and up the stairs, taking my phone with him, no doubt to explain to Scott what an awful mother I am. Again.

I delay changing out of my work clothes, for fear that Jacob will hear me going up the stairs and accuse me of listening in to his conversation, and instead I go into the kitchen, putting the kettle on. I'd rather open the bottle of wine that's in the fridge, but that can wait until after Jacob's gone to bed.

I've got some haddock fillets in the fridge and decide to make Jacob's favourite; fishcakes. He's loved these since he was little, and although they're a bit of an effort to make, I know he'll like them… not that I'm trying to bribe him with food, perish the thought.

I'm just mashing the potatoes, when I hear him coming down the stairs.

"What's for dinner?" he asks, putting my phone down on the work surface beside the hob.

"Fishcakes," I reply, waiting for him to jump for joy, like he normally does.

"Fishcakes?" He turns his nose up. "Why can't we have sausages for once?"

"We do have sausages sometimes…"

"Veggie sausages," he says, pulling a face. "They're not like the ones Dad makes."

"That's because your dad eats meat," I explain.

"Then why the fuck don't you?"

I drop the potato masher. "Jacob!" I shout. "Where on earth did you pick up language like that?" I know the answer to my question already, because while I appreciate that children can overhear these things in the playground, I also know that they then have a tendency to use the words in all the wrong places, dropping them into sentences in inappropriate situations… whereas this is exactly the kind of thing his father would say. He glares at me but doesn't answer. "I won't tolerate you swearing," I continue. "Now, go to your room until dinner's ready. And when you come down, I expect an apology." His scowl darkens, but I stand my ground and, after a moment's pause, he turns and goes back upstairs, his feet stamping on each tread.

It takes me a few minutes to calm down, and before I return to cooking the dinner, I grab the wine from the fridge, open the bottle and pour myself a glass, taking a very long drink, despite my shaking hands, as I wonder – not for the first time – where it all went wrong.

I have a long soak in the bath before going to bed, mulling over Jacob's half-hearted apology, our silent meal, and his tantrum just before bedtime, when I could tell he only just managed not to swear at me again. I know I'm going to have to speak to Scott about this, but it's not a conversation I'm looking forward to. I know he'll somehow try and make it my fault, and I'm really not sure how much more of him I can take.

I lay my head back on the rolled up towel behind me and try to forget about Scott, at least until tomorrow, when he'll be coming to collect Jacob for the weekend… and no doubt teaching him more bad behaviour in my absence. I shake my head… how can I possibly hope to relax when I'm thinking like that? I need to fill my mind with happier thoughts, of something more calming… so I close my eyes and a vision of Adam Barclay drifts into my head, a self conscious smile settling on my lips as I recall my dream, his lips touching mine, his hands exploring…

"Oh, for God's sake." I sit up, splashing water over the edge of the bath. "What's the point?" I mutter and climb out, wrapping a towel around me. Thinking about Adam, dreaming about Adam, isn't going to help, because that's just a fantasy – and it's not a fantasy I want to see become a reality either. Yes, he's attractive. Okay, he's more than attractive. But if there's one thing this evening has taught me, it's that men are men… even when they're five year old boys. And I don't for one second believe that Adam Barclay is any different to the rest of them. He might seem pleasant enough on first acquaintance, but so did Scott... and look where that got me.

Friday nights are always frantic. Well, they are when Scott's collecting Jacob anyway.

I have to pick him up from after school club, and then get him home, fed and changed, before Scott arrives at seven. He always makes a big deal of the timings, pointing out that he has to finish work early in order to get to us by then, even though it was his choice to move his pick-up day from Saturday in the first place.

It's the only time when Jacob and I eat separately, but it's easier to just cook him something quick, and then eat by myself later on, when I'm less nervous and can relax more.

Tonight, I'm giving him veggie sausages and chips, which is the closest thing to a compromise I can think of. He looks at his plate and then turns to me, but doesn't say a word, smothering everything in tomato ketchup and wolfing it down, while I go through his school bag and find his reading book, which he'll need to take with him.

"Don't forget I need my PE kit for Monday," Jacob says, stuffing a chip in his mouth.

"Can you eat properly please," I tell him. "And your PE kit is already washed, dried and folded, back in your bag and sitting in the conservatory, ready for Monday morning."

"Well, put it by the front door, then. Otherwise I'll forget it."

"Jacob," I say, standing above him, "will you stop speaking to me like I'm your servant. I'm not. Your PE kit can stay in the conservatory over the weekend. And I'll put it by the front door on Sunday night. I'm not going to spend the next two days tripping over it." I sigh. "I'm going upstairs to pack your rucksack... finish your dinner and then come up and get changed."

I don't bother to wait for his reply and leave the room, climbing slowly up the stairs and going into his room, which is a tip.

His rucksack is in the corner, propped up against the wall and I pick it up, putting it on his unmade bed, before turning and rescuing the scattered items of clothing from the floor and putting them in the laundry basket behind the door. I know I should make him do this, but I'm too tired for another argument. Once I can be sure I'm not actually going to trip myself up just walking around his bedroom, I find him a couple of pairs of jeans, two t-shirts, a hoodie and a sweatshirt and start packing his bag, sitting down on the edge of his bed.

"I don't want that one," he says, coming into the room, ketchup smeared around his lips. He walks over and pulls the hoodie from the bag. "I want the blue one."

I look around the room and find the article in question hanging on the back of the chair in the corner. "Bring it here, then," I murmur and he goes over, picking up the top and handing it to me. As I fold it though, I notice there are stains down the front of it.

"You can't take this; it's not clean."

"Then why didn't you wash it?"

"Because you didn't put it in the laundry. It's not my job to go through your clothes, checking what's clean and what's dirty, Jacob. You're old enough to be able to put things in the laundry basket, or put them back in the wardrobe."

He sucks in a breath and glowers at me as I throw the blue hoodie into the laundry basket, and refold the grey one, putting it into his rucksack, and adding the t-shirts.

"Go and wash your face," I tell him. "You're covered in ketchup."

"Because it's the only thing that makes your sausages taste of anything."

I ignore his jibe and get up again, fetching him some underwear from his top drawer and finish the packing, closing the zip on his rucksack.

"I've left you out some clothes to change into," I tell him, nodding to the things on the bed. "I'll take this down." I pick up his bag and go to the door. "Shout if you need anything."

"I'm not a baby, Mum."

"No, you're not." *When you were a baby, you were so much nicer.* I struggle to remember what he used to be like sometimes, but I know he wasn't like this.

Downstairs, I put his reading book into the front pocket of his rucksack, and leave it on the bench in the dining room. It's almost a quarter to seven, which is good – Scott should be here any minute, and we're ready in time. Hopefully tonight will go smoothly for once, and I can settle down to a stir-fry and maybe a movie... and some peace and quiet.

Jacob comes running down the stairs and into the dining room, wearing the blue hoodie I just put into the laundry.

"What are you doing?" I ask him and he looks up at me. "Go upstairs again and take that hoodie off. I left the red one out for you."

"I told you. I like the blue one."

"Yes, and it's got a stain down the front of it. You can't wear that."

He moves closer, glaring at me. "I'll wear what I fucking like... alright?" I step back, recoiling from his jabbing finger and the look of hatred in his eyes.

"Jacob, stop it! Stop swearing at me." I kneel down and take hold of his arm. "I won't let you speak to me like that, do you hear?"

"How are you going to stop me?"

"Well, I'll call your father and tell him not to come and get you, for one thing."

His eyes flicker. "You can't stop me from seeing Dad. He told me... you're not allowed to."

He wrenches his arm away and storms from the room, leaving me staring at the space he's just vacated, feeling powerless, impotent, and ashamed of myself for being so weak.

I feel a tear hit my cheek and brush it away as I stand up, going into the kitchen to grab a piece of kitchen towel and dry my eyes. There's no way I'm going to let Scott see I've been crying. He'll be merciless.

I sit down at the dining table, resting my head in my hands, taking deep breaths to calm myself and resolve not to think. It'll only make me cry, and I can do that later, when I'm alone and tears don't matter.

"Where's Dad?" Jacob's voice makes me jump and I look up at the clock on the mantelpiece, to see that it's gone seven-thirty already. I didn't even know I'd been sitting here for so long.

"He must be running late. It's probably just the traffic."

"Can I put the TV on?"

I'm surprised he's bothered to ask, and although I normally don't let him watch television at this time of night, I nod my head and get up, going to sit in the living room with him, just to make sure he's not watching something inappropriate.

He flicks through the channels, settling on a programme about dinosaurs, which has just under half an hour left to run. I'm not that interested myself but he is, his little face absorbed by the detailed computer graphics, and for a while I sit and stare at him, wondering how he can be such a monster one minute, and such an angel the next... and whether all children are like this.

Eight o'clock comes around, the programme finishes and there's still no sign of Scott. Ordinarily, if it was a weekend when Jacob was staying here, I'd be putting him to bed, and I curse Scott under my breath. Even if he arrives now, it's going to be gone ten o'clock before they get back to Bristol, and although I'm sure Jacob will fall asleep in the car, it's not good for him to have his routine disrupted like this.

"Where's Dad?" he asks again, sounding more uncertain this time.

"I'll try phoning him, shall I?"

I'd normally do everything I can to avoid speaking to Scott, but the sound of Jacob's worried voice is enough to make me put my own feelings to one side, and I go out into the hall and get my phone from my bag, connecting a call to Scott before I've got back into the living room. It goes straight to voicemail though, so I leave a message – a more polite message than I would have left, if Jacob hadn't been sitting on the sofa looking up at me, his eyebrows raised expectantly.

"Hi, Scott," I say into the phone, "it's Jenna. I'm just wondering where you are and what time you think you'll be getting here. Can you call me back... Jacob's getting worried."

I hang up and put the phone down on the coffee table.

"I'm not worried," Jacob says, although his voice gives him away.

"I know. I just said that so Dad would call back quicker. You know he doesn't like to think of you being worried about anything."

I've sometimes wondered at my capacity for lying, especially when it comes to Scott. I've told Jacob so many fibs over the years, about how his father will always put him first, will always care for him and keep him safe… knowing that the only person Scott really cares about is himself, and possibly whoever he happens to be sleeping with at the time. Possibly.

Another fifteen minutes roll by and, although Jacob is fairly interested in the nature programme on television, which is about insects, he keeps looking out of the window every so often.

When it gets to half past eight, I pick up my phone and try calling Scott again. Jacob turns to look at me expectantly, but once again it goes to voicemail and unable to see the point in leaving another message, I hang up.

"I'll text him," I say, smiling at Jacob, in what I hope is an encouraging way.

He doesn't smile back, but turns his attention to the television once more.

Unrestrained by being overheard, I type out what I'm really thinking.

— Scott, where the hell are you? You're over an hour and a half late and Jacob's upset. If you're not here by nine, I'm putting him to bed and you'll have to stay in a hotel overnight – because I'm damned if you're going to wake him up, just because you can't be bothered to stick to the schedule. At least have the manners to call me and let me know what's going on, so that I can tell your son.

"What did you tell him?" Jacob asks, looking over at me again.

"I just asked where he is and when he'll be here," I paraphrase, knowing I can delete the message later, and that Jacob can't unlock my phone anyway… or read well enough yet to completely understand my message.

"He will come though, won't he?" Jacob sounds almost scared now and I get up from my chair and go to sit beside him. He surprises me by letting me give him a hug.

"I'm sure he'll do his best," I lie. "And if he can't make it tonight, he'll be here tomorrow."

"Tomorrow?" He leans back, staring up at me.

"We'll give him another half an hour, and if he's not here by then, I think it's best if you go to bed…"

"But I don't want to go to bed." His bottom lip starts to quiver and I hug him tighter.

"I know, but you can't stay up all night."

"I can."

"No, you can't. And I'm sure Dad will be here in the morning."

"Why's he late?" he asks accusingly, like it's my fault.

"I don't know, but I'm sure he's got a good reason." God, I hate lying to him, being as I'm fairly sure the 'reason' will be blonde, in her late teens or early twenties, and too hard to say 'no' to, even for the sake of his son.

There are tantrums, and then there are tantrums, and last night's was a tantrum on an epic scale. Even though I'd explained to Jacob that he'd have to go to bed, when it came to it, he fought me. He kicked, hit, and even punched me in the stomach… hard enough to hurt. It was the first time he'd ever been violent with me, and although I was quite shocked by the severity of his actions, and I'd normally have told him off, I didn't have the heart. His dad had let him down and he was hurt, and he wanted to hurt someone back. I was the one in the way. I've never seen him cry so much and I've never hated Scott more, not even for all the things he did to me. Hurting our son is inexcusable; it's unforgivable.

So, instead of telling Jacob off, I lay in bed with him and held him until he stopped crying and fell asleep, and then I went downstairs and turned off the lights, locking up the house, before sending Scott another text message:

— Your son is in bed, having cried himself to sleep. I hope whoever she was, it was worth it.

It was tame, pale by comparison with what I wanted to type, but I was too tired and too fed up to bother. Taking my phone upstairs, I went to bed and it was only as I switched off my bedside lamp that I realised I hadn't eaten anything all evening.

This morning, things haven't been much better, not helped by the fact that, when Jacob woke up, he came running into my room, wanting to know if I'd heard from Scott and, bleary eyed from a lack of sleep, I checked my phone to find that he still hadn't responded to either my calls or my messages. Jacob ran back to his room and slammed the door, and I could hear him crying, even from my bed. I had to go to him, but he didn't want me; he wanted his dad, so after a few minutes of trying to comfort him, I suggested we get up and dressed, assuring him that Scott would be bound to arrive soon, keeping my fingers crossed that he couldn't let his son down that badly... could he?

It's now nearly ten o'clock and I've still heard nothing. Jacob is sitting in the living room, sulking and watching cartoons, and I'm scrubbing the kitchen to within an inch of its life. I've decided that, if Scott doesn't arrive by lunchtime, I'll take Jacob out somewhere, to try and make up for it.

The doorbell rings, and I hear Jacob let out a yell of glee. "Wait," I call, throwing my cloth into the sink and getting to the hall, just as he pulls open the door, his shoulders dropping as he sees that, rather than his father, it is Adam Barclay who's standing on the doorstep.

"Oh God." I step forward, pushing my fingers back through my hair. "I'd completely forgotten."

Adam looks from me to Jacob, and then back to me again, his confusion evident. "I can come back another time," he offers.

"No... no, it's fine." Jacob is still standing, watching the two of us and I place my hand on his head. "Why don't you go and sit back down," I say to him, and he shrugs and wanders disconsolately back into the living room, as I look up at Adam. "Come in."

He smiles and steps inside, waiting while I close the door and then follows me through to the dining room, although I pause at the living room door, just to check that Jacob is alright, which he seems to be.

"I really do apologise," I whisper to Adam once we're in the dining room. "Jacob's dad didn't turn up last night, and he didn't call, or answer my texts, so Jacob's upset and it's..." I feel tears welling in my eyes and turn away, looking out of the window and into the pointless conservatory – or lean-to – embarrassed that I'm about to cry in front of a complete stranger.

"Is there anything I can do?" he asks, and I'm suddenly aware that he's moved closer, that he's standing right behind me. I can feel the heat from his body seeping into mine, even though he isn't touching me. "I mean, there probably isn't, but…" He stops talking and I turn to face him, just about holding back my gasp as I notice the depth of concern in his eyes.

"Thank you for offering but…"

"Mum!" Jacob shouts, interrupting me. "Dad's here."

I tense, pursing my lips, my anger bubbling to the surface.

"Jacob… can you let me answer the door?" I call, although he's already running into the hallway and I know I'm too late. I look at Adam, mouthing, "Sorry," and he smiles and shakes his head, stepping back to let me pass, and I leave the room, steaming mad and ready for a fight.

Chapter Ten

Adam

I've been looking forward to coming back here since Wednesday, almost to the point of counting the hours. And I know why… I haven't been able to think about anything, or anyone, since I set eyes on Jenna, and it's a relief to finally be ringing her doorbell and know that we'll get to spend some more time together – alone. We may have had a slightly weird conversation – once we'd established that Jenna isn't married, that is – but I liked it. And I want more.

I wait, impatient to see her again, but as the door is pulled open, my heart sinks, as I'm faced with her son… Jacob.

I know Jenna said his father was picking him up last night and, judging from the expression on the boy's face, he's disappointed to see me. I'm about to ask if his mother is at home – although I know she will be – when she appears from the dining room. She's dressed in jeans and a blue, grey and white flowery, long-sleeved top, and she looks divine.

"Oh God," she says, her eyes locking with mine before they widen in surprise as she moves closer, and she lets her hand drift up to her hair, her fingers brushing through it. "I'd completely forgotten."

I'm not sure whether I should feel hurt by that, but she looks so stressed and worn out, that I can't feel anything other than sympathy… and confusion.

"I can come back another time," I suggest, just to be helpful.

She shakes her head slightly. "No, no… it's fine."

Her son is still standing between us, watching our conversation and Jenna puts her hand gently on his head. "Why don't you go and sit back down?" she says, and he shrugs a little petulantly before going back into the living room, as Jenna turns her attention to me. "Come in." She smiles and steps to one side, giving me enough space to enter the house, where I wait for her to close the door, and then follow her through to the dining room, noticing that she stops momentarily at the living room door and glances inside, presumably to check that her son isn't doing something he shouldn't be.

"I really do apologise," she murmurs quietly as soon as we're alone in the dining room, turning to face me. "Jacob's dad didn't turn up last night, and he didn't call, or answer my texts, so Jacob's upset and it's…" As she speaks, tears form in her eyes and before I can say or do anything, she turns away again, lowering her head, and moves to the window, her back to me.

Seeing her like this hurts me, with a sharp pain deep in my chest. I want to reach out and pull her into my arms, and hold her, comfort her, tell her it'll be okay. But I can't. Even if she has bewitched me. I can't make any assumptions.

"Is there anything I can do?" I ask instead, moving closer, hoping that I can reassure her somehow, without touching her. "I mean, there probably isn't, but…" She turns at that moment, our eyes meeting, and as her lips part in something that sounds like a half-gasp, I'm almost certain I feel a connection between us.

"Thanks for offering but…"

"Mum!" Her son's voice breaks into the moment and she starts slightly. "Dad's here."

I notice her whole body seems to tense and she purses her lips, her eyes darkening at the same time. She looks angry, ready to boil over.

"Jacob," she calls out, "can you let me answer the door?" Even as she speaks, though, I hear his footsteps rushing down the hallway and she looks up at me. "Sorry," she mouths, the smile momentarily returning to her lips, and I step aside before it fades, as she leaves the room.

Left to myself, I wonder if I should go out into the back garden, or at least into the kitchen, because at the end of the day, she is still a client, even if I want her to be more, and she's entitled to some privacy. But before I have the chance to decide what to do, I hear voices…

"Why don't you take your bag, Jacob, and go and get into Dad's car?" That's Jenna talking, sounding cheerful enough, although I can hear something strained, even strangled, in her voice.

"Okay," he says. "See you Sunday."

"Have a good weekend." She's raised her voice, so I assume Jacob has already left the house and is making his way to his dad's car. For a moment, I half expect her to come back, but then she says, "How dare you," her voice a low whisper, but loud enough for me to hear.

"How dare I what?" There's a slightly mocking tone to the man's voice and, forgetting about moving away, about giving them some privacy, I actually move closer, standing right by the dining room door.

"How dare you let Jacob down like that. How dare you not answer my calls and messages."

"You divorced me, remember?" he says, and I feel my muscles tighten at the tone he's now using, which is sneering and contemptuous. "That means I don't have to answer to you anymore."

"Answer to me? When did you ever answer to me?"

"Why can't you fucking well let it drop?" he says, raising his voice, and I take a step forward, almost revealing my presence, before I stop and hold myself in check. This isn't my fight… even if I'd quite like it to be.

"Can you please stop using language like that?" Jenna sounds exasperated and I wonder how many times she's asked that of him. "And can you stop teaching Jacob to do it as well? He's started swearing at me now…"

The man laughs, interrupting her. "I'm just trying to get him to stand up for himself… to be a man, rather than a wimp."

"No, you're not. You're teaching him to be rude and obnoxious, like you are. And you still haven't explained why you weren't here last night, or why you didn't return my calls and let Jacob know that you weren't going to make it."

"Because I was busy, that's why."

"Yes, I know you were busy. That much was obvious, and I can imagine what with too."

He laughs again. "You've got to stop this petty jealousy, Jenna. You had your chance…"

I've never wanted to punch anyone before in my life; I've never even considered using violence, not even against Nathan, but I think I'd make an exception in this man's case.

"I'm not jealous," Jenna replies firmly. "But we have an arrangement… and you're supposed to stick to it, not just turn up whenever you feel like it. Aside from the fact that it upsets Jacob, I do have a life too, you know?"

"No you don't." I can hear the humour in his voice and wish I could show my face and wipe the smile from his.

"Yes, I do. I'm in the middle of meeting, as it happens."

A meeting…? She could have phrased that better, if she'd wanted to score points. She could have called it a date. I wouldn't have minded. Not in the least.

"Who with?" he asks, picking up the bait that she didn't even drop.

"It's none of your business, Scott."

"Yes it is… if you've got strangers coming into the house while my son is living here, then I'm entitled to know—"

"You're entitled to know nothing," she interrupts. "Just because you can't keep your trousers up for more than twenty seconds, doesn't give you the right to come into my home and dictate how I live my life." She takes a breath, but not a very long one. "Now, I think you'd better leave… and next time you decide your latest blonde is more important than your son, could you at least have the manners to let me know?"

I hear the door slam and move quickly back into the room, trying to look nonchalant and like I haven't just overheard every word of what's been said.

"I'm so sorry," Jenna says from the doorway, her cheeks flushed and her eyes sparkling with anger.

"Don't be."

She pushes her fingers back through her hair again, this time making it slightly dishevelled, and leaving me torn between straightening it, or messing it up some more. I don't do either, and that's not because she's a client, but because she looks far too vulnerable. Her conversation with her ex has made it clear that he must have cheated on her, and that explains the guarded look she's got in her eyes right now. It's a look which makes me realise that, if she's ever going to be anything more to me than a client – which I sincerely hope she is – then I'm going to have to take it slow, and earn her trust. Because whatever he did to her, it hurt… and I think it still does.

"Would you rather I came back later on?" I ask. "I'm free all day, so I'm happy to go away and come back this afternoon, if it helps?"

She shakes her head, smiling up at me.

"No. That's very kind, but you're here now, and I could do with the distraction."

"Of me being here?" I say, without thinking. *Was that really appropriate, Adam?*

She blinks a few times and blushes. "I meant of going through the prices."

"Yes. Of course. Sorry."

"Don't apologise. After the display I just put on with my ex, you've got nothing to apologise for."

Deciding that speaking only seems to be getting me in trouble, I pull the quotation document from my folder and set it down on the table, turning it around for her to see. She glances at me, smiles and sits down on the bench, reading through the document. I remain standing, moving away slightly and pretending to look out of the window, through the lean-to, and into the back garden. I'm not really concentrating though, being as the only thing I'm really aware of is Jenna.

"This all looks fine," she says after a few minutes. "Would it be okay if I thought about it for a few days?"

"Of course." I turn round to face her. "Although there is one thing I need to measure." I may not have been concentrating when I looked out of the window, but I've just remembered something rather obvious, and I pull out the small tape measure that I always carry with me and go into the kitchen, taking the measurements of the doorway that leads into the lean-to. There's no actual door, however, and therein lies the problem.

As I come back into the dining room, Jenna looks up at me. "Is everything alright?"

"Yes. It was just something I'd forgotten. It doesn't affect the quote."

"I see." I approach her, taking a business card from my folder, and handing it to her.

"That's got my mobile number on it. Just give me a call when you've decided what you want to do."

I wonder for a moment whether I might never hear from her again; whether between us we've embarrassed ourselves too many times for her to want to see me any more.

As we say goodbye on her doorstep and I drive away, I feel a shadow cast over me, like something miraculous and wonderful has ended, even before it had begun, as though I've lost her, even though I never had her... and I wonder if I'm destined to be haunted by another unattainable woman for the rest of my life, just like the girl on the beach.

In spite of my despair, Jenna continues to frequent my dreams, and I'm finding it harder and harder to focus on work. If I'm not careful, Dad will notice soon and I'll have to think up an excuse for living my life in a daydream of 'if only I'd...' and 'I wish she'd...'.

I've just parked my car outside the office on Wednesday lunchtime, having returned from a site visit, when my phone rings. It's not a number I know, but during working hours, that could mean anything, and I pull on the handbrake and answer the phone at the same time.

"Adam Barclay..."

"Hello, Adam. It's Jenna."

My heart spins in my chest, a warm glow filling my body as a smile forms on my lips. "Hi, Jenna. How are you?"

"I'm a lot better than I was on Saturday morning. I do apologise again for that scene... for what happened."

"You don't need to apologise. Honestly."

"Thank you."

"You don't need to thank me either."

There's a short silence, and then she says, "I suppose I'd better tell you why I'm calling… I've decided to go ahead."

My smile widens uncontrollably. "Excellent." I try really hard not to give away my delight that our mutual embarrassment hasn't caused a permanent rift between us.

"The thing is," she adds, with a note of caution and I feel my grip tighten on the phone, "I forgot to mention the timescale."

"The timescale?"

"Yes. I've been so preoccupied with everything else, I forgot to point out that I'm going to need the work completed by the end of July." I feel the blood drain from my body and land in my boots. *July?* Is she kidding? "I know a project like this would normally take three to four months…" she adds. *Yes, if you don't count the kitchen construction, it would, and as long as you don't have any bad weather, or hiccups along the way.* "But it's really got to be done before the school holidays start. Do you think that's going to be possible?"

I think about all the jobs we've already got scheduled in, from now until the summer, and even beyond that, and shake my head. "I'm not sure," I say out loud, wondering how I can make it work. "Look, I've only just got back to the office. I'll take a look at the schedules and see what I can do. If we're going to complete by the end of July, we'd have to start next week."

"That soon?"

"Yes. You said yourself, the basic construction is three to four months, but then there's the kitchen to be built as well, and if you've got a definite deadline we have to allow a contingency for bad weather…"

"Yes." She sounds hesitant.

"Don't worry about it," I add quickly. "I'll call you back later this afternoon."

"I'm sorry I didn't mention it before," she says.

"That's okay. I'm sure you've got a lot on your mind."

I get out of the car as I'm speaking, and go into the office. "I'll hear from you later?" she asks.

"Yes. I'll get back to you before the end of the day. I promise."

"Thank you, Adam."

I like the way my name sounds when she says it, but try not to think too much about that as I end the call and look up at my Dad, who's staring at me.

"Who was that?" he asks.

"That was Jenna," I reply, and then wish I could engage my brain before speaking. Why did I use her first name?

"Jenna who?"

"Jenna Downing."

I can almost see the cogs ticking in his head, as the name rings bells and he tries to place it.

"You mean that client you went to see last week?"

"Yes, Dad."

"You're on first name terms with her already, are you?" He's trying not to smile, and isn't really succeeding.

"She asked me to call her Jenna, if you must know. She uses her ex's surname for the sake of their son, but she doesn't like it, so…" I let my voice fade, wondering why on earth I've just given him that much information.

"So, she's divorced, is she?"

"Yes."

"With a son?"

"Yes."

"Sounds complicated."

"Nowhere near as complicated as her job just became."

"Why's that?" he asks, sitting forward.

"Because she's just told me that she's happy to go ahead, but that she needs the work completed by the end of July."

Dad shakes his head. "No way. We can't do it, son."

I ignore him and go over to the wall, looking at the schedule that's mounted there and scratching my head a couple of times.

"Okay…" I muse, thinking out loud. "If I pull Don and Mitch from the Armstrong job…"

"That won't help you," Dad interrupts, getting up and coming to stand beside me. "You need at least three men working full time on a job like Ms Downing's, and we don't have three men available at the moment… besides, it's not fair on Mr and Mrs Armstrong."

"Oh, they won't mind. Not after the favour we did for them the other day."

"What favour?"

I turn to face him. "Their roof took some damage in the storm and I got Jason and Lewis to go up and fix it for them… free of charge."

He nods his head. "I see."

"And now, what goes around comes around," I add. "We don't really need a five man crew over there any more, so pulling Don and Mitch off…"

"Doesn't solve your problem," he interrupts again. "Like I say, you need at least three men working full time, probably even overtime, if you're going to stand a chance at—"

"I know that. I'll be the third man."

"And the overtime?" He turns, folding his arms across his broad chest. "Who's going to pay for that? You certainly didn't build it into the costings, and you can't expect Don and Mitch to work for nothing."

"I know… I'll do the extra hours, if they're needed."

He shakes his head, then looks back at the schedule. "Can I assume that Ms Downing is attractive?" he asks.

"No. She's beautiful."

"Hmm," he muses. "It's a good job you're my son."

"Why's that?"

"Because at least Michelle is unlikely to actually hurt you when you explain to her why I'm having to come back to work full time for the next few months."

"When *I* explain to her?"

He turns to me again. "Yes. You don't think I'm going to tell her, do you? This is your idea… your mess… your complicated girlfriend."

"She's not my girlfriend."

He smiles. "Yet."

"Maybe never," I point out. "She might not be interested and, like you said, it's complicated."

"Have a bit more faith in yourself, son," he says, then turns away and goes back to his desk, sitting down. "I'll give Mitch and Don a call and tell them they'll be on a new site from Monday morning… and I'll let you break the news to Ms Downing, shall I?"

I sit down myself, looking across the office at him. "Thanks, Dad."

He shakes his head, and then picks up his phone, and I do the same, connecting a call to Jenna, who answers on the second ring.

"That was quick," she says, with a definite smile in her voice, which makes my lips twitch upwards.

"Well, we aim to please," I reply, feeling relieved and relaxed that I've found a way to make this work… to give myself a chance.

"That sounds like you might have good news for me?"

"I have indeed. I've managed to jig the schedules around a bit, and we can be with you on Monday morning."

"Really? You can do it?" She sounds almost as thrilled as I am, although I try not to read anything into that. She wants her extension built by the summer, after all. I'm just facilitating that.

"Yes."

"Will you… will you be there yourself?" she asks, and I wonder at her slight hesitation, and at the question itself.

"Yes," I reply. "I'm going to be working on site. Just so you know, our normal starting time is eight o'clock, so that we don't disturb your neighbours…"

"But I'll have left for work by then," she interrupts.

"Well, I can come round earlier if you want. Give me a time that suits you and I'll be there."

"Is seven-thirty too early?" she asks. "It's just that it would be nice to see you…" She coughs and I can't help smiling, wondering if she meant to say that. I hope so. "I mean, it would be nice to see you before I leave, to make sure you know where everything is."

"Seven-thirty is fine."

"That's perfect," she says. "I'll leave you with a back door key and you can let yourselves in to use the kitchen and the bathroom."

"Thank you. That's kind…"

"It's the least I can do when you're helping me out."

"While we're on the subject of kitchens," I add, thinking out loud, but also not wanting our conversation to end just yet, "I should probably point out that you're going to be without one for a while, once we knock through internally, and take out your old units. So you'll need to plan for that."

"That won't be a problem," she replies. "Jacob and I can go to my parents' house to eat – or even to stay, if necessary."

"Well, it won't be for a while yet, so you'll be able to give them some notice of your arrival... but what about Jacob's school? I mean, do your parents live locally?"

"Oh yes. They live in a village about fifteen minutes away... called Carven Bay."

I sit back, smiling to myself. "Well, what a small world. That's where I live."

"You do?"

"Yes."

"It's a magical place, isn't it?" I can actually hear the enchantment in her voice. It makes me smile even more.

"Yes, it is. Were you born there?" I ask, my natural curiosity about her getting the better of me.

"No, we moved there when I was sixteen, but I fell in love with it straight away... who wouldn't, with a beach like that?"

"I know. It's my favourite place to be." How can I never have met her before? I thought I knew virtually everyone in Carven Bay... but it seems not.

"Did you grow up there then?" she asks.

"Oh yes. I lived in Newquay for a few years, but I couldn't wait to get back to Carven Bay." I look up at my dad, hoping he's not going to take that personally, but he's ensconced on the phone, and isn't listening, thank goodness.

"I know the feeling. Jacob and I moved back with my parents after I left Scott, but when it came to finding a place of our own, I couldn't find anywhere I could afford."

"I know. It is expensive. Luckily, because I live alone, I only needed a one bedroom place, otherwise I doubt I could have managed it either." Why did I tell her that? Was that a not very subtle way of letting her know that I don't have anyone in my life? I hope she doesn't think I'm being pushy or presumptuous.

"So whereabouts do you live then?" she asks, not having seemed to have noticed my comment at all.

"In one of the apartments overlooking the beach."

"Oh, lucky you."

"I know. And I really do appreciate it."

I hear someone talking in the background. "I'm sorry," she says, "I'm going to have to go. My boss needs to go over something with me."

"Of course. I'm sorry. I should have realised you'd be at work, and not kept you talking for so long."

"Oh, don't apologise," she replies.

"I'll see you on Monday," I add, before she can hang up.

"Yes… seven-thirty."

"I'll be there."

I put my phone down and lean back in my chair, smiling to myself.

"You're looking cheerful," Dad remarks from the other side of the office and I look over at him.

"I'm feeling cheerful."

He smiles. "That makes a change."

He's not wrong. I can't really remember the last time I felt like this… it was over fifteen years ago, after all, and my memory isn't *that* good. I give him a slight smile, before opening my laptop.

"What's she like?" Dad asks, getting to his feet and going over to the small kitchen area in the corner to put the kettle on.

"Beautiful."

"You told me that already. I mean what's she really like?"

"She's a breath of fresh air," I reply, letting out a sigh. "She feels like everything I've been looking for."

He turns and stares across the room at me. "Then make it work, son," he says.

"I'll do my best."

"And what's her little boy like?" he asks over his shoulder as he opens the cupboard to fetch the tea bags.

"Noisy, disruptive, rude… inconsiderate."

He faces me once more. "Sounds like your brother."

I smile. "He's exactly like my brother."

He shakes his head. "Good luck," he smirks and then chuckles, going back to making the tea again.

"Dad?" I say, after just a few minutes. "Can I ask you something?"

"Of course." He doesn't turn around this time.

"Why didn't you and Michelle ever have more kids? Was it because you saw what happened with Nathan when he was little… you know… how troublesome he was? Did it put you off?"

He turns now and moves back across the room, leaning back against his desk, opposite me. "No, son," he says quietly. "It has nothing to do with that." He lets out a deep breath. "We'd have loved to have more children… especially Michelle. But she had a bad time giving birth to Amy… they couldn't stop the bleeding, you see."

I sit forward, shutting my laptop again. "What happened?"

"There wasn't anything they could do… cutting a long story short, they had to do an emergency hysterectomy."

"Oh my God…" The words fall out of my mouth. "I had no idea."

He smiles. "Well, you were only little at the time. You wouldn't have understood. And… well, it's not something that comes up in conversation, so I suppose we've just never found a reason to tell you."

"No…" I muse to myself. "I'm sorry, Dad."

He shakes his head again. "Why? We've been very blessed… and very lucky." He pushes himself off the desk and stares down at me. "We've got two fabulous children, *both* of whom make us very proud."

And with that slight bombshell, he goes back to making the tea.

It's been an odd weekend, spent on tenterhooks, waiting in almost breathless anticipation for the moment I'll see Jenna again, and now that time has come, I find I'm really quite nervous as I wait for her to answer the door.

"Hello," she says, smiling, and that now familiar feeling hits my chest again. She looks so beautiful, with her hair put up, wearing a smart suit, and a dash of make-up on her face – although personally, I think she looks better without it, like she was on Saturday morning, and I'm inclined to say, I prefer her casual clothes to her work outfit, but even so… she's absolutely stunning.

"Good morning." I smile back.

"Come in." She steps aside and I quickly remove my work boots, carrying them through with me into the dining room. "You look very different," she remarks, which I suppose is true, being as I'm wearing slightly worn combat trousers, a t-shirt and a thick jumper – nothing like the usual smart jeans and shirts she's been used to seeing me in.

"Well, I came prepared to work," I reply. "But then you look different too."

"I wish I could say I felt comfortable, but I don't."

Jacob is sitting at the dining table, eating a bowl of cereal, and he glances up, noting our conversation, I think, and glaring at me.

"Are you finished?" Jenna asks, turning to him.

"Yes," he replies, pushing his bowl away.

"Right. Go and clean your teeth and fetch your school bag."

He leaves the room, giving me a hard stare over his shoulder, before he climbs up the stairs.

"I—I've got a key for you," Jenna says, going into the kitchen and returning with a key fob, which she hands to me. "It's to the back door, but I was thinking that it might be easier for you, if you came in that way in future? There's an alleyway that leads down the back of the houses, and the number is on the gate. You can just let yourselves in and get started… even if I'm not here."

I nod my head, pocketing the key at the same time, and deciding that, key or no key, I'm going to make an effort to get here early every morning, just so I can see her.

"And I've done my best to clear out the conservatory… I mean, the lean-to," she adds, looking up at me, with a beautiful smile. "But I couldn't move the washing machine and tumble dryer."

"That's okay. I'll move them now. Where do you want them put?"

"I suppose they can come in here for now," she says. "I won't be using either of them for a while. I've arranged to go over to Mum's at the weekends to do our washing there."

I nod my head. "Okay. Well, I'll get them shifted."

She picks up Jacob's bowl from the table and goes through to the kitchen, placing it in the sink. I follow, dumping my boots, and going on into the lean-to, where I unplug the tumble dryer, before lifting it from its place on top of the washing machine, and carrying it back through.

"Are you alright?" she asks as I pass, putting down the Star Wars lunch bag that she's only just picked up. "Do you want some help?"

"No. I'm fine." I put the dryer down in the dining room. "It doesn't weigh much."

"Really?" She joins me and I smile.

"Well, not as much as your washing machine will, anyway."

Jacob comes back down the stairs, dumping his school bag on the bench. "Where's my PE kit?" he asks.

"By the front door, where it usually is on a Monday morning," Jenna replies, and I wonder why she doesn't ask him to say 'please', or 'thank you'… why she lets him talk to her like that. But then, I don't suppose it's any of my business.

She turns back to face me. "I—I was wondering," she says, looking back into the kitchen. "I assume you'll dismantle the conservatory first?"

"Yes."

"But won't that mean there's no door between the kitchen and the outside world? I mean, it looks like there might have been one once, but there isn't one now and…"

I can almost hear the fear in her voice and I instinctively take a step closer. "I thought about that," I explain. "That's why I took those measurements the other day. The gap is smaller than usual, but I've managed to source a door that will fit without too many adjustments. Mitch and Don are picking it up this morning from one of our suppliers, and we'll make sure it's fitted and secure before we go tonight. Don't worry… I won't leave here until I know you're safe."

She blushes and rests her hand on my arm, burning a hole there. "Thank you, Adam," she whispers, and I sigh deeply, wishing I could tell her that I've fallen so hard for her that all I want to do – other than spend the rest of my life just looking at her – is to keep her safe.

Chapter Eleven

Jenna

Trevor took me with him to meet a new client this morning, which was one of the reasons I put my hair up and why I'm wearing my best suit. I always wear something smart to work, but when I'm meeting clients, I pull out all the stops. The Jamesons are a lovely couple, probably around my age, who've just moved to the area, having bought a small two-bedroomed bungalow, which they're looking to extend to add a couple of bedrooms and a larger kitchen, being as Mrs Jameson is pregnant, and they already have a toddler.

"You'll have to start on their plans straight away," Trevor says as we get into his Toyota Prius for the short journey back to the office. I'm reminded of Adam, being as this is the same model of car that he drives, but I stay focused.

"Okay. That's not a problem. I finished the Campbell's plans on Friday. I left them on your desk." He went home early on Friday for his daughter's birthday party, so probably wasn't aware that I'd already completed the project.

He nods, checking the traffic and pulling out. "Yes, I noticed this morning when I got in to work." We get to a junction and he stops for the traffic lights. "How's your own building project going?" he asks, making conversation now. "When do they think they'll be able to start?"

"They started this morning."

He turns to face me. "Really? That was quick. Last I heard, Barclays were snowed under with work."

That's odd. "Well, they seem to have fitted me in," I murmur.

He shrugs. "Maybe someone cancelled... it happens."

I nod and settle back into the seat, thinking about Adam's arrival this morning. He looked different in his work clothes – less smart, obviously, but more... rugged – and it was hard not to admire him, especially when he was lifting my tumble dryer from the conservatory through to the dining room. He did it with such ease, his muscles flexing... Dear God. What's wrong with me? I haven't reacted to a man like this since I was sixteen years old and I first saw the wolf man. But I'm not a teenager anymore. I know better than that now. I know that men are men, and however nice they might seem at the beginning, they're hard-wired to let you down, to lie, and to hurt you.

If only I didn't find him so easy to talk to...

I spend the day working on the Jameson's project, keeping busy and trying not to think about Adam, reminding myself, whenever I find his image filling my head, that he's a man... and what men can do, as a result of which, the hours fly by and, before I know it, it's time to collect Jacob from after school club. Ours is generally a nine-to-five office, but Trevor has been very good about allowing me to be flexible with my hours. So, I get in to work at eight-thirty, having dropped Jacob at school, and driven across town to the office, and I finish at four-thirty, which allows me enough time to get back to school and pick him up before five, when the club finishes.

The traffic is light this evening and we get home at just a few minutes after five o'clock, Jacob having filled the short journey from school by telling me how he scored two goals in football, and that he's been moved up to the top group for spellings, which means that, as well as learning ten new words this week, he's also been given a word search to do. Whatever problems he may be developing – courtesy of Scott – I can't fault his effort at school, or his delight in doing well.

"We'll make a start tonight, shall we?" I suggest as we get out of the car and I notice Adam's Toyota is still parked where it was this morning, a smile forming on my lips, unbidden.

"Okay," Jacob replies, dragging me back from my momentary lapse, "but can I have something to eat first?"

"You can have a banana."

"A banana?"

"It's good brain food," I tell him and he looks up at me as he drags his rucksack from the back seat, almost forgetting his lunch bag, but reaching in for it at the last moment.

"You're making that up," he says, narrowing his eyes.

"No, I'm not. I was reading about it… there are studies showing that bananas help with brain function."

His eyes widen now. "Seriously?"

"Yes… so there!" I grin down at him and he smiles back, and I wish it could always be like this. Like it used to be, before Scott's influence overtook mine.

I let us into the house, switching on the hall light, and going through to the dining room, where I can hear noises coming from the back garden.

"What's that?" Jacob sounds fearful and clutches my hand.

"Don't worry. It's just Adam."

"Who's Adam?"

"Don't you remember? He's the man who was here this morning. The man who's doing the building work."

"Oh… yes." He lets go of me and goes through to the kitchen, his fear forgotten, as he picks a banana from the fruit bowl and starts trying to peel it.

"Bring it here," I suggest, pulling the clips from my hair and shaking it out, before peeling Jacob's banana and handing it back to him. "You sit and eat that, while I go and see how Adam's getting on outside, and then we'll make a start on your spellings, alright?"

Jacob nods his head, sitting down at the dining table, surprising me with his obedience, for once.

I go through to the kitchen and, without thinking, walk straight into the door that now fills the space which used to be open, leading out to the conservatory.

"Ouch!"

The door opens outwards and Adam stands before me, his trousers dusty and his sweater discarded, leaving him in just a plain grey t-shirt, despite the near freezing temperature. He's wearing a tool belt now, slung low around his hips, which just seems to make him even more attractive... at least it does to me.

"Are you okay?" he asks, moving into the light, closer to me.

"Yes. I just wasn't expecting there to be a door here."

"Even though I'd told you there would be?" He smiles at me.

I nod my head and smile back, rubbing my elbow, where I caught it on the door as I glance over his shoulder. "It's all gone," I say, a little dreamily.

He steps back, allowing me to move outside and join him. "Yes," he replies. "I'm afraid your lean-to is no more."

I look around at the space it once occupied. "Well, I can't say I'm sorry, although it looks so big."

"Most people say that," he says, then stops suddenly and smirks, his eyes sparkling as he looks at me in the dim light, and I can feel myself blushing at the double-entendre. "It's because it's not enclosed," he adds, to rectify the situation.

"I see." I move further into the garden, noticing that we're alone out here. "Your colleagues have already gone then?"

"Yes. They went about half an hour ago, when the light faded." I look up at him. "I waited behind to let you know about the door."

"The one I just walked into, you mean?" I ask, and we both smile.

"Yes, that would be the one."

"Well, I know about it now."

He moves closer again. "Yes, but that was only part of the reason I stayed," he adds, his voice dropping, and I feel a pool of heat settle at the pit of my stomach, as I hold my breath, waiting... "I need to give you the key."

"The key?" I breathe, gazing up at him.

"Yes... to the new door."

I feel like such an idiot – what did I think he was going to say? That he'd stayed here just to see me? Why would he? I look away for a second, hoping he hasn't noticed my embarrassment. "Yes, of course," I mumble.

He holds out his hand, offering me a key, and I take it from him, being careful not to touch him.

"I hope I'm not being presumptuous, but I've kept the spare one myself…" He pats his trouser pocket but then holds out a second, more familiar key. "And this is your old one," he adds. "Although you won't be needing it anymore."

I shake my head. "I suppose it was a bit pointless giving that to you in the first place really."

"No, it wasn't. If we'd had to leave your house today for any reason, before dismantling the lean-to, then I'd have needed to secure the property, wouldn't I?"

"I suppose so…"

He steps closer still, so he's only a few inches from me. "Are you alright?" he asks.

How can I tell him that I'd built up a stupid, juvenile hope in my head; that I'd thought he was going to tell me he'd waited here just because he wanted to see me? How can I tell him that I feel foolish… disappointed, and let down? Even though it's not really his fault. It's mine.

"I'm fine. It's just been a busy day." That's not a lie, even if it's not entirely the truth either.

He stares at me for a second, then nods and steps away again, grabbing his sweater from the wide kitchen window ledge.

"I'll see you tomorrow morning," he says, throwing it around his shoulders, evidently immune to the cold.

"You'll be here early again?"

He nods. "If that's okay with you… I—I thought I'd come round before you leave for work, just in case there's anything we need to go through."

My lips twitch upwards, and I make a conscious effort to control them, not to read anything into his actions. I'm a client… and he's very definitely a man. And I need to remember that.

I make a start on Jacob's spellings as soon as Adam has left, through the back gate, going inside and sitting at the dining table with him. We're doing basic homophones, such as 'flower' and 'flour', where the words are spelled differently but sound the same. Jacob finds them confusing to start with, although there are pictures and clues to help, and he argues that some of the standard spelling rules that Miss Eden taught him last year don't seem to apply – which, I have to admit, they don't. Unfortunately, being unable to do something perfectly affects his mood, so when he gets one wrong, he slams his hand down on the table, in a fit of rage, knocking his glass of water over. I tell him off, because his reaction was unnecessary, and his response is to lash out, punching me hard in the arm.

"It's just water… what's the fucking problem?" he yells at the same time.

"Jacob! Don't swear at me."

He glares at me. "Why not? Dad says they're just words, and they don't hurt anyone."

"I don't care what Dad says. In this instance, he's wrong. They're not just words."

His eyes narrow. "What do you know anyway!"

I open my mouth, then close it again, reminding myself that I promised not to say anything against Scott within Jacob's hearing, despite the temptations, and instead I leave the room, going into the kitchen and taking a few deep breaths to calm myself down. I'd already worked out that Scott was behind Jacob's altered behaviour – and he as good as admitted it himself – but now I know for sure. How I'm going to get Scott to stop it is another matter though, being as he doesn't listen to a word I say… and our son is rapidly going down the same road.

A tear falls onto my cheek and I rub it away. I'm not a crier. I never have been, but it feels like Scott's still calling the shots, still wearing me down, still belittling me, even though we're divorced. He's controlling me through Jacob… and what's more, I think he knows it.

Today, I only managed a brief conversation with Adam before Jacob dragged me out to the car, fretting about being late for school. I fought my feelings of disappointment on the drive into work, telling myself over and over, that even if it feels like I have no control over my son, or my ex-husband, I can at least try and do better at controlling my responses towards Adam, and not keep making a fool of myself. Nothing can ever come of it anyway, because I'm not going to get involved. That's the last thing I need right now.

My day is busy again, not helped by the fact that Holly, who works alongside me, is off with flu and I'm having to cover her work as well, although I do manage to get away on time and pick Jacob up from after school club. He's not in such a good mood today, and when we get home, he stomps up the stairs, without saying a word. I've got no idea what that's about, but I'm sure I'll find out later. There's no point in trying to talk to him now; he'll only shout, and probably swear… and if avoiding the issue makes me a coward, then so be it.

I noticed when we got back that Adam's car wasn't parked outside, and I actually felt relieved. At least I can be myself this evening, rather than behaving like a silly teenager, so I follow Jacob upstairs, ignoring his closed bedroom door, and go into my own, flicking on the light and closing the curtains before removing my jacket, blouse and skirt, leaving them on the bed, and pulling on a pair of jeans, and a thick jersey top, with an embroidered panel at the front. I didn't put my hair up today, so I give it a quick brush, and turning off the light, go back downstairs to start getting dinner ready.

Going through the dining room, I leave the light off, only switching one on when I get to the kitchen, where I open the fridge, looking into the salad drawers to see what we've got available for tonight. I'm just contemplating veggie fajitas, when a gentle knocking on the back door makes me jump out of my skin and I slam the fridge door shut in shock, letting out a startled yelp. Peering through the glass panel, I see Adam looking back at me, a concerned expression on his face.

"Sorry," he says, as I open the door to him, "did I scare you?"

"I didn't think anyone was here. Your car's not out the front, so I assumed you'd gone for the day."

He smiles. "I parked down the side, being as we're using your back gate to come and go. It seems silly to walk all the way round from the front."

I nod my head. "I see."

"But I didn't mean to scare you," he adds.

"Don't worry," I reply, my heart rate finally returning to normal. "Was there something you needed to see me about?"

He stares at me for a second, then blinks a couple of times. "No... I—I just stayed behind to... um... to clear up a bit. That's all." He pushes his fingers back through his hair.

"And how's it going out there?" I ask, trying to peer out beyond him, even though he's blocking the doorway.

He steps aside, although I still can't see much in the darkness. "We're just digging out the foundations," he replies. "It's nothing exciting at the moment."

"And I suppose you're having to do that all by hand, are you?" My garden is far too small for large equipment to be brought in.

He smiles. "We certainly are. It's been a while since I've worked this hard..."

"Are you suggesting that you don't normally work very hard then?"

His smile broadens. "Not like this, no. And there's nothing like manual labour to remind a guy that he's thirty-five, not twenty-five."

"Thirty-five isn't old," I remark.

"Not for some things," he replies, and I notice that sparkle in his eyes again, but I make a conscious effort not to respond, even though my mouth has gone dry and my skin is tingling. "Well," he adds after a moment's silence, "I'd better be getting off home. A long, hot shower beckons."

"Hmm... that sounds lovely," I murmur, and his eyes flicker again, making me blush.

"I'll see you tomorrow morning," he says, and this time, I don't question him, mainly because I'm worried about what I'll say next to humiliate myself.

The rest of my week has run true to form. Holly still isn't back, so work has been hard going. Jacob's moods have been up and down; one minute he seems like the normal, lovely little boy I can still vaguely remember, and the next, he's an obnoxious monster, the mirror of his father. And as for Adam… well, I've managed to avoid making a fool of myself again, but only by making a conscious effort to control our conversations, and keep in mind that, no matter how beautiful he is on the outside, no matter how much his smile makes my insides melt, and no matter how easy it would be to just fall into his dark brown eyes… he's still a man.

By the weekend, I'm frazzled, and I hate to admit it, but there's a part of me that wishes it could be Scott's turn to take Jacob, just so I could have a rest. Still, I manage to get through it by spending Saturday at my parents' house, catching up on the laundry, and then Sunday doing the grocery shopping and housework. Jacob has to come shopping with me, which he hates, and I bribe him with a few treats just to get round the store. When we get back, I let him have an hour on his Playstation – a Christmas present from his father, needless to say – while I unpack the groceries and clean the kitchen, before taking him to the park. I always feel guilty that my weekends with him are filled with chores, while his weekends with Scott are fun-packed and thrilling, but it can't be helped. If I don't do the chores at the weekend, they don't get done.

Kicking a football around the park seems to have tired Jacob out, and after dinner, he falls into bed, exhausted, leaving me free to take a long, well-earned bath.

I'm lying back, my head settled on a towel, my eyes closed, trying not to fall asleep, when there's a crashing, splashing sound and I startle, sitting up, just as the pain hits me and I glance down, seeing the blood ooze from the cut on my leg. For some reason, it takes me a second or two to react, to realise that the shower head has fallen from the wall, bringing its fixing and the surrounding tiles with it, and that one of the tiles has cut my leg.

It's not a bad cut – at least I don't think it is – but it's bleeding profusely and I jump from the bath, grabbing a towel and holding it over the wound, pressing down hard and sitting back on the edge of the bath. I remain there for ten minutes, hoping that will be long enough, before I remove the towel and examine the cut, to find it's actually quite a neat injury, only about two inches long and not that deep, fortunately.

The bleeding has just about stopped and I get to my feet, examining the hole in the wall where my shower once was.

"Oh for heaven's sake," I mumble, feeling my shoulders drop and taking a deep breath, but resolving that I'm not going to cry. What would be the point? Crying won't clear up the bathroom, or get a dressing put on my leg, will it? It's not like there's anyone else here who can do those things for me, while I sit back and feel sorry for myself, so I put on my robe and go downstairs, where I find the first aid kit and apply a large dressing to the cut on my leg, before going back, draining the bath and doing my best to clear up the mess that's inside it.

As I lie in bed, I let a few tears fall, wishing I could be stronger, wishing that I didn't miss having someone to share moments like this with. I know it's not a big deal; it's only a shower head and a few tiles, and it could have been worse – it could have been Jacob in the bath, not me – but sometimes having to do everything myself is so utterly draining. I didn't ask to be alone. I was married. I even thought I was happily married, compared to a lot of people... until I woke up to reality and discovered I wasn't, and that I never had been.

Despite my best intentions, for the first time in ages, I sob myself to sleep.

This morning has been a nightmare so far.

I forgot to re-set my alarm, to allow for the fact that having a bath this morning would take longer than having a shower, so by the time I get downstairs I'm running late. Jacob is in a foul mood and won't do a thing I say, and by seven-thirty, I've already had enough.

I'm just laying out Jacob's breakfast in the dining room, when I notice Adam walking down the garden towards the house, glancing around at the foundations. He looks up, notices me, and smiles, and although I do my best to smile back, I can feel tears pricking my eyes – presumably the last remaining ones I managed not to cry last night. Humiliated by my inability to keep it together for more than ten minutes, I go back into the kitchen to finish making the tea.

"Is everything okay?" Adam's standing at the back door, holding it open, but not actually coming inside.

I open my mouth to say yes, but find I'm shaking my head, and then before I know it, he's right there. He's kicked off his boots and is standing in front of me, looking into my eyes.

"What's wrong?" he asks. "Is there anything I can do?"

I shake my head again. "No… it's nothing. I'm just being pathetic."

He smiles. "I doubt that. Tell me what's happened."

"It really is nothing… it's just that my shower broke last night when I was in the bath… and a few of the tiles came down with it, and cut my leg…"

"You're hurt?" he says, his brow furrowing.

"It's not a bad cut." I look down and raise my leg slightly, holding it out to the side, showing him the dressing, which I replaced after my morning bath. "It could have been a lot worse." He sighs. "It was just a bit of a shock, that's all… and of course, it meant I had to take a bath this morning, instead of a shower… and now I'm running late."

"Then let me help," he says. "What can I do?"

I smile up at him. "Nothing, but thanks for offering."

"So, I can't help you get breakfast ready, or make Jacob's packed lunch while you drink your tea?"

"How do you even know Jacob has a packed lunch?" I ask, surprised.

"Because I noticed his lunch bag," he replies. "I didn't think Star Wars was quite your style."

"No, it's not."

"So… what can I do to help?" he perseveres.

"Nothing… honestly. I'm just having a weak five minutes, that's all." I feel embarrassed now for letting him see me with my guard down.

"There's nothing weak about accepting help," he says softly. "You don't have to do everything yourself."

I recall my thoughts from last night and let out a half laugh. "I think I do, being as there's no-one else here to do them with me."

He shakes his head slowly, then takes a step back. "I'll let you get on," he murmurs, turning away and I know I've offended him. Even so, he gets to the door before my conscience pricks at me.

"Sorry," I say, my voice just about loud enough for him to hear. "That was ungracious of me."

He turns back and smiles. "No, it wasn't. I shouldn't have interfered."

"You weren't. You were trying to help, and I was rude."

"You weren't rude, or ungracious. And standing here talking to me won't get Jacob's lunch made." He slips his boots back on, opening the door again. "I'll get back to work and leave you to it."

He's gone before I can say anything else, and I stare at the space he's just vacated, feeling guilty, until Jacob appears, asking why there's no juice in his glass, dragging me back to reality and the fact that we're running even later now than we were before.

Getting out of the car this evening, I'm brought back to the recollection of this morning's conversation with Adam, which I've tried to avoid thinking about all day. I've been torn between pangs of remorse and shame, coupled with a deep sense of humiliation – the last of which seems to be becoming a regular occurrence around him. As I close the car door, I just hope I can manage to avoid any further awkwardness tonight – or that he'll have decided I'm too ungrateful for words, and will have gone home already.

I let us in, making sure Jacob takes off his shoes before he runs upstairs to his room, and with a feeling of some trepidation, make my way through to the rear of the house, which is in darkness, allowing me to see out of the dining room window and down the garden, to where Adam is shifting some bricks, oblivious to my presence, his head bowed as he toils away in an area lit up by a couple of high powered lamps. I watch for a few minutes, my thumb nail in my mouth, marvelling at the broad expanse of his back, straining against the thin material of his t-shirt, before I decide to announce my presence by switching on the light. Blinded to the outside world now, I shrug off my jacket, laying it over the bench by the dining table to take upstairs later, and go through to the kitchen, surprised to find Adam already waiting at the back door.

"Can I come in?" he asks, opening it.

"Of course." I turn to face him, but avoid looking him in the eye, focusing on the space beneath his chin instead. He kicks off his boots and closes the door, then takes off his tool belt, laying it on the draining board, making me wonder what's coming next.

"Can… can I show you something?" he asks, sounding nervous.

"Um… okay."

I glance up and he smiles, nodding his head and then makes his way into the dining room, which confuses me. He turns at the door and looks back, presumably to make sure I'm following, which I am, and then starts climbing the stairs.

"Excuse me, but what's going on?" I ask, taken aback. "Where are you going?"

"Upstairs," he replies, stating the obvious. "I realise I'm taking liberties, but will you humour me?"

I take a breath and reach the conclusion that, having been so rude to him this morning, I owe him that much, and put my foot on the first tread, following him to the top of the stairs, where he opens the bathroom door, switches on the light, and then steps back to let me enter.

"You want me to go in?" I ask and he nods, smiling. I pass him, going inside, and stop dead when I see that a brand new shower head has been mounted on the wall, the tiles around it replaced and neatly grouted. It looks better than it did before and I turn back to him, my mouth open in surprise. "Did you do this?" I ask.

"Yes." He comes into the room, standing beside me. "I came up here after you'd left this morning and checked out what I'd need, and then I went to one of our suppliers and got the parts and the tiles, and fixed it while Don and Mitch got on with digging the foundations outside. I —I hope you don't mind?"

"Mind? I'm so grateful…" As the word leaves my mouth, I burst into tears.

"Oh, God," he says and steps closer. "Don't cry, Jenna. I didn't mean to upset you."

I shake my head and reach behind me for some toilet paper, using it to wipe my nose and eyes. "I'm sorry."

"Why? You've got nothing to be sorry for," he replies.

"This is just so kind of you." I glance up at the shower head, admiring his handiwork, and then take in the fact that the shower screen and bath are sparkling. "You cleaned my bath too?"

"I made a hell of a mess," he says, his smile returning. "It was the least I could do."

"Well, it's a poor reward, but would you like to stay and have a coffee, while I make a start on Jacob's dinner?" I'd quite like to invite him to stay and eat with us, but I'm not sure how Jacob would react to that, and I don't think I could handle any more of his moods or tantrums, especially not in front of Adam.

"I'd love to," he replies, and steps back so I can exit the bathroom ahead of him.

Downstairs, I boil the kettle and get out some vegetables from the fridge, and some spices from the cupboard.

"What are you making?" he asks, leaning against the back door.

"Vegetable curry." I turn and look at him.

"Are you vegetarians?" he asks, sounding interested, rather than critical, like Scott does.

"Not entirely. We eat fish." He nods. "What about you?"

"I suppose I'm quite similar," he replies. "At least I have been for the last few years."

I smile at him, then start making the coffee. "I—I can't thank you enough for fixing my shower," I say quietly, feeling self-conscious again. "You'll have to tell me how much I owe you."

"You don't owe me anything."

I pause, the coffee scoop in my hand, poised mid-air. "But I must do…"

He shakes his head. "No."

"Well, you'll have to add it to my bill then," I say, tipping the coffee into the cafetière.

"Or we could just call it a favour," he replies.

"I—I can't possibly accept." I put the scoop back into the tin and turn to face him again.

"It's a bit late now," he remarks, grinning. "The work's already done."

I watch him carefully, feeling nervous. "So... what do you expect in return?" His face falls and I know I've offended him. For the second time today.

"You don't get it, do you?" he says, stepping forward, coming closer to me.

"Get what?"

"I didn't do you a favour in the expectation of receiving anything in return. I did you a favour – I fixed your shower – because I wanted to help you out. I don't have an agenda, Jenna. I'm not like that."

"I—I'm sorry," I stammer, feeling tears prick my eyes again. "It's just... I suppose I've got used to Scott... to my ex..." I let my voice fade, wishing I hadn't started that sentence, that I hadn't been about to reveal that Scott never did anything without expecting something in return... and that it took me too long – far too long – to work that out.

"Hey... there's nothing for you to be sorry for. Really. Just don't use the shower for twenty-four hours, while the grouting dries, that's all." He smiles down at me.

"Thank you," I murmur, despite the lump in my throat.

"It's okay... just chill."

I shake my head. "I'm not very good at chilling."

"I had noticed," he says.

I lean back on the work surface, folding my arms. "To be honest, that's one of the reasons I'm having all this work done. I'm planning on working from home, hopefully to spend more time with Jacob and reduce the stress in my life. My boss would only agree to the plan though, if I had a designated space set up, so once all of this is complete, I'm going to convert the living room into an office. It's not ideal, I suppose, but I'm hoping that the space out here will provide enough room to live in, and give us the best of both worlds..." I fall silent yet again, surprised that I've told him so much. But then, I seem to keep doing that around him, for some reason...

"Can't your ex help out?" he asks, taking an interest. "I mean, with Jacob?"

"Scott?" I shake my head. "You must be joking. He does what he pleases, when it pleases him. And that doesn't include helping me out."

Chapter Twelve

Adam

I drink the coffee Jenna hands me and watch while she chops up some mushrooms, sweet potatoes and cauliflower, adding them to a pan of roasting spices that smell incredible.

Today has been weird. It started with seeing Jenna through the window and realising that she was upset about something. My natural instinct was to want to help, but then she rejected me… well, she rejected my offer, anyway, which I have to say hurt a lot more than I expected it to. I know she thinks she has to do everything by herself, and maybe she's trying to prove a point – to herself, or to her ex, I'm not sure – but she doesn't have to prove a damn thing to me. I'd intended to just walk away from her, to go back into the garden and give us both some time to ourselves, but then I saw the look on her face when she said she was sorry, and I couldn't. She looked so hurt herself and I knew then that I could never leave her hurting… no matter what.

It was then that I decided to repair her shower. It seemed to me like such a simple thing to do; it only took a couple of hours, but I knew it would make a huge difference to Jenna's life, so I picked up the parts and got on with it. All afternoon, I wondered about just leaving when she got home, and letting her discover the surprise for herself, but I wanted to see her face, so I took her up to the bathroom… and she burst into tears. It wasn't quite the reaction I'd hoped for, although she didn't cry because she was sad – even I know that – she cried because she was grateful, and I think that was the worst part of all. It certainly made me want to hold her, even though I knew I couldn't, and standing in her bathroom, watching her cry was the hardest thing I've ever done in my life.

As for her thinking that she had to do something in return, as payback for me fixing her shower… well, that was really informative. It told me something about Jenna, but a lot more about her ex and their relationship, which her comments afterwards only confirmed. She's obviously used to being with a man who's out for whatever he can get. She's got used to living her life like that, I guess… and he's let her.

"I really can't thank you enough," she says, stirring the vegetables in the pan and looking up at me.

"You don't have to," I reply, finishing my coffee. "It wasn't a big deal."

"Well, it was to me. I mean, it *is* to me."

"I know… that's why I did it," I confess and her eyes widen as I put my cup down on the draining board. "And now, I should be going. I've got a shower of my own that's calling to me." She smiles, letting the wooden spoon she's been holding drop to the side of the pan. "And if you're going to say 'thank you' again," I add, putting my boots back on, "you can forget it."

"I was going to say that I'll see you in the morning," she replies, her lips twitching upwards slightly.

"In that case, feel free to speak." I smile at her, resting my hand on the doorknob. "Enjoy your curry."

"Thank you."

I shake my head, smiling more widely, and she giggles, and I know that today was a day well spent.

I can't believe it's Friday already and another week has gone by.

It's been a week in which I've cherished my mornings and evenings, when I get to snatch a few brief minutes in the day to be with Jenna. We haven't really had time for any long conversations, but sometimes just to stand and watch her, just to be with her, in the same room, on the same street, in the same town, is enough.

The weather hasn't been that kind to us this week either, as it rained solidly on Wednesday and Thursday, and although today has been much better, we're still a bit behind.

Jenna arrives back at just after five, putting on the light in the dining room and I notice that she hasn't changed out of her work clothes like she sometimes does. She's still wearing a tight, fitted black skirt and white blouse, presumably having taken the jacket off, and her hair is tied up behind her head. She looks lovely like this, but I still think I prefer her when she looks more relaxed, in a flowing dress, or jeans and a blouse, her hair loose around her shoulders. She's talking, presumably to Jacob, and then she turns and disappears from sight and I let out a long sigh, feeling like a love-sick teenager, thriving on momentary glimpses of the girl I crave.

I grab my sweater and put it around my shoulders, making sure I've tidied everything away for the weekend, and feeling desolate that I won't see Jenna for two whole days now… which stretch before me like a prison sentence.

I open the back door and call out her name.

"Two seconds," she replies from somewhere in the house, and then a minute later, appears. "I'm sorry," she says, as I think about the fact that she starts a hell of a lot of her sentences with an apology. I don't comment though, because she's looking particularly stressed this evening.

"I just came to say I'm leaving for the night… Are you okay?"

"Yes… it's just that it's Scott's night to collect Jacob."

"And you're worried he won't turn up again?" I ask.

"No." She shakes her head. "He sent me a sarcastic text this afternoon, telling me he'd be on time, so I'm not worried about that."

"Then what's wrong?"

"It's just I need to get Jacob ready, and he's in a horrible mood because he came third in the spelling test, which is evidently my fault…"

"Third isn't so bad," I reason, remembering some of my results at school.

"That's what I told him, but he wasn't convinced."

I nod my head, unsure what to say, uncertain if I should offer to help, partly for fear of being rejected again, but also because I'm worried her gratitude might push her over the edge and into tears again. "Well, I'll get out of your hair," I murmur eventually.

"Thanks," she replies – and again, I contemplate how often she says that word when she has no need to. "I'll see you on Monday."

"I'll be here... have a good weekend."

"You too."

I doubt it, not if I can't be with you.

All the way home, I can't stop thinking about Jenna. About the sad look in her eyes, the sorrowful tone of her voice, the fact that she seems so lonely, and that the men in her life seem to treat her so badly. Her ex obviously has a lot to answer for, not just for the fact that he cheated, which in my view makes him an idiot, but also because of the way he behaves towards her now, talking down to her, mocking her, belittling her. And even her son is rude to her, regarding her as little more than a slave, it seems to me.

By the time I let myself in, throwing my keys into the bowl on the shelf by the door, and kicking off my boots, I'm already wondering how I'm going to get through the next two days without seeing her, and I try to distract myself by taking a shower... except that was a dumb idea, because all I can think about is what it would be like if Jenna was to shower with me. I brace my arms against the cool tiles and let the water flow over my head, trying not to imagine her perfect body bound with mine... and then when that doesn't work, I shut off the water and wrap a towel around my waist, going out into the kitchen and chopping vegetables for a stir-fry, like my life depends on it.

Maybe I'll hit the waves, I muse as I start cooking, wearing a bathrobe now. I haven't had time to surf for ages and it looks like it could be a good weekend to get out there, based on the forecast, anyway. Surfing always used to help me forget things when I was younger, so maybe it'll work now.

I dish up my stir-fry into a bowl and take it with me into the living room, sitting down on the couch and flicking on the television. I channel hop as I eat, not really watching anything, and contemplate going to the pub after dinner, rather than sitting here all evening thinking about Jenna, because no matter how hard I try, I can't think of anything else. The need to see her is overwhelming...

My phone is sitting on the table, staring at me and, as I finish eating, I pick it up, twisting it around in my hand, then turning on the screen and idly pressing the 'contacts' icon and letting my fingers scroll down to the letter 'J', where I stored Jenna's number at the beginning of her project. I sigh, turning my phone around once more, and then press the little green phone button, holding my breath.

"Hello?"

"Hi... it's Adam."

"Hi," she replies, sounding confused, which isn't surprising. I'm pretty confused myself.

"Are you okay?" I ask. "It... it's just that you seemed a bit stressed earlier." It sounds like a reasonable excuse for a phone call... kind of. At least it might if I meant something to her and wasn't just the guy who's building her extension.

"I'm fine," she replies. "Scott's been and gone, thank goodness."

"So he made it on time?"

"Yes."

I suck in a breath. "Does... Does that mean you're free this evening?" I ask, the words pouring out of me in a bit of a rush.

"Yes, it does."

"In that case, would you like to come out for a drink with me? It's Friday night, after all, and I think we already established, you need to chill."

"Didn't we also establish that I'm not very good at chilling?" she says and I feel my heart sink.

"We did," I reply, "but it's never too late to try something new."

There's a long silence, before she eventually says, "Okay," and I let out the breath I've been holding, as I smile and lean back on the sofa.

"I'll drive back and pick you up," I suggest.

"No, why don't we meet somewhere... do you know The Smuggler's Rest?"

"Here in Carven Bay?" I ask, just to make sure we're both talking about the same place.

"Yes. I can meet you there in… an hour?"

"Sounds perfect."

"I'll see you there," she replies and we end the call.

It's only when I'm getting dressed a short while later that it dawns on me that she might not turn up. Maybe she said 'no' to me collecting her and arranged to meet me instead, because she's got no intention of spending the evening with me.

God, I hope not…

I get to the pub ten minutes early, just to be on the safe side, wondering if I've ever been this nervous before. I'm not even sure whether this is a date, but I feel like I'm thirteen all over again… only so much worse. Back then, my worst fears had been butting heads, or clashing teeth, when I kissed Shelley. Now I feel like my entire future depends on what happens in the next couple of hours.

So… no pressure then.

I order a pint and find a table in sight of the door, where I sit and wait… and wait. And twenty minutes later, I reach the firm conclusion that I was right. Jenna's not coming.

For a moment I'm reminded of that time all those years ago when the girl failed to turn up at the beach, and how I went back, day after day, waiting and watching… hoping she'd be there. Only she never was. I can still remember how that felt, how…

"I'm so sorry I'm late." Jenna's voice cuts through my memories and I jump to my feet.

"Don't worry," I say, smiling. "I was about to give up on you."

"Oh God… were you?" She bites her bottom lip, her eyes glistening and I take her arm, pulling out the chair beside mine and sitting her down.

"No," I reply. "I was joking." I wasn't, but she doesn't need to know that, and she's clearly not good at taking jokes – not at the moment anyway. She's too fragile. "Let me get you a drink," I offer.

"I'll have a white wine spritzer," she replies. "I'm driving, so I'd better not have my usual bottle of wine, and a straw…"

I chuckle and she smiles back, relaxing a little, I think. I hope.

I get her drink, returning to the table and I notice that she's removed her coat, putting it over the back of the chair, and that she's wearing a gorgeous blue dress, with tiny white flowers on it, which is fitted at her slim waist. Even in the dim lights of the bar, I can also see that she's wearing a light touch of make-up – not that she needs it – and I smile to myself, wondering if she put it on for my benefit, or for her own. I really hope it was for herself, partly because I hate the idea that she thinks she has to try to look good for me. She doesn't. But more importantly, I'd just like this to be about her, because in the short time I've known her, I've never been aware of her doing anything that wasn't about putting someone else first.

She raises her glass to mine and I clink them together, before we both take a sip.

"So, Jacob left alright then, did he?" I ask, breaking the ice.

"Yes. Scott seemed to be in a hurry to be somewhere else tonight, so he didn't hang around to hurl insults, for a change." She stops talking, raising her hand to her mouth and I'm pretty sure she's blushing too. "I'm so sorry," she says, lowering her hand again. "That wasn't meant to come out."

I reach out, taking her hand in mine now, and relishing the feeling of her soft skin as she lets me hold onto her, not pulling back, but allowing me to rest our clasped hands on the table. "It's okay. I'm happy to listen, if you want to talk about your ex… or vent about him."

"Really? You'd let me vent about Scott?"

I smile at her. "If it helps, then go for it." I get the distinct impression she needs this, that she's held it all in for too long and she needs to let it out.

She takes a breath, using her other hand to raise her glass to her lips, and sipping her wine, before she looks up at me. "I don't even know where to start," she says eventually. "I—I mean, where do you start with a man like Scott? I caught him in bed with our babysitter."

Wow. That was unexpected. "You did?"

"Yes. It's such a cliché isn't it? It's almost as bad as him having an affair with his secretary, and I'm sure if he'd had a secretary, he would have done that too…" Her voice fades and she takes another sip of her drink.

"What happened?" I ask, moving a little closer and lowering my voice.

"We were living in Bristol at the time and we'd planned a weekend down here at my parents'," she says, shaking her head. "Except we hadn't. *I'd* planned a weekend at my parents', in which Scott was meant to be included, but he cancelled at the last minute, saying he had to work. I left by myself – well, with Jacob, who was two at the time – and I'd have been none the wiser to what Scott was up to, if Jacob hadn't forgotten his favourite toy, and we hadn't had to go back for it. I went into our bedroom… and there they were…" She closes her eyes and I know she's imagining the scene, so I tighten my grip on her hand and she opens her eyes again, focusing on me. "I left," she says simply. "In fact, I ran. I grabbed Jacob from the living room, and I just ran…"

"Where did you go?"

"I came down here to Mum and Dad's."

"Even though you knew that was the first place he'd look for you?" I ask, surprised.

"Well, if I'm being honest, I didn't expect him to follow me."

"Why?"

"Because he seemed to be having too much fun with our nineteen year old babysitter at the time."

"He must have followed you though. Surely…" The guy can't have been a total idiot.

"He did. He arrived that evening, presumably after he'd finished with Ella."

"Is that the babysitter?"

She nods her head. "He wanted my forgiveness, but…" She pauses for a long moment, staring off into the distance, like she's remembering something, before she continues, "I'm not a complete fool. There was no way I could forgive him."

"So you filed for divorce?"

"Yes. He threatened to take Jacob from me, told me no man would ever want me again… threw the usual insults at me and set about making my life a misery… oh, and turning Jacob into a miniature version of himself." She stops talking abruptly again. "God, I sound so bitter, don't I?"

"I think you have every right to sound bitter."

She shakes her head. "I have to try and control it though, in case I forget and say something regrettable in front of Jacob. I—I always promised myself that I wouldn't let my anger overflow into hatred, even if Scott does make it really hard sometimes…" Her voice fades and she looks away, as I reach over with my free hand and place a finger beneath her chin, turning her face back to mine.

"You're doing a fantastic job," I murmur.

"I wish…" she whispers, her voice cracking.

"Hey… considering what he put you through, I think you're incredibly tolerant of your ex, and it can't be easy having to still see him so often."

"No," she replies, her voice gaining in strength. "It would be a lot simpler if I could just cut him out of my life altogether… but I can't, for Jacob's sake."

"And that's why you're doing a fantastic job," I reply and she smiles, accepting the compliment, for once.

Chapter Thirteen

Jenna

I stare into his eyes, his finger still poised on my chin, my hand still clasped firmly in his, and let out a long, deep sigh. I'm sure I've ever felt so relaxed with anyone before, certainly not so relaxed that I could just blurt out all of that, anyway. I mean, I know I haven't told him everything. I haven't told him about all the other women Scott slept with, and how that destroyed me, and made me hide behind my walls. That's too much. I feel it reflects so badly on me as a wife… as a lover… that I couldn't satisfy my own husband, even though we were having sex so often. I can't possibly tell Adam about that, or how it feels to know and appreciate my own inadequacies, even if he is so sympathetic and kind.

"Can I get you another drink?" he asks, breaking into my thoughts.

"Yes, thank you." I think I need one.

He releases me and I sit back as he gets up and goes over to the bar, and I'm surprised to find that I miss him. That's the most pathetic thing ever, I know. He's just a few feet away from me, looking perfect in his jeans, white shirt and black leather jacket… and I miss him. I miss his touch, his presence, the reassurance of him, even the smell of him. I miss him more than I've ever missed anyone in my life… and yet if I got up and stepped two or three paces, I could touch him.

"Here you are," he says, putting our drinks down and bringing me back to reality with a bump.

"Thanks," I reply, taking a sip and turning to him. "So... what about you?"

He frowns, looking at me over the rim of his glass. "What about me?"

"Well, I've told you my awful life story, now it's your turn." I don't want him asking any more questions – not yet, anyway – and this seems like a good way of avoiding it

He shrugs. "I'm not sure my story is as exciting," he says softly.

"Well, that's probably a good thing, isn't it? There is such a thing as too much excitement."

"There is?" His eyes sparkle and he puts his glass down, twisting in his seat, so he's facing me and we're closer together again. "To start with, I've never been married…"

"Lucky you," I cut in, then check myself. "I'm sorry. I'm interrupting your story, and imposing my somewhat jaded views of marriage on you."

He shakes his head. "Don't worry. I can see why your views might be jaded. Mine aren't entirely positive."

"Why's that?" I ask, turning in my own seat.

"My parents got divorced when I was quite young," he replies. "And they did a good job of it, I suppose. But they both re-married pretty soon afterwards and I ended up feeling like I had two separate families, but didn't belong with either of them. Of course, I realise now that it was more about perception than anything else… that they didn't actually do anything wrong. It was just how I saw things as a child, whose life had been turned upside down. But even so, I think that made me a bit wary of relationships."

I stare at him, a little surprised that he's as open as he is. "You mentioned having a half-brother?" I prompt, being as he's fallen silent for a moment.

"Yes. And a half-sister. Amy. She was great – she still is – but my relationship with Nathan was tough. I ended up moving out of my mum's house when I was sixteen, because I couldn't stand living there with him any longer."

"Where did you go?"

"I moved in with my dad and his wife, Michelle… and Amy."

"I see." I take a quick sip of my drink. "And has your relationship with your brother got better now you're both grown up?"

He pauses and lets out a long breath. "Nathan died a few years ago."

I shift right to the edge of my seat, letting my hand rest on his arm. "I'm sorry, Adam," I murmur. "I didn't realise."

"Why would you?" he says.

"But I feel awful now." I do. I feel terrible for being so insensitive.

"It's okay." His voice is soft, kind, disarmingly gentle. "Honestly."

"Do you want to change the subject?" I ask. "We can talk about something else, if you'd rather."

He shakes his head. "No. It hardly seems fair of me to get you to unburden, and then not to tell you about myself."

"You don't have to."

He tilts his head slightly. "Yes, I do."

We wait a moment, while he sips his beer, and then he replaces the glass on the table and looks back at me. "There was a girl," he says quietly. "Her name was Jade." I have no idea what this has to do with his brother – or if it has anything at all to do with him – but the look on his face is captivating, and I listen intently. "I met her at Nathan's twenty-first birthday party. I was thirty at the time… and Jade was one of Nathan's friends. Actually they shared a house at uni together." He pauses, staring at me. "She was twenty."

I sit back a little, in an involuntary action, reminded for a second of Scott and Ella.

"It wasn't like your husband," he says quickly. "Well, I don't think it was, anyway. But we hit it off straight away and… and we spent the weekend together."

I nod my head, wondering how exactly he thinks this is so different from Scott.

"Just the weekend?" I ask.

"No," he says. "It lasted longer than that. She had to go back to university, with Nathan and the rest of his friends, but we decided we wanted to try and make a go of things, in spite of the distance between us."

"Was that a problem? Being so far away from each other, I mean?"
I can't help recalling the time that Scott and I spent apart, and what I
now know he did in my absence.

"Not really. We talked a lot on the phone, and met up when we
could, which wasn't perhaps as often as we'd have liked, but even so,
I went to stay with her in Kent, and she spent a week with me at New
Year, and then she introduced me to her parents when I spent a
weekend at their farmhouse in Suffolk."

"So it was quite serious then?" I ask, surprised.

"Well, I was never completely sure about that," he says quietly.

"Why not? It sounds pretty serious to me."

"Sometimes I thought it was, but at other times, I thought all she
wanted was… a physical relationship."

I'm momentarily reminded of Scott again, and the fact that all he
seemed to want was sex – and not just with me. I remember, when he
was explaining about his other women, that all he seemed to be
interested in was his 'needs'. "Oh… I see," I murmur. "And you
didn't?"

He smiles, looking closely at me. "I like sex as much as the next man,
Jenna, but not to the exclusion of everything else… not to the point
where there's literally nothing else."

"And there was nothing else?" I ask, feeling intrigued, because now
he's starting to sound like the exact opposite of Scott.

"No."

"Why didn't you talk to her about it?"

"Because, by the time it had become a real issue for me, she was
coming up for the end of her course, and although I've never been to
uni myself, I could tell how stressed she was. It was something that I
decided could wait. We… we'd planned for her to come and stay down
here for the summer while she worked out what she wanted to do with
her life, and as far as I was concerned, that was going to give us a chance
to really spend some time together. I knew there was the possibility that,
at the end of it, we'd find we weren't suited, or that she'd realise her
future lay elsewhere – or that I would – but at least we'd know…" His
voice fades.

"So what happened?"

"The plan was that her dad was going to collect her from uni in Kent and drive her back to Suffolk, where she'd spend a week or so with her parents, and then I'd drive there and pick her up. None of it was really set in stone, but that was the basic idea… only the day after her final exam, I got a call from a policeman."

"A policeman?"

"Yes. He was at my mum's house and he asked me to go round there, which I did, obviously, and then he said that Nathan had been in a car accident, and that he and his female passenger had been killed."

"His female passenger?" I ask, picking up on Adam's expression.

"Yes." He nods his head slowly. "To start with everyone assumed he'd been travelling with a girlfriend none of us knew anything about, because they both had a suitcase in the car with them… and then it became clear that the 'girlfriend' was Jade."

"Oh… my God."

"Neither of them had left a note for anyone, or said anything to their friends about where they were going, but it didn't take a genius to work out that they were leaving together." He focuses on me, his eyes piercing into mine. "The thing I'll never know of course is, whether Nathan talked her into it because he wanted her for himself, or whether it was Jade's idea, because she didn't want to be with me anymore, or whether it was mutual, and they just fell in love… or in lust, or whatever it was."

I lean into him slightly. "I'm so sorry Adam."

He tilts his head again. "Don't be. I wasn't in love with her. I knew that even then. It just hurt, being rejected, and lied to, and deceived… And then there was the funeral."

"Which one?"

"Jade's. I—I've never told anyone about this, except for my dad, and even then, I didn't exactly tell him. He knows about it because he was there when it happened, so you have to promise not to say anything."

"Of course."

He smiles. "It was… I don't know… probably about three or four days after Jade's death. I was at work with Dad and the phone rang. He took the call, and it was Jade's father, Christopher, asking to speak to me about the funeral, so Dad handed the phone over and I spoke to him. To be honest, my first thought was, how on earth he'd tracked me down. Jade's parents didn't even know my surname, let alone the name of the business, so I was sitting there wondering whether he'd intended to work his way through every building company in Newquay until he found me, when he announced that the funeral was the following Tuesday… and that I wasn't welcome."

"He did what?" I'm stunned.

"He said that our family had brought them nothing but trouble, that we were the cause of Jade's death and they didn't want me there."

"But that's ridiculous," I point out. "You had nothing to do with what happened."

"I know, but he accused me of not doing enough, of not seeing how unhappy she must have been with me, if she'd felt the need to run away with my brother. That wasn't really fair, in the circumstances, but they were hurting. Their daughter had just been killed and they wanted someone to blame. I was an easy target."

"So you didn't go?"

"No. I wanted to, but I had to obey their wishes. I couldn't have created a scene at her funeral, no matter what she'd done."

"That was very considerate of you."

He shrugs. "It was hard for them. They couldn't see that Jade was the one who'd cheated and lied, because whichever way you looked at it, she'd done that much at least; they weren't willing to accept that I hadn't done anything to her, other than wait for her to finish uni so we could try and work out if we had a future together… and it was easier for them to blame me, rather than face reality. Besides, I was in a bad enough place already, so what harm did it do? I—I told Dad about the conversation when I put the phone down, and he wanted to call Christopher back and give him a piece of his mind. I wouldn't let him though, and we talked it through, and agreed that we wouldn't tell anyone else, just in case it got back to Mum. I think she secretly blamed Nathan herself, at least for part of it, because she kept asking me not to, and she'd have hated to know that someone else felt the same."

"Did you blame him?" I ask. "Do you now?"

"At the time I think I was too confused to blame anyone. And now… well, life's too short to blame people for things that can't be changed."

I feel so ashamed of all the times I've hated Scott for the things he's done, I can't bear to look at Adam, and I lower my head, fighting back tears.

"Hey," he says, placing his finger beneath my chin again and raising my face to his. "What's wrong?"

"You're so much stronger… so much better than I am," I murmur as he starts to blur.

Chapter Fourteen

Adam

This date – if it is a date – isn't going as I'd planned at all.

I'd hoped that we'd spend a quiet evening talking, sharing a few drinks, that Jenna would be able to relax with me, chill out a bit, and see me as someone other than the man who's building her extension – someone she might want to spend some more time with, maybe.

Instead, all we've done is talk about our pasts, about her ex-husband, and the fact that he cheated, about their divorce, and about Jade and Nathan. It's not what I had in mind at all.

And now, on top of all that, it looks like she's about to cry, because for some reason, she's got it into her head that I'm somehow 'better' than she is.

"No, Jenna," I whisper, moving close enough that she'll be able to hear me, regardless of everyone else in the pub. "That's not true at all." She looks me in the eye, the doubt behind hers obvious. "Jade and I only spent a couple of weeks together, if you add up the actual time we were in each other's company. Obviously I considered us to be a couple, regardless of how often we were able to see each other, and I was faithful to her, even if she wasn't to me. But the point is, you can't make a comparison between our relationship and the one you had with Scott. They're completely different things. I mean… you met him when you were… how old?"

"Sixteen," she mumbles, surprising me.

"Okay… and you loved him."

She tilts her head. "I thought I loved him," she murmurs. "But how can I have done, when he did that to me?"

"You loved him," I say firmly, because I know she did. "Even if your love has now turned to hate, you loved him then." She hesitates and then nods her head. "And that's what I'm trying to explain here. I didn't love Jade, and I'm not better than you. Not at all. I just have a different set of experiences."

She looks at me for a while, studying my face, it seems, and then leans back, putting some space between us. "Can you excuse me?" she says. "I'm just going to Ladies'."

"Okay." She glances around, noticing the sign for the toilets and then gets to her feet, taking her handbag with her. "You are coming back, aren't you?" I ask, feeling nervous.

"Yes." She smiles slightly and moves away.

Left to myself, I take a sip of my beer and shake my head. What an evening… I'd worked out that her ex had cheated, just based on their argument, but to know that she caught him in bed with someone else… and someone much younger, as well, that had to hurt. I think it might also make her slightly suspicious of me too, considering that I've just told her about Jade, who was significantly younger than me, although I hope she realises that I'm nothing like her ex; that I'd never knowingly hurt her… or anyone else for that matter. But especially not her.

"Sorry about that." She sits back down again, putting her bag beside her on the floor and smiling at me. "I just needed a few minutes."

"That's okay," I reply. "I do understand."

She sits forward, looking around the pub. "I like it in here," she remarks, making it clear she wants to change the subject, and I don't blame her.

"I haven't been here for a while. I think they've redecorated it."

She turns back to face me. "So, it's not your regular then?"

I smile. "I don't think I have a regular. I'm not that sociable, really."

"No, neither am I," she says, wistfully.

"So, what do you like doing?" I ask.

"My life revolves around Jacob, for the best part – well, Jacob and work – but when I get any time to myself, I just like to sit in the living room, with the fire blazing and lose myself in good a book… preferably with a glass of wine."

"Would this be the living room you're about to convert into an office?" I ask.

"Yes, I'm afraid it would." She seems sad at that prospect.

"And there's no way round that?"

"No. There are only two bedrooms, and although the loft is big enough, I can't afford to convert that and have the extension done as well… and you've seen my kitchen…" She smiles.

"Yes, I have." I smile back.

"In which case, you know it's too small. And besides, this is the quickest fix. I—I need to be able to spend more time with Jacob," she adds, almost like she's thinking out loud, and I move closer to her. "If I'm not careful, Scott's influence will completely undermine everything I've tried to do with him, and I'll lose him completely."

"Lose him? You mean Scott will try and take him away?"

"No, what I mean is that Jacob's behaviour is becoming intolerable and I'm struggling to maintain any control over him. He's running the house – and my life – already, and it seems to me that it'll only get worse as he gets older. I need to try and nip it in the bud, while I still can; while we can both still remember that he was once a much nicer little boy than he is now… before it's too late."

"It's not too late," I murmur, taking her hand in mine again. "Remember? I told you earlier… It's never too late."

She manages a smile and then reaches out for her drink, finishing it, before she glances at her watch. "Did you know it's ten-thirty?" she says, leaning back.

"No… I had no idea."

"I probably should be going. I've got to do the shopping first thing, and then get to my parents' house to do the laundry."

"You really know how to live, don't you?"

"Well, it's got to be done." She smiles, bending to pick up her handbag, and then gets to her feet. I stand as well, leaving my half-finished beer on the table, and help her with her jacket, before following her out of the door and into the car park. "I'm around the back," she says.

"Then I'll walk you to your car." She looks like she's about to object, but then changes her mind and nods her head, and we start walking around the side of the pub, to the rear car park, which is illuminated by fairy lights that adorn the surrounding trees. "I hope the stories of our pasts haven't spoiled the evening for you," I say, keeping my fingers crossed behind my back.

"No... not at all. I've had a lovely time."

Somehow I find that hard to believe, but I don't say anything, other than, "So have I."

"Really?" she asks, more forthright than me, clearly. "Even though I've done nothing but moan about Jacob and Scott all evening?"

We've just reached her car and I take her hand in mine, pulling her to a halt and turning her to face me. "I don't mind you talking about Jacob... or about Scott, if it helps you to relax and unwind a bit. It's good to get to know you... and I'd like to get to know you even more, if that's okay with you?"

She looks up at me, puzzled, I think, her eyes sparkling in the lights, her beauty taking my breath away, and acting on impulse, I lean down, gently brushing my lips against hers. She sighs, then moans, and I change the angle of my head, cupping her face in my hands, taking a step closer, my feet either side of hers, our bodies touching for the first time, as I deepen the kiss. I feel her hands move up my arms, resting for a moment or two on my biceps, before moving up around my neck, fisting my hair, then pulling it. Hard. She opens her mouth to me, unbidden, and I claim her with my tongue, walking her backwards until she hits the side of her car, pinned against it by the weight of my body, as I move one hand to her waist, resting it there for a moment, but then moving it up slightly so my thumb can brush against the side of her breast. She gasps, then moans again, deep and sexy this time, and I gently bite her bottom lip, before breaking our kiss and leaning back slightly, looking down at her flushed face, her eyes alight. She's breathing hard, but so am I, and she lowers her hands, although she lets them rest on my biceps once more, leaving them there, as she lets out a long, slow sigh.

"Can I see you again?" I murmur, rubbing her swollen bottom lip with the side of my thumb.

"Y—You'll see me on Monday," she replies, stuttering and lowering her eyes to stare at a space just below my chin.

"I know that… but that's not what I meant. I meant, can I see you again?" I ask my question with emphasis, because I know she knows exactly what I mean.

She hesitates, looking even further down now, at one of the buttons on my shirt – probably the second one, I'd have said – and after the pause becomes worryingly long, I place my finger beneath her chin, not for the first time tonight, and raise her face to mine, seeing what looks like uncertainty in eyes again. "What's wrong?" I ask her. "Have I done something to make you doubt me?" I wonder if this is to do with Jade, and with Jenna's memories of her ex-husband and their young babysitter; if she's seeing similarities there which are giving her pause for thought.

"No," she replies quickly, moving her hands up again, so they're on my shoulders now. "It's nothing to do with you… not really. It's just that Scott took a lot from me. I never thought I'd want to…" She looks me in the eyes. "I—I suppose I've put up walls… barriers…"

I nod my head. "I know, and I can understand that. He took your confidence, and your self-esteem, as well as your faith in men… and probably a whole lot of other things besides. But the thing is, I like you, Jenna. I like you a lot, and I'd really like to help you break the walls down and let the sunshine back into your life again."

She stares at me, tilting her head, studying me for what feels like a long time, and then says, "I like you too, Adam, but I thought Scott loved me and he hurt me so much… and then there's Jacob to think about. I mean, it's complicated… I can't have a casual relationship, not that I'd be any good at that anyway…" She sounds panicked, anxious, and I hold her tight.

"Who said anything about casual?" I say calmly. "I'm not talking about casual, Jenna."

Her eyes widen. "But that's the problem. Don't you see? I—I don't know you well enough to let you in… to commit to anything serious."

"Well, we could take things one step at a time, couldn't we? As a start, you could commit to agreeing to see me again, couldn't you? You could commit to getting to know me better, so I can prove to you that you can trust me? How does that sound?"

"One step at a time?" she muses and leans into me. "Can I think about it? Would that be okay?" She looks up at me again.

"If that's what you need, then of course it's okay."

"Thank you," she says softly, letting me go and reaching into her pocket for her keys, then unlocking the car as I take a step back.

"I'll see you on Monday morning," I add, opening the driver's door for her.

"Yes. I'm not sure I'll have an answer by then, but…"

I reach out and cup her face in my hand again. "You don't have to give me an answer by Monday. Take as much time as you need. I'll wait."

She sighs again, leaning into my touch, and then gets into her car, looking up at me. "Thank you for a lovely evening," she says.

"No… thank you."

"Enjoy the rest of the weekend."

I close her door, wondering how on earth I'm going to even think straight for the rest of the weekend, and stand watching as she drives away, knowing that at least one thing I've just said to her was a barefaced lie, because I don't just like her… I love her. I've loved her since the moment I first saw her, which makes this the second time in my life that's happened. I just hope this time there's a better outcome.

I haven't slept that well, because I spent most of the night thinking about Jenna, wondering if she was thinking about me, about how long it will take her to decide whether she trusts me enough to give us a chance, what I'll do if she says 'no'… how I'll live without her.

It wasn't the best night.

I get up and go to make myself a coffee, standing in the kitchen and trying to work out how to spend my Saturday. I'd hoped to maybe go surfing, but the weather's not looking that great, and I suppose I ought to tidy the flat and do some laundry… which just reminds me that Jenna's going to visit her parents today to do hers. I shake my head, trying to stop myself from thinking about her all the time. Ninety-nine percent of the time is enough, surely?

Except, evidently it's not, because my phone is on the island unit and, before I've even realised what I'm doing, I've picked it up and typed out a message to her, pressing 'send', without even contemplating the fact that she might think I'm hassling her, even though I'm not. I just wanted to thank her for a lovely evening and ask if she was okay this morning. There's no harm in that, is there?

I pour myself a cup of coffee from the machine and stare at my phone, willing it to beep, to announce the arrival of a text. It doesn't and, by the time I've finished my coffee, I've decided that maybe my message was a step too far. She wanted time to think, which suggested I should probably leave her alone, not text her at the first opportunity. Should I send her another message apologising?

"Dear God, no," I say out loud, shaking my head and putting my cup into the dishwasher, before going into the bathroom to shower, just as my phone beeps, and I run back to the kitchen, grabbing it, flipping it around, nearly dropping it, and eventually unlocking the screen to find a message… from Jenna.

— *You don't need to thank me. I had a lovely evening. I'm fine, thanks. Hope you're okay too. Jenna.*

I suppose she answered my questions, and she said she had a lovely evening, so that's promising. And she didn't tell me to back off either… which feels like a positive. But then I am clutching at straws, and I know it.

I put the phone back down, resisting the temptation to reply and have her thinking I'm desperate, even though I am – well, I'm desperate for her to let me break down those walls, anyway – and I go back to the bathroom and have a quick shower, coming back out with a towel around my waist, my hair dripping onto my shoulders, and make my way into my bedroom, just as the phone beeps again.

I stop, and double back into the kitchen, wondering who it can be this time. It won't be Jenna, that's for sure…

— *Hello again. Sorry, to trouble you, but I was wondering if you're going to be free tomorrow morning? I'm at Mum and Dad's today – as you know – but could we maybe meet for coffee tomorrow? If you're free, that is? If you're not, don't worry. Jenna.*

I can't stop myself from smiling, staring at the message and reading it through again, just to make sure I haven't mis-read it. She wants to meet me tomorrow. She's definitely saying that. There's no mistake. Obviously it might not mean anything, but if it doesn't, why ask? Why not just wait until Monday?

— *I'd love to see you tomorrow. Where would you like to meet? Adam*

Her reply is immediate.

— *Can you come to my place? Jenna*

— *Of course. What time? Adam*

— *Is ten-thirty okay with you? Jenna*

— *Ten-thirty is perfect. See you then. Adam*

I wait a few minutes, but she doesn't reply. She doesn't need to though, because I'm going to see her tomorrow, and that's enough for me. It's more than enough.

I arrive at Jenna's house at ten-thirty on the dot, and stand waiting for her to answer the door, feeling nervous and hopeful, in equal measure. I'm probably more nervous than I would normally be, because on the spur of the moment, I stopped off on the way over here and picked up some flowers… tulips to be precise. Lots of them. I'll admit, I kind of got carried away, and standing here now, my arms full of them, I'm wondering if I've overdone it.

She opens the door and her eyes widen, right before she smiles at me, and I stare for a moment at her beautiful face, the floral dress that's clinging to her body, the way she's put her hair up, leaving a few loose strands brushing against her cheeks. "Hello," she says softly, tilting her head at the array of flowers I'm holding.

"Hi… um… these are for you." I think that was kind of obvious, but I hand the tulips over anyway. She manages to take them and her smile widens.

"They're beautiful. But you didn't need to buy me flowers."

"Yeah… I did."

She steps aside and I enter, passing her and resisting the urge to kiss her, to feel her body against mine again, mainly because I'd crush the flowers she's cradling so gently, and I wait instead for her to close the door and lead us into the dining room.

"I'll put these in water and get us some coffee," she says, going through to the kitchen and returning a couple of minutes later, carrying two cups.

"Thanks." I take one of them from her – the one with milk in it – and we stand for a moment.

"I really am grateful for the flowers," she says, looking up at me.

"You don't have to be."

"It is ever so kind of you though."

Has no-one ever bought her flowers before?

She hesitates, taking a sip of coffee, and then says, "Would you… would you mind taking a look at the kitchen with me?"

"Why is something wrong with it?"

"No…" She starts walking away. "It's just that I've been giving it some thought."

"I see… and?"

"And I'm not sure I want a mass-produced, manufactured set of units in here anymore." She puts her cup down on the work surface, where I notice the tulips, arranged in two enormous vases, and I can't help smiling, before turning back to her. "I think I want something a bit more unique, with a rustic feel to it, ideally made of wood…" She glances around and I start to wonder whether this is the purpose of my visit; to advise her on kitchen cabinets. I hope not. "The problem is, I'm not sure how to go about looking for something like that, or if I'll be able to afford it on my budget."

I nod my head, placing my cup beside hers. "Well, I could build it for you."

She blushes. "I—I didn't ask you over here to get you to do that," she says, flustered.

"Why did you ask me over, Jenna?" Her blush deepens and she looks away, my heart sinking. "Is this just about your kitchen? I mean, if it is, then that's okay. I'm…"

"It's not just about the kitchen," she interrupts, and I step towards her, capturing her face in my hands and kissing her deeply, our tongues clashing, as I move her backwards to the work surface, her fingers knotting in my hair, her breasts heaving against my chest, my groans echoing around the room. It seems there are no half-measures for us, not that I want there to be. I crave her, after all…

"We are still taking things one step at a time, aren't we?" she says, as we pull apart, her hands clasped behind my neck.

"I don't know… are we?" She tilts her head, puzzled. "I mean, I'm happy to, you know that. But have you reached a decision yet? Do you want to take things one step at a time with me?"

"Yes." How can one simple word make the whole world so much brighter?

I smile down at her. "You're sure?"

"Yes. That's why I asked you round here…" Her voice fades and she blushes again.

"So it had nothing to do with your kitchen then?" I ask, teasing her just a little bit.

"No, not really. It's just that… I realised all of a sudden yesterday morning, that I wanted to take my first step with you, and I didn't want to wait until Monday morning to do it. That's all. The kitchen was just my excuse to see you."

I shake my head, kissing her gently, but pulling back before I get carried away again. "You don't need an excuse to see me, although I'll still build your kitchen for you…"

"You will?"

"Yes… if you'll have lunch with me."

She doesn't take much persuading and, after we've had another coffee, and a few more kisses, I drive us out to a pub I know, about half an hour away from Newquay.

I order our food at the bar, and when I come back to our table, by the window, bringing our drinks with me, Jenna returns the conversation to her kitchen.

"How much do you think it's likely to cost?" she asks, once she's gone through what she's looking for in a little more detail, and we've discussed a few options. "It's just that it's Jacob's birthday soon…" She falls silent for a moment, then adds, "I don't bother trying to compete with Scott when it comes to extravagant presents, but my beloved son is insisting on a huge football party at the leisure centre, next weekend – with his entire class on the guest list."

"Jenna… don't worry about it." I place my hand over hers, sensing her rising panic – at least it sounds like panic to me. "I'll work something out."

She tenses and narrows her eyes just slightly. "If you think you're paying…"

"What?" I interrupt. "What are you going to do? Buy a massed produced kitchen that you'll hate, just to prove a point?"

"I'd rather not, but I will if I have to."

"Those walls are really thick, aren't they?" I shake my head, smiling at her.

"Sorry?"

"The walls you built around yourself… they're really thick."

"They've needed to be," she replies, tears forming in her eyes, our conversation suddenly much more serious, as I move my chair slightly, so I'm closer to her.

"I know. And I do understand. But why don't you let me do this for you? Look on it as the next step; as the first layer of bricks coming down… What do you say?"

"Are you giving me any choice?" she asks.

"Of course. You always have a choice."

She looks up at me, then lets her head rest on my shoulder. "In that case, as you're giving me a choice, I'll accept… gratefully."

I kiss the top of her head. "You don't have to be grateful. I'm more than happy to build you a kitchen, if it means I get to spend some more time with you."

She tilts her head up, looking at me. "Do you want to then?" she asks. "Spend more time with me, I mean?"

"I think you know the answer to that," I reply, leaning down and kissing her, only stopping when the polite cough of the waitress bringing our lunch interrupts a perfect moment.

We sat in the pub for several hours, talking about Jenna's work, and mine, touching on her problems with Jacob, my parents' divorce and their relationships, and the fact that her parents had met and married fairly late in life, making them a few years older than my own. By the time we glanced out of the window and realised it was getting dark, I felt like I knew a lot more about her… not as much as I wanted to, but more. And I've always liked the idea of 'more'.

I drove us back to Jenna's house, noticing that she got increasingly anxious with every passing mile, which she eventually revealed was due to the fact that Scott was due to return with Jacob. I offered to come in and wait with her, but by the time I'd parked up, we'd decided it was better for her, if I just left her to get on with her usual routine. So, I kissed her goodnight and waited for her to go indoors, before driving back home, feeling a whole lot better than I had forty-eight hours earlier, when she'd said she needed time, when she wasn't quite so sure about me.

She seems much more certain now. Okay, so she's shy and nervous. And I'm very well aware of the fact that I have to take it slow with her. She's buried herself, well and truly, behind her walls, but that's only to be expected, given what her ex did to her, and the way he treats her now. The thing is, I know that I can help her overcome whatever fears she's holding on to. I know I can help her to be herself again, to smile, and relax and be the carefree woman I know she really is. One step at a time, we'll get there. I know we will.

This morning, I think I actually have a smile on my face when I wake up, and I don't think that's ever happened before… well, it might have done, perhaps, the morning after I met 'the girl' on the beach, when I was expecting to see her again that day… the day she didn't turn up. Still, I'm not going to think about that now. She's in the past, and Jenna is very much in the present, and I get up and go through to the shower, about as happy and carefree as I think it's possible to feel.

Getting to Jenna's place, I let myself in through the back gate as usual, spotting Jacob through the dining room window, already sitting at the table, although I notice that he's not wearing school uniform, but his home clothes, and I realise it must be the Easter holidays. He's hunched over a bowl of cereal, spooning it into his mouth, and I feel a little disappointed that I probably won't get to kiss Jenna before she leaves for work – not with Jacob around – but remind myself that this is how it has to be, that she needs it to be slow, steady, considered, and that Jacob is a huge factor in everything we do.

"Good morning," Jenna's voice snaps me back to reality and I glance up, seeing her treading through the earthwork and coming towards me. She's never done this before. She's never come out to greet me, always busy indoors with breakfast, or making tea, or getting Jacob's lunch ready, and I've had to go in to her. And I was going to, once I'd snapped out of my daydream.

"Hello." I step closer to her as she smiles up at me, and I'm so tempted to kiss her, it almost hurts. There's an awkward pause while she stares into my eyes and I look down into hers. "I—Is something wrong?" I ask, feeling tense.

Her shoulders drop slightly and she shakes her head. "No," she mutters, and then turns away as I grab her arm and pull her out of sight of Jacob, pushing her hard up against the kitchen wall and kissing her, my body pressed against hers, her moans echoing with mine as she twists her fingers into my hair, pulling it, keeping me where I think she wants me. It really is all or nothing with us, it seems, but I pull back after a minute or two, breaking the kiss, mindful of Jacob, and look down at Jenna to see she's blushing, biting her bottom lip.

"I wanted to do that the moment you came out here, but I realised Jacob would be able to see us and thought it best not to."

"Oh God," she says, clamping her hand to her mouth. "I should have thought."

"It's okay." I caress her cheek with my fingertips, as she shudders against me, making me smile. "I know it's not just you we're taking it slowly for. I know Jacob needs to get used to the idea of you seeing someone and that it's best to take that one step at a time too. So, for now, we'll have to restrict ourselves to seeing each other when he's at his dad's."

Her face falls. "Are you serious?" she murmurs.

"Yes. I don't think it's wise for us to go out with each other, or for me to spend huge amounts of time here while Jacob's at home, do you?"

"No, I suppose not."

"I should probably point out however that, in between Jacob's visits to his dad, whenever we can, whenever we're alone, I'm going to take every single opportunity I can to kiss you." I lower my voice as she looks up, smiling, and I put my words into actions.

Chapter Fifteen

Jenna

The last few weeks with Adam have been incredible.

I somehow managed to make it through Jacob's sixth birthday party, although I'm not sure how. It was loud and tiring, and I was grateful the leisure centre provided a couple of people to supervise, because the idea of trying to control twenty-six kids, all of whom seemed to be completely hyper, was too much for me, even with Mum and Dad there to help. Jacob had insisted on inviting Scott to the party, but fortunately, he couldn't come. I wanted to invite Adam – for moral support if nothing else – but that would have been impossible. So, I satisfied myself with a long phone call to him after Jacob had gone to bed. Somehow it didn't feel quite the same.

We don't get to see that much of each other, and it's still early days in our relationship, but spending time with Adam is just so relaxing. I feel safe, and comfortable, and happy for the first time in a really long time, and I'll admit, I've become very attached to him. I look forward to even the brief moments we get to spend together during the week; I love his kisses, which are gentle, and yet forceful at the same time; I miss him when I can't see him, although I enjoy our phone calls and texts in between, and I relish our weekends together... like this coming one, when Jacob is due to go to his father's again.

I feel awful for wanting Jacob to go away, especially as during the Easter holidays, I'd booked him into lots of clubs, or arranged for him to spend time with my parents, which I know makes him feel like I don't want him around. The fact is though, that I have to work, even if the arrangements resulted in him being so much more bad tempered and moody than usual throughout the whole school holiday and into the new term, being as he seems to be determined to make me suffer at the moment. It's a situation that's not being helped by the extreme heat, which is unusual for the middle of April. Even the temperature at night has been quite high, and I think he's struggling to cope with it – as are we all, especially as the air conditioning at work has broken down, and we're sweltering.

Today is Friday though and, as I shower and get dressed in my lightest skirt and blouse, I can't help smiling. I know I should be sad that Jacob's going to Scott's tonight and that I won't see him until Sunday evening, but even so, I'm looking forward to a weekend of peace and quiet... and to being able to spend some time with Adam – despite the fact that we haven't made any definite plans yet.

Jacob's in a really grouchy mood this morning, so once I'm sure he's actually awake, I leave him to get dressed by himself, slightly fearful of his temper these days – although I'd never admit that out loud, not to anyone. Not even Adam.

I go downstairs to start getting the breakfast ready, wondering if Adam will have arrived yet, touching my fingers to my lips and recalling his kiss last night, just before he left to go home. It was brief, but intense... and very memorable.

I glance out of the window at the bright, sunny morning, feeling disappointed that the garden is empty; there's no sign of Adam yet, and I go through to the kitchen, putting on the kettle, getting Jacob's bowl from the cupboard, filling it with cereal, and taking it back in to the dining room, along with the milk, before coming back and starting to make my tea. I startle at the knocking on the back door, turning to see Adam looking at me through one of the narrow glass panes, a smile on his face.

"You do have a key," I point out, as I open the door to him.

"I know. But I don't like using it when you're here." He glances over my shoulder. "Are we alone?" he asks.

"Yes... well, sort of. Jacob's upstairs still."

"Good," he murmurs, taking a step closer, pulling me into his arms and kissing me. I reach up, around his neck, grabbing his hair in my hands and holding him as his tongue delves into my mouth, his body pressed firmly against mine. There's an urgency to his kiss, as always, and yet it's soft and sweet at the same time, and I'm breathless in moments, looking up into his eyes as he finally pulls back, his hands settled on my hips, mine on his shoulders.

"I'm so glad we've got the weekend to ourselves," he whispers, his eyes fiery, and I feel a pang of doubt, my stomach flipping over with uncertainty.

"Why?"

He smiles. "Because I've missed you. That's all." I relax, sighing into him. "One step at a time," he whispers in my ear, just as we hear Jacob's footsteps on the stairs and pull apart. "I haven't forgotten," he adds, winking.

"Where's my orange juice, Mum?" Jacob's voice rings out from behind me.

"I'm just getting it." I move away from Adam and get a glass from the cupboard, filling it with juice from the fridge before handing it to Jacob, who turns to leave. "Um… I think you forgot something, didn't you?" I remind Jacob of his manners, even though he ignores me and continues on his way.

"Don't you ever say 'please' and 'thank you'?" Adam asks, at which Jacob stops and turns back, scowling at Adam, who holds his gaze until Jacob mutters a very ungracious, 'Thank you,' in my vague direction, and then stomps off.

"Sorry," Adam whispers. "I shouldn't have said that."

"It's fine," I tell him. "Actually it was kind of nice to have someone backing me up, for a change."

He smiles and puts his arm around me, whispering, "I just want to help. But if I overstep the mark, then tell me. Okay?"

I nod my head, and lean into him, grateful for his support, even though he has no idea how bad Jacob can really be.

Today has been a good day, helped by the fact that Trevor called in an engineer, who fixed the air conditioning, so by lunchtime, although the temperature outside was getting up towards the mid twenties, we were lovely and cool. And with the forecast for next week saying the heatwave is due to continue for the foreseeable future, I think everyone at work was relieved, not only that we no longer had to suffer, but also that it's Friday… and the weekend beckons.

As I drive to Jacob's school to collect him, I can't help looking forward to the next two days, wondering if Adam's made any plans, and hoping that this evening goes smoothly, without any setbacks from either Jacob or Scott.

My hopes are short-lived though, when I go in through the school gates to find Jacob, sitting on the low wall that surrounds the play area, a sulk etched on his lips.

"What's wrong?" I ask, walking over to him, as Mrs Swann, who is in charge of them today, catches my attention.

"Ms Downing?" she calls and I glance up. "Could I have a word with you?" I feel my stomach lurch, wondering what can have gone on.

"Of course." Jacob doesn't react, and I veer in the direction of Mrs Swann, who is standing in the shade, in a pretty summer dress, her long blonde hair tied in a ponytail behind her head, and a sympathetic expression on her face.

"I'm sorry to have to bother you," she remarks, looking over my shoulder to where Jacob is sitting, "but we've had a few problems with Jacob this afternoon."

"Oh?" I wait for her explanation.

"I heard him swearing at one of the other children," she says quietly. "And I'm afraid it's not the first time."

"Oh God… I'm so sorry." Despite my earlier good mood, I feel my shoulders drop and blink back the tears that are already welling in my eyes.

She smiles, looking even more compassionate now. "These things happen… and we know Jacob's home life can be… well, difficult, sometimes." She's struggling to find the right word, but all she's actually doing is making things worse.

"His home life is fine," I retort, taking a deep breath. "It's the time he spends with his father that's the problem."

She leans back slightly, the colour rising in her cheeks. "I didn't mean any offence, Ms Downing, I was just…"

I shake my head, holding up my hands. "It's not your fault. If I'm being honest, he's started swearing at home as well, but I'm at a loss as to what to do about it, when his father actively encourages him." I don't really know why I told her that, except that I don't want her, or the other teachers, to think that I'm happy with Jacob's behaviour, when I'm not.

"I've spoken to Jacob," she replies, raising her eyebrows at my candour, but not commenting on it. "I've explained to him that swearing is not acceptable, and I've made him apologise to the other children."

I doubt that will do much good, but I thank her for being so lenient.

"We'll see how it goes for now, shall we?" she says.

"I suppose so." That doesn't seem like much of a solution to me, but I suppose what she's trying to say is that it's not really her problem, or the school's; it's mine. And I need to sort it out.

I turn back to Jacob and walk over to him. "Come on then." I keep my voice low and firm as he gets to his feet, picking up his school bag, and follows me through the gate and to my car.

Once he's strapped in, I get behind the wheel, and grip it firmly. "I'm not impressed, Jacob," I tell him. "This has got to stop." He doesn't reply, and I look in the rear-view mirror, to see him scowling back at me. "And you can wipe that look off your face too."

His grimace deepens, and I know I'm losing him, the road before me blurring with the tears that I refuse to cry in front of him. Should I stop him from seeing Scott? Can I even do that? Should I go and see Scott, try and talk to him, explain the situation and get him to stop whatever it is he's doing? Would he even listen to me? I feel so lost, so helpless…

I look out of the side window so Jacob won't see me wipe away my tears with the back of my hand, and set off for home, all thoughts of a perfect weekend forgotten.

I let us into the house and tell Jacob to go upstairs and shower.

"I don't want to shower," he replies, speaking to me for the first time since this morning.

"I don't care. It's hot. You need to shower."

He purses his lips and, for a moment, I think he's about to let rip at me, but instead he stomps up the stairs and into his bedroom, slamming the door behind him.

"I'll be up there in five minutes to pack your things," I call after him, going through to the dining room, and dumping my handbag on the table, before opening up the window.

I can hear Adam – or maybe it's him and his colleagues – but I don't really have time to go out and see him now, as much as I'd like to, and instead I walk back to the living room, opening the window in here too, just to get some air into the house.

Climbing slowly up the stairs, I weigh up the pros and cons of trying to talk to Scott tonight when he comes to collect Jacob, or whether I should call him on a separate occasion, maybe arrange to meet somewhere neutral to have a conversation; whether there's even any point in doing either.

I open the door to Jacob's room to find him standing in a bright red t-shirt, bending to pull on a pair of navy blue shorts.

"You can't possibly have showered already, Jacob."

"I told you, I don't want a shower." He turns away from me, and I reach down, taking his arm and turning him back, feeling my anger rise.

"And I told you… you're taking a shower."

"I hate you, you fucking bitch!" he shouts at the top of his voice.

"Jacob…" I whisper, my voice cracking. How could he? How could he say that to me? I hear my phone beeping, but ignore it.

"I don't want to shower," he says, his voice still raised.

"Fine!" It's my turn to yell now. "Be smelly. See if I care."

I grab his rucksack and stuff clothes into it, not caring whether they're screwed up or not, not caring about anything really. Why would I, when my son hates me so much, he talks to me like that?

"There." I zip up his bag, not daring to look at him. "Finish getting dressed and come downstairs."

Without glancing back, I leave the room, taking his rucksack with me, and go down the stairs, just as my phone beeps again and I let out a sigh, walking through to the dining room and fishing it from my bag, dropping Jacob's rucksack as I read the message that's waiting for me:

— *Won't be able to make it this weekend. Something's come up. Scott.*

That's it? That's all he's going to say? He's letting his son down, and changing everyone's plans, and he thinks he can just send a stupid message like that?

My boiling blood overflows and I connect a call to him, surprised that he answers on the second ring.

"What do you want, Jenna?" he says as a greeting.

"I want to know why you're letting Jacob down," I reply.

"I explained. Something came up."

"Another blonde, I presume?"

There's a pause and then I hear a slight laugh. "Your jealousy is getting a bit embarrassing, Jenna."

"Oh, grow up, will you? This isn't about me, or you. It's about Jacob. He's been looking forward to seeing you, and now I'm going to have to tell him that you're not going to make it." A thought occurs to me. "Well, do you know what? I'm not going to."

"You're not going to what?" he asks, sounding confused.

"I'm not going to tell him… you are. If you're going to disappoint him, then you can be the one to explain it to him." I move to the foot of the stairs as I'm talking. "Just hang on, Scott," I say, then hold the phone away from my ear. "Jacob!" I call. "Come down here. Daddy's on the phone for you."

Jacob's bedroom door opens and he flies down the stairs, taking the phone from me. "Hi, Dad," he says into it, his smile broad, his eyes sparkling. It breaks my heart to see the difference in him when he's talking to Scott, compared to the way he speaks to me, but I try not to let it show as he looks up at me, his smile slowly fading.

"There's no-one there," he says, handing me back the phone again.

"Scott?" I say into the mouthpiece, but Jacob's right. The line is dead.

I re-dial his number, which goes directly to his voicemail, and I know that he's turned off his phone. Despite that, I quickly tap out a message to him.

— *You are a despicable coward, not worthy of your son, and I hope you're pleased with yourself.*

Pressing 'send' doesn't make me feel any better, because I know he won't get the message for ages; not until he's brave enough to turn his phone back on, anyway. And in the meantime, I've got to break the bad news to Jacob.

He doesn't take it well, pushing against me, even though I've got my arms around him.

"You did this, didn't you?" he says, glaring at me. "This is because I was bad at school, because I wouldn't have a shower…" His voice trembles.

"No, Jacob. Something came up at Daddy's work. Honestly."

He shakes his head. "Daddy wouldn't let me down," he mutters and I desperately want to tell him the truth; that his daddy has done nothing but let him down since the day he was born.

"It's no-one's fault," I add, wondering why I'm continuing to lie for Scott. "And it's nothing to do with what happened at school. I promise."

He pushes himself away from me and stomps into the kitchen. "I don't want to spend the weekend with you," he says, raising his voice. "I want to go to Dad's."

I follow him slowly, noticing the tears in his eyes, my heart breaking yet again, but for him this time, not for myself.

"Is everything okay?" Adam's voice makes me stop in my tracks as he opens the back door, stepping into the kitchen, between Jacob and myself.

"Yes, it's fine."

"No, it's not!" Jacob yells and runs from the room, pushing past me.

"What's happened?" Adam asks, glancing over my shoulder to where Jacob has just disappeared through the dining room door, and up the stairs, and then turning back to me again.

"Scott," I reply. "He's just informed me that he won't be able to have Jacob for the weekend."

"Why not?"

I run my fingers through my hair, sucking in a breath and focusing properly on Adam for the first time, taking in the fact that he's not wearing anything on his top half, and that the sight of him is a little distracting. He's tanned, perfectly formed, with more muscles than should be legal, and I want to kick myself for being so easily diverted from the problem at hand. "He… he didn't say," I explain, "and when I asked him to tell Jacob, rather than leaving it to me, he hung up."

"You mean, he didn't talk to him at all?"

"No." I shake my head. "This evening was already going really badly, but what I'm going to do now, I don't know…"

"What was wrong with this evening?" he asks, taking a step closer to me.

"How long have you got?" I try to make light of the situation, even though I'm not really in the mood.

"As long as you need," he replies, and I sigh, closing the gap between us and letting my head rest on his chest. He puts his arms around me and, after a while, I look up at him.

"Jacob's teacher told me, when I collected him from school, that he's been swearing at the other children." I close my eyes for a second, then open them again, to find Adam's looking down at me expectantly, concern written on his face. "He's been swearing at me too, for a while now, but it seems it's getting out of hand, so I was wondering on the way home, whether I should try and talk to Scott about it, not that I think it'll do any good… And then when we got back here, I asked Jacob to take a shower, and he refused, then shouted at me, called me a bitch, and told me he hates me." I hear my voice crack as Adam's arms tighten around me.

"Come here," he murmurs and holds me close. It feels good to be hugged and I savour his strength, hoping some of it might rub off on me, because I think I'm going to need it over the next couple of days, which reminds me…

"This rather spoils our weekend, I'm afraid." I look up at him, leaning back in his arms.

"Don't worry about that," he says, pushing a stray hair away from my face and tucking it behind my ear.

"I won't be able to see you."

He smiles. "I'd worked that much out for myself, but I'm sure we'll live… at least until next weekend."

"I'm sorry."

He shakes his head. "You've got nothing to be sorry for," he says firmly.

"Except I really should go and check he's alright… that he's not destroying his bedroom in a fit of temper."

"Okay. Well, I've got a few more things I can be doing here, so I'll hang on for a while, just to make sure you're okay."

"You don't have to…" My voice fades.

"Yes, I do."

He leans down and kisses me, just gently, pulling back before we get carried away with ourselves, and then he turns away… and that's when my heart stops beating. Literally. It stops and turns to dust, as I take in the tattoo on his back. It's in the form of a wolf's head, staring out at me, its Celtic knots and lines forming a unique and unmistakable design… one that I've never forgotten since that day on the beach, when I was sixteen years old.

I'm catapulted back in time to a younger version of myself, and to a younger man, who caught my eye, made me smile, made me promises… to meet me, to teach me to surf… and then never turned up. And left me disappointed and dejected. I shake my head, holding back my tears as Adam walks down the garden. How can I have been so wrong about him? He's no different to Scott; no different at all. For all his words, he's just as unreliable, conceited and selfish as every other man, and I clamp my hand to my mouth, capturing the sob that I can't hold back any longer.

How could I have been so stupid as to think that Adam might be different?

Whatever that meeting might have meant to me... and it meant everything... I clearly meant nothing to him.

He doesn't even remember me.

I turn and walk slowly through the dining room, feeling dazed, overwhelmed by my discovery, wanting to be grateful that at least I found out now, before it's too late, before I committed myself even further. Taking the stairs slowly though, I find it a struggle to face the fact that it's over... Because it is over. It really is. I can never trust him now. Not when I know he could let me down so easily. He's done it before... and he'll do it again.

Upstairs, I find Jacob lying on his bed, face down.

"Jacob?" I say quietly and he surprises me by turning towards me, his tear-stained cheeks evidence enough of his feelings. "I'm sorry the weekend's been spoiled for you."

I go and sit down beside him and wait, hoping he'll maybe put his arms around me, or clamber onto my lap for a cuddle. He doesn't, but he doesn't shout at me either, or tell me to leave, which is a sort of break-through, I suppose. And I'll take anything I can get at the moment.

"Shall we try and think of something we can do together?" I suggest and his face brightens slightly.

"Like what?" he mutters.

"I don't know... but while we're thinking, why don't we have some fish and chips for dinner?"

He smiles. "Fish and chips? Really?"

It's a rare treat for us and his reaction makes me smile, in spite of myself.

I nod my head and reach over, ruffling his hair. "Just let me get changed and we'll go and get them, shall we?"

He nods, cheering up, easily pleased it seems... like most men, I suppose.

I leave him to himself for a few minutes, while I go through to my bedroom and take off my work clothes, which I leave on the bed, and change into a long, white sundress, removing my bra at the same time, being as it's just too hot to wear one.

I take a while longer, brushing out my hair, in the hope that Adam will have given up and gone by the time I get back downstairs, because I'm not sure I can face him tonight.

I'm not sure I can admit – even to myself – how much he meant to the sixteen year old me, or how much he was coming to mean to me now… or how much it hurts that he doesn't remember me. Because I meant nothing to him. And no doubt, when someone more interesting comes along, I'll mean nothing all over again.

Chapter Sixteen

Adam

I know I said to Jenna that I was okay with the weekend plans being changed – well, cancelled – but I'm so disappointed. The thing is, I can't show her that, because she seems to be feeling guilty about everything, including Jacob's behaviour, which is entirely down to her ex-husband, and for which she always has to pick up the pieces. I think a weekend to ourselves would have done us both good, and the only saving grace we've got is that I'm assuming Scott will want to see Jacob next weekend, which is only seven days away, and that we can see each other in between, even if it is only briefly.

I've cleared up the garden, put away all the tools, packed up my car and put my t-shirt back on, even though it's still boiling hot, and I'm now just waiting for Jenna to come back down. I know I can't stay for the evening, which is what I'd really like to do, but I just want to make sure she's okay before I go home.

I lean up against the wall and check my phone for messages. Amy's sent one, saying that she's going to be at Dad's on Sunday and is there any chance I can pop by at lunchtime? I haven't seen her since she moved in with her boyfriend, Mike, in Okehampton, just after Christmas, so I send a reply, saying I'll do my best. Now that my plans with Jenna have been cancelled, it shouldn't be a problem, but I don't want to make any promises, just in case.

As I put my phone back in my pocket, I glance up and see Jenna walking through the dining room, and into the kitchen, wearing a long, flowing white sundress, which is beautiful, although one look at her face makes my heart stop. I thought she looked upset when she went upstairs, but now she looks completely devastated and I wonder if Jacob has been rude to her again.

Stepping into the kitchen, I ask if she's okay, and she keeps her back to me, telling me she's fine, her voice flat and emotionless.

"Jenna? What's wrong?"

"Nothing. I'm spending the evening with Jacob... so..." Could she be any more dismissive, I wonder.

"I know," I interrupt. "I gathered that." She turns and glares at me, and I know that, regardless of what she's saying, something is very wrong. "What did I do?" I ask, because every instinct in my body is telling me that whatever is going on now has nothing to do with Jacob, or with Scott. This is about us.

She opens her mouth to speak, just as Jacob comes into the room, wanting a drink. Once again, he doesn't bother with a 'please' or a 'thank you', but Jenna doesn't pick him up on that, and neither do I. As much as I want to help her, I'm far too distracted at the moment, by whatever it is that's changed between us. Because something definitely has. Jenna gets a glass from the cupboard then turns around again, seemingly surprised to find me still standing there, staring at her, "We'll see you on Monday, then..." she says quietly. "Thanks for your hard work this week."

What the hell is happening here? She's thanking me? Like I'm the hired help, all of a sudden?

She starts to pour Jacob some orange juice and I watch her, even though she's taking her time, and ignoring me in the process. Once she's done though, she hands Jacob the glass and turns away, dismissing me completely.

"Jenna?" I say quietly.

"Can you make sure you shut the back gate properly on your way out?" she asks, her voice cool and offhand, as she wanders away towards the front of the house.

I stare after her, wondering how I came to be the villain of the piece all of a sudden, but I'm unable to do anything, paralysed by Jacob's presence in the house. I know if he wasn't here, I'd follow her, pull her into my arms and demand to know what's going on. But I can't do that. I can't let him see that his mum is breaking my heart. So for now, I'm going to have to let her.

I've been home for over an hour. I've showered, put on some shorts and a t-shirt and sat on the sofa, staring into space, trying to work out what changed between the moment when I was holding Jenna in my arms, and the time when she came back downstairs. Did she maybe speak to someone on the phone? Perhaps Scott did something else to upset her... except that doesn't make sense, because she'd have told me if it had been something like that. No, this was definitely something I did. That much was obvious. The problem is, I didn't do anything... not that I know of.

I pick up my phone from the coffee table and look up her number, connecting a call to her, which unsurprisingly goes straight to voicemail.

"It's me... Adam," I say, adding my name just in case. "Look, I don't know what happened this evening, but I need to speak to you. I need to work this out, so can you call me. Please?"

I hang up, wishing I could have added 'I love you' to that message, although that probably wouldn't have been playing fair... not that I'm playing.

I wait for half an hour, but my phone just lies on the table, mocking me, so I pick it up again, and this time I type out a message.

— If you don't want to talk to me, then can you at least reply to a text? Can you tell me what I did to hurt you? Because I think I did, only I don't know how, and I want to make it right again. Adam x.

By nine-thirty, I've had no response to either of my messages, and I'm getting desperate.

I suppose that men do strange things out of desperation, and in my case, that involves getting into my car and driving back over to Jenna's house, in the hope that Jacob will have gone to bed, and that I can persuade her to open the door and talk to me... because I know for certain that I don't stand a hope in hell of sleeping until I can get to the bottom of this.

It's just after a quarter to ten when I park, pulling up behind Jenna's car and letting myself in through the front gate, before ringing her doorbell.

"Who's there?" Her voice rings out and I smile, pleased that she didn't just open the door at this time of night.

"It's me."

"What do you want, Adam?" I suppose at least she knows who I am, which is something.

"I want to talk to you."

"Well, I don't want to talk to you, so can you leave, please?"

She sounds angry, upset… and hurt, and I shake my head. "No. Not until you've explained to me what it is that you think I've done to you."

"You didn't *do* anything," she says, her voice laced with sarcasm, "except be a man, of course."

"What does that mean?"

"You see if you can work it out."

"How am I supposed to do that, when I've got no idea what you're talking about?" I gaze up at the door between us. "And do you think you could open the door?" I add. "Because at the moment, your neighbours can hear everything we're saying."

"No," she replies. "I don't need to open the door, because we've got nothing to say to each other."

"Yes, we have… and if necessary, I'll just go around the back and let myself in."

"You wouldn't dare."

"I would. I need to see you… and I'm not leaving until I have. You can let me in, or I'll do it myself, but either way, we're going to talk."

There's a moment's silence and then slowly, the door cracks open and she stands before me, beautiful in her sundress, her hair a little dishevelled and her eyes red and swollen from where she's so obviously been crying.

"Oh, Jenna," I murmur, stepping into the house. "What's wrong?"

She looks up at me and bursts into a flood of noisy tears. I take a step towards her, reaching out, but she clenches her fists, and without warning, starts raining punches onto my chest as she sobs, and I let her, for about ten seconds or so, before I grab her wrists, halting her.

"Feel better now?" I ask.

"Don't be so patronising."

"I'm not. But I haven't done anything wrong, so why are you hitting me? Is this to do with Scott?" I ask. "Are you taking your problems with him out on me?"

She sucks in a breath, pulling her arms way from me and folding them across her chest, anger pouring off of her. "No. But you're no better than him," she hisses, rage sparking in her eyes.

"Excuse me?"

"You don't even remember me, do you?"

"Remember you? What are you talking about?"

"Exactly what I just said. You don't remember me."

"Am I supposed to? Have we met before?"

"Yes. But clearly it meant nothing to you."

I shrug. "Okay, explain it to me then." I'm beyond confused now, and lean against the wall beside me, folding my own arms and waiting, as she looks down at her feet for a second, then back at me, her anger seemingly abating as she blinks back a fresh wave of tears.

"Do you remember me telling you that I moved to Carven Bay when I was sixteen?" she says.

"Yes."

"Well, when we'd been here for a few days, my parents suggested I take a walk on the beach, just to blow away the cobwebs and unwind… so I did. It was late in the afternoon, and I wandered down the pathway and out into the bay, where I sat on a rock. There was a group of surfers…"

"Oh God… It's you," I whisper, feeling lightheaded, the room spinning, and a lump rising in my throat. "It's really you. You're the girl…"

"What girl?" She looks puzzled by my interruption.

"The girl on the beach… the girl who wanted to learn to surf… *the girl*." She nods her head, looking sad, but I reach out to her and pull her into my arms, holding the evidence that miracles can happen, as I gaze into her tear-filled eyes. "I'm so sorry," I murmur, running my fingers down her soft cheeks, although my hands are shaking and I'm grinning like an idiot, unable to believe she's really here. With me. "I'm sorry I didn't recognise you straight away. I should have done, especially when I saw your eyes, but I didn't… and I'm sorry." She's staring, bewildered. "Have you known all along?" I ask. "Have you been waiting for me to remember? Is that why you're upset? Because it was taking me so long?" I hold her close to me, even though she's stiff in my arms. "How did you recognise me?"

"I didn't, not until this evening, when I saw your tattoo," she mumbles, pulling back from me.

I let her go, my smile fading, and move away for a moment, before turning back. "Hang on a second. Can I get something straight? You've been giving me a hard time all evening, giving me the cold shoulder, ignoring my calls and messages, and hitting me just now, because I didn't remember you, or at least didn't recognise you, because I'll be honest here and admit that I've never forgotten you, not ever. But now I find out that you didn't recognise me either, until you saw my tattoo? Why exactly does that make me the bad guy?" She lowers her eyes and I go back to her, placing my finger beneath her chin, and raise her face to mine. "Be fair, Jenna," I whisper. "Our memories were always going to have faded. A lot has happened in between – for both of us – and being left with an impression of each other is perfectly reasonable. Let's face it, we had one conversation, nearly fifteen years ago, for less than an hour."

"I know," she replies, looking into my eyes. "I know that. I completely understand that. But you're missing the point. It's not about who recognised who first, or how, or when." Her voice fades.

"Okay, what is it about?"

She starts to cry again. "You let me down," she sobs, trying to pull away from me, although I don't let her.

"How? How did I let you down?"

"You didn't come back. You said you'd come back the next day, and you didn't," she wails.

"Yes, I did. I went back to the beach the next evening, and every evening after that, for weeks… but I never saw you again." She stops crying, gulping back her tears and staring at me. "I looked for you, every single day. You weren't there."

"Yes, I was. I went back the next morning," she whispers. "And the morning after."

I stare at her for a moment, and then a slow smile forms on my lips. "The morning?" I query and she nods her head. "But I was working. I couldn't spend all day on the beach – worst luck. I used to go there after work, and most weekends – I still do, when I'm not with you." I move closer to her, one hand in the small of her back, the other on her waist. "I was looking forward to seeing you again, so much… and when you didn't show up…"

"But I did," she says.

"Okay, okay," I whisper. "The point is, it was no-one's fault. No-one let anyone down. It was just a misunderstanding, that's all."

"That's all?" She cries, and bursts into tears again. I move my hand up, holding her head against my chest, stroking her hair, until she leans back again and I see the depth of her sorrow in her eyes. "Don't you see? I—If you'd been there, or if I'd been there, things might have been so different. My life might have been…" She starts to sob again, uncontrollably, and I lean down, lifting her into my arms and carrying her through to the living room, where I sit on the sofa and lower her onto my lap, holding her there and letting her cry. It's hard not to confirm her statement, hard not to tell her that, if she'd been there, or if I'd been there, then her life wouldn't have turned out the way it has. But then neither would mine… because there's no way on this earth I'd ever have let her go.

Very slowly, she starts to calm, to take longer and deeper breaths, until she's able to sit back, her face streaked with tears, and look up into my eyes. "I'm sorry," she whispers.

"What for?"

Her brow furrows. "For being so horrible to you, for hitting you…" She rubs her hand across my chest, where her fists pummelled into me just a short while ago. "Are you okay?" she asks.

"I am now." I cover her hand with mine, holding it against me.

"You're right," she says softly. "I suppose it was just a misunderstanding… that and bad timing. You weren't being intentionally male."

"Intentionally male?" I repeat, biting my lip, trying not to smile. "What does that mean?"

"It means you weren't intentionally letting me down."

I lean forward and kiss her forehead. "I would never do that, Jenna."

She lets her head rest against me again. "I was looking forward to seeing you too," she whispers and I let that smile burst onto my face again. "And I really did want to learn to surf."

I pull back slightly and look down at her. "Well, as I've believe I've said before a couple of times, it's never too late…"

"What for?"

"To start again… and to learn to surf."

Her eyes widen, but then she shakes her head. "No, I'm too old now."

"No you're not. You've just got to let go of your misconceptions… and trust me."

She tilts her head slightly. "Are we still talking about surfing?"

"Not necessarily."

She opens her mouth to speak, but I lean down and capture her lips, crushing her body to mine as I let the relief wash over me. An hour ago, I didn't know if I'd ever get her back, and now, not only is she in my arms, but it turns out, she's the woman of my dreams. She's 'the girl', and she's here. And, as I change the angle of my head, deepening our kiss, I work out why it is that I fell in love with her so quickly, the moment she opened her door to me, just a few weeks ago… it's because I was already in love with her and I have been for nearly half my life already.

We stop kissing eventually, breathless, flushed, gazing at each other as though for the first time, even though I know her face intimately, as I'm sure she does mine.

"It's been such an awful evening," she murmurs, on a soft sigh.

"It's improving though, isn't it?" I ask, and she nods her head, smiling.

"I've still got Jacob and Scott to worry about," she adds, and then pauses as though in deep thought.

"What's wrong?" I ask and she blinks a few times, focusing on me properly.

"I was just wondering why on earth I ever got together with Scott," she muses.

"Because you fell in love with him…"

"Yes, but why?" she interrupts. "I mean, I know he was good looking, but the only time he was ever nice to me was when he was…" She stops talking suddenly and blushes.

"What?" I ask, even though I'm fairly sure I know what's coming. "When he was what?"

"In bed with me," she whispers. "Why did he do that?"

"Because he was manipulating you?" I suggest. "If Scott couldn't see how gorgeous and sexy and beautiful you are, and wasn't prepared to tell you that every single time he saw you, regardless of where you were, then he was blind, as well as stupid… and we both know he was stupid." She giggles. "Your laugh is beautiful, Jenna. Like you. I thought that, right from the first moment I saw you that afternoon, walking onto the beach, looking a little bit lost." I lean slightly closer to her. "You've haunted my dreams ever since, you know."

To my surprise, and disappointment, she shakes her head. "Don't say things like that. I'm sure you've been with lots of other women in the last fifteen years."

"Not *lots* of other women. And I'm slightly ashamed to say that being with them didn't stop me from thinking about you, and from dreaming about you, and I've had some amazing dreams about you over the years. Of course, lately, I've been dreaming about you as you, rather than you, as the girl, because I thought you were two different people, but now I know you're not, that makes perfect sense." I pause for a second, then ask, "Did you ever dream about me?"

She purses her lips, then bites the bottom one, and says, "At the beginning, yes."

I smile. "Only at the beginning?"

"Well… okay, and recently too," she confesses, and then tilts her head. "I thought it was odd that the sea featured in my dreams about you, but now I know who you are… that you're the wolf man…"

I pull back, looking down at her. "The wolf man?"

She blushes. "Yes… I called you that in my head, being as I didn't know your name."

"Wolf man?" I query again.

"Yes. Because of your tattoo." I nod, understanding now. "Did you come up with a name for me?" she asks.

"No… to me, you've always been 'the girl'."

"The girl?" She sounds almost disappointed, and I lean closer again, my lips almost touching hers.

"Yes… *the* girl. As in, the one and only girl. The only girl I've ever really wanted; the one with whom no other has ever compared."

She starts to smile. "No other?" she echoes.

"No… not until I met you again."

Her smile widens, but before she can speak, I close the gap between us, kissing her, feeling her arms come around my shoulders, in that familiar way, her fingers brushing through my hair as she moans and sighs, and without breaking the kiss, I lift her, twisting around and lying her down on the sofa, then I move on top of her, supporting my weight, but letting her feel my body along the length of hers. She doesn't hesitate, but parts her legs, cradling me between them, the sounds of our longing filling the room, until I pull back and gaze down at her flushed face, her eyes alight with undisguised need, even as I turn us onto our sides, facing each other and raising myself up on one elbow, looking down at her.

"One step at a time… remember?" I whisper, struggling to keep control. "And I think we've taken enough steps for one evening, don't you?"

"Probably," she mutters, although I sense a note of reluctance in her voice, which makes me smile as I place my hand around her waist, pulling her closer to me.

"So, what are you going to do this weekend?" I ask her, changing the subject, but with an idea in mind.

"I'm not sure. I told Jacob we'd do something together to make up for Scott letting him down, but I don't know what yet, and we couldn't come up with anything earlier." She nestles into me. "Normally, we'd go to my parents' on Saturday to do the laundry, but…"

"Could you do that on Sunday?" I ask.

"Why?" She twists, looking up at me.

"Because I've got a suggestion." She doesn't reply, but waits, her face serious. "Things kind of changed between us tonight… and I'm not just talking about that kiss." I smile down at her. "I think we both know that finding out that you're the girl and I'm – evidently – the wolf man, makes a difference, doesn't it?"

"Yes," she whispers.

"And I think it's time we took the next step in our relationship, don't you?" She tenses in my arms, and I know she's misunderstood me. "It's okay… I'm not talking about what you think I'm talking about. I know you're not ready yet. Not completely." Her body might be, but the rest of her still has some catching up to do. She sighs and smiles at me, and I smile back. "I was just going to suggest that, if you don't have any other plans, then maybe we could do something together tomorrow… all three of us."

She takes a long breath, staring at me. "What did you have in mind?" she asks.

"I'd like to teach you to surf. And I don't see any reason why Jacob couldn't learn too. I wasn't much older than him when I first got on a board."

"And how long did it take you to learn? Because I feel it's only fair to warn you, Jacob isn't the most patient of children."

"Well, I took to it kind of naturally, but most of my friends knew one way or the other, whether they were going to be able to master it, after their first lesson."

"I see." She's trying so hard not to smile, and the effort makes her look even more beautiful than usual. "So you took to it naturally, did you?"

"Yes."

"Somehow I'm not surprised."

"I promise you it's one of very few things in my life that I've not required some kind of tuition or guidance with."

Her eyes sparkle slightly, and she bites her bottom lip, gazing up at me. "And you really… you really think I could surf?" she says, surprising me with her insecurity, her reaction so different to the almost boundless enthusiasm she showed when I last made this offer, to the teenage version of Jenna.

"There's only one way to find out. But you've waited nearly fifteen years, and I think that's long enough, don't you?"

Chapter Seventeen

Jenna

I lean up on my elbow, turning to face him. "We don't have any boards."

He smiles. "Well, do you have swimming costumes?"

I'm reminded of the last time he asked me that question, on the beach, so many years ago, and the confusion that followed when he thought my negative answer meant I didn't own one at all. The memory makes me smile too, as I nod my head.

"Okay then. I've got boards…" He thinks for a moment, then adds, "Although I suppose we ought to take into account that the water's going to be cold, because it's only April."

"But it's boiling," I reason and he shakes his head.

"The air temperature doesn't mean a thing."

"So, what are you saying?"

"Well, I'd normally wear a wetsuit…"

"You weren't wearing one when I saw you on the beach."

"No," he says, "because it was September, and the water's warmer then. But at this time of year, it'll be freezing."

"So you're suggesting we get wetsuits?"

"You don't have to, but you'll probably be more comfortable." He seems to think for a moment. "I guess we could go to one of the bigger beaches, if you'd prefer. You'd be able to hire wetsuits there, instead of buying them."

I shake my head. "Hmm… and I'd have a much bigger audience for my humiliation when I fall in the water every time I try to stand on the board… No, I think we'll grin and bear it at Carven Bay for tomorrow, and see how it goes. We can always get wetsuits if it works out."

"Okay. But can you try and have a little more faith in yourself?"

"Faith in myself? I can't even remember what that feels like," I say, almost to myself.

"I know," he says softly, holding me tighter. "But this is something that you really wanted when you were younger, so don't let what's happened in between take that away from you."

He's right. I know he is. And not just about my desire to learn to surf. Something did change between us tonight. I'm not sure whether it was discovering and acknowledging who we really are and that we have that connection from the past – and that it meant something for both of us. Or whether it was the way he just kissed me, which felt different to every other time, in a good way. Letting him in at that moment felt like the right thing to do, even if I knew I wasn't ready for it to go further – not yet, and certainly not on the sofa, while Jacob's asleep upstairs. We have to be responsible. Especially where he's concerned…

Adam sits up, bringing me with him and holding onto me.

"I know you're nervous," he says, his voice low, but gentle.

"I'm not."

"Yes, you are. I can see it in your eyes. What are you nervous of, Jenna? And don't say 'learning to surf,' because it's more than that."

"It's just that spending the day together, with Jacob, is a big step."

"I'm not unaware of that. And if it's too soon…"

I shake my head, because I'm not being entirely honest with him, and I have to be. "It's not. At least, it's not, as long as we're mindful of him."

"We will be."

He sounds so reassuring. "That's not the only thing I'm wary of, Adam."

"What else is worrying you?"

I take a deep breath. "I gave Scott everything when we were together… and I mean everything, and he threw it back in my face in ways that you can't even begin to imagine." I'm not sure I'm ready to explain that, so before he can ask me to, I continue, "He hurt me so much, and the thought of letting someone get close enough to do that to me again…" I let my voice fade, lowering my eyes, even though I'm relieved I've admitted my fear to him.

"You're forgetting one thing," he whispers and I look up at him again.

"What?"

"That I will never hurt you. I couldn't." He takes my hand in his and raises it to his lips, kissing my fingers and staring into my eyes. "You can trust me, and I intend to prove that to you. Because as far as I'm concerned, this matters, Jenna… it mattered before I knew who you really are. But now, it matters, like it's never mattered before."

His words leave me reeling, but just as I'm trying to work out how to respond, he gets to his feet, looking down at me. "Think about tomorrow. See what Jacob wants to do, and let me know in the morning, okay?"

"And if I say 'no'?" I ask, feeling fearful.

"What do you mean?" He sounds confused, even though I think my question was a simple one.

"Well, if I say no to coming surfing, what happens to us?"

He frowns. "Nothing happens to us." He sighs and runs his fingers back through his hair. "I mean, obviously I'll be a bit disappointed, but I understand that this is a really big step for you, and if you're not ready yet, then we'll just wait… until you are. And, in the meantime, we can spend the weekend doing our own thing; we can talk on the phone and text each other, and I'll see you on Monday morning as usual. I'll admit that I may get here ten minutes early, but…"

"Why?" I ask, intrigued.

"Because I'll have missed you, so I'm going to need to kiss you for at least that long… maybe longer." His eyes sparkle as he smiles, and then he holds out his hand and I take it, letting him pull me to my feet and into his arms.

"Um… Are you leaving?" I ask, looking up at him, because it feels like he is.

"Yes," he replies.

"Did I do something wrong?"

"No, of course not. But I'm trying to prove to you that you can trust me."

"And you need to leave to do that?" I ask.

"To be honest... yes." He smiles. "You look very alluring in this dress, and maybe a little vulnerable too... and that's quite a heady combination. Added to which, I've had fifteen years of dreaming about you, letting my very vivid imagination run riot. So, if I'm going to earn your trust, I think I'd better do it from my place... at least for tonight."

As he finishes speaking, he leans down and kisses me deeply, his tongue searching for mine, his hands wandering up and down my back, his groans echoing in my mouth, as my fingers knot in his hair, holding him in place while our breathing deepens and my skin tingles in anticipation... My head may want to wait, may be screaming at me to hold back, to give our relationship more time; but my body is positively crying out with need and, as Adam bites gently on my bottom lip, I move closer to him, and he presses our bodies together, letting me feel his arousal against my hip. I gasp at the intimate contact and he pulls back, looking down into my eyes.

"Sorry," he whispers. "Like I said, you're a heady combination."

I'm breathing deeply, unable to reply, so I smile instead and he leans down again, his mouth beside my ear.

"Dream of me," he murmurs.

I think that's a given...

I awake feeling hot, which could be due to the fact that the sun is already streaming in through my window, and I forgot to leave it open last night. The fact that I'm also flustered, and very turned on, is because I've been having an extremely sexy dream about Adam. Now I'm awake, of course, it all feels like a bit of a blur, as dreams often do in the cold light of day, and as hard as I try to grasp the details, they drift away on the tide. But I can still recall the sound of waves crashing on the shore, his words – very specifically, him telling me to lie down, before he peeled my bikini from me – the feeling of his strong body on top of mine, his firm hands, his deep kisses, our skin touching…

"Mum?" Jacob's voice makes me jump and I shake myself back to reality.

"Yes?" I sit up on the edge of the bed, then go to the door, opening it, to find Jacob standing on the landing between our two rooms.

"Can I go and watch TV?" he asks, looking a bit downcast.

"Okay. But before you do, I've got something I need to talk to you about…"

He sighs. "What have I done now?"

"Nothing. It's just an idea for something we can do today, that's all." He tilts his head to one side, but doesn't look overly enthusiastic, and waits for me to continue, "How would you like to go surfing?"

"Surfing?" He's stunned. I can tell from the wide-eyed look on his face, and the way his mouth is hanging open.

"Yes."

"Where?"

"At the beach, of course." I smile down at him.

"But I can't surf," he points out.

"No. Neither can I… but I thought we could learn." His face lights up and he runs to me, throwing his arms around my hips. "Can I take it you're pleased about that idea?" I ask and he looks up, nodding his head.

"I'll go and get dressed," he says, all thoughts of Saturday morning television forgotten, it seems.

"Okay… I've just got a quick phone call to make, and then I'll shower, and after that, we should be able to leave… so once you're dressed, you can watch television until I'm ready."

"Okay, Mum," he calls over his shoulder, and I have to smile to myself, seeing the 'old' Jacob for the first time in ages, as I turn back to my room, going inside and closing the door, before I settle on the bed, and pick up my phone from the bedside table.

Adam's is the first name on my contacts list, and I connect a call to him, sitting back and resting my head against the pillows.

"Hi," he says, his voice a gentle whisper against my ear.

"Hello."

"How are you?"

"I'm fine. How are you?"

There's a moment's pause, before he replies, "As much as I love making small talk with you, can you just put me out of my misery?"

I chuckle. "Okay... what time would you like us to come over?"

"Right now?" he says and I laugh.

"Well, I need to shower first. I've only just woken up."

"You're not an early morning person then?" he replies and I glance at the clock beside my bed and notice that it's already after nine.

"Well, normally I am – as you already know, being as you see me most mornings – but I must have overslept for some reason."

"Would that have had anything to do with your dreams?" he asks, and I'd swear I can actually feel his breath tickling my ear this time. It makes me shudder as I recall both my dreams and the reality of his kisses last night, and I hold the phone tighter.

"It might have," I reply.

"Good."

"You're assuming you featured in my dreams, are you?" I ask, pursing my lips to stop myself from smiling, even though he can't see me.

"Not necessarily," he replies. "I never assume anything when it comes to you. But why don't you tell me about them anyway..."

"Absolutely not."

He laughs. "In that case, I know I featured in them."

"You're hopeless... you know that, don't you?"

"I think you mean hopeful, Jenna." His voice is serious again now and I know I'm blushing.

"You didn't answer my question," I remind him, changing the subject.

"What question? There was a question?" he says and I shake my head, smiling.

"Yes, there was. What time do you want us to come over?"

"I seem to remember telling you to come over right away," he replies. "But I suppose, to be practical, I'd better let you shower first, so shall we say ten-thirty?"

"That's perfect."

"No, you're perfect."

I blush again. "Do you want us to bring anything?"

"No… just yourselves and your swimming costumes… oh, and maybe a couple of towels. I've got everything else."

"What about food?" I ask.

"Like I said… I've got everything else."

"Already?" I'm surprised.

"I went shopping really early this morning," he says quietly.

"Before you even knew if we were going to come over?"

"Don't get angry with me." He sounds apologetic and I can't help smiling again. "I wasn't making assumptions. I had to go shopping anyway, and I just picked up a few extra things, that's all. If you'd called and said you couldn't come… well, let's just say I'd have been having some very nice lunches for the next few days."

"I see."

"Are you cross with me?" he asks, sounding worried now.

"No."

"Good."

"But if you don't give me your address, you'll be eating that very nice lunch all by yourself."

He chuckles. "I'll text it to you… I don't want to hold you up. Not now I know you're coming over here."

"Okay."

We end the call, and I go into the bathroom, showering quickly and returning to my bedroom wrapped in a towel, my hair dripping down my back, before it dawns on me that I have a problem; and it's a big one.

In thinking through the whole idea of spending a day with Adam, I've forgotten one very important detail. I've forgotten that, when I left Scott, I left behind all of the obscene bikinis he bought for our honeymoon, bringing just the other three, and while they're perfectly wearable, they're still quite skimpy.

I pull them from my bottom drawer, where they've languished for the last few years, and deciding that the blue one is probably the nicest, I hold it up, letting out a long groan, as I take in the four triangles that make up the garment, all held together with ties, and I wonder if I'll even be decent.

"I suppose there's only one way to find out," I mutter to myself, and let the towel drop to the floor, putting on the bikini, adjusting the ties at my hips, and the ones behind my back and neck, making sure they're tight, and then studying myself in the full-length mirror that sits beside my chest of drawers, feeling myself blush.

Okay… so, everything is covered, but the silvery snaking stretch marks are still visible – just – while the pale blue material leaves almost nothing to the imagination. And Adam's already told me that he's got a very vivid one of those.

"Oh God…" I murmur and sit down on the edge of the bed.

I know we're taking things one step at a time, but is this a step too far? And is it too soon to be showing him this much of myself… especially when we'll be spending the day with Jacob?

I pick up my phone and twist it around in my hand, wondering whether to call and cancel, although how I'll explain that to Jacob, heaven only knows. Or maybe I can find out from Adam whether I can change my mind about the wetsuits?

I press the button at the bottom of the screen, trying to decide what to do, and notice that I've got a message, and that it's from Adam. Clicking on it, I read…

— *My address is Flat 6, Bayview Lodge. It's right down on the seafront. You can't miss it. Is it sad that I'm pacing the floor because I can't wait to see you, even though I only left you less than twelve hours ago? Adam x*

I can't help smiling as I tap in the 'reply' box and start typing:

— *I'm not sure if it's sad or not. But I'm sure you should have better things to do with your time. Jenna*

His reply comes through straight away.

— *No. I don't have anything better to do than to wait for you… And why are you wasting time texting me, when you should be getting ready to come over here? xx*

I glance down at my bikini, realising there's not a lot I can do about the situation, and I shrug my shoulders. After all, what have I got to lose

– other than my self respect? And I don't have much of that anyway. Scott took it all.

— *We'll be half an hour, okay? Jenna*
— *Okay. I think my floors can survive that long. Adam xx*
I suck in a breath and, before I can change my mind, I type back…
— *xx*
And he replies…
— *Thank you for that. xx*

I park at the front of Adam's smart apartment building and, once Jacob has climbed out of the car and I've grabbed our bag containing the towels and my underwear and spare clothes for Jacob, I take his hand and we go over to the main entrance, where I press on the button next to the number '6'. It takes just a few seconds for Adam to reply and for his disconnected voice to instruct me to push on the door and go up to the second floor, after which there's a buzzing sound and the door clicks open.

Upstairs, Adam is waiting for us outside his flat, dressed in grey board shorts and a white t-shirt and he looks me up and down, in my navy blue sundress, which is shorter than most of the things I usually wear, being knee-length, but is more practical for a day at the beach, and he smiles appreciatively.

"Hi," he says, his eyes sparkling.

"Hello."

He looks down at Jacob and repeats his greeting, although my son remains silent and I squeeze his hand to get his attention.

"You remember Adam, don't you?" I say, feeling nervous.

"Yes." He looks at me. "He's the man who's doing the work on our house."

"That's right. He's going to teach us to surf."

I glance up at Adam, and it's impossible to miss the slight frown that crosses his face, or its meaning. I know I should probably have explained that Adam is more than the man who's doing the work on our house, and teaching us to surf, but I'm not sure what to call him. He's the man who fills my dreams; the man who kisses me like his life depends on it, and who's taking things one step at a time with me – just because it's what I need him to do. But how do I explain that to a six year old? How do I put that into an introduction? 'This is the man that Mummy really likes... a lot'? Or maybe 'This is the man that Mummy could easily fall for, if she wasn't so scared of getting hurt'? I doubt Jacob would understand either... and yet 'This is Mummy's boyfriend' doesn't feel right either; not when Adam and I haven't even talked about it.

"Are we ready?" Adam says, breaking into my thoughts and I nod my head.

"If you are."

"Just two seconds," he says, disappearing back into his flat, and then returning with a cool bag slung over his shoulder and a bag in his hand, four beach mats rolled up and poking out of the top of it. "I've packed us a picnic," he explains, closing the door and pocketing his keys, before leading us back to the stairs.

"Don't we need boards?" I ask.

He turns and smiles. "We do. But I don't store them in my flat... you'll see why in a minute."

We get outside and cross to the garage block on the other side of the car park, going to the third one along, which Adam opens, to reveal a series of racks, containing at least half a dozen surf boards.

"If I kept these in the flat," he says, turning to me, "I'd have to sleep out here."

"Why do you have so many?" I ask.

"I've just never been very good at getting rid of them."

He puts down his bags and moves inside, picking up a smallish board, then turns to Jacob, offering it to him. To my utter shame, Jacob snatches the board, but before I can say anything, Adam takes it back again, glaring down at Jacob, who stares up defiantly. "That's my property. It's my oldest board, so you treat it with respect, young man. Do you hear?" Adam's voice is quiet but firm and Jacob stares a little longer, until Adam continues, "That means you say 'please', you say 'thank you' and you don't just snatch. Got it?"

There's a short pause before Jacob slowly nods his head and Adam hands him back the board, but he doesn't let go and they both look at each other until Jacob eventually mutters, "Thank you."

Adam finally releases the board, then goes back into the garage, selecting another from the opposite rack, and bringing it to me. "Thank you," I whisper and he chuckles, his eyes twinkling.

He turns back, closing the garage door again.

"What about you?" I ask. "Aren't you taking a board?"

"No," he replies, picking up the bags again. "I'll be taking care of you two, not surfing myself."

I like the sound of having Adam take care of me, and for a moment, I just stare at him, mesmerised.

"Come on, then," he says, eventually, and we head across the quiet road and down the pathway, onto the beach.

I keep hold of Jacob's free hand until we're halfway down the path, and then I let him go and he runs ahead, at which point, Adam turns to me.

"I'm so glad you could come," he whispers and I smile up at him.

"I'll remind you of that when you've tried teaching me to surf," I joke to try and keep the atmosphere light – even if only because Jacob is still within view.

We come out onto the bay and the breeze catches my hair. Even though it's only the end of April, because of the exceptionally warm weather, there are already several groups of people on the beach. Among them are a few families, and some youngsters, with surf boards of their own, which reminds me of the day I met Adam…

"If we sit over here," he says, distracting me and moving to the right, further onto the beach, "there's some flat sand where we can practice."

"Practice?"

He looks down at me. "Yes… you don't think I'm going to let you just jump on a surfboard and leap into the sea, do you?"

"Well, no… but we practice on the sand?"

He nods his head, setting the bags down and I lay my board beside them. "That's how you start, yes."

We unfurl the beach mats he brought with him, before I reach into my bag, pulling out the sun cream I packed earlier.

"Jacob!"

He's put down his board next to mine and is running around with his arms outstretched, pretending to be an aeroplane, I presume. Whatever he's doing, he's ignoring me, that's for sure.

"Jacob, come here," I call again and this time he stops, deliberately looks at me, and then starts running around again.

Exasperated and embarrassed, I go over to him and, after a few minutes of chasing him around, I manage to grab his arm and drag him back, kicking and screaming, to the place where we're sitting.

"Just let me put some sun screen on you," I say, holding onto him, trying to get him to be still.

"I don't want to." He folds his arms, a tantrum clearly building.

"Fine." Adam's voice rings out and I turn to see him pick up the smallest board – the one he gave to Jacob – and start walking away from us, towards the path that leads back to his flat.

"Where are you going?" Jacob says, breaking away from me and taking off after him, grabbing at the board before Adam's even gone three or four paces.

Adam stops and looks down at him. "What did I tell you?" he thunders. "You do *not* snatch my board."

Jacob stops what he's doing. "But where are you going?" he asks.

"There are rules when you're on the beach," Adam says, his voice quieter, but somehow even more threatening now. "And the most important rule of all is that you do whatever your mother says. If you can't do that, then I'll take your board back, and you can sit on the beach mats while I teach your mum how to surf."

Adam turns away and takes another step, but Jacob reaches up, grabbing at Adam and not the board.

"I'm sorry," he says and my mouth drops open in shock. When was the last time I heard him say that?

"Don't tell me, tell your mum. She's the one you should be saying sorry to," Adam says, turning back to me, but not moving. Jacob looks

up at him and Adam returns his gaze to my son. "Well? Go on then…"
He stands still, waiting, and eventually Jacob comes back to me.

"Sorry," he says, looking mournful.

I nod my head. "Okay," I reply, feeling a little breathless as I remove Jacob's t-shirt and start applying the sun cream. I glance up after a moment and see that Adam's returned Jacob's board and is now sitting on one of the beach mats, staring at me, and I have to smile, because it's the only way I can show my gratitude at the moment. He smiles back and then looks away, out to sea, making me wonder if Jacob's behaviour is forcing him to regret his decision to spend the day with us, or even have second thoughts about our budding relationship… if that's what this is.

"Please tell me you've put your swimming costume on under your clothes," Adam says and I look up at him again. He's staring at me once more, a smile on his lips, his eyes filled with a deep intensity. "Because if not, you're going to have to go back to my place to change."

I smile as I turn Jacob around and smother his back with cream. "No. I thought that one through this morning."

"Good."

Adam stands and peels off his t-shirt, revealing his magnificent chest and for a moment, I freeze, my hand poised on Jacob's back, as I stare at the vision of perfection before me.

"Mum?" Jacob twists around. "That's enough, isn't it?"

I look down at him. "Just let me rub this in." I concentrate on what I'm doing, and finish the job at hand, before letting Jacob go and noticing that Adam has placed our boards out on the flat area of sand.

"Do I need to get undressed?" I call over to him, admiring his tattoo and the way his muscles flex when he moves. He turns slowly and looks at me, smiling.

"Well, I'm not going to say 'no'," he replies. "But you don't actually need to. Not if you'd rather stay as you are for now."

I nod my head and move forward, joining him and Jacob as Adam starts to explain that the first thing we need to do is to learn how to stand.

"I can already stand," Jacob says.

Adam ignores him and shows us what he means. "You need to work out your balance," he adds, looking at me. "Find a position that feels comfortable for you." He smiles. "And don't worry about looking like a fool. Everyone has to go through this bit…"

"Except those who are naturals," I murmur, loud enough for him to hear, and his smile widens.

Jacob, who's standing beside me, starts to mess around, pretending he's on a tightrope, and wobbling, before falling down dramatically and rolling in the sand.

"If you're not going to take this seriously," Adam says, coming over and standing above him, "then you can go and sit down. Because there's no way I'm letting you in the water until you've learned the basics. So, you either do this my way, or you don't do it at all."

Jacob stares at him, then slowly gets to his feet, and this time does everything Adam says, letting Adam adjust his position, and finding his balance perfectly.

As for myself, once Adam has dealt with Jacob, he comes over to me, standing behind me with his hands on my hips, through the thin material of my dress, and twists me around slightly. "You need to face forwards," he whispers, his voice deep and soft in my ear.

"I do?"

"Yes."

I lean back into him just slightly and he chuckles. "And don't do that, or you'll fall off the board."

"I'm not on a board," I point out.

"Not yet," he adds, letting me go.

Once we've been doing that for a while, Adam brings the boards over and demonstrates how you go from lying down, to standing, explaining that you can lead with either foot, and that it's a matter of personal choice which one you prefer.

"Some people find it just comes naturally to lead with one or the other; and some people try them both, and find that one feels easier," he says, going to Jacob and helping him push himself off the board and jump to a standing position, without his feet falling off either side. I watch, smiling at my son's obvious enjoyment, before Adam leaves him to practice and comes across to me.

"I think you might need to take your dress off for this," he says and, seeing his point, I go back to the beach mats and pull my dress off over my head, taking my time over folding it and putting it in my bag, before I turn around, straightening, and look back at Adam, who's staring at me, frowning.

I walk slowly back to him, feeling self conscious.

"What's wrong?" I ask him as I approach, the blush creeping up my face.

"Nothing."

"Oh?" He could have fooled me.

He shakes his head, confirming my thoughts that something is clearly bothering him, then goes back to the beach mats, returning with his t-shirt. "Here… put this on."

He hands it to me and I stare up at him, wanting to ask why I need to be covered up, except I'm scared of his answer, so I pull on his t-shirt, finding that it smells of spice and leather, and vanilla, and Adam, and that it covers me perfectly, down to the middle of my thighs, which is obviously what he intended.

Adam lets out an audible sigh and I struggle to control the lump in my throat as he leads me back to the board again. "You need to lie down," he mutters.

No, I need to run and hide. But, being as that isn't really an option, even if only because Jacob's here, and is thoroughly enjoying himself, I lie down on my front, focusing on learning to surf. Or at least trying to.

"Now, when you feel comfortable," he says, standing beside me, "place your hands on the edge of the board and jump up… just like I showed you before."

I do as he says, trying to ignore my embarrassment and remember his instructions as I jump to my feet, although all I do is succeed in slipping from the board, right into his waiting arms.

"Are you okay?" he asks, holding on to me.

"Yes, thank you."

"Mum… you're such a loser," Jacob cries, laughing, as he performs yet another perfect jump, which makes me feel like such a… well, loser, frankly.

"Ignore him," Adam says. "Do you feel like trying that again?"

"Why not? I suppose I may as well humiliate myself completely." I start to lower myself down again, but Adam stops me, pulling me upright.

"What do you mean 'humiliate' yourself?" he asks, his eyes fixed on mine.

"Well, who do I think I am? Trying to surf at my age, and wearing a bikini like this, when I'm covered in stretch marks, and…"

"What on earth are you talking about?" he interrupts.

"You tell me. You gave me your t-shirt, didn't you?" I snap, then immediately wish I could bite back the words.

"Yes," he says quietly, "but clearly not for the reason you think." He puts his hands on my shoulders and turns us so Jacob can't see my face, and then touches my cheek with his fingertips. "I gave you my t-shirt because I'm not sure how robust your bikini is when it comes to jumping around. That's all. If you're thinking I had any other motive…"

I blush, alarmed by the fact that there are tears pricking behind my eyes. "I'm sorry," I mutter, feeling deeply ashamed now by my outburst. "I—I wouldn't normally have worn anything like this, but I only have three bikinis, and this is the nicest one."

"It is a *very* nice bikini." He smiles, moving just a little closer.

"Well, it's a bit impractical… although compared to the ones Scott bought me for our honeymoon, it's positively Victorian."

"Can I assume they were a bit skimpy?" he asks and I laugh.

"Skimpy is an understatement. They were little more than strips of fabric." I hold my thumb and forefinger an inch or so apart, just to demonstrate how little my bikinis actually covered.

Adam's brow furrows. "Tell me you went somewhere really private for your honeymoon," he murmurs and I look down, shaking my head.

"Not entirely, no."

"You mean, he… he liked showing you off in public?"

"He seemed to, yes." I bite my lip, remembering Scott's reaction to me wearing my bikinis on our honeymoon. "Although, looking back, I can't believe I actually let him do that…"

He sighs deeply. "You weren't comfortable with it, then?"

"No. I consoled myself that all the other women at the resort were wearing similar outfits, and some didn't wear anything at all, and to be honest, Scott had booked the honeymoon and done all the packing, and he hadn't really taken anything else for me to wear, so I didn't have a huge amount of choice." I let my voice fade as Adam places his finger beneath my chin, raising my face to his.

"Keep the t-shirt on, Jenna. Please…" I lean back, feeling hurt and maybe a little disappointed. "Stop it," he says.

"Stop what?"

"Overthinking."

"I'm not," I reply, even though I know I was.

"Yes you are. You're assuming that, because I've given you my t-shirt, and asked you to keep it on, that means I don't want to see you in your bikini, when in reality, I'd happily spend every second of my day just gazing at you, because you look more and more beautiful every time I see you and, regardless of what you wear, or what you don't wear, that's not going to change. Not as far as I'm concerned." He pauses, then adds, "But your body is yours, Jenna, and yours alone. Obviously, one day, I hope you'll want to share it with me, but that will always be on your terms, and no-one else's. Okay?"

I smile up at him, nodding my head, wishing we were alone – completely alone – so that I could kiss him, and as I stare into his sparkling eyes, I wonder if the feeling's mutual.

Adam's made us a choice of wraps and sandwiches, with tuna or cheese and salad fillings, together with some raw veggies, breadsticks and hummus, and fresh fruit.

I'm just about to tell him how delicious it all is, when Jacob interrupts, asking, "Why haven't we even been in the sea yet?"

Adam smiles. "We will. You just have to be patient."

Jacob scowls a little, but fortunately is distracted by food, and I glance up to see that Adam's now looking at me, and I roll my eyes, which makes him smile even more.

Once we've finished eating, we pack away, and Adam gets to his feet.

"Is it time to go into the water now?" Jacob asks, jumping up and joining him.

"No," Adam replies. "We have to run through a few more things first."

"More?" Jacob whines.

"Yes," Adam says, before I can tell Jacob off. "Come up here onto the softer sand."

"Why?" Jacob's being annoyingly inquisitive.

"Because you need to learn how to fall properly."

Jacob laughs. "I know how to fall over."

He demonstrates by flopping down on the sand and playing dead.

"I don't think that's what Adam had in mind," I point out, bending down and lifting him to his feet.

"No, it's not," Adam confirms and moves away to an area about ten or fifteen feet away, where the sand is more churned up, and definitely softer underfoot.

I look up at him, wondering what's coming next as he stands, facing us.

"When you feel yourself falling from the board…" he begins.

"You're assuming we're going to fall?" I ask, trying not to smile.

He grins. "Everyone falls… and when they do, they need to do it without getting hurt."

"How can water hurt you?" Jacob asks, surprising me by taking Adam seriously for once.

"You'd be amazed," Adam replies. "Water is really dangerous stuff. You need to treat it with respect at all times."

Jacob turns, wide-eyed, gazing at the shoreline, before looking back at Adam again, as he goes on to demonstrate the 'proper' method of falling from a surfboard, which appears to be backwards.

"Make sure you cover your head with your arms," he adds, continuing his demonstration.

Jacob gets into the spirit of things, falling back, curling up and covering his head, exactly as Adam did.

"Well done," Adam chimes, coming over and pulling him to his feet again. "Now it's your mum's turn."

"You want me to fall down?" I look up at him.

"Yes. I need to know you're capable of doing this…" His voice fades and they both watch me, expectantly.

"At the risk of sounding like my son, I think I know how to fall, without having to demonstrate it." Adam moves right next to Jacob and folds his arms across his chest; an action which Jacob mirrors, and I find it hard not to laugh at them. "Okay… I'll do it." I hold my arms up, then tuck my head down and let myself fall backwards. Fortunately the sand is soft and I uncurl myself to find Adam standing above me, blocking the sun with his massive frame and holding out his hand. I take it and he easily pulls me to my feet again.

"Perfect," he whispers, winking, and then turns back to Jacob. "Okay, let's try that a couple more times, and then we'll be good to go."

"You should have brought your board," I remark to Adam, as we stroll down the beach, keeping an eye on Jacob has he careers ahead of us.

"No. I'm here to supervise you two. But don't worry, I'm having more than enough fun as it is."

I scowl at him, although I can't help smiling at the same time. "I thought you were enjoying this far too much."

"Nowhere near as much as I'm going to when you discover how cold the water is," he chuckles.

He wasn't kidding either. The sea is absolutely freezing and as the first wave washes over my feet, I yelp in surprise. Jacob laughs, pointing at me, but Adam takes my hand.

"It gets better," he says. "Just give it time."

Jacob's already heading into the surf, and I nod towards him, unable to hide my fear. "Adam… watch him, will you? Please?"

He smiles. "Of course." And turning away, he lets go of my hand and wades after my son. I watch as he grabs Jacob's board, holding it while he climbs on, then pulls him out a little further into the waves. They talk, although I can't hear what they're saying, and Jacob lies down, just as he did on the beach earlier. Then after a while, he starts to paddle. Adam swims beside him, taking long strokes, issuing instructions at the same time, and then all of a sudden, Jacob's standing and I can't wipe the broad smile from my face as he balances perfectly, his arms outstretched… for a full ten seconds, before he crashes into the sea, falling perfectly, his head cradled in his arms. Adam reaches for him, pulling him to the surface, but Jacob is completely undaunted, laughing and throwing his head back in glee.

"Did you see me, Mum?" he yells and I nod my head, just before he looks up at Adam, and they turn away again, repeating the process.

After the fourth attempt, Adam leans down and says something to Jacob, and then turns away, wading over to me again.

"You can't leave him," I say, feeling nervous again.

"I've told him to just paddle on the board for a while, and keep to the shallows," Adam replies quite calmly. "But don't worry. I'm still watching him." He leans closer. "I won't let anything happen to him, I promise."

I smile up at him. "Thank you."

He shakes his head. "You don't need to thank me." He takes my board, and then my hand. "It's your turn now."

"Really? I can't just stand here and watch?"

He laughs. "No. The whole point of today was that you wanted to learn to surf. Remember?"

"Hmm…"

I let him lead me further into the water until he stops, my teeth chattering with cold as he holds the board still. "Climb on," he says.

"That's easier said than done," I reply, although I manage it eventually, lying down straight away, just because I feel safer.

"Now," he adds, dragging me out a little deeper, "when you start paddling, watch for the waves and remember everything I've told you."

"Everything?" I reply, turning and smiling at him.

He shakes his head, grinning. "Yes. Everything." He lets go of the board. "You're on your own now."

I feel a couple of light waves carry me forward and then start to paddle, looking over my shoulder at the same time. As I see a slightly bigger wave approaching, I grab the sides of the board and hoist myself up, mistiming it completely as the wave washes over the board, tilting it up and knocking me sideways into the water. I submerge for a few seconds, shocked by the ice-cold water, and suddenly I feel a pair of arms come around me, pulling me upwards onto my feet, and then Adam is holding me hard against his chest. I feel embarrassed, partly because I made such a hash of my first attempt at surfing, but also because I know – without even looking – that Adam's white t-shirt will be glued to my body, revealing every inch of me.

He pulls back slightly, looking down at me, and I'm just wondering how to cover myself when I realise he's not looking at my body. He's looking at my face, and his eyes are dark with anger... or is it fear? I can't be sure.

"What were you thinking?" he growls. "I told you to remember everything I said, and you forgot every single word of it."

I bite my lip, blinking back my tears. He's never spoken to me like this... "What did I do wrong?" I whisper.

"You didn't fall properly. I told you – fall backwards, tuck your head in. Your board nearly wiped you out, Jenna."

"I'm sorry," I mutter and he pulls me close again, his arms tight around me.

"No, I'm sorry," he says, his voice much gentler, a whisper against my ear. "I didn't mean to snap at you." He leans back again, the darkness gone from his eyes now, replaced with a deep, intense softness. "Please... please will you be more careful?"

I stare up at him. "Would it help if I said I knew you'd catch me?" I ask, desperate to alleviate my sense of guilt.

He sucks in a breath and replies, "Yes. It would. Because I will always catch you." He looks away for a moment and then turns back. "You still scared the hell out of me though."

By the end of the afternoon, not only am I frozen to the core, but I'm pleased to say that I've managed to master standing on the board, and staying there for about five seconds. I've fallen in more times than I care to think about, but I've done it 'properly', as Adam would say, having learned my lesson, just from the look in his eyes and the fear in his voice.

We make our way back to our spot on the beach, shivering but satisfied, after a thoroughly enjoyable day. The sun is starting to go down, and I wrap Jacob in a towel to help him warm up, as he turns to Adam and asks if he did okay.

"You did," Adam replies, water dripping from his hair and down his chest. "You did really well."

"I did better than Mum, didn't I?" Jacob says. "She was being a girl."

Adam moves closer to him and crouches down. "There's nothing wrong with being a girl," he says quietly. "One day, you'll work that out, and you'll realise that without them, boys would be nowhere."

I smile to myself, and start to pack up.

"We can go back to my place to change," Adam suggests. "It'll be easier. And a lot warmer."

He's not wrong. The thought of changing out of my wet things and into my clothes on the beach fills me with dread and I nod my head in agreement.

"That sounds perfect."

Adam starts rolling up the beach mats and I ask Jacob to pass me the sun cream, which is right by his foot. He ignores me and continues to stare out to sea.

"Jacob," I repeat, feeling ashamed of him again. "Didn't you hear me?"

He turns and glares at me, then looks away, letting me know he's heard, but has no intention of doing what I've asked.

Adam appears from behind me. "Forgotten the rules already, have you?" he says, going over to Jacob and standing above him.

Jacob looks up. "What rules?"

"Remember I said you had to do what your mum told you to do?"

Jacob shrugs, and Adam bends down, picking up the sun cream and holding it out to Jacob, who stares at him. "You've got it now," he remarks. "Why don't you give it to her?"

"Jacob!" I can't believe he just said that, but Adam doesn't even flinch. Instead, he stands completely still, the tube in his hand, poised, waiting…

"I've got all night," he says eventually, and Jacob huffs out a sigh and takes the bottle from Adam, bringing it to me.

"There!" he says, gruffly and storms back to his place again.

Adam looks over and I mouth 'sorry' to him, but he shakes his head and goes back to rolling up the beach mats.

"We're dripping all over your floors," I say to Adam as he closes the door of his apartment, guiding us from the hallway into a large, luxurious living area, with a kitchen off to the left.

"My floors are used to it," he replies, smiling. "Now, being as we're all covered in sand, who wants to shower first?"

"Me!" Jacob puts his hand up, dropping the towel that he's kept wrapped around him on the walk back from the beach.

"Okay." Adam puts down the bags by the island unit, which effectively separates his stylish kitchen from the rest of the living space, and turns around again. After a whole day spent together, I ought to be getting used to his bare chest, as well as his tattoo, but I can't help staring – and judging by the smile on his face as he catches my eye, I think he's noticed. "The bathroom's this way."

He leads us back into the hallway, opening the door to the right. I've brought our bag, containing our dry clothes and I look up at Adam as he stands to one side to let us pass.

"Thank you," I murmur.

"You're welcome." He smiles down at me. "There are towels in the cupboard. Feel free to use my shampoo and soap… and I'll leave you to it."

He moves away and, although I miss his presence, I focus on Jacob, ushering him into the sumptuous bathroom, with a double width shower at one end and roll-top bath at the other.

"Wow," Jacob breathes, making for the shower and dropping his trunks unceremoniously at the same time, while I hunt out a couple of towels.

"Let me set the water temperature for you," I call after Jacob, putting the towels on the closed toilet seat, and just managing to get to the shower before him, turning on the water and adjusting it. "Okay… in you get."

He clambers in and turns to me, his hand on the glass door. "You don't have to stay," he remarks.

"But…"

"Mum…" He sounds impatient. "I shower by myself at Dad's. It's just you who insists on fussing around me."

I feel the rebuke and nod my head. "Okay. I—I'll leave your clothes out. Just call if you need anything."

He ignores me, standing under the shower, his head tipped back, and I rummage through the bag, finding his dry clothes and putting them with the towels, before going back out into the hallway. I'm wet, cold, and fed up… and without warning, I burst into tears.

"Hey…" Adam is right beside me in an instant, and he pulls me close to him. "What's happened?"

"Jacob… what else?"

"What's he done now?" he asks, leaning back a little and looking down at me.

"Oh, it's nothing really."

"It's clearly something." He pulls away and takes my hand. "Come with me," he says and leads me into his sitting room, which has practical wooden floors, that I'm still dripping over, a beautiful, curved grey leather sofa, positioned in front of the full length windows that look over the bay, and a small dining table and chairs. It's homely, and yet refined. And very grown up.

"You have a lovely flat," I remark, looking around.

"Don't change the subject," he says. "Tell me what Jacob did."

I lean into him, resting my head on his still naked chest as he puts his arms around me. "He didn't want me to stay in there with him," I murmur.

"And…?" He sounds confused.

"And I'm probably making a fuss over nothing. It's just that when we're at home, he usually has a bath, and because I'm paranoid, I usually stay with him – or at least I stay close by. But he just told me to leave, and informed me that when he's at Scott's he showers by himself." I raise my head, looking up at Adam. "It just means he's growing up, I suppose. I shouldn't be so sensitive."

He smiles. "You're not being sensitive… or paranoid. You're being a mum." He moves closer. "And I'm sorry if I've interfered today. If I'm not helping things, then I'll back off."

I shake my head quickly, and reach up, touching his cheek with my fingertips. "No. No… you are helping. Well, you're helping me, anyway."

"I just don't like the way Jacob speaks to you. He… he reminds me of Nathan."

"Your brother?" I query.

"Yes. I think I told you he behaved pretty badly when he was growing up?"

"Yes. You said he made Jacob look like an angel. Are you revising your opinion now you've spent more time with him?"

Adam shakes his head. "No. But I can't help remembering how Nathan used to treat our mum, the way he used to talk down to her, answer back to her, swear at her and hit her… or that he ended up taking drugs."

"Well, Jacob already does most of that," I murmur, almost to myself.

"Has he hit you?" Adam steps closer and I nod my head.

"He only does it when he's angry, or upset."

Adam's face darkens. "That's no excuse. If he does it again, Jenna, you have to tell me."

"I will. But… can we backtrack for a moment? Did you just say your brother was into drugs?" Fear trickles down my back and I shiver.

"Yes. It was nothing heavy… at least not that I knew about."

"Oh, God…"

He sighs. "Hey… just because my brother was an idiot, doesn't mean Jacob will go the same way as he did."

"If Scott has anything to do with it, he will," I reply and Adam's eyes widen.

"Is he a user?" he asks.

"Of drugs? No. Of people. Yes." I shake my head, lowering it again. "The problem is, Scott is Jacob's only real male influence. We don't see enough of my dad for him to really help out, and I wouldn't want to worry my parents. They're getting on a bit now, and they've already done so much for us… but I'm scared that if Jacob doesn't straighten out soon, I won't be able to pull him back." I hear my own voice crack, and Adam tightens his grip on me.

"You will," he whispers. "He's not inherently bad. He's just being led astray."

"By my stupid, selfish ex-husband." I look up again, raising my voice slightly. "I—I swore I'd never say a bad word against Scott when we divorced – at least not to Jacob, anyway – but all Scott does is undermine me. He lets Jacob do whatever he wants, whenever he wants; lets him eat and drink rubbish, stay up late, and watch films that are far too old for him. As a result Jacob thinks Scott is a God and I'm a monster."

"You're not a monster," he says, comfortingly. "I can see chinks of goodness and innocence in Jacob that I never saw in Nathan. Not once. And that means he can be led back."

I shake my head. "I don't think he wants to be. I think he worships Scott far too much."

Adam pulls back from me, clasping my face with his hands, his fingers twisting into my wet hair as he lowers his lips. "You worry too much," he murmurs, and then closes the gap between us again. His lips crush mine, hard and almost bruising, and I cling to him, sighing as he moves closer and lets me feel his arousal. Unlike last night though, he doesn't apologise… and I don't mind that in the slightest. I need his desire more than ever.

We break apart, breathless, staring at each other, and he smiles, his thumbs brushing against my skin.

"Mum?" I jump and Adam pulls back sharply as we turn to see Jacob standing in the doorway, fully clothed, looking dishevelled, his hair a mess. "What are you doing?"

Chapter Eighteen

Adam

Jenna steps away from me, and I let her go, watching as she walks over to Jacob.

"Nothing," she says softly, crouching in front of him. "Mummy was just tired, that's all. Adam was giving me a hug."

A hug? I suppose he might fall for that, being as I had my back to him and was blocking his view for the best part, but I can't help thinking it would have been better if she'd told him the truth, explained that we're seeing each other. In fact, I think she should have introduced me as her boyfriend when they arrived, rather than going along with his description of me as the man who's working on their house, but she obviously didn't want to do that, which I suppose means she's not ready to tell him about us yet…

"Adam's shower's really great," Jacob says, his misgivings clearly forgotten. He looks up at her. "It's your turn," he smiles, coming further into the room, leaving her crouched on the floor, and she gets slowly to her feet, glancing back at me.

"Will you be okay?" she asks, tilting her head and biting her lip, as she nods towards Jacob, who's wandered over towards the windows, looking out at the view, I guess.

"We'll be fine." I smile at her, in what I hope is a reassuring way.

"I'll be ten minutes."

"Take your time." I'm pretty sure I can handle a six year old for a short while.

The bathroom door closes and I turn to Jacob, who seems preoccupied with what's going on outside the window.

"Do you want something to drink?" I ask him, and he turns to face me, his eyes narrowing slightly, making me wonder whether he believes we were just hugging, or whether he's guessed there's something else going on – which there is.

"Yes," he says.

"And what comes next?" I move closer to him, waiting.

"Please," he says, getting the message quickly, even if his voice is laced with sarcasm.

"Do you get very far with that attitude?" I ask him, folding my arms, although he doesn't reply and, after a few minutes, I give up and go into the kitchen, pouring him an orange juice.

I take it back and hand it to him, keeping hold of the glass until he says a reluctant, "Thank you."

After he's taken a sip, he looks up at me. "We're not at the beach now," he says, defiantly.

"So?"

"So you can't tell me what to do." He sounds angry, bitter even, and I shake my head, before bending down so my face is on the same level as his.

"No... we're not on the beach, but you're in my home, young man. So you'll do as you're told." His eyes widen at the tone of my voice, as a blush spreads up his face. "Now, why don't you sit down and finish your drink?" I suggest, and he does.

I go back to the kitchen, emptying out the cool bag and filling the kettle with water, just as Jenna comes back into the room, her hair damp, but combed, looking flushed and beautiful in her navy blue dress.

"Is everything okay?" she asks, glancing from Jacob to me.

"Everything's fine."

She smiles, shy I think, and then hands me my t-shirt. "I should probably give you this back," she says. "Thank you for letting me borrow it."

"The pleasure was mine, believe me." I take it from her and throw it into the washing machine.

"We… we should be going," she adds, looking over at Jacob again. "We've had a lovely day, but Jacob's tired."

"Okay." I can't help feeling disappointed. I'd hoped to persuade her to stay for at least a cup of tea, and maybe even for dinner too. We could have ordered in. Still, she seems determined to go, and I look at her closely, wondering if something's wrong. She seems tense and uneasy, but I'm not sure why. "Are you…" I whisper, but she shakes her head quickly, the motion interrupting my question and I nod as she turns away to tell Jacob they're leaving.

Once they've gone, after a very brief goodbye, and a forced 'thank you' from Jacob, I feel more lonely than I think I've ever done before. The day seemed to go so well. I thought we had fun together, and I know that seeing Jenna relaxed and laughing gave me more pleasure than I've had in a long time… and yet it all seems to have ended so badly.

I sigh deeply and head for the bathroom, taking my time in the shower, trying not to think about how empty my arms feel; that she's only been gone for five minutes, and I want her back here already… that I want her back here for good.

Shutting off the shower, I wrap a towel around my waist and go into my bedroom, finding a pair of shorts and a t-shirt, smiling to myself as I remember how fabulous Jenna looked at the beach. I know she misunderstood my reasons, but I have to admit that, although she looked incredible in her bikini – and she really did – there was something even sexier about her wearing my clothes. It felt intimate, somehow, even if it was just a t-shirt.

I get dressed, going back into the kitchen, where I left my phone on the work surface, and I notice that the screen is alight. Picking it up, I see there's a message, and that it's from Jenna, and my heart flips in my chest, a smile forming on my lips as I read…

— *Call me later? xx*

I focus on the kisses, recalling our messages this morning, where she seemed reluctant to add them, and then finally sent a text that was just two kisses, and nothing else, which was so sweet of her, and which made my heart burst at the time, before I quickly tap out a reply.

— *What time? xx*

I stand, leaning back on the island unit, holding the phone in my hand, for a full ten minutes, before she replies.

— *Any time after nine. xx*

I nod to myself and put the phone down gently, before pouring myself a beer, and cooking some pasta with a simple tomato and chilli sauce, and sitting in front of the television, channel hopping while I eat.

It seems to take forever for the time to tick around to nine o'clock, but when it does, I pick up my phone and connect a call to Jenna, which she answers straight away, with the word, "Sorry."

"Don't be," I reply, hearing the sadness in her voice. "It's okay."

"But I am sorry," she continues, as though I haven't spoken. "I should never have introduced you like that this morning, and I got it completely wrong when Jacob caught us together. I—I hadn't thought it through, but I should have done, shouldn't I? I'm his mother, after all." She pauses and then adds, "I've told him now though," taking me by surprise.

"About us?" I just need to make sure we're talking about the same thing.

"Yes."

"What happened?"

"I just decided that I needed to be honest with him, so I told him the truth."

"Which is?" I ask, feeling intrigued about her perspective of our relationship.

"That we're seeing each other. That… that is the truth, isn't it?" She sounds scared, and I smile to myself.

"Of course it is." I sit back on the sofa, putting my feet up. "How did he take it?"

"Well, I'm not sure he understood to start with, because it was slightly awkward."

"Why?"

"Because he's only six, and I didn't know what to call you that he'd understand."

"What did you settle on?" I ask.

"I didn't. Not really. I just explained that we're together; that we're spending time getting to know each other…" She falls silent.

"Well, that sounds perfectly reasonable." She doesn't reply. "What's wrong Jenna?"

"I'm just… I'm… I mean, I know it was the right thing to do, telling him the truth, but I'm nervous now, because I know he'll tell Scott." I can hear the fear in her voice.

"So what? Does that matter?"

"No, not really… except that he's bound to make trouble."

"Hey… don't worry. There isn't any trouble he can make that I can't handle, just as long as you're okay." She stays silent. "Are you okay?" I ask.

"I think so," she says, calming slightly. "Well, I am if I'm forgiven for messing up earlier."

"There's nothing to forgive, not as far as I'm concerned. You're in a difficult position with Jacob and I understand that."

"Sure?"

"Positive."

I hear her sigh. "I'm so tired."

"Is that from the surfing, or the stress?"

"Both," she replies, but I think I can hear a smile in her voice this time, which is a relief.

"Then can I suggest you go to bed and get some sleep?"

"I suppose so." She sounds disappointed.

"And can ask two more things of you?"

"Okay…"

"Can you stop worrying… and can you dream of me?"

Hanging up a few minutes later, after we've eventually said goodbye, I lie back, my arms behind my head, and stare at the ceiling, thinking to myself that we've taken another step forward, because at least now, Jacob knows about us. Okay, so it seems Jenna is worried about Scott's reaction – for some reason that I really don't understand myself, being as it's got nothing to do with him. And obviously, I don't actually know how Jacob and I are going to get along, once I start spending more time with his mum... so I guess maybe I shouldn't congratulate myself too soon on taking that step.

After all, I might just trip over.

"Hello, stranger." Amy kisses my cheek, grinning up at me. "It's been ages since I've seen you."

I'm a bit late getting to Dad and Michelle's because I overslept. I've been awake half the night, thinking about Jenna, wondering why she's so scared of Scott's reactions all the time, and worrying about Jacob, and my relationship with him, and how to make it work better for all of us. I never thought I'd have a problem like that, but there you go... I guess you just don't know what life is going to throw at you. Unfortunately, although I've lain awake half the night, I haven't reached any conclusions, although I have decided to maybe try and find the time to talk to Michelle. She's been where I am, at least where Jacob is concerned... and I'd value her opinion.

"Well, you're the one who moved to Okehampton," I reason, kissing Amy on the other cheek.

"It's only an hour away." She lets me go so I can shake hands with Mike, who's smiling at her benevolently. He's the opposite to Amy in colouring, having very pale blond hair, and light blue eyes, but it's easy to see from the expression on his face, that he's smitten. Totally.

"Give your brother a break," he says.

"Yeah... give me a break. I'm a busy man." I nudge into her.

"So Dad tells me."

I glance over at my dad, who's standing by the barbecue, with Michelle, on the other side of the patio. The table between us is laid already, with a few salads and some bread in the centre.

"Why? What's he been saying."

She smiles, her eyes sparkling, and links her arm through mine. "Oh... nothing much... just that you've got yourself a girlfriend at last."

"I've had plenty of girlfriends."

"They weren't proper girlfriends. They were women you went out with." She's not wrong. The difference between Jenna and everyone who came before her is like night and day.

Amy drags me over to the barbecue, with Mike following.

"I hear you've been talking out of turn, Dad," I say, as we approach and he turns to me.

"Just telling it how it is, son. Just telling it how it is."

Michelle looks up at me, smiling. "Now you're here, we may as well eat."

"Yeah, sorry I'm so late."

She shakes her head. "That's okay. We know how… preoccupied you are."

They all laugh and eventually, I have to join in.

My seat is beside Michelle's and, after we've been eating for a while, I turn to her. "Can I ask you something?"

"Of course." She puts down her wine glass and gives me her full attention.

"What's it like, taking on someone else's child?"

She blinks a couple of times, clearly surprised by my question and, right at that moment, the whole table falls into silence, everyone turning towards us. I'd hoped to have this conversation in private… but it looks like that won't be happening now.

"Why do you ask?" she says.

I take a deep breath. "Well, it seems it's no secret that I'm seeing someone, so I might as well tell you, in case Dad hasn't… the lady in question is called Jenna, she's divorced, and she's got a son."

"And you're serious enough about her to be asking a question like that?" Michelle queries.

"Yes." I don't see the point in trying to hide it. Why would I? It's the truth.

She smiles, and reaches out, resting her hand on my arm. "I can only speak from my own experience, but I never had a problem with it. I knew about you right from the beginning, and I just accepted that you were part of the deal."

"That's not really what I meant," I say, trying to explain myself a bit better. "I've known about Jacob since before Jenna and I started seeing each other. But what I'm asking is, how do I manage my relationship with Jacob? What's the best way of dealing with him?"

"I suppose that's something you and Jenna have to decide between you," she replies, smiling slightly. "In our case, I agreed with your dad from day one that I wasn't going to try and be your mother. But at the same time, if you'd been the kind of child who'd misbehaved, I would have told you off." She leans into me. "Is that what you're asking?"

"I suppose so... kind of."

"What's wrong, son?" my dad pipes up from the other end of the table.

I turn, letting out a long sigh. "Nothing... and everything."

"That's not very helpful. Is there some kind of problem with Jenna's son?" he asks.

"Do you remember me telling you that Jacob reminded me of Nathan?"

"Yes."

Everyone turns, staring at me. They all know what happened with Jade and how I felt about that, and that I rarely mention my brother's name these days. So, they're watching me, waiting to see what I'm going to say next.

"Well, he is. In lots of ways. But then, at other times, he seems like a nice kid."

"And?" My dad stares at me, clearly knowing there's more. "What's the problem?"

"It's Jenna's ex. He gets access every other weekend, and he just seems to let Jacob run riot. As a result, when he's with Jenna, he doesn't listen to a word she says, and she told me yesterday afternoon, that he's started hitting her."

"Jacob?" Dad clarifies.

"Yes. If it was the ex who was hitting her, I'd take care of it. It's not so easy when it's her son."

"No," he muses. "But you can't do nothing."

"I know."

"Can I say something?" Michelle leans forward, getting my attention.

"Yes."

We all turn to her.

"Go with your gut. If you see him doing something that's wrong, then talk to him. If he needs chastising, then do it… and talk to Jenna, so she knows you're on her side."

"I have. I don't want to risk losing her, so I've been doing all of that. I'm just not sure whether I'm doing it very well." Did I really just say that out loud? Michelle's smiling at me, so I guess I must have done.

"Don't look so worried," she says, leaning into me a little. "You'll be just fine. You'll do a lot better than I did, anyway."

"Excuse me? When did you ever get anything wrong?"

"Oh, I got a lot wrong over the years, believe me… but I think the worst thing I did was focusing too much on Amy when she was a baby. I—I was just so devastated I wouldn't be able to have any more children, and so thrilled to have her, that I became completely besotted with her… and I think I ignored you."

"We both did that," my dad says, from the other end of the table, sounding sad, the emotion reflected in his eyes.

"You didn't." I can still remember it feeling like that at the time, but I hate the idea that they feel guilty over it.

Michelle gives me a hard stare. "Yes, we did."

"You had good reason."

"Maybe. But that doesn't make it right." She gives my arm a firm squeeze. "You're a good man, Adam. Lead by example. *Show* Jacob how to behave properly and you won't go far wrong."

I feel hugely embarrassed now and am starting to wonder if I should ever have started this conversation. To cover my humiliation, I pick up my wine glass and take a sip, and I catch Amy's eye over the rim, smiling as she gives me a wink.

"Would you like me to ease your discomfort?" she says.

"Be my guest." I've got no idea what she's talking about, but I'll welcome anything that shifts me out of the limelight.

"In that case…" She grins now, looking from Dad to Michelle. "Mike and I have an announcement…"

I arrive at Jenna's on Monday morning, parking my car down the side street and going in through the rear gate, the garden bathed in glorious sunshine. The back door must be open, because I can hear someone moving around in the kitchen and I make my way down the path and through the growing extension, looking in through the door, to where Jenna is standing with her back to me, preparing Jacob's packed lunch.

"Hello," I say quietly.

She flips around. "Hi," she replies. "I didn't hear you coming."

I move inside and pull her into my arms, holding her tight. "I missed you yesterday," I whisper, leaning down and kissing her gently.

"What did you get up to?" She rests her hands on my chest.

"I went round to my dad's for a barbecue. We talked about you for a while."

She's surprised. "You did? I wasn't aware your family even knew I existed."

"Well, Dad does, obviously."

"Yes, but only as a client. He doesn't know about us, does he?"

I smile at her. "He guessed something was going on, when I moved all the schedules around and shifted half our work force, so I could fit your job in… and he's covering for me at the office while I'm here."

She stares at me. "I had no idea…"

I brush my fingertips down her cheek. "I wanted to see you again, Jenna. I wasn't about to pass up the opportunity." I lean down and kiss her, just quickly. "Anyway, Dad had mentioned you to my step-mother, and to Amy…"

"Who's Amy?"

"My half-sister? Remember?"

"Oh, yes."

"So, he'd mentioned you to them, and I felt it was only fair to fill in the gaps." Although I'm not going to tell her what happened during our conversation about Jacob, I can tell her the outcome of the afternoon.

"They want to meet you."

"They do?"

"Yes. You and Jacob."

"Do they know what they're letting themselves in for?"

"I've told them you can be difficult, but they're willing to take the risk," I joke and she slaps my arm playfully, giggling. "The afternoon turned into a bit of a celebration in the end, actually."

"Oh yes?"

"Yes. Amy brought her boyfriend with her, and they announced that they've got engaged."

Amy's announcement took me by surprise, if I'm being honest. As the product of a broken marriage, I suppose I've always had a rather jaded view of the institution, and on the few occasions when I've discussed it with Amy, I've always had the impression that she felt the same, but I guess she must have changed her mind, because she was clearly elated. And because of that, I'm pleased for her.

Jenna's staring up at me. "What are you thinking?" she asks.

"Nothing." I recall Jenna telling me on our very first date that her own perspective of marriage was similar to mine, which isn't surprising. And now isn't really the time to open up that discussion. "How was your Sunday?" I ask instead, and her smile fades. "What's wrong?"

"Nothing." She echoes my earlier response, but then continues, "We went to Mum and Dad's and I did the laundry while Jacob played in the garden. He spent the whole of lunchtime telling them about surfing with you." She glances up at me.

"And?"

"And after he'd mentioned your name for about the tenth time, they wanted to know who you are and what's going on between us…"

"So?"

"So, I told them about us as well." She bites her bottom lip, and I pull it free with my thumb. "I hope that's okay," she adds.

"Of course it is," I reply. "How did they react?"

"They were pleased," she says, although she still looks a bit withdrawn.

"What's wrong, Jenna?" I ask.

"Scott called to speak to Jacob," she sighs.

"While you were at your parents'?"

"No. After we got back. He does that sometimes on Sunday evenings… you know, on the weekends when Jacob's here. Only this time, Jacob took the phone up to his bedroom." She looks me in the eyes. "It was fairly obvious he wanted to speak to Scott in private, so he could tell him about you… well, about us."

"So what if he did? You've got nothing to worry about, Jenna. You're divorced. You're entitled to live your life however you want, and we're not doing anything wrong." Why can't she see this?

She smiles, although she doesn't look entirely convinced, so I bend and kiss her deeply, only pulling away when I hear Jacob coming down the stairs.

"I'll see you later," I whisper, moving towards the back door.

She nods and then returns to her chores, and I stand, just for a second, wishing it didn't still feel like there's a huge Scott-shaped barrier between us.

Once Dom and Mitch have started work, I set off in my car again, and spend the morning sourcing the wood that I'm going to need to make a start on Jenna's kitchen. I visit a few suppliers, eventually finding what I'm looking for, and placing the order. It will be available in two weeks, and that ties in perfectly with the construction work. I've already decided to build the units on site; not because I have to, but because it gives me an excuse to spend more time with Jenna.

It's late afternoon, by the time she comes home, with Jacob in toe, seemingly hot and sulky. Mitch and Dom have already gone for the day and I'm just clearing up, killing time so that I can see Jenna before I have to leave.

She comes outside and I notice that she's changed from her work clothes into a pair of denim shorts and a sleeveless blouse, and I can't help my eyes from wandering, or the smile that spreads across my face as I see that she's doing the same. I'm not wearing a t-shirt, and her eyes are fixed on my chest as she walks towards me, which reminds me of her reaction at the beach on Saturday, and how often I caught her staring, when she thought I wasn't looking.

"Hi," I say as she gets nearer.

"Hello." She smiles up at me.

"Good day?"

"Not bad."

"Well, I've had an excellent day."

She turns and studies the walls of her extension, which are almost at full height now. "It looks like it," she replies.

"Oh, that's nothing," I say nonchalantly. "I'm talking about your kitchen."

She looks back at me. "Oh?"

"Yes. I've sourced and ordered the wood, and I've decided that I'll build everything here…"

"Okay." She seems quite pleased about that idea. "So, when will the kitchen go out of action?"

"Probably in about three or four weeks' time," I suggest. "It's hard to be precise yet."

"I see. Well, I won't warn my parents about it at the moment, not until we've got a definite date. They're already doing so much for me and I don't want to mess them about."

I move closer to her, so we're almost touching. "Okay," I murmur, "but…" I let my voice fade, uncertain how to phrase my question now I've started it.

"But what?" she asks.

"Well, I know you'll have to eat somewhere else while you don't have a kitchen here, but do you have to eat with your mum and dad all the time?" She looks confused. "Couldn't you and Jacob come and eat with me sometimes… at my place?"

Her eyes widen. "Really?"

I smile. "Yes, really. Jacob knows we're together now, so why not? I get that you'll still want to see your parents some evenings, and that they'll want to see Jacob too, but to give them a break – and so we can see each other – I'd love to have you both come to me."

She leans into me. "Thank you," she whispers. "I think I'd like that."

"Mum?" Jacob's voice rings out from inside the house and Jenna instinctively pulls back, even though I keep hold of her.

"Yes?" She turns as he appears in the gap where the door to the extension will be, and then she takes a step away from me and I let her, despite my frustration.

"I want a drink."

She goes to move towards him, but I grab her hand, my anger rising in an instant as I look down at Jacob. "What do you say?" I ask him.

He glares at me. "We're not at the beach," he sneers, "and we're not at your place. So you can't talk to me like that. You're not my dad."

Jenna turns and looks up at me, and I see the sorrow in her eyes, which makes me wonder for a second, if she wishes I was Jacob's dad, and how different things might have been if I were.

I soften my features and smile at her, before returning my gaze to Jacob and walking over to him, crouching down. "No, I'm not," I reply firmly. "But if I were, you'd never speak to me like that again. And you'd treat your mother with more respect too."

I stand and turn away, not giving him the chance to reply, and walk back to Jenna.

"Will you be okay?" I ask.

"Yes," she says softly, and I lean down and kiss her cheek, before moving down the garden, grabbing my t-shirt and letting myself out of the back gate.

It gets to nine o'clock before my guilt over what happened with Jacob gets the better of me, and knowing that he'll be in bed, I call Jenna, just to make sure she's okay.

"I'm fine" she says, answering my question, but before I can talk to her about Jacob, she adds, "Scott called again though."

"He did? Is that usual?"

"No. I think he's checking up on me via Jacob."

"Checking up on you?" I repeat. "You're not his to check up on, are you?" I feel the need to ask, just for reassurance, I suppose.

"No, I'm not," she says vehemently.

"And do you mind me calling to check up on you?"

"No."

Does that mean she's mine? I wish I could ask that question outright, but I'd rather do it when we're face-to-face, not over the phone, because I'd like to tell her I'm in love with her first, and then ask if she's willing to consider herself 'mine'.

We talk for a while, and when I ask, Jenna reassures me that she's absolutely fine with me telling Jacob off, when it's required. She apologises for his attitude, which isn't necessary. It's not her fault that her ex is leading him astray. And then she says she's grateful to have someone backing her up, and that feels good. I don't need her gratitude, but I like the idea of supporting her, and helping her. However, when I suggest making plans for the weekend, she seems really reluctant – pointing out that Scott might throw a spanner in the works again, and that she doesn't want to make any arrangements, just for him to ruin them. I suppose I can see her point, to an extent, but I have to admit to feeling a bit disappointed by the fact that Scott now seems to be dictating our time together, even when we're supposed to be alone.

And, more importantly, that she's letting him.

This morning, I find Jenna in the kitchen again and I let myself in, turning her around, cupping her face with one hand and crushing my lips against hers, pulling her close to me and letting her feel my body's instant reaction to her, my arousal pressing into her hip. I know I apologised the first time this happened, but I'm damned if I'm going to apologise anymore. I want her. And while I'm happy to wait, I'm not ashamed of how she makes me feel. She moans into me and I deepen the kiss, changing the angle of my head and caressing her cheek with my thumb, just as the sound of Jacob's footsteps on the stairs comes between us, forcing Jenna to pull back sharply, stepping away from me.

"He knows we're together," I whisper, moving closer to her again, but she shakes her head, frowning and pushes me back quite harshly, just as Jacob comes into the room.

"When are we going surfing again?" he asks and I turn to see he's looking directly at me.

I stare at him for a moment or two, then turn to Jenna. "I'll see you later," I tell her, kissing her gently on the cheek, before going outside, completely ignoring her son.

I'd like to say I feel guilty for doing that, but I don't. His attitude is getting to me and, if I'm being honest, Jenna's is starting to as well, albeit in a completely different way. I thought that telling Jacob about us would make a difference. I thought we'd be able to be more open and more 'together', but it seems not. If anything, it feels as though our relationship is even more distant than it was before. It's like she's ashamed or something; more concerned about her ex-husband's reactions than how I might feel. And at the moment, I'm feeling confused. No matter how 'together' we are when we're alone, no matter how great her kisses feel, or how she reacts to me when I touch her, it's not enough for me. I need more than that. I always did. And I'm not talking about sex; I'm talking about so much more than that. It's always been about 'more', especially where Jenna's concerned.

I have a very dissatisfying day, mainly because I can't stop thinking about Jenna, and how different she is when we're alone, compared to how she is around Jacob, and more than anything, how much influence she's allowing Scott to have over her life and our relationship. On top of that, it's also really hot, so I let Mitch and Dom go early, which gives me an excuse to spend some time alone, not that I know why I thought that would help… it just means I can think even more.

At just after five, I hear the front door of the house slam, and I know Jenna will be home, so I carry on clearing up, pretending to be busy until she comes out, like she has done for the last few evenings, hoping we'll be able to spend a few minutes together, that maybe she'll ask me to call later on, because regardless of my day of doubts and fears, I still need her more than anything.

"Hey…" Jacob's voice interrupts my thoughts and I turn to see him standing just inside the extension.

"Are you talking to me?" I ask.

"Well, you're the only person here, so yes." He steps out into the garden, taking a couple of paces towards me. "You didn't answer me this morning."

"No."

"So? When are we going surfing again?"

"We're not."

I turn away, but he grabs my wrist. "Why not? I'm going to Dad's for the weekend, but we could go after school…"

I stare down to where his small hand is clutched around my arm. "Let go," I growl, and he releases me. "We can't go, because the surf's dropped; we were lucky to catch the waves we did at the weekend." I stare down at him. "You'll probably have to wait until the autumn now before you can surf again."

He pouts, folding his arms. "You're making that up."

"No, I'm not. But regardless of that, I don't want to take you surfing. I don't like the way you talk to your mother. In fact, I don't like the way you treat people in general, so if you want to come surfing with me ever again, then I suggest you spend the summer learning some manners, and some respect for other people. And then, when the surf picks up again, I might consider it."

He blinks a few times and I wonder if he's about to cry, but he doesn't. Instead he turns and walks back to the house, his head bowed.

I wonder if I should have spoken to him like that, but then I think of Jenna and the sorrow in her eyes, and my doubt fades. Whatever is going on between us, she needs my help with Jacob, and I've got no intention of letting her down. Not now… not ever.

I assume she must have gone upstairs to change and I wait outside, fairly sure that Jacob won't welcome my presence in the house, not after what I've just said to him. I'm just putting my t-shirt back on, when I hear the sound of breaking glass, coming from the house and, without a second thought, I run, leaping up the unmade back step, though the extension and into the kitchen, where Jacob is standing, looking guilty as sin, with a broken glass by his feet.

"It wasn't me," he says straight away.

"Don't lie," I reply, moving closer. "Your behaviour is already bad enough, don't add lying to it as well." He bites his bottom lip. "Are you suggesting the glass jumped off the shelf?" I ask. "Because there's no-one else here, is there?"

He shakes his head. "I dropped it," he mutters.

"Well, accidents happen." I soften my voice in an instant, because he's finally being honest, and he does seem genuinely sorry. "Now, you need to move out of the way, and let me clear up the broken glass. Are you hurt?" I ask, just to make sure.

"No. But you're not going to tell Mum, are you?"

"I'm not. But you are."

I crouch and start picking up the shattered pieces of glass, placing them on the draining board, just as I hear Jenna's footsteps on the stairs, and I glance up and see Jacob looking worried. "Tell your mum," I urge him. "She won't be cross." And he steps into the dining room to forestall her.

"What's happened?" Jenna asks, looking beyond Jacob and seeing me in her kitchen, clearing up the broken glass from her floor.

"I dropped a glass," Jacob whispers, although I can just about hear him. "It broke."

I stop what I'm doing and watch them as Jenna kneels down in front of him, taking his hands and examining them. "You're not hurt, are you?" she asks. "You didn't try and pick up the glass?"

"No." He shakes his head and looks over his shoulder at me. "Adam's doing it."

Jenna looks up, smiling, and then pulls Jacob into her, hugging him.

"Are you angry?" I hear Jacob ask.

Jenna laughs. "Of course not. As long as you're alright, that's all that matters." She pulls back. "Now, why don't you sit up at the table, and I'll get you a drink."

He steps away and looks back at me. "Thanks, Mum," he says and Jenna's mouth drops open as I smile quietly to myself.

Jenna's late back today. It's nearly half past five before I hear the front door close, and she comes straight out into the garden looking hot and flustered.

"What's wrong?" I go straight over to her, my t-shirt flung over my right shoulder.

"I've had the worst day," she replies and leans into my bare chest, as I pull her into a hug, feeling relieved that she came to me; that when she wanted solace, she sought it with me… "I made a real mess of a set of plans," she continues, looking up again. "My boss hauled me in and roasted me over the coals about it."

"Oh dear."

I hug her tighter, hoping that helps a little. "The thing is," she adds, "I know I only made the mistake because Scott called."

"He did?" I feel my muscles tense, but make a conscious effort to relax, in the hope that she won't notice.

"Yes."

"He called you at work?"

"Yes. He's been texting me for the last couple of days, but today he phoned instead. He said it was to remind me that he's taking Jacob on Friday, and to make sure he's ready on time, but that's stupid. I don't forget things like that."

"So it was just an excuse to talk to you?"

"Yes, I think so."

I wonder about asking why she hasn't told me about his text messages, and more importantly, why she doesn't just tell him to get lost, but she's got tears in her eyes, and I guess now may not be the best time.

"It was after his call that I messed up, and then Trevor called me into his office, and I ended up crying… which was embarrassing, for both of us, really."

I hold onto her, stroking her hair, for a couple of minutes, and then pull back, looking down at her. "Why don't you go and have a soak in the bath?" I suggest.

She sighs. "Because I can't. I've got to make the dinner, and Jacob's got spellings to practice for a test tomorrow…" Her voice fades.

"Okay... well, why don't I make your dinner, and while I'm doing that, I can help Jacob with his spellings. I may only be a surfing builder, who's never set foot inside a university in his life, but I did learn how to spell − at least well enough for a six year old."

She laughs, trying not to cry again, I think. "You'd do that?"

"Of course I would."

"And you don't mind?"

"No. Now... stop talking and go and run a bath."

She leans up, kissing my cheek, running her fingertips down my jawline, her eyes locked with mine, and then she turns and goes back inside the house.

I follow, a few seconds later, pulling on my t-shirt before I get to the kitchen, and kicking off my boots, before washing my hands and checking out the contents of Jenna's fridge, where I find some salmon fillets and vegetables. I can make something out of that... and I set to work.

I've finished slicing the onion and peppers when Jacob comes out, with a small blue exercise book in his hand. "Mum says I have to practice my spellings with you," he says quietly, gazing up at me.

"That's right." I put down my knife, taking the book from him. "What are we looking at?"

He reaches up, flicking through a few pages until we get to the last one with any writing on it, which contains a list of ten words.

"Do you write them down, or speak them?" I ask him as he leans on the door of the fridge-freezer.

"Write them. There's spare paper in the drawer in the dining room." He nods over his shoulder.

"Okay... you get yourself set up." He hesitates for a second, narrowing his eyes at me, but then turns and disappears into the dining room. I carry on with preparing vegetables, and when I look up, he's sitting at the table, poised, so I glance down at the book. "How do you spell 'night'?"

"Which one?" he asks, and I check, noticing that further down the list is the word 'knight'.

"The one that comes after day," I say, hoping that'll make sense.

He calls out when he's finished writing and I give him the next word, followed by a brief explanation, having learned my lesson, and we proceed through the list, until we get to the end and I wipe my hands on a tea towel and go through to him, checking over what he's written down. His handwriting is a bit messy – but no worse than any other six year old boy, I would imagine – and I read through his answers, congratulating him on getting them all correct. He beams up at me, clearly pleased with himself.

"Come and get your exercise book," I tell him, "and then why don't you set the table for you and your mum?"

He looks up at me, as though confused. "Set the table?"

"Yes. Put out the knives and forks."

He nods and climbs down from the chair, following me back into the kitchen, where I hand him his book, together with two knives and two forks. Before he moves away, however, he stops and looks up at me again, a quizzical expression on his face. "Why are you doing this?" he asks.

"Doing what?" I look down at him and turn, leaning back on the work surface.

"Helping Mum… Is she doing something for you?"

I crouch down now. "No, she's not." That's not strictly true, because she's doing a lot for me, just by being in my life, but I'm not going to start explaining that to him. "What makes you ask that?"

He shrugs and I work out for myself that *quid pro quo* must be how things work in Scott's world.

"I offered to help your mum," I explain, "because she's upset, not because I expected something in return from her. You should never give anything to someone – whether that's time, friendship, money, a present, or your love – in the expectation of receiving something back."

He stares at me now, seemingly bewildered, then says, "Did you upset her then?"

I smile. "No. I hope I never upset your mum… not knowingly, anyway. She had a bad day at work, that's all." I decide against mentioning that his father contributed to his mother's tribulations, because I recall Jenna saying that she vowed never to say anything bad about Scott to Jacob, even if there's very little that's good about the man, from what I've gathered.

"I don't understand," Jacob says, with a rather cute, puzzled expression on his face now. "If you didn't cause the problem, then why do you have to put it right?"

His dad really does have a lot to answer for, but rather than pointing that out, I put my hand on his shoulder and edge a little closer to him. "Because, when your mum came home, she'd been crying, and when a girl is crying, or she's sad, especially if she's a girl you care about, then you should do whatever you can to make her feel better – even if it's not your fault."

He sighs heavily and looks at me, as though deep in thought, and then nods his head, before turning away and going back into the dining room to lay the table, while I return to making dinner for the woman I want to make feel better – more than anything.

Chapter Nineteen

Jenna

The last few days have been absolutely horrendous and, if it wasn't for Adam, I'm not sure how I would have got through them.

I took the decision to tell Jacob about my relationship with Adam, or at least to try to, although I got sort of muddled about what to call him, which I don't think helped. I'm not sure whether Jacob was confused, or whether he just wanted to talk about it to someone, but he told Scott the very next day, during their call, and since then my charming ex-husband has been making my life a living hell. To start with, he just called in the evenings, at home. Then he started sending text messages as well, and then he phoned me at work, which he's never done before. And that threw me so much, that I ended up making a mistake on the plans I was finishing off for Holly. Fortunately Trevor saw it before the clients came in for their meeting, and was able to cover it, but he called me into his office afterwards and I ended up bursting into tears. That had to be one of the most humiliating things I've ever gone through – certainly in my professional career, anyway – and although he was kind about it in the end, I still feel awful, even two days later.

My only solace is that at least it's Friday and Scott will be arriving at seven o'clock to pick up Jacob. He's made a point in his phone calls – of which there have been several now – and in his numerous text messages, of telling me that he'll be on time, so at least I know he won't be letting Jacob down this week. And then I'll have the whole weekend with Adam. We'll be able to have more than ten minutes together at a time; in fact, we'll have two whole days, which means we can talk, and I can apologise properly for everything that's happened since last Saturday. I can say sorry to him for not properly acknowledging our relationship to Jacob in the first place, and for being so pathetic and tearful all the time, which is caused entirely by Scott's interference. I know I shouldn't let Scott have that much influence in my life, but no matter how hard I try, he always seems to get the better of me, and I give in to him for a quiet life, and so as not to upset Jacob.

I need to thank Adam too, because I didn't get a chance at the time, for cooking us dinner the other night, and then not even staying to eat with us. He was so kind in making the offer and letting me go and have a relaxing half hour in the bath, but I have to admit, I'd expected him to stay. I was really surprised when I came downstairs, feeling a lot better than I had when I went up, to find he'd cooked for us, but was ready to leave. I felt so guilty, but he reassured me everything was fine and, since then, has made a point of checking up on me all the time, to make sure I'm okay; being kind and considerate, and generally the exact opposite of Scott.

I'm a little early getting to Jacob's school, but that's because Trevor told me I could finish at four today, instead of four-thirty. I'm not sure if he's still feeling sorry for me about what happened earlier in the week, but I'm also not sure if I really care. The point is, it's the weekend, and once Jacob's gone with Scott, I can spend all my time with Adam. I smile to myself as I lock the car, remembering that, although I haven't been shopping yet, I do have a bottle of Chardonnay in the fridge, and it occurs to me that Adam might be able to come back later this evening, after Jacob's gone, and maybe help me to drink it, and perhaps share a take-away as well. I know it's not exactly the most thrilling of evenings, but after the week I've had, it sounds absolutely perfect... no ex-husbands causing trouble, no sons being naughty, no interference at all. Just the two of us. Together. All I'll have to do is try and stay awake long enough to enjoy it.

I go in through the school gate, where the children are playing in the playground, and look around for Jacob, surprised that he's nowhere to be seen. On a hot day like today, he's normally outside enjoying the good weather. For a moment, I'm overwhelmed with panic. Surely Scott wouldn't have come down and taken him out of school without telling me, would he? Surely the school wouldn't have just handed him over. They don't know Scott, so…

"Mrs Swann?" I call out to the teacher on duty, hearing the anxiety in my own voice.

"Yes, Ms Downing?" She turns to look at me.

"Where's Jacob?"

She smiles, which only makes me more nervous. No-one ever smiles when they're talking about Jacob… not these days.

"He's in the school office," she replies. "Go on in." She nods towards the main entrance and I turn, wondering what he's done wrong now and why he's been sent to the school office. Preparing myself for the next disaster, my insides start to churn as I contemplate how I'm going to cope with something else going wrong this week. I make my way down the short corridor and in through the first door on the right, where I find the school secretary, Mrs Hutchins, attending to another child – a little girl, who I know is called Charlotte. She's cut her knee, by the looks of things, and Jacob is standing beside her, patting her shoulder, in a solicitous six year old way, and telling her it'll be alright. I'm absolutely stunned by Jacob's act of kindness and, for a minute, I just stand, leaning on the doorframe, staring, until I come to my senses and walk further into the room, asking if I can help. Mrs Hutchins looks up at me, smiling.

"No, it's fine," she says. "Charlotte fell over and cut her knee, but it's nothing major – she's more shocked than anything else. And Jacob has been very helpful."

Even Mrs Hutchins sounds surprised, but then why wouldn't she? Jacob isn't renowned for being helpful, and I wait while they finish tending to Charlotte's cut knee, before asking Jacob if he's ready to go.

"Yes," he replies, then turns back to Charlotte. "Are you sure you'll be alright?" he asks, sounding very solicitous.

"Yes, thank you," she says. "I'll see you on Monday."

He nods and I cover my mouth with my hand to hide my smile, because their little interchange is so sweet, before taking his offered hand in mine and leading him back out to the playground, collecting his rucksack along the way.

Once we're in the car and on our way home, I look at him in the rear view mirror, as he's watching something out of the window.

"So what happened at school then?" I ask.

"Nothing," he replies. "I didn't do anything wrong. Charlotte tripped up the steps and fell over and I took her indoors and stayed with her – that's all."

We stop at the traffic lights and I turn around. "I'm not cross," I tell him. "I'm proud of you. Well done." He smiles. "That's a really nice thing to have done."

"Adam told me to do it," he says, surprising me even more. "Well, kind of." The lights change and I move forward. "Dad is coming tonight, isn't he?" he adds.

"Yes."

"Great! He said he's going to buy me a new game for my Playstation this weekend. We're going into town for it, and he said he's going to take me out for lunch"

"Did he now?" I find it hard to keep the cynicism out of my voice. It's typical of Scott to buy Jacob's affections, and it rather spoils the moment for me.

Jacob runs into the house and straight up the stairs, just like he normally does on a Friday night, eager to get ready for his dad's arrival, and I let him, walking through to the dining room myself, putting my handbag down on the table, and going outside into the back garden, where Adam's sweeping up the brick dust from the path.

"Hi," I call, standing and watching him.

He looks up, smiling and lets his broom fall to the ground, stepping over to me and pulling me into his arms, kissing me briefly.

"I have a question for you?" I say, my hands resting on his bare chest.

"Oh yes?" He looks intrigued.

"Yes… Did you tell my son to look after little girls when they fall over?"

His brow furrows and he slowly shakes his head. "No," he replies.

"Well, he says you did." I tell him about what happened at school, that Jacob helped Charlotte when she fell over, and stayed with her while the secretary dressed her scraped knee, and a smile spreads across his lips.

"Oh… that probably stems from the other night," he says cryptically, and I stare up at him, waiting for an explanation. "Remember when you came home and you were upset, and I made you dinner?" I nod my head. As if I'm going to forget that day in a hurry… "Well," he continues, "Jacob and I got talking and I was telling him that, when someone you care about is upset, then you should do what you can to help them out – to make it better – even if it's not your fault."

I feel tears welling in my eyes and he moves closer, his feet either side of mine.

"What's wrong?" he asks.

"It's nothing… well, I suppose it's just that it's the first time in years that Jacob's shown any consideration for anyone else." I lean in close to him and whisper, "Thank you," into his chest, before looking up into his face. "Why are you doing this?" I ask.

"Doing what?"

"Helping me out so much?"

He smiles. "Well, the rule I quoted at Jacob stands for me too, not just for him. You've been upset about his behaviour, and that means I have to do whatever I can to make it better."

"Even though it's not your fault?"

"Yes. And besides, it's never too early for a young man to learn that, when he grows up, people are going to judge him based on how he treats them. If he wants to get anywhere in life, he needs to learn to show some respect – and that starts with you, more than anyone else."

As he finishes speaking, he leans down and kisses me again and, although I wish he'd deepen the kiss, he doesn't. He pulls back instead, looking down at me.

"Have you got any plans for this evening?" I ask him.

"No… well, other than going home and having a shower."

I nod my head. "How would you feel about going home and having a shower… and then maybe coming back here?"

"I'd love to."

"Scott will have picked Jacob up by then," I explain, "and I've got a bottle of wine in the fridge. I was thinking we could maybe get a take-away…?" I let my voice fade, wondering if I should be dictating the course of our evening like this, although the smile on his face tells me he doesn't mind.

"That sounds perfect," he says, just as Jacob runs out of the back door, coming right up to us. I instinctively pull away from Adam, stepping back to look down at Jacob.

"How was school today?" Adam asks, after a brief silence.

"Fine." Jacob's smiling up at him and Adam ruffles his hair.

"Well, have a good weekend with your dad, and I'll see you on Monday."

"Okay."

Adam looks back at me again and mouths the word 'later', and then goes down to the end of the garden, grabbing his t-shirt on the way and pulling it over his head, before letting himself out of the back gate.

"Where is he, Mum?" Jacob sounds distressed and I can tell he's only just holding back his tears.

"He's only thirty minutes late. He's probably just held up in traffic," I lie, because I'm fairly sure Scott is playing some kind of game with me. He's made such a big deal all week about the timings for tonight, so it doesn't make sense that he'd be late, unless he's deliberately trying to catch me out… or trying to catch me with Adam, anyway. "Why don't you go and play a game on your Playstation for a while?" I suggest, hoping to take his mind off things.

He nods and turns away, although the expression on his face tells me he won't be preoccupied by anything for long, and I feel my blood boiling, knowing that Scott is trying to mess with my life, and is using Jacob to do it.

About ten minutes later, the doorbell rings and, try as I might, I can't get there before Jacob, who flies out of the living room and into the hallway, yanking open the door.

"Dad!" he yells, just as I arrive behind him to see Adam standing on the doorstep, looking confused as Jacob adds, "Oh, it's you," sounding disappointed.

"Yes," Adam says quietly. "It's me."

Jacob turns away and goes back into the living room, and Adam looks at me. "Scott's late," I whisper, in the hope that Jacob won't hear.

"Shall I go?" Adam murmurs.

"No." I shake my head and hold out my hand, which he takes, letting me pull him into the house.

He puts his arms around me, which feels really comforting, even though he keeps the hug brief. "Do you want me to try and keep Jacob occupied?" he asks.

"He's on his Playstation at the moment." I nod towards the living room.

"Well, I'll go and see if he wants to play something with me. It might help to take his mind off things."

I follow him into the living room, standing in the doorway, watching as Adam sits down beside Jacob on the sofa.

"Have you got another handset?" he asks and Jacob nods, pausing his game and getting up to fetch the spare handset from the cupboard under the television, before bringing it back and giving it to Adam.

"I'll have to switch to two-player mode," Jacob says, his voice a little brighter than it was earlier. "Just a second…" He fiddles with the handset, and the screen changes, splitting in two, and before I know it, the two of them are battling it out on the screen, laughing and nudging shoulders, as they try to outscore each other.

I can't help smiling at the change in Jacob, and I stand, leaning against the doorframe and watch them, until the ringing of the doorbell brings me back to a harsh reality.

"Dad!" Jacob yells, the game forgotten, as he drops his handset and leaps to his feet. My position at the door gives me an advantage though, and I'm able to beat him into the hallway and make it to the front door a second or two ahead of him, opening it to find Scott standing there, looking smug.

"You're late," I manage to say, just as Jacob barges past me and launches himself at Scott, who picks him up and hugs him briefly, lowering him to the ground and placing his hand on our son's head, rather proprietorially.

His eyes narrow, although he's smiling. "Don't tell me you've got plans," he says.

"Whether I have plans or not is none of your business," I reply, hoping Jacob doesn't tell him that Adam's sitting in the living room right this minute. The last thing I need is a scene…

"Then whose car is that?" Scott asks, pointing to Adam's Toyota, which is parked behind mine. "Is your boyfriend here already?" I feel myself blush, but before I can say anything, he steps forward, too close for comfort, and continues, "Jacob's been telling me about a guy who's been teaching him to surf. He seems to be quite impressed with him."

I purse my lips to stop myself from smiling, although I feel rather ashamed of the fact that, while I'd assumed Jacob had been telling his father bad things about Adam, he's actually been doing the exact opposite – or so it seems.

"Got something interesting in mind for the weekend, have you?" Scott adds, before I can reply, and then laughs. "Don't blush, Jenna. It doesn't suit you. You're no innocent, and don't pretend you are. So… where is the golden boy then? I hear you've been letting him discipline Jacob as well?"

"Well, he needs it sometimes," I retort, embarrassed, my anger rising even further.

"Not from your boyfriend, he doesn't." Scott raises his voice. "I'll take care of showing my son how to behave, if it's all the same to you."

I'm suddenly aware of Adam's presence behind me, and I turn to see him standing in the doorway to the living room, his face like thunder.

Looking back at Scott, it's clear he's noticed Adam too. "Well, aren't you going to introduce us?" he says, sarcastically, nodding at Adam, and keeping his eyes fixed on him at the same time.

"No."

Very slowly, he moves his gaze to me. "Oh… I think you should, being as you've obviously moved this guy into my son's life… and presumably into my bed as well."

His bed? How dare he?

I take a breath, ready to yell, but then suddenly remember that Jacob is standing between us, and I bend down to him.

"Your shoes are upstairs," I tell him. "Go and put them on and you'd better check that Mummy packed your pyjamas as well."

He nods his head and runs for the stairs, as I stand upright again, glaring at Scott. Before I can say anything though, he starts, "What do you think you're doing, moving another man into the house?" He steps closer, his foot on the threshold. "Do you really think it's wise to let Jacob get close to someone else, when you know full well it won't last? Let's face it, we both know your boyfriend's going to move on, as soon as he finds out what you're really like… how dull, and prudish, and frigid you are; that you're all promise and no delivery." A part of me wants to remind him that he once said that sex with me was the best ever, but I can't be bothered. He'll only find a way to turn it into an insult. "You always were one massive disappointment," he adds, living up to expectations. "But to include Jacob in your sordid little flings… I mean, what kind of mother are you, for fuck's sake?"

He stops talking at last and although I can feel the tears pricking my eyes, I'm damned if I'm going to cry in front of him.

Chapter Twenty

Adam

I want to hurt this guy. Badly. Who does he think he is? He and Jenna have been divorced for years, and he's talking like he still has some kind of hold over her. *His* bed? He gave up the right to call it that when he cheated on her and broke her heart. It stabs at my own to know she loved him enough to let him do that to her, although now I've seen him, I can understand it better. He's one of those super good looking guys, with charisma oozing from every pore and it's easy to see them as a couple… a perfect couple.

"Who do you think you are, Scott?" I can hear the emotion in Jenna's trembling voice.

"The father of your son," he replies, moving closer to her, to the point that I step forward myself. "And I don't like the set-up you've got going on with this new guy."

"I don't know what you're talking about. There is no 'set-up'. It's not like that. Adam and I aren't… I mean, there's nothing… we're not…" She falters and I feel the ground shift beneath me. Can she really be justifying herself – denying our relationship – to *him*?

"I'm glad to hear it," he smirks, just as Jacob comes down the stairs again, his rucksack over his shoulder, and I watch as he goes up to Jenna, and she hugs him goodbye, before he leaves with his father, not another word being exchanged.

Jenna stands for a moment, with the door open and I move back down the hallway wondering why she didn't put Scott in his place, why she made our relationship sound so casual, to the point of non-existence; whether that's her real perception of us.

Eventually, she closes the door and leans back against it, still breathing hard.

"I'm sorry about that," she says, calming a little, although I'm anything but calm myself.

"Can I ask you something?"

"Of course."

"Why did you make it sound like there's nothing going on between us?" She looks down at the floor and I feel a dark shadow crossing over me. "Jenna? What's happening here?"

"Nothing," she says defensively, although she still won't look at me.

"In that case, why wouldn't you tell him that we're a couple? You did it with Jacob, and you told your parents too… so why won't you just admit it to Scott?"

She lets out a long, deep sigh, finally making eye contact with me, although I'm not sure I like the uncertainty I see on her face. "You don't understand," she says. "It's not as easy for me as it is for you."

Is that even an answer? "Sorry? I don't understand what you mean."

"You and I don't have the same kind of history," she murmurs.

"No, we don't. I seem to remember telling you that – or something like it – myself. But that doesn't mean I can't appreciate your past with Scott. I understand that trusting someone new is hard for you… harder than it is for me."

"Then why…?" She looks confused now. "Why don't you understand how difficult this is for me?"

"I do. That's what I'm saying." I take a half step closer to her. "I may not have been married before, or even been in a serious relationship with anyone, but I trusted Jade, and – more importantly – I trusted Nathan, even if we never got on that well, because there are some things you simply don't do, and stealing your brother's girlfriend is one of them. But even though what they did hurt me, I did eventually work out that, if I could, I'd rather have them both back, and both alive, than have to live with the knowledge that the consequence of them feeling that they had to run away, rather than just talk to me, is that they're both dead." I raise my voice, getting more wound up as I'm talking, and have to take a breath, before continuing, "It may not be the same as getting a divorce, but it's a damn sight more permanent, Jenna."

"I'm sorry," she whispers and I can see the tears in her eyes, even from here. "I didn't mean to be insensitive."

I move closer still to her. "Can't you see? Can't you see what I'm trying to say?" She looks at me blankly. "You're not the only person in the world to discover that someone who you trusted isn't what you thought they were. You have to learn from these things… and move on."

"I know that," she snaps, raising her own voice a little now. "It's just that I have Jacob to think about and it's hard, having to see Scott all the time."

"I understand that. But it won't always be like this…"

"You think?"

"I know. Not if you let your walls down and let me in." She stares at me, blinking, like she doesn't understand. "Why won't you take away that last barrier? Why won't you put Scott behind you and let me in properly? Take that one last step…"

"Are you talking about sex?" she interrupts.

"No. I'm not talking about sex. I'm talking about trust. You have to trust me."

A tear falls down her cheek and, although I want to move forward and hold her, I don't. I wait. And eventually she looks up at me. "It's not that easy," she whispers. "I built my walls to protect myself, Adam. I need them."

"To keep me out?" I ask.

"To keep *everyone* out."

I nod my head, biting back the hurt. "I'm not saying you have to tear them down in one go. Not completely. Why… why don't we look on it as me putting in some windows for you? You need to let some light in sometimes. I can make you happy, Jenna. I know I can. I can definitely make things better with Scott and with Jacob. But you have to let me."

She stares at me, and I can see the conflict in her eyes, torn between her past and her future, but she doesn't say a word and after a minute or so has gone by, I let out a long sigh of despair. We're getting nowhere here, and I'm not even sure she wants to. Not really. I think she's so buried behind her walls, she's forgotten how to live. Or at least how to trust. And how to love.

"I'm going," I say quietly, moving towards her, because she's blocking the door.

Her eyes widen and I can see the panic shining in them. "You're leaving me?"

"No." I shake my head. "I'll never leave you, not in the way you mean. But I can't make you stay with me either, not if you don't want to."

"What do you mean?" she whispers.

"I mean that, after what I heard tonight, I need to know whether you're really interested in trying to make things work with me, or not."

"Of course I am," she whimpers and I'm so tempted to stay, even though I know I can't.

"I know you're scared, Jenna. And that you think I'm going to hurt you, like Scott did… and, if I'm being honest, that really hurts, because you're not giving me a chance. You're judging me, based on his behaviour, even though I've told you, over and over, that I'll never do anything to hurt you."

"He said that too," she says, gulping back her tears.

"Hmm… but you're forgetting – again – that I'm not him." I sigh, pushing my fingers back through my hair, and feeling like we've just gone round in a full circle, for the umpteenth time. "I think it's best if I go now."

"Will I see you again?" I can hear the crack in her voice.

"That's up to you, Jenna. Entirely up to you. I—I don't think I should work on your extension anymore though." She lets out a slight sob, clasping her hand to her mouth. The need to hold her is crushing my heart, but I ignore it. Whatever happens next between us, I know it has to come from her. She has to want this enough to take that last leap of faith with me, or we're never going to work this out. "I'll move the schedules around again and get someone else to cover for me, and I'll give you some time to yourself to decide what you want. If that's not me, then I guess I'll have to find a way to live with that. Although God knows how." I take a step closer. "But if you decide you're ready to be with me, then you're going to have to mean it, and you're going to have to put your faith in me entirely, because in all the time I've known you, I've never done anything not to deserve your trust – and I never will."

I step towards her, place my hands on her waist, and move her gently aside. She lets me, and I open the door, looking down at her tear-streaked face. For a moment, I wonder about staying, about kissing her and holding her close to me, and telling her it'll be okay. But then I realise I can't – because I don't know that it will be. I don't know that anything will ever be okay again. I've reached a point where I need answers, and they can only come from her.

"If you want me," I whisper, my hand still resting just above her hip, "then you just have to call me. I'll be waiting."

"How long for?" she asks, swallowing down her tears, and it takes me a moment to work out that she's probably assumed I'll go straight out and find someone else to share my bed with… because that's what Scott would do.

I don't react, or respond to that thought. Instead I tell her the truth. "Forever." She narrows her eyes, disbelieving. "I mean it, Jenna. I wish to God you'd believe me for once, but I don't cheat, and I don't lie. Like I said when you wanted to learn to surf, you need to have some faith in yourself… even if it seems you don't have any in me. You're the only woman I've ever really wanted, and it's been like that since the first time I met you, when you were sixteen years old. I've never had a serious relationship, because I've never found anyone even close to my memory of you. So, the answer to your question is, I'll wait forever, if I have to. I'm used to it."

The drive home is a bit of a blur, but I make it, and fall onto the sofa, staring out at the view of the bay, more scared than ever.

I'm still holding my keys and, with every breath, I think about running straight back out of the door and driving back to her, telling her that I love her, and begging her to give me a chance to prove it to her.

But every time I'm tempted to jump up from the sofa, I stop myself. I have to let her do this. She has to make the choice and know it's the right one for her.

And I just have to wait, and hope. Because now I've found her again… now I've had a taste of what 'more' really feels like, I honestly don't think I can live without her.

Chapter Twenty-one

❦

Jenna

Even as Adam walks away, I want to call him back, to beg him to forgive me, to take me back and give us another chance… but I can't.

I watch him drive away, then close the door and fall to the floor, crying my heart out.

"What's wrong with me?" I wail. He's offering me everything I've ever wanted; everything I've wanted since I first saw him nearly half a lifetime ago, and I'm risking it all because of what Scott did… well, and because of my own fear.

"I'm scared." Saying it out loud makes it feel more real, especially as I now know what it is I'm really scared of. Adam's made it clear that he'll wait – he even said he'll wait forever – but no man can do that, and I'm terrified that he'll be the same as Scott in the end; that he'll discover I'm not enough, and he'll stray too… and I know I couldn't bear that.

I don't know how long I've sat on the floor, but it's dark by the time I get to my feet and go around the house, locking up and switching everything off. Upstairs, I get undressed and fall into bed, wondering about my plans for a quiet night in with Adam. As it is, I haven't even eaten… and I don't care.

Lying, staring at the ceiling, I can't stop thinking about him, about what it's going to feel like on Monday to have three strangers working on the extension. I wonder what it will be like not to have him kiss me first thing in the morning; what it might be like to come home after a bad day, and not feel his strong arms around me. I try to picture my life without Adam in it, and start crying again, the tears soaking into the pillow, as I recall all the times he's made me laugh, the things we've done together, the kindness he's shown to me and to Jacob. He's such a special man and I know I'm lucky to have him in my life… and I know that I love him, more than I ever loved Scott. But how can I have a relationship with him? How can I risk my heart again, knowing that if he lets me down, I'll break for good this time?

"Adam? Where are you?"

I wander along the beach, the waves lapping gently over my feet. There's no-one in sight and I search the horizon, looking for him.

"Adam? I can't find you…"

The sky darkens, a storm gathering, coming closer.

"Adam? I'm scared…"

I wake, with a start, sitting upright in the bed.

"Adam?"

I'm alone, the dawn light peeping around the edges of my curtains, but the terror of my dream casts a long, dark shadow, the stark loneliness overwhelming me.

I leap out of bed and run to the bathroom, throwing off my pyjamas and jumping into the shower.

I ring the buzzer twice and wait, wondering if Adam was lying when he said he'd wait… whether he's not here, but has spent the night somewhere else… with someone else.

I'm just raising my hand to ring again, when I hear his voice.

"Hello?"

"It's me… Jenna," I say into the intercom.

"Hi. Um… come on up."

He sounds a bit unsure and my earlier doubts return, my stomach leaden. God… please don't let this be a repeat of Scott and Ella… please.

The door buzzes and clicks, and I push it open, going up the stairs to the second floor, where Adam's waiting for me on the threshold of his flat, wearing a pair of cotton shorts and nothing else. His hair is a mess and I stand, staring at him.

"Are you okay?" he asks.

"Yes. Sorry… did I wake you?"

"Yes. But then it is only six-thirty in the morning."

"God… is it?" I didn't even check the time before I left home. "I'll go," I mutter, turning to leave.

"Like hell you will." He grabs my arm, pulling me back. "Come in." He drags me inside, closing the door behind us.

"I'm sorry," I mutter. "Are… are you alone?" I feel myself blush at the question.

"Of course I'm alone. Who else would be here at this time on a Saturday morning?" He stares at me and then frowns. "You think I'd have another woman here – or anywhere, for that matter?" I don't answer and stare down at his chest instead until he moves forward, clasping my face in his hands and raising it, so I have to look at him, seeing the hurt in his eyes. "I've told you, Jenna. I. Do. Not. Cheat."

"I know, but… after last night."

"You mean last night, when I told you that I don't lie either… right before I told you that you're the only woman I've ever wanted, and that I'll wait forever for you?"

"Yes."

"You get the concept of forever, do you?" he says, smiling now, and I suck in a breath.

"Yes. And when you put it like that, I feel really stupid."

"Not stupid," he says softly. "Just insecure… even if you've got no reason to be. Not with me." He takes my hand and leads me into his living room. "Why don't I get you a coffee?" he suggests. "And you can admire the view, while I take a shower."

"Sorry?" I turn to him, confused. "You want me to watch you take a shower?"

He chuckles. "No… although I wouldn't dismiss the idea completely." His eyes glint mischievously and I can't help my lips from twitching up slightly. "What I actually meant was that you could sit in here and look out at the bay, while I go into the bathroom and take a shower… I get the feeling you've come here to say something?" I nod my head and he returns the gesture. "And in that case, I think I'd rather be showered and dressed first… if that's okay with you?"

He directs me to his sofa and brings me a coffee within minutes.

"I'll go and shower," he says. "I won't be long."

"Okay."

He takes a step away, but then stops. "You won't leave, will you?" He sounds worried.

"No."

"Good." He smiles and turns, walking quickly from the room.

He returns about fifteen minutes later, wearing jeans and a white t-shirt, and for a moment, I wonder if it's the one I wore the other day, before I notice his damp hair and the sparkle in his eyes, and as he comes to sit beside me, I smell his divine scent too.

"Are you okay?" he asks, his voice low and soft.

"Yes."

I put down my half empty cup and turn to him, taking a breath. I've been rehearsing what to say, but now I'm here and he's in front of me, I feel tongue-tied, knowing that our conversation is going to get personal – very personal.

Still, it's got to be done, because it's the only way forward, and I want to move forward. So, I take a deeper breath as he watches me, waiting.

"I've been thinking," I say to start with.

"Yes?" I move closer to him and he smiles. "What have you been thinking?"

"God, this is so hard," I murmur.

"What is?"

"The conversation we need to have."

His face falls. "Should I be scared?"

"I don't know… but I am."

He shifts along the sofa so he's right next to me. "You have nothing to be scared of. Not as long as I'm with you." He twists around, cupping my face in his hands, and looks into my eyes. "I love you, Jenna," he murmurs and I stare at him, stunned, even though my heart feels so light, it's floating skywards, and taking me with it. "I know I'm not playing fair," he adds, sighing, "especially not when you've come here to tell me something, which is obviously quite difficult… but I've been dying to say that to you for so long."

"I—I love you too," I whisper, marvelling at the change in his expression as his eyes widen, a smile forming on his perfect lips. "Although I'm afraid I only worked it out properly last night… sorry."

"Hey… don't be sorry. I didn't say it so I could hear you say it back. I wasn't expecting that at all. I just wanted you to know. I wanted you to understand the reason why you don't need to feel scared; the reason why you don't have to worry about telling me anything, or about how I'll react, or about me hurting you, or lying to you… it's all because I love you."

He's staring into my eyes, his own filled with the honesty of his words, and I know I have to tell him the truth. "I'm still scared."

"Why?"

"Because I went into my relationship with Scott believing that he loved me too. I thought he'd never hurt me, or cheat, or lie… and he did. And if you did that to me… then…"

"But I won't," he says. "I won't do any of that. Why won't you believe me?"

"Because it's just words."

He pulls back slightly. "No, it's not. I've never been in love before, other than with you the first time I met you. But no matter who I've been with, regardless of the fact that I didn't love them, I've never cheated on anyone. That's just who I am. You don't have to believe me, but you could try trusting me enough to let me spend the rest of my life proving it to you."

I smile at him. "Well, I thought about that."

"You did?" He frowns, although his lips are twitching into a smile.

"Yes. Last night, after I'd spent a while thinking about how it would break me if you ever cheated, I focused on how my life would be without you in it… which was pretty awful. And then, when I finally managed to go to sleep, I had the most dreadful dream."

"About me?" he asks, concerned.

"Yes." I hesitate for a second, before continuing, "I suppose I ought to explain first that, in my other dreams about you, the ones I had when we met before, and the ones I usually have now, we're always on the beach, and we're… um…" *God, I wish I'd thought this through.*

"Intimate?" he guesses.

"Yes."

"Sounds like my kind of dream," he replies, his eyes sparkling.

"Well, last night was very different. In my dream, I was still on the beach, but this time, I was alone. I was trying to find you, but you weren't there. And there was this dark, threatening storm coming towards me, and no matter how hard I looked for you, I couldn't find you. And I woke up this morning, feeling so scared, I decided I had to come here… and face my fears, or at least talk them through with you, instead of hiding behind my walls all the time." I look down at my hands, which I've clasped in my lap. "I—I know I'm not easy to live with," I murmur.

"Yes, you are." He puts one of his hands over both of mine, squeezing them.

"No. I'm a pain in the neck, with a lifetime of baggage."

"Even if you are, you're *my* pain in the neck… and I'm pretty good with carrying baggage… it comes from working on building sites for so many years."

I chuckle and lean into him as he places his finger beneath my chin, raising my face and lowering his lips to mine.

"No, Adam. We need to talk." He stops instantly but doesn't move away, his face just inches from mine. "This isn't going to be easy."

"For which one of us? You, or me?"

"Me… and maybe you too."

He sighs. "Okay… can I assume we're talking about Scott?"

"Yes. I need you to know the reason he cheated, because until you do, until I know that you're sure about what you're letting yourself in for, I can't make a commitment to anything, no matter how much I love you."

He smiles again. "You don't need to explain that to me," he says. "I already know why Scott cheated."

"You do?" I can't hide my surprise.

"Yes. Because he's an idiot."

I chuckle again, even though I'm shaking my head. "No, that's not the reason."

"Yes it is."

"Adam. Please… you have to let me explain."

He sits back a little, pulling me into his arms. "Okay, but if you think it had anything to do with what he said last night, about you being prudish and frigid, then you can think again."

"But… but that's precisely it. That's the reason behind it. It's because I didn't give him what he wanted. I—I wasn't enough…"

Adam leans away from me slightly and I turn to face him. "I'm going to assume Scott told you this?"

"Yes."

"Which just makes him even more of an idiot."

"No… you don't understand."

"Okay," he sighs, "explain it."

"This is the part where it gets difficult," I begin, taking a deep breath.

"You've got to trust me enough to tell me," he replies softly and I look him in the eyes and know that I do.

"When… when Scott and I first started going out with each other, we didn't have sex for a long time, because I didn't want to rush into things. I was quite young, I suppose, and I wasn't ready. But when it eventually happened, he was like a different person."

"In what way?" he asks, holding me closer.

"Do you remember I told you once that he was only ever nice to me when we were in bed – well, that's what I'm talking about. He used to pay me compliments, say lovely things about me and my body and whatever it was we were doing… but only ever when we were in bed." I feel myself blush and bite my lip, embarrassed, but plough on regardless. "Because of that, I didn't mind having quite a lot of sex with him – several times a day, if necessary."

"Necessary?" he says, querying the word.

"Well, I've never found sex in itself that enjoyable, to be honest, so 'necessary' feels like the right word in this context." I think for a second.

"I suppose that's why Scott called me those names…"

"Whoa," he says, sitting up a little and looking down at me. "Hold on a second. I've obviously never made love to you, but I have kissed you, and I know how you respond, and I can assure you that you are very far from being prudish, or frigid. Don't ever think of yourself like that… And if you didn't enjoy sex with Scott, then that's not your fault, it's his…"

"I'm not sure about that," I reply, feeling even more embarrassed now. "But I need to finish my story."

He smiles and hugs me again, sitting us back into the sofa once more.

"We… we first had sex about seven months into our relationship… there, or thereabouts." I get back to where we were before he distracted me. "But then, the following year, we both got into different universities. I went to Bristol and he went to Surrey, and we realised that would mean spending most of our time apart. I'll admit I was worried about that, but he reassured me we could handle the separation, that our relationship was strong enough to stand the test, and I believed him. It was hard, but we got through it, meeting up whenever we could and spending weekends together."

"And then what happened?" he asks, when I pause for breath.

"Then Scott got a job in America."

"America?"

"Yes. I was absolutely devastated, but again, he was adamant that we'd be okay. It was just for a year, and he didn't want to turn down the opportunity…" I let my voice fade, remembering his argument at the time.

"How did you manage?" he asks.

"I went to visit him three times during the year and we spent a week together each time – mainly in bed, I have to say." I blush, although Adam just looks at me, straight faced, listening intently. "And then, when he came back, we moved in together."

"Here? In Carven Bay?"

"No." I shake my head slowly. "No… his job was in Bristol, so I resigned from Cole and Simpson and moved there."

"You gave up your job for him?"

I nod. "I found another one really quickly, and not long after that, he proposed and we got married."

"How old were you?" he asks.

"Twenty-three."

"So, quite young."

"Yes, but we'd been together for nearly seven years; it seemed like the next step."

He smiles. "Maybe… but you hadn't spent very much time together during those years, had you?"

"No… and you're interrupting the story."

"Sorry."

I nestle into him. "We got married," I continue, "and although we'd agreed beforehand that we'd wait before having kids, Scott changed his mind and decided we should start a family straight away. Jacob was born within the year, and that's when things got really hard…"

"How?" he asks, holding me tighter.

"I don't think either of us was really prepared for the changes a baby would bring to our lives. We were both really tired and we argued a lot. Scott was going for promotions at work and feeling the stress of that, so it fell to me to make the effort in our relationship… I—I lost my pregnancy weight, which he seemed to find an issue, and I went back on the pill, and we agreed to start going out together more. And after that, things got better… until I found him in bed with our babysitter." I stop talking and Adam leans forward slightly, looking down at me.

"Are you alright?" He sounds concerned, and I can't help smiling up at him and nodding my head.

"Just about." I pull him back down close to me and snuggle up, my arms around his waist. "As you know, I left him," I whisper. "And I took Jacob with me, and came down to my parents, but Scott followed us. I was so… so angry, and disappointed, but I had to know the truth. I had to know if he was just having a fling, or if it had been going on for some time. I had to know if it was just sex, or if it was love… so, I told him he had to be honest with me about what had happened, if he wanted to save our marriage. I had absolutely no intention of staying with him, because the idea of letting him touch me, or come anywhere

398

near me, made me want to be physically sick, but the need to know everything was overwhelming… morbidly so. Surprisingly, he seemed to want to save our relationship, so he agreed to tell me the truth…"

"Which was?" I can hear the hesitation in Adam's voice, but I daren't look up.

"Ella – the babysitter – she wasn't the only one he'd slept with. During the course of our argument, he reluctantly informed me there had been a lot of others."

"Define 'a lot'."

"Over the ten years of our relationship, at least fifteen." He stiffens beside me. "It started before we went to bed the first time," I explain quickly, "because I'd made him wait."

"You made him wait?" he interrupts. "I knew the guy was an idiot, but seriously… didn't he get it?"

"Get what?" I still can't look at him, but I mumble into his chest anyway.

"That it's a privilege to wait for you."

I can't believe he just said that and I hug him tighter. "Well, he didn't think so… and you're interrupting again."

"I'm sorry."

I shake my head, then carry on, desperate to get to the end now. "He told me he didn't like waiting and he went with a girl at college instead. He—he didn't seem to realise that I'd be hurt when I found out that my first time hadn't been 'our' first time. Although even I didn't think about that when he first told me. It only dawned on me later, because at the time he was telling me, he also went on to explain that, even though he broke up with that girl once he and I started sleeping together, he then started seeing someone else…"

"He did what?" Adam pulls back, gazing down at me.

"I—I'm not sure how to put this… I don't want you to think badly of me."

"That's not possible. And whatever it is you need to say, just say it."

I suck in a breath, blurting out the next words. "Scott said he… well, he needed someone more accommodating than me. That was his word."

"Accommodating? What did that mean?"

"Oh… God…" I mumble, staring out of the window at the view over the bay. "He liked… um… oral sex," I whisper, not daring to look at Adam. "Only the first time it happened, he… well, he made me kneel in front of him and forced himself down my throat. And he… well… you know… in my mouth. I hadn't been expecting that… and I didn't like it."

"I'm not surprised. I'm going to hazard a guess that he told you that this other girl didn't mind him doing that with her?"

I nod my head. "He said he reciprocated, but that was all they ever did. They didn't have sex."

"Oh, and I presume he thought that made it okay?"

"In his eyes, it did. Because I wasn't giving him what he wanted."

"That's a convenient way of looking at it… for him."

"Can I finish my story?" I murmur. "I need to get it over with."

He nods his head, pulling me back, and I put my feet up, so I'm lying in his arms again.

"So, what happened after college?" he asks.

"He told me that when we were at uni, he found the separation too difficult; he missed having sex, so he convinced himself that, if I didn't know about it, it didn't matter… and he slept with roughly ten other girls during the three years we were apart, even while he was lying to me and telling me how strong our relationship was." I sigh, taking a breath. "His time in America was different though… he didn't sleep around then. He had a proper relationship instead, with just one woman. Her name was Mandy."

"Did he love her?" Adam asks.

"He said he didn't, but by that stage of his confession, I didn't really care. As far as I was concerned, our marriage was already over, so what did it matter? He reassured me that, after he came home from the States, he'd been monogamous for a while, which was nice to know, being as that's when we first moved in together, and got married… but then I got pregnant and, in Scott's eyes, I was 'too fat', so that's when he started sleeping with someone at his office. He saw her until after Jacob was born and I lost weight, and he decided I was worthy of his attentions again, and then he moved on to the babysitter – which he claimed was an accident."

"An accident? He accidentally had sex with your babysitter?"

"Well, he claimed it wasn't intentional... it wasn't meant to happen."

"But the others were?" he asks.

"I think so, yes... because I wasn't fulfilling his requirements. He said he needed more sex than I was offering, either because we were living apart, or because I was pregnant, or fat, or tired, or both, and he couldn't just put his needs on hold... I think that's what he said."

I finally lean back and look up at him. He's staring down into my eyes, his own dark, almost angry and I feel my fear rising, tears forming in my eyes.

I've told him everything; my inadequacies, my humiliations, my rejection. I've held nothing back... but judging from the look on his face, I think I might have gone too far.

I think I might have lost him.

Chapter Twenty-two

Adam

I stare down at her glistening eyes, my anger building, to the point of boiling over, just as she starts to speak again.

"I—I understand that men sometimes have different needs to women, but please try and see this from my point of view. I can't be in a relationship where sex is going to be used to control me. And I won't be cheated on again… I can't." Her voice cracks and I shake my head, pulling her back into my chest again and hugging her close.

"Hey… you have nothing to fear, Jenna. I like sex. I like sex a lot. But I know better than anyone, that it's not enough to sustain a relationship – not on its own. There has to be more to it than that, and I've been looking for the 'more' ever since I first saw you and realised it even existed."

She leans back and looks up at me. "What do you mean?"

"I mean that, the first time I saw you on the beach, I knew there was something different about you. I knew you were what I'd been looking for ever since I'd first taken an interest in girls… I just hadn't realised until then what it was I'd been searching for."

"And what is it?" she asks. "What is this 'more'?"

"It's a need."

"A need? Do you mean a sexual need?"

"No. It's got nothing to do with sex. It's a need to make you feel happy and safe and wanted… and loved… because you are." She smiles, even though there are still tears brimming in her eyes. "I know I've struggled to hide my arousal from you, but answer me truthfully, have you ever felt pressured into having sex with me?"

She shakes her head. "No."

"And you never will." I shift slightly pulling her even closer to me, but still focusing on her face. "Like I said just now, waiting for you is a privilege. And I'll keep doing it for as long as you need me to… for as long as it takes. I love you… and only you."

She leans into me and I hug her tighter.

"Scott used sex to manipulate me," she murmurs, "and, because it was the only time he was nice to me, I craved it. But then at other times, he could be absolutely vile. I wasn't always aware he was doing it at the time, but the way he controlled me… it was so devious. I spent a lot of my time treading on eggshells, never knowing what to say, or what kind of reaction I'd get…"

"You don't need to do that anymore. I want you to be honest with me."

"That's kind of the point of this whole embarrassing conversation," she says, pulling back slightly and looking up at me. "Even if it is so muddled and difficult." She blinks a few times, then adds, "Like I said, I've got baggage…"

"It's fine. You just have to talk to me and let me share the load."

"I'll try. Honestly, I will." She rests her head on my chest. "I know my relationship with Scott might seem a bit odd to you, but I want you to know that it's all about Jacob. I know you were having doubts last night, but you have to understand, I don't have any feelings for him anymore. In fact, I often wonder how I ever did… he makes my life so miserable…" She sounds too sad for words.

"That stops now," I tell her firmly. "He doesn't get to call the shots, Jenna. Not when I'm around."

I hear her long sigh and wait for a moment until she says, "The… the thing is, I need you to bear in mind that my memories are still there…"

"Memories of him?" I ask, fear creeping up my spine.

"No... not in the way you mean. I'm talking about my memories of how it felt when I opened the bedroom door and found him in bed with Ella... the sounds they were making, the sight of them together... it still haunts me... and when he told me about all the other women he'd slept with... I felt so betrayed, so inadequate. And I know you've told me you won't cheat – and I believe you – but I can't guarantee that I won't get suspicious, or jealous, or distrustful from time to time. It's going to be hard... it's going to be strange for me, letting down my walls..."

"What about putting those windows in instead?" I suggest. "As a first step?"

"No." She looks up at me again. "I want more than that. I don't want to just look out at you. I want you on the inside."

My heart flips over in my chest and I cup her face with my hand. "We'll deal with it. I will never give you cause to feel jealous or suspicious of me, but if you do for some reason, then you just have to tell me. Don't keep your feelings to yourself. Share them with me. That way, I can reassure you that you have nothing to fear – because you never will have. I won't hurt you – not in any way; not physically, not emotionally. Not ever."

She leans up, narrowing the gap between us and kisses me, her lips soft against mine as she moans into me. I change the angle of my head and deepen the kiss, unable to resist her, and she lets me, opening up, our tongues clashing as the heat between us rises in an instant, like it always does. I alter my position and push her gently down onto the sofa, nestling in the cradle of her open thighs, raising myself above her. She weaves her fingers into my hair, pulling it, holding me in place, her breathing ragged, and I force myself to stop, gasping in a breath.

"If... if you want me to stop, then I'll stop. If you need more time, I'll wait, but..."

She gazes at me. "No more waiting, Adam... I want you..." she whispers and my heart soars, and without taking my eyes from hers, I balance on one arm, raising the other one and undoing the buttons of her blouse, revealing her perfect, full, rounded breasts. She's not wearing a bra and I lean down, capturing one hardened erect nipple between my teeth, biting gently as she squirms and sighs beneath me.

She arches her back into me and I know I have to see her, to touch her… so I kneel up, slowly undoing her shorts and pulling them down, together with her delicate lace underwear, standing to complete the process, then sitting her up and removing her blouse, so she's naked before me, as I pull my t-shirt over my head and drop it to the floor. I'm just undoing the button on my jeans, when I realise how wrong this all is and I stop.

"No," I murmur, and Jenna gasps, clutching her arms around herself, tears forming in her eyes and I know I've screwed up. "Hey…" I lean over her. "Don't cry."

"Why not?" she says. "You've stopped. Now you've seen me close-to, with all my stretch marks and flaws, you don't want me. You've changed your mind."

Could she be any more wrong? "No, I haven't." I move closer to her, my lips barely an inch from hers. "Nothing I've seen has made me want to do anything, other than make love to you for the rest of my life. I can't honestly say I noticed your stretch marks. I was too distracted by how perfect you are… but if you've got any, then they're a part of who you are, and I wouldn't change single inch of you."

"Then what's wrong? she asks, sounding doubtful still.

"Nothing. Except I'm damned if our first time together is going to be on the couch. We're not teenagers, Jenna. Please… let's do this properly…"

I stand again and hold out my hand and, after just a second's hesitation, she takes it, letting me pull her to her feet, and lead her towards my bedroom. She stops after a few paces, however, pulling me back.

"What about my clothes?" she says, glancing back to the pile of clothing on the floor.

"Don't worry… you won't be needing them."

In my bedroom, she sits nervously on the edge of the bed, her eyes lowered, still trying to cover her very ample breasts with her arms, and I quickly remove my jeans and trunks, before joining her, shifting backwards slightly.

"Come here," I say softly and she turns, looking at me, letting her arms fall as she edges back and a little closer. "I want you more than anything, Jenna, but if you've changed your mind…"

"I haven't," she whispers, interrupting me, and I smile at her, pulling her into my arms, feeling her naked skin against mine.

"Before I end up losing my mind," I murmur, despite the fact that I'm already half way there, "do I need a condom?"

She shakes her head. "I'm on the pill," she murmurs. "And before you ask, I had all the necessary tests done after Scott told me what he'd done. He assured me he'd used protection with all the other women, but I didn't trust him."

I'm not sure I like hearing Scott's name when we're in bed, but I suppose it's necessary for us to talk about the past… just this once. "I don't blame you," I tell her. "And I had a medical last year for my insurance. I got tested then, and… well, I haven't been with anyone since. Actually, I haven't been with anyone since Jade, to be honest."

Her eyes widen. "Really?"

"Yes… and speaking of that, I feel it's only fair to apologise in advance."

"What for?"

"For the fact that this could well come to a conclusion a lot more quickly than either of us might like." I smile down at her, and she bites her lip, making me want to kiss her.

"You have nothing to apologise for," she replies eventually.

"Tell me that afterwards."

"I—I hope I don't disappoint you," she whispers.

"You couldn't, not ever."

As I'm speaking, I let her go, sensing her fears and understanding them better now, after our conversation.

"Do you want to sit?" I offer and she frowns, confused.

"I am sitting," she says.

"I know you are… but you're not sitting in the right place."

I nod towards my erection and she glances down for the first time since I undressed, quickly returning her gaze to me, her eyes wide – almost fearful.

"On that?"

I chuckle. "Yes."

"But it's so…" She stops talking, a blush creeping up her cheeks.

"So what?"

"Well – frankly – huge."

"Thank you," I whisper, and she smiles, and then, without a word, twists around, straddling me.

I clutch her waist as she slowly lowers herself down, hitching in a breath and biting her lip as I penetrate her.

"Okay?" I ask, holding her still.

"Yes," she murmurs, her eyes locked on mine. "It… it just stretches…"

"And do you like the stretch?"

She sighs, "Oh… yes…" and I let her go, leaving her to her own devices, watching as she lowers herself a little further, feeling her tight walls surround me, her mouth forming into a perfect 'O', as she places her hands on my shoulders, while I raise my own further up her back, pulling her hard into me, feeling her breasts crush against my chest. "Oh, God… that feels so good." Her voice is a hoarse whisper against my ear, but I'm concentrating, deep inside her now, and she rests for a moment, before she raises herself up again, starting to move.

I think I've always known that making love with Jenna would be like nothing else I've ever experienced; that there would be no holds barred. Our first kiss was enough to tell me that. But the reality is so much more, and within seconds, we're both breathless, desperate, wild with longing and desire.

She leans back slightly and I release her, my hands resting on her waist once more as she takes me, her fingers digging into my shoulders. It's a struggle, but I fight the urge to climax, with every move, grateful that, within a few minutes, her breathing alters and I feel her thighs start to quiver.

"Adam?" she says my name, like a question, like she's not sure what's happening. "I'm… Oh, God… I'm…" She throws her head back and screams, and I hold onto her as she grinds her hips hard onto me, literally riding out the waves of her orgasm, until eventually it subsides and she flops forward onto me. "I—I've never… I've never," she stutters, then leans back, staring into my eyes, disbelieving. "I've never done that before, not during sex."

She look so pleased with herself, her eyes on fire, a smile etched on her perfect face, and I lie down, bringing her with me, then keeping us connected, roll her onto her back, raising myself above her.

"Well," I murmur, kissing her, "it wasn't a one-off… so let's see if you can do it again, shall we?"

She sucks in a breath and nods her head, grinning and raising her legs as I start to move inside her. She matches my rhythm in an instant, and within moments, the only sounds I can hear are her repeated moans and gasps of pleasure and my own groans of satisfaction.

I know I can't last much longer, but it seems I don't need to. She brings her hands up, placing them behind my head and twisting her fingers into my hair, just as she comes apart for a second time, thrashing beneath me, crying out my name, and I'm pushed over the edge into ecstasy, pouring my love deep inside her.

To avoid collapsing onto her, I roll us onto our sides. "I love you," I whisper, holding her close to me, savouring her soft body, naked against my own.

"I love you too," she breathes, sighing gently.

"That was magical."

"You're magical," she says, leaning back and looking at me. "How did you do that?"

I smile at her. "I didn't. That was you…"

She shakes her head. "That doesn't make sense. Nothing like that ever happened when I was with Scott…" I pull her close again, wishing she hadn't mentioned his name – again – and she nestles down into me.

"How about a shower?" I suggest, just in case she decides to make any more comparisons – favourable or otherwise – as I lean back, noticing her face has fallen. "What's wrong?"

"I—I thought we might be able to do that again," she whispers, seemingly embarrassed. "But you clearly don't want to…"

"Yes, I do."

"But you just said…"

"I suggested a shower because I want to make love to you in there."

Her face betrays her surprise, and she blinks a few times. "In the shower?" she murmurs.

"Yes. Have you never done that before?"

She shakes her head. "No. Scott never did anything like that... not with me, anyway."

I pull out of her, taking care to be gentle about it, and then sit up and look down at her perfect, prone body. "Can I say something?"

She frowns. "What's the matter?" I hesitate and she sits up too, placing her hand on my arm. "What did I do, Adam?"

"You didn't do anything... and I'm not trying to be controlling, and neither do I want to dictate anything to you, but do you think we could make a rule... and stick to it?"

"A rule?"

"Yes. When we're making love, or in bed together, or being intimate anywhere else for that matter, whether that's in the shower, or the kitchen, or the living room... I really don't want to talk about your ex-husband."

"I'm sorry," she whispers, changing position and straddling me once more. "That was insensitive of me to bring him up..."

"Don't worry about it."

"But I shouldn't have mentioned him," she says, still sounding worried, despite what I've just said, and I reach out, cupping her face in my hand as she looks into my eyes. "I love you," she says, with heartbreaking sincerity.

"I know you do." I kiss her, deeply. "And I love you too. Now... how about this shower?"

She smiles and I move us both to the edge of the bed, placing my arms beneath her legs so the backs of her knees are resting on the insides of my elbows, then I stand, lifting her with me and she squeals, leaning into me and clutching hold of my neck.

"Do I bend like that?" she asks, looking up at me.

"You do," I confirm.

"I feel very exposed." She smiles, biting her bottom lip as I carry her from the bedroom, across the hallway, into the bathroom, and straight into the shower.

"Good." I turn on the water, before lifting her and lowering her onto my erection. "That's the whole point."

Her eyes seem to flutter and she sucks in a long, slow, satisfied breath. "Oh, God… you're so big again," she breathes.

"Yes. Because I want you."

"You do?" She smiles.

"Want me to prove it?"

"Yes please…"

With her legs hooked over my arms, I rest her against the tiles and start to move. Hard. And I don't stop until the sound of her screaming echoes off the walls.

"I suppose we ought to get dressed," Jenna says as she finishes drying herself off, and I drop my towel, moving closer to her, so we're almost touching, and I feel her breathing change.

"Why?" I ask. "Why bother? Jacob's away for the weekend, and we'd planned to spend our time together anyway, hadn't we?"

"Yes," she whispers.

"So, what's the point in getting dressed? You can just stay here. As you are."

She doesn't reply, but lowers her eyes and moves away from me.

"Hey… what's wrong?" I reach out and pull her close to me, but she comes with some reluctance. "Jenna?"

She leans back in my arms. "I know I'm not supposed to mention Scott, but I'm going to have to, if you want me to explain."

"Okay."

"It… it's just that he used to like me to wander around with no clothes on. He used to watch me… even when he was fully clothed… even if I was just doing the housework or the laundry. Sometimes I didn't mind, because it meant he was actually paying me some attention, but most of the time, I found it a bit degrading."

"I don't blame you. Although I didn't mean I wanted to sit around watching you. I meant I want to be naked with you. Together. But if you feel uncomfortable walking around my flat with no clothes on… well, that still doesn't mean you have to get dressed."

She tilts her head. "It doesn't?"

"No. Because I think we've already established you look both very comfortable and absolutely incredible when you're wearing my t-shirts. So why don't you put one of those on? If you want to?"

Her lips twitch up in a cute smile and she nods her head, and I take her hand and lead her back into my bedroom, where I open one of the drawers and pull out a grey t-shirt, handing it to her.

"Are you going to wear anything?" she asks, holding it and staring up at me.

"Do you want me to?"

She hesitates, her eyes grazing over my body. "I like this," she whispers, running her hand down my chest and across my stomach. "And I like the wolf too."

I remember her nickname for me, and smile. "Anything else you like?" I ask, teasing her.

"Yes," she says, her eyes twinkling as she lowers her hand, and then a gasp escapes her slightly parted lips, when she discovers that I'm still aroused. "Oh God…" She shudders, her eyes fluttering closed for an instant, and I chuckle.

"You want more?" I ask.

"Can we… can we…"

"Wait a while?" I guess and she nods her head. "Of course we can. You're not sore, are you?"

She shakes her head. "No. I'm hungry."

I laugh. "You're hungry?"

"Yes. I didn't have breakfast, and… well, we've been kind of busy this morning."

I glance at the clock on the bedside table. "Well, it is after twelve. Would you like some lunch?"

"I'd love some," she beams and pulls my t-shirt on over her head, which makes me groan slightly as I pull her into my arms.

"You're so sexy," I whisper.

"I'm not," she refutes.

"I think you'll find that such things are in the eye of the beholder… and I'm telling you, you're sexy." I kiss her. "And if we're going to wait a while, despite the obvious temptation of you wearing one of my t-shirts, then I'm going to put on some shorts."

I turn and grab some out of the next drawer down, pulling them on, but noticing Jenna's pout when I stand up again.

"If you look at me like that for much longer," I whisper, holding her close again, "I'll forget about waiting, and I'll forget about lunch… and I'll take you back to bed. Right now."

"That's a very tempting idea…"

"Except you're hungry?"

She grins, nodding her head. "Yes, I am."

After a lunch of cheese and salad sandwiches, we take a cup of tea into the living room and lie out on the couch, with Jenna curled up on top of me. We've barely been here for ten minutes though, when her breathing alters, and I realise she's fallen asleep on me. I smile to myself and turn slightly, which makes her moan and snuffle in a really adorable way, then I cradle her in my arms and watch her as she dozes for the next couple of hours, thinking about how much my life has changed in the last twenty-four hours, and what I did to deserve this.

Last night, I really wondered if I'd ever see her again; if I was asking too much of her; if my life was over. But this morning, being woken by my doorbell, then hearing her voice, knowing that, if she was going to end it with me, she'd have done it by text or by phone, and that her arrival could therefore only mean one thing… I don't think I've ever felt so happy, or so relieved in my life. I'm not going to say that hearing her story was easy, but I know why she needed to tell me. And I'm glad she did, because now everything's out there, I think I understand her better.

As for making love with her… despite the slight hiccup of her mentioning Scott's name, I already know that what we have is different, and that it's strong enough and bright enough to burn, unceasing, for a lifetime.

She wakes slowly, coming to, and looks up at me. "Did I fall asleep?"

"Just slightly." I lean down and kiss her forehead.

"I'm sorry."

"Hey, don't be sorry. You're tired, you needed sleep, and I liked holding you while you slept. It felt right."

"Yes," she murmurs, nestling into me again. "It did."

I raise her face to mine and kiss her deeply, letting my hands wander up inside her t-shirt as she sighs into me. She feels so good, and although I love her wearing my clothes, I need to be naked with her again, so I quickly remove her t-shirt and my shorts, and we spend the next couple of hours just enjoying each other, kissing and caressing... discovering, whispering, and loving. She doesn't hesitate to let me taste her, and my God... is she sweet. And loud. And afterwards, once she's calmed, she looks at me, uncertainty clouding her eyes as I hold her close.

"You don't have to do anything," I tell her.

"But that doesn't seem very fair."

I turn us onto our sides, facing each other. "Look, I know what you told me earlier... about what he did to you and... well, I think I need to explain something to you."

She hesitates for a moment and then nods her head.

"Firstly, no man – no man – worthy of that title would ever force a woman to do what he did to you. And secondly, you never have to do anything with me that makes you feel uncomfortable. I love the taste of you... I love the feeling of you coming on my tongue, and I will do that to you as often as you want, but I don't ever want you to feel that you have to... reciprocate." I use her word, because I can't think of another.

She lets her head rest on my shoulder. "It would be different with you though, wouldn't it...?"

"Of course... it would be on your terms, for one thing."

She nods her head and looks up at me as her hand wanders south. "My terms," she whispers, like she's toying with the idea, but I grab her wrist and roll her onto her back, nestling between her thighs.

"It can wait... forever if necessary," I murmur, kissing her deeply, and she moans into my mouth as I enter her.

"Would you think me awful if I said I'm hungry again?" she says a long while later, once we've both got our breath back, as she sits up, her hair beautifully dishevelled.

"No. Shall we order in a take-away?"

She blushes, just for a moment, perhaps remembering our intentions last night, before everything fell apart. "Okay," she whispers.

"Hey... don't think about it."

"How can I not think about it? I—I thought that was what we'd be doing yesterday evening... I thought we could sit and watch a movie, and maybe talk, and kiss and... it all went so wrong." There's a hitch in her voice, and I pull her close to me, feeling her soft body against mine.

"No, it didn't. And it wasn't your fault... And, in any case, look where we've ended up."

"Together?" she queries.

"Very together." I kiss her again.

"Very together," she repeats in a soft whisper as I break the kiss, before getting up and finding my iPad, so we can check out take-away menus.

I wake to early morning sunshine and gaze down at Jenna, who's lying in my arms, her head resting on my chest, a smile on her lips and I wonder if she's remembering last night. I smile too, recalling that we came to bed after our Thai take-away, and that we made love relentlessly, our bodies entwined, taking each other to new highs, over and over, until sleep finally claimed us in the early hours.

I lean down and kiss her, gently as she mumbles something, then slowly opens her eyes, gazing up into mine, her smile broadening.

"Good morning," she whispers.

"Good morning."

She shifts slightly, my arousal nudging into her hip.

"Last night wasn't enough for you then?" she teases.

"Evidently not."

Her eyes sparkle and, without saying a word, she pushes me onto my back and moves on top of me, lowering herself down and sucking in a deep sigh as she joins us together again.

"I thought you might want a break after yesterday." I hold her hips as she starts to move.

"No, not from you… I love what you do to me. It's so different…" She falls silent and I wonder if she was about to mention Scott's name, even as she sits back slightly. "I'm not doing this just to please you," she adds, out of the blue, grabbing my attention.

"I'm glad about that."

She smiles down at me. "I'm not doing it to feel complimented either."

"Good… because my compliments are like my love… unconditional, and completely genuine."

"I'm doing this because you make me feel alive… I had no idea it could be like this…"

I grab her, pull her down and roll her onto her back, taking control. Taking her.

"We don't have to be in bed for me to make you feel alive, Jenna. I can do that anytime. Anywhere."

"I know… but as we are in bed…"

She reaches up, pulling me down to her and kisses me with a fierce and hungry passion.

And I kiss her back.

Apart from half an hour or so in the shower, we spend most of the day in bed, both of us knowing, I think, that Jacob is coming home this evening and that, for a while at least, our time together will be limited.

That said, we don't spend every moment of the day making love. We do a lot of talking too, about us, about how we feel. It's hard sometimes for me to find the words to tell her what she means to me… what she does to me. But I think she understands. I hope she does, anyway.

At just after five o'clock, Jenna asks me to fetch her clothes, which I folded up and put on the coffee table yesterday lunchtime.

I watch her dress, noting the change in her; the fact that she's more tense, less talkative.

"Are you okay?" I ask.

"Yes… I'm a bit sore, but…"

I smile. That wasn't what I'd meant, but I suppose at least it means she's not dwelling on Scott, and the thought of seeing him later. "Sore in a good way?" I ask, going over and standing in front of her.

"In a very good way."

As she does up her shorts and pulls on her blouse, I realise I should probably put something on myself, and I grab my own shorts and a clean t-shirt from the drawer.

"Come with me," she says suddenly, and I turn to face her.

She's standing, her blouse unbuttoned, her breasts exposed, staring at me, her face filled with uncertainty. I walk straight to her and hold her in my arms.

"You want me to come home with you?"

"Yes. Please."

I smile, cupping her face with my hand. "You don't have to say 'please'. If you want me there, then I'll be there."

Once we're dressed, I pick up my keys and she finds her bag, which is by the sofa, and we head out of the door and down the stairs. Outside, I pull her into a hug, kissing her hard, our bodies fused, until we both pull back, breathless.

"Is it always going to be like that?" she asks, staring into my eyes.

"Yes… Always." I smile down at her and she smiles back. "I'll see you at your place," I whisper.

She looks bewildered, gazing up at me. "Sorry? I thought you were coming with me."

"I am."

"Then I don't…"

I realise the misunderstanding, holding on to her. "I can't come in your car, Jenna."

"Why not?"

"Because I'll need to drive back here later. I can't stay the night with you – not yet. We need to give Jacob some more time to get used to the idea of us being together before we do that. I mean, I know he's aware of us, but I don't think it's a good idea for him to see me coming out of your bedroom, or out of the shower first thing in the morning… do you?"

She shakes her head. "I should have thought of that myself."

"It's okay. Look, I'll follow you back to your place, and I'll spend the evening with you, and, if you're okay with it, perhaps I can start spending more of my evenings with you, after I've finished work…"

"Do you mean you're going to carry on working at my house?"

"Of course I am. I only said I couldn't, because the thought of seeing you every morning and every evening, and not kissing you, or holding you, was too much for me. But as it is… there isn't anything or anyone that could keep me away from you." She leans into me. "So, will it be okay if I spend my evenings with you?"

"Of course it will."

"I'll cook dinner sometimes, if you like, so you can help Jacob with his homework, or put your feet up. And then, when Jacob's got more accustomed to having me around, when you think he's ready, maybe I can stay over?"

"That sounds perfect," she murmurs.

"It does." She seems sad, in spite of her words, and I cup her face in both of my hands, locking eyes with her. "It's going to be hard not sleeping with you, and not waking up beside you, but we'll still have our weekends, when Jacob goes to visit his father, and I think we need to give him some time to get used to the idea of his mum having a boyfriend, don't you?"

"Boyfriend?"

"Yes… although I suppose that does sound a bit juvenile at our age doesn't it? Still, at least it's a word that Jacob will understand… unless you think calling me your fiancé might work better?" Her mouth drops open in stunned silence, although I have to admit, I'm kind of surprised myself. "I'm sorry. That was really lame as proposals go, wasn't it? I've never done that before… I've never even thought about it before, actually. I'm not really the marrying kind, and I'll understand if you'd rather pass on the suggestion. Let's face it, you don't have the best experience of marriage, so if you want to say 'no', I won't take it personally, I promise. And it won't make any difference to our relationship... I just..."

"Have you finished making excuses for your proposal yet?" she interrupts, smiling.

I pretend to think for a moment. "Yes, I think so."

"Good." She takes a breath. "If I'm being honest, I never thought I'd want to marry again... actually, I never thought I'd want to be with another man again... but I do. I want to be with you more than anything, and now you've made the suggestion, I really rather like the idea of being married to you. I like the idea of being yours."

"You'll always be mine, and I'll always be yours," I tell her firmly. "We don't need to be married to prove that."

"Are you withdrawing your proposal now?" she asks.

"No. Never."

"Good. Because I accept."

I smile. Then I grin. And then I kiss her. Hard.

Jenna turns to me as soon as we enter the hallway of her house, and throws her arms around my neck.

"Thank you for a perfect weekend," she whispers. "It started off so badly, but it's ended better than I'd dared to hope."

"I was so scared I'd lost you when I left here on Friday. I wasn't sure how I was going to live without you if you didn't want me back... but now I don't have to be scared anymore... and maybe next time Jacob goes to stay with his dad, we can go out and buy you a ring, and make this engagement thing official."

"Engagement thing?" she jokes, smiling up at me.

"Yes. Don't mock. I told you, I'm not the marrying kind..."

"Then why did you propose?" She leans back in my arms.

"Because I love you. But that doesn't make me an expert on the subject."

"Well, you might need to become an expert on something," she muses, serious now. "And fairly quickly."

"What's that?"

"How we tell Jacob that I'm going to change my name…" She bites her lip, looking doubtful.

"You don't have to," I say, understanding the situation at once. "If you need to keep using Scott's name, for Jacob's sake, then I don't mind."

"You don't?" She's surprised – bordering on shocked – and I smile down at her, moving closer.

"When my mother remarried," I explain, cupping her face with my hands, "she took her new husband's name, and that meant I was the only person in the house with the surname of Barclay. It felt odd… and I can still remember how isolating it was. I don't want to do that to Jacob, or to make you have to choose. You don't have to decide now, and we can talk it through with Jacob, if you like, but I'll go along with whatever you want. It's just a name, Jenna. It's being with you that matters, not what we call each other."

She shakes her head, tears forming in her eyes. "I don't deserve you," she whispers.

"Yeah, you do," I reply. "You've just spent the last two days proving that to me… very spectacularly." I lean down to kiss her, just as a car drives past outside and she tenses in my arms.

"What's wrong?" I still, our lips almost touching.

"He's due any minute," she says quietly.

"Scott?"

"Yes."

I nod my head. "He can't hurt you. He can't hurt us. I won't interfere between the two of you, but I won't let him hurt you either. I'll be right behind you."

"I know you will," she whispers and leans against me. "You've always been there to catch me, haven't you?"

I smile to myself and nod my head as I stroke her hair, relishing our last few moments together. For now at least. "I suppose falling in love is kind of like learning to surf, isn't it?"

She pulls back and looks up into my eyes. "How would you know?" she says. "You didn't learn to surf. You were a natural."

"I wasn't talking about me. I was talking about you." I move closer, our bodies moulded, the memory of our perfect weekend suffused into our very core. "Learning to surf and falling in love are all about trust. In both cases, you had to learn to have some faith in yourself, and to believe in me, and know that I was never going to let you fall, without being there to catch you. And to keep you. Forever."

Printed in Great Britain
by Amazon